Dear Reader,

Welcome to the third story in THE MASTER VINTNERS series. While in Adelaide in May 2010, when I sat having lunch in an Italian restaurant with a friend and dreaming up the first two TMV books, I never imagined that it would lead me to fall in love with a whole new population of characters. The extended Masters family, and their offshoot of friends, have provided my imagination with challenges and story ideas that have kept me occupied for some time.

I was lucky enough to visit a few of the vineyards outside of Adelaide and to admire the beautiful settings, taste the carefully crafted and delicious wines and bask in the ambience of all that is amazing when you visit a country that is not your own. It seemed only fitting, to me, to give those stunning vistas and experiences a longer life in my own heart and mind than the short time I was able to be there.

In *One Secret Night,* Ethan Masters discovers a shocking family secret. It's a measure of how difficult he finds this information to deal with when he uncharacteristically divulges it to a woman he meets only in passing, and expects never to see again. Their secret night turns into a firestorm of passion and emotion as he and free-spirited Isobel Fyfe learn what it's like when opposites attract…and fall in love.

I hope you'll fall in love with Ethan and Isobel, too!

Happy reading,

Yvonne Lindsay

ONE SECRET NIGHT

BY
YVONNE LINDSAY

MILLS & BOON

This book is dedicated to dear friends who helped me brainstorm when my brain was a tranquil place with nothing happening—a lovely thing to have but not when you're nutting out a plot!
Nalini, Peta and Shar—big thanks for all your help.

One

His mother was alive.

Ethan Masters walked blindly through Adelaide's city streets, the staggering knowledge continuing to ricochet in his mind. A mind already struggling to come to terms with his father's recent unexpected death. He'd thought that would be the hardest thing he would ever have to face. But this discovery today, that the man Ethan had idolized and revered above all others had lied to him and his sister for the past twenty-five years, was much worse.

Grief mingled with a sharp sense of betrayal sliced through him anew—its blade serrated and leaving behind a raw pain that throbbed incessantly deep inside his chest. He didn't know what to do with the information he'd been given today. Part of him wished he'd never learned the truth. In fact, if he hadn't discovered an anomaly in his father's personal accounts he would still be none the wiser. The family solicitor's reluctance to explain had only made him more determined to discover where the monthly payments had been going.

So, now he knew. The woman who had abandoned him and his sister, Tamsyn, had accepted money to stay away, happy to let her children think she'd died in the car accident that had spared their lives.

Even worse, his father's siblings, Ethan's uncle Edward and aunt Cynthia, had colluded in the lie.

It went against everything—*every* family institution—he'd been brought up with. Bad enough that his memories of his parents had been tainted. But to know that so many people he trusted had gone behind his back…it was more than he could take. Maybe he should have gone straight home after his meeting in the city—confronted his aunt and uncle, told Tamsyn the truth. But if he himself found it next to impossible to weigh the information he'd received today, how could he expect to face his sister with the news?

The very idea of telling Tamsyn sent a shudder down his spine. Tamsyn was, by nature, a caretaker. She wanted everyone to be happy, and she worked darn hard to achieve that goal. Always had, even as a child. It was one of the reasons why her branch of the family business was so sought after and came so highly recommended. This news could well destroy her. He couldn't bear to see that happen. He hadn't spent the past twenty-five years of his life being her champion to fall at this hurdle now. No, this was his problem to deal with and he needed to work out his next move before facing everyone. He'd reach that decision a darn sight faster without the various demands of the family business, not to mention his extended family buzzing around to distract him.

A flicker of exotic color and movement caught his eye. A young woman who stood out from all the somber office workers marking the end of their working week by spilling from nearby buildings. Small, slender and blond, her dress a multihued swirl that clung briefly to outline her buttocks and thighs as a passing vehicle threw a gust of air in her direction. An incongruously large and cumbersome pack was settled on her back, yet she carried it as if it weighed nothing at all. Intrigued, Ethan watched as she slipped through the doors of a nearby pub and out of sight.

Without a second thought, Ethan followed her footsteps. He pulled himself up short as he entered the building and firmed his lips into a grim line. For someone who hadn't wanted distraction he'd certainly found it in the noisy confusion of pub patrons—a blend of tourists, students and office workers. For a second, he considered leaving. But what the hell, maybe concentration would come more smoothly after a drink. Straightening his shoulders, he headed to the bar. He scanned the crowd all the while, but he saw no sign of the colorful butterfly that had drawn him here.

Minutes later, Ethan listened to the beat of the music energizing the people on the dance floor—people whose lives were clearly far less complicated than his had so rapidly become—and deftly swirled the red wine in his glass. He watched as the rich ruby liquid ran in tiny rivers down the inside and inexorably into the bowl.

"Not to your taste, sir?" the barman asked from across the gleaming wooden bar.

"It's fine," Ethan admitted, belatedly adding his thanks.

He continued to scan the crowd reflected in the mirror over the bar, and allowed his thoughts to wander. Rolled the truth around in his head that the life he'd lived since the accident had been based on untruths.

Looking back, he remembered that his father had been different after the crash. That bit more remote, that bit more stern and demanding of excellence in those around him. That bit less trusting. But once he'd recovered from his own injuries, Ethan, in his six-year-old mind, had rationalized that by believing his father was sad and lonely, just as he and Tamsyn were. So he'd tried his hardest, with everything, to be all his father demanded and more. And all for what? To discover that John Masters had been living a lie for the past twenty-five years and worse, had coerced everyone around him to do the same.

Even knowing it *had* been achieved, Ethan struggled to see how his father had carried it off. It was the stuff of soap operas, not his life. At least, not the life he'd thought he had.

He lifted the wine goblet and took a mouthful, letting the burst of berry and clove explode on his tongue before swallowing. Not bad, he conceded, but it stood in the shadow of his most recent international-award-winning Shiraz. Then the alcohol hit his stomach, reminding him he hadn't eaten since leaving The Masters, his family home and seat of their renowned winemaking business, early this morning.

"Deep in thought?"

The ultrafeminine voice caught his attention and he turned to take in the features of the slightly built blond-haired woman who'd inserted herself at the bar next to his chair. The butterfly. Up close he could see she was a little older than the average student here but she definitely didn't fit in with the corporate types, either. Her eyes were a bright, clear blue, her skin a honeyed light tan. Her eyebrows rose ever so slightly, awaiting his answer.

"Something like that," he responded.

"They say a problem shared is a problem halved," she offered with a welcoming smile. "Want to talk about it?"

Her lips glistened with the shimmer of a tinted gloss that perfectly complemented her skin. Her blond hair gleamed and fell in a short waterfall to shoulders exposed by the bright floral halter-necked dress that clung softly to her body. A bolt of sexual energy surged through him, but hard on its heels was a heavy dose of reality. Despite the fact he'd followed her in here, he wasn't the kind of guy who was into pub pickups. Hooking up with a stranger wasn't the answer to his problems. He wasn't ready for this—for her.

"No, thanks."

His response was more brusque than he'd intended. He was just about to add to it, to somehow soften what he'd said, when she gave him a thin smile, the warmth suddenly leaving her eyes as his "not interested" message got through loud and clear. He turned away slightly, feeling absurdly ashamed of himself, as she placed her order and waited for the barman to deliver it. He hadn't meant to be rude. After all, upon seeing her outside, hadn't he come in here seeking her?

Although she wasn't in his direct line of vision, he found himself acutely aware of her. Of her long, tapered fingers drumming on the wooden bar—her nails surprisingly short and practical—of her light summery fragrance wafting enticingly toward him in the air-conditioned environment. And particularly, of the gentle sway of her body in time to the beat of the music pumping from the bar's speakers. He should apologize, but as he turned to do so he discovered she'd already downed the shot she'd ordered and now threaded her way back through the crowd.

Relief that she'd moved on mingled with an odd sense of loss. Ethan took another sip of his wine and swiveled on his chair. Leaning back against the edge of the bar, he surveyed the writhing mass of people dancing on the floor. His eyes were immediately drawn to the blonde. She moved with inherent grace to the throb of the beat of the music and he was forced to acknowledge an answer-

ing throb in his own body. It had been too long since he'd
relaxed and let his hair down. He should have encouraged
her friendly overture rather than snubbed her. He scanned
the room again before his eyes returned to her. He'd been
too quick to turn away from her before and now he couldn't
take his eyes off her.

A guy staggered up from a group of business types
with a mounting collection of empties on their table, and
made his way through the throng on the dance floor. He
stopped behind the blonde woman, placing his hands on
her hips and dancing suggestively behind her. Ethan felt a
wave of possessive anger claw through him before pushing
it back where it belonged. She wasn't his to worry about,
he told himself. Even so, he still couldn't turn away—
especially when she carefully placed her hands on her
new dance partner's and took them from her body. Ethan
stiffened on his chair. Having the other guy touch her was
all well and good if she was happy with it, but when she
so clearly wasn't…

The guy stumbled a bit, then righted himself only to
grab at the woman's hand and turn her around to face him.
He leaned forward to say something close to her ear. An
expression of disgust slid across her face and she shook her
head while trying to disengage his hold on her. This was
wrong on so many levels it made Ethan's blood boil. *No*
always meant no. Before he knew it, he was off his stool
and edging his way through the dancers, his eyes firmly
trained on one target and one target only.

"Sorry I'm late," he said, bending and placing a kiss on
the startled woman's cheek. He turned slightly, placing his
body firmly in front of her, and faced her wannabe beau.
"She's with me, mate," he said, his stance and his expression saying in no uncertain terms that it was time for the
other guy to back off.

To his relief the man gave him a drunken apologetic smile and returned to his table. Ethan turned back to the blonde.

"Are you okay?" he asked.

"You didn't need to do that. I can take care of myself, you know," she replied haughtily.

For some reason the thought of this svelte creature, who didn't even come up to his shoulder, "taking care of herself" made him laugh out loud. "That much was obvious," he said when he managed to get his mirth under control.

He was surprised when her face creased into a smile and she laughed along with him.

"I suppose I really should just say thank-you," she said, still smiling.

"You're welcome. You didn't look as if you were enjoying his company."

"No, you're right, I wasn't." She held out her hand. "I'm Isobel Fyfe."

"Ethan Masters."

He accepted her hand, instantly aware of the daintiness of hers in his much larger one. His fingers tightened reflexively as every one of his protective instincts roared to the forefront of his mind. He didn't let her go as he leaned forward slightly, his masculine bulk shielding her from those around them.

"Can I buy you a drink, or perhaps dinner somewhere else?" Ethan asked as he was jostled by the crowd. "It's a bit of a crush in here."

For a minute he thought she'd refuse but then she nodded.

"Dinner. Let me get my pack. The barman's holding it for me."

Ethan led her back toward the bar, her hand still in his. When she retrieved her large and well-worn backpack from behind the bar, Ethan automatically reached to relieve her of it as they made their way to the front door.

"It's okay," Isobel said. "I can manage. I'm used to it."

"Yes, but at least let me salve my male conscience by carrying it for you. I promise I won't lose it."

"Oh, well, when you put it like that." She smiled, handing the dusty pack, still with airline luggage tags attached, over to him. "Besides, it really doesn't match my shoes."

Ethan cast a glance at the high-heeled sandals she wore and had to agree. "Are you okay to walk in those or should we take a taxi?"

"Where were you thinking of going?"

He named a Greek restaurant farther down Rundle Street. "It's not far."

"Then let's walk," she said, slipping one small hand into the crook of his free arm. "It's a beautiful evening."

Ethan slung the pack over one shoulder, hardly caring for the creases it would generate in his Ralph Lauren Black Label suit.

"That wasn't your usual haunt, was it?" Isobel asked, nodding her head back toward the pub they'd just vacated.

"That obvious?" he asked with a smile.

For a moment he withstood her silent perusal as she eyed him carefully. The sense that she was checking him out in more ways than one made his blood begin to hum in his veins, sending warmth spreading out to his extremities.

"Yes," she answered succinctly.

Intrigued, he pressed her as to why.

"A few things," she said as they came to a stop at a street crossing and waited for their signal. "But mainly it's your demeanor. You've got this air about you. Some would say that it's probably wealth and privilege but I think there's more to it than that. You look like you aren't afraid of hard work." She took both of his hands in hers and turned them this way and that, examining them carefully before letting them go and tucking her hand back in the crook of his arm. "Yes, well tended but not in a prissy way. And yet there's an air of entitlement about you, or command, if you'd rather think of it that way. You're willing to work hard, but you're used to giving orders and having them immediately obeyed."

Ethan gave a short bark of laughter. "And you can tell all that just by looking at me?"

She shrugged—a delicate motion of her slender shoulders. "You asked," she replied simply. "Are we crossing?"

Her question reminded him that they were supposed to be going to dinner. He took a minute to clear his mind as they strolled across the intersection and down the sidewalk. How had this happened? he wondered, supremely conscious of her hand nestled at his elbow and the feminine sway of her hips as she walked along beside him. How had he gone from having a drink to unwind, to escorting a woman he'd only just met to dinner? How long had it been since he'd acted on impulse like this?

The answer to the last question was simple. Never.

Isobel felt the tensile strength of the forearm beneath her fingers and relished the tingle of anticipation it set up deep inside. The finely woven wool of Ethan's suit—she'd missed catching his last name in the noise back at the bar—was just a veneer to the man who wore it. Her senses fizzed with the same sense of excitement she got when she knew she'd captured a particularly good photo—that prickling spider-sense that she was on the verge of something greater than she'd experienced before. And, having made it a lifestyle choice to grab every moment and make it a worthwhile one, dinner with Ethan was just the ticket.

She wasn't the kind of girl who was free with her favors,

but she wasn't one to let the opportunity to spend a fun evening with an attractive man fall by the wayside, either.

Her instincts had told her he was straight up—that she had nothing to fear from him—and instinct had never let her down before. Besides, she had little reason to believe that anything would happen beyond an entertaining meal together. This guy was totally not her type. Too self-assured, too dominating and too darn good-looking for her equilibrium. Still, the evening promised to be interesting, if nothing else.

They arrived at the restaurant and she was immediately struck by the deference paid to him by the staff. After they were seated at the table, her pack secured safely on the floor between them, she couldn't keep the smile from her face.

"What's so funny?" he asked, reaching for his water glass and taking a long draw of the sparkling liquid. No mere tap water for him.

She dragged her gaze from the movement of the muscles in his tanned throat and reached for her own glass, lifting it to her lips.

"It's amazing. You just take it all for granted, don't you?" she eventually said.

The look of puzzlement that crossed his face, pulling his heavy dark brows together, was all the answer she needed.

"I don't follow."

"They treat you like royalty," she said with a small laugh. "And you don't even notice."

"I'm a regular, and I tip well," he replied, looking a bit put out.

"It wasn't a criticism," she said softly. "I'm sure they respect your patronage."

It only took a second for her double entendre to hit its mark, whereupon he surprised her by chuckling out loud.

"You don't pull your punches, do you?"

Isobel shrugged. "I believe in calling a spade a spade, even when it's a face card."

"So you gamble?" he probed.

"Only when I know I'm going to win," she conceded, looking down at her menu rather than meeting his dark-eyed stare across the table.

She thought for a minute of her last assignment. Her photography work gave her a chance to capture and highlight the best in people—and the worst. She was good enough to catch plenty of both, and not everyone was pleased with the results. Her most recent job had turned dangerous when the nation she'd been visiting had politely, but firmly, requested she remove herself from within their borders. It was clear that if she ignored them, their next request would not have been so civil.

On that particular assignment, she'd taken a gamble and she'd thrown in her hand before things got uglier. But she'd be heading back, as soon as she completed her next cookie-cutter job—one of the dull but easy assignments that gave her a measure of financial security. The new catalog shoot would be a walk in the park compared to her usual work and even though it wasn't as challenging on a social or emotional level as her preferred projects, it would ensure she had sufficient funds to head back to the war-torn country she'd just left to finish what she'd started.

"Do you win often?"

His voice was soft, like velvet, and she felt something deep inside her answer its challenge.

"As often as I can."

"It's hardly gambling when it's a sure thing," he commented before picking up his menu.

"You can't blame me for playing it safe." She nodded

toward the printed card in his hands. "What do you recommend?" she asked.

"Everything's good here but the lamb, in particular, is my favorite."

"Good. I'll have that then."

He closed his menu and put it down. "Just like that? You don't want another half an hour to peruse your choices and change your mind a half dozen times?"

"Why? Is that what you usually do?" she teased, knowing full well the answer would be an emphatic no.

He gave a slight shake of his head. "I prefer not to waste time. I'll order for us both."

"Thank you. I'd like that."

She watched carefully as he called the waiter over and placed their order, including a bottle of wine. Again the staff showed him that same respect they had before.

"You must tip *really* well," she mocked with a laugh. "I swear that guy was about to offer you his firstborn child."

"Hardly," Ethan responded drily before realizing that she was still teasing. "Ah, I see, you think it's fine to bait me? Okay then, I'll bite. Since you're clearly not in the habit of bribing waitstaff into providing good service, what do *you* do with your money?"

"My money?" Isobel pulled a face. "What I don't use for travel I try to use to help support worthy causes."

"Seriously?" His face pulled into a frown. "That's very philanthropic of you."

"I barely make a difference," she said, a note of sadness creeping into her voice as she remembered the helpless futility of some of the people she'd tried to help. "For myself, I've learned to need very little."

"What about when you grow older? How will you support yourself then?"

"I'll worry about that when it happens." His frown deepened, prompting her to ask, "You don't approve?"

"I didn't say that. Different strokes. I'm involved in a family business. We work together, socialize together—we're all striving for a common goal. With the business we have, we're looking forward to the future every day. I can't imagine just living in the day and not planning ahead. But then, as a family business, there are plenty of other peoples' futures at stake than just my own."

"I'm the only one affected by my decisions," she said simply, "which definitely has its advantages."

Ethan smiled back at her, and she knew that in some way, even if it was small, he probably envied her freedom. Most people did, but without realizing that it came with its own personal cost at the same time. Ethan clearly had a network of people to help and support him, while Isobel was very accustomed to being on her own.

She took advantage of the companionable silence between them to study him some more. In the subdued lighting of the restaurant, his lean features were all shadows and light. His nose a long straight patrician blade, his upper lip narrow but with a perfect bow to it, the lower lip fuller, enticing. His hair was worn short and controlled but she could detect the faintest of hints of curl in it and she wondered what he'd look like if he let it grow out a bit more, let himself look a little less disciplined and a lot more wild. Her fingers itched to reach for her camera in her pack and to shoot off a series of pictures of him.

The tingle that had started in her body earlier ramped up a notch, sending swirls of heat spooling through her belly and lower. The strong shadow on his jaw showed he was probably a two-shaves-a-day man, but somehow she knew she liked him better like this. Less polished, more primal. She squeezed her thighs together as a surge of desire arrowed direct to her core, and in that moment Isobel knew she was probably going to sleep with Ethan whatever-his-last-name-was tonight and, more, that she wanted to—very, very much.

Two

The food was delicious and she was glad she'd left Ethan to make their selections. She slipped up a little sauce from the edge of her plate with a finger and licked it off, her eyes closing briefly to enjoy the blissful flavor just that bit longer. When she opened them again, she caught Ethan staring at her. That earlier thrill of desire jolted through her again and she saw a flare of reciprocal interest light in his eyes.

What would he be like as a lover? she wondered as she broke eye contact and reached for her wineglass. He wasn't her usual type, which was probably a male version of herself—free-spirited, unfettered, casual. No, Ethan was definitely different. He exuded stability and strength, not to mention an unfair dose of sex appeal, and she found the combination fiercely compelling.

"Tell me about your travels," he said, leaning forward

to top up her wineglass with a little more of the very fine merlot they'd enjoyed with their meal.

So far they'd kept their conversation very general and superficial. So much so that neither of them really knew much about the other. Isobel preferred it that way. She didn't like to share too much of herself—at least not more than she was prepared to. She found so many people were critical of her attempts to expose some of the better-kept secrets regarding atrocities against children and families overseas. It was safer, she'd found, to be judicious with the information she shared.

She found it easy to fill the next hour with flip conversation of some of the funnier exploits she'd experienced. Ethan leaned back in his chair and laughed heartily at her recitation of her reaction to a giant centipede coming out of the hole in the ground she'd been using as a toilet during a trip through Nepal. Her own lips turned up in response to his unfettered joy. He had a great laugh, she decided. She liked it when a man could really give in to mirth. It was, in her mind, a good indicator of just how much he'd give in to anything else he was passionate about. Right now, she hoped that was her.

"Can't say I have anything in my experience to equal or better that," he said through his laughter. "And none of that puts you off or makes you want to take a more mainstream route?"

"No." She shook her head. "You don't really *see* the world as other people are forced to live it when you do that."

"Interesting choice of words."

"What?"

"Forced. Aren't most people living the life of their choice?"

She gave him a pitying smile. "You don't really believe that, do you?"

"I believe it's up to each individual to choose his own path."

"In a perfect world, maybe. Not everyone has the privilege of a perfect world."

Ethan considered her words before responding. "You're right. I'm being too general and thinking only in terms of here and my life, my choices." His face suddenly became serious and she felt his withdrawal as if it were a physical thing when in reality, he was no farther away from her than he'd been two seconds ago. "Even I don't have control over everything in my world."

He said it so bleakly, Isobel wondered for a moment what had happened to him that was so terrible. She reached across the table, pressing her fingertips lightly on the back of his hand where it rested on the pristine white tablecloth.

"I'm sorry," she said simply.

"Why sorry?"

"You strike me as the kind of guy who likes to be in charge of what happens."

"Yeah, I am," he admitted with a rueful smile. "And at least I can be in charge of how I react to what happens, right?"

They turned their conversation to more general topics after that, Isobel wringing more laughter from Ethan and reveling in the fact that she could. Seeing that glimpse of vulnerability in him had only made him even more attractive to her. It took a strong man to admit his weaknesses and she was hardwired to appreciate a strong man.

They'd been lingering over their coffee and dessert when she saw Ethan look at his watch. Around them, the restaurant had all but emptied.

"It's getting late," Ethan said. "Is there anywhere I can drop you off?"

"Oh, I'll be fine. I'll just check into the nearest hostel or hotel," she answered blithely, though she was admittedly a little sorry that their evening was drawing to a close.

The attraction she'd felt toward him all through the meal had only sharpened as she'd spent more time with him, and she wondered if perhaps he was too much of a gentleman to expect their evening together to lead to anything more. As much as she respected honor in a man, she wasn't feeling particularly honorable herself right now.

"You haven't booked anywhere?"

"No, I just flew in this afternoon. But it's no problem. There are a few places within walking distance of here, aren't there?" She could see Ethan bristle at the thought and she couldn't help the chuckle that bubbled from her at the expression on his face. "I can look after myself, you know."

"Like you did back at the pub?"

"I would have shaken him off eventually."

"Yes, it certainly looked that way." His delicious mouth firmed into a straight line.

"Hey, it's not a problem. I can get the restaurant to call me a cab if you're that worried. I only need a place for a night, anyway."

One night? One night of no questions, no answers. No recriminations. He would probably never see her again. One night of freedom, of passion. Ethan's mind expanded on the idea with the velocity of bush fire and with more than a hint of its searing heat, as well. He spoke before he could overthink the situation and talk himself out of the idea that had bloomed in his mind. If she went for it, all well and good. If not, no harm, no foul.

"Why not stay with me? I mean, I have an apartment

here in the city. There's more than enough room for you, as well."

To his surprise her smile widened.

"I'd like that." She hesitated a moment before continuing. "I'd like to stay *with* you tonight."

A knot of tension coiled tight in his gut. Did she mean what he thought she meant or had his simmering libido simply heard what it wanted to hear? In his whole life he'd never had a one-night stand—had considered them to be the mark of a person with little control, and even less respect for themselves. But his body burned in a way it had never burned before. Still, he felt obligated to be a gentleman about this.

"I have a couple of guest rooms. You can take your pick."

"Oh, I don't think that will be necessary," she replied softly. "Do you?"

He swallowed and shook his head. "Not if you're comfortable with that."

She laughed, the sound thrilling across his raw nerves like a soothing caress. "Oh, I expect to get really *un*comfortable, don't you? Come on, let's go."

Ethan was unused to someone else taking the lead but he couldn't deny the primal surge of attraction that flooded his body at her confidence. For once, the important decisions didn't lie solely with him. He didn't have to be the responsible one. He could just relax into doing what felt right. And this felt very, very right.

Without taking his eyes from her face, he gestured to the waitstaff for their bill. It felt like forever before the account was settled, with his usual generous tip added. Then he was hefting Isobel's pack up over his shoulder again. With his free hand he reached for her, threading their fingers together—the palm-to-palm contact hinting at the intimacy yet to come.

The short cab ride to his apartment building was executed in silence, the distance between them in the back-seat of the cab miles rather than mere feet. But the instant they alighted, Ethan drew Isobel to him again. She looked up at the midrise apartment building and flicked him a wicked smile.

"Penthouse, right?"

He gave a small groan. "Guilty as charged."

"I love a view," she replied as they entered the building and took the elevator to the top floor. They entered a private foyer and Ethan watched as Isobel walked across the hardwood floors through a double-story-height room. She came to a halt in front of the wall of glass that looked out through the darkness, over Kurrangga Park and beyond.

"This is definitely a view," she said softly before turning around to face him. "But I think I like this view better."

She crossed the floor toward him as he placed her pack on the floor behind one of the oversize cream leather couches. As he straightened, her small hands slid around his waist beneath his jacket.

"Yeah, I definitely like this view better."

Isobel lifted herself on tiptoe and her lips caressed his ever so gently, like a butterfly kiss. As soft and near ephemeral as her touch was, the impact on his senses was so strong that it was as if someone had ignited every nerve in his body. He could feel her warmth even though she barely touched him. His nostrils flared as he breathed in the light essence of her scent. It wasn't enough. His hands reached for her, pulling her hard against him, absorbing her as her curves settled against the hard planes of his body. He lowered his head, watching as she lifted her face to him, her eyelids fluttering closed, her lips parting ever so slightly.

And then he kissed her as he'd been unconsciously dreaming of doing from the moment he'd first seen her. She was the perfect balance to him, light to his darkness, pliant to his inflexibility, warmth to the coldness that had settled deep inside him today. Resolutely he pushed all remembrance of what had led him to cross the same path as Isobel from his mind. She was here. He was here. That was the only thing that mattered in this moment.

Her lips were smooth and soft, her tongue a tiny dart that met his and tangled in a hot mess of need and desire. Her hands ripped at the buttons of his shirt, sending them bouncing onto the floor. She pushed the fabric open, baring his chest and belly to her touch. Her fingers spread across his skin, leaving a searing trail wherever she touched.

Ethan lifted his hands to her hair, letting the shoulder-length, silky strands run through his fingers as he reached to cup the back of her head and draw her even closer. He pressed his hips against her lower belly, instinctively seeking some relief for the increasing pressure that built in his groin. She pressed back and he groaned. He felt her hands skim across his belly to the belt of his trousers, where nimble fingers slid the leather free from its buckle, and began to unfasten his waistband. And then, mercifully, her hand was gripping him through his briefs, her fingers firm yet gentle at the same time. But he didn't want gentle. Not yet.

He ground against her hand and felt her answering response as she gripped him tighter. At the same time his fingers worked against the knot that bound the halter of her dress at the nape of her neck. The fabric finally gave way. Ethan pulled back from her slightly, allowing the top of her gown to slide down over her breasts, exposing them to his hungry gaze. Her nipples were a delectable, soft, peachy-pink, drawn into taut buds that begged for his mouth. He cupped one breast in his hand, rubbing the hard nub of her nipple with his thumb as he bent his head to its partner, drawing the tender flesh into his mouth and rasping its tip with his tongue.

A shudder passed through Isobel's body, a soft mew of pleasure emitting from between her lips. Ethan transferred his attention to her other breast, laving it with the same attention before he pulled back and bent slightly to slide one arm behind her knees and sweep her up into his arms. Her hands linked behind his neck and she pressed her lips against his chest as he strode to the master bedroom. Her teeth scraped across one nipple, making him almost stop in his tracks as a jolt of sheer lightning passed through his body. But he regained his focus, eventually shoving open the door that led into the bedroom where he slowly lowered Isobel to her feet.

She shimmied her dress over her hips, stepping out of the pool of fabric at her feet, even as she reached for him again. Dressed only in heels and the barest scrap of silk panties, she shoved his jacket off his shoulders and then dispensed with his shirt the same way. Ethan tugged down his pants and kicked off his shoes. He skimmed his socks off as he pushed his trousers away and reached for Isobel.

They tumbled to the bed together in a tangle of arms and legs, each trying desperately to get closer to the other, all the while touching and exploring the skin now exposed to them. He wasn't sure later how she engineered it, but she ended up straddling him, her legs trapping his thighs as she leaned down to trace his collarbone with the tip of her tongue before moving lower until she licked and nipped again at his nipples. His skin had never felt this sensitive, his responses this intense. He'd never felt so powerless, nor so empowered at the same time.

Even so, it wasn't in him to simply lie there, supine. Ethan stroked his fingertips over the tops of her thighs, then followed the line of her hip as it curved down along the edge of her panties and into the shadowed hollow of her core. He slid one finger under the flimsy covering, tugging the material aside and exposing her as a true blonde in the dimly lit room. She was wet and hot as he traced his finger around her moist flesh, dipping into her center. She ground against his hand, moaning her pleasure. He pressed his palm against her, even as he slid a second finger inside the scalding grip of her body. Again she pushed against him, her hips moving in a tight circle.

She ceased her exploration of his torso, sitting more upright, allowing him deeper access to her. He looked up at the vision of sheer femininity that hovered above him. Her eyes were open, staring straight into his, as if she could see into his very soul. Her breasts were small, perfect globes that shimmered in the half-light, her nipples drawn into concentrated buds. He stroked his fingers along her inner passage, pressed more firmly with his palm. Her body began to tremble, her stomach muscles—already flat and toned—tightening visibly as her whole body grew taut. And then he felt her crest the pinnacle of pleasure. Her inner muscles squeezing in paroxysms of satisfaction, her thighs shaking, a keening sound of fulfillment escaping from her, even though she had caught her lower lip between her teeth.

Ethan rose up and deftly moved her so she was beneath him, his hands now drawing her panties off her body, his fingers tracing the long, lean muscles of her legs. Once the lacy scrap was discarded, he slid her high-heeled sandals off her feet, massaging the instep of each foot before running his hands back up her legs again. The well-trimmed thatch of hair at the apex of her thighs glistened with the evidence of her gratification, and he nuzzled at the blond hair, inhaling the musky scent of her before exposing the swollen nub of flesh hidden inside. He traced a circle around the shining pink pearl with the tip of his tongue.

"Too soon," she protested weakly, her body still quivering with the aftereffects of her orgasm.

"Trust me, it's not soon enough," he argued, closing his mouth over the tumescent bead and gently scraping his teeth over its surface.

Isobel all but leaped off the bed, her hips surging upward in response to his action. Ethan swirled his tongue around her again, soothing her, before repeating the action with his teeth. She may have been in control of her last peak, but he most definitely would be driving her to her next. He increased the pressure of his tongue and began to suckle firmly. The next time he softly closed his teeth on her he felt her break, her body at first stretched as tight as a bow before the arrow of physical delight flew free, turning her muscles slack and supple beneath him.

He brushed his tongue over her again, then again more soothingly, until he finally withdrew from her and dragged himself up and over her.

"You okay?" he murmured, his hands now stroking her belly, tracing her rib cage and moving slowly to rest against one breast. Beneath his hand he could feel her heart hammering in her chest.

"Okay? Yeah, I think I'm just a bit more than okay," she said, smiling as she caught his face between her hands and kissed him. "But what about you?"

She flexed her pelvis against him.

"We're going to take care of that right now," he said. Supporting his weight on one arm, he reached with the other into the drawer of the nightstand.

He shook out the box of condoms he withdrew and grabbed one packet.

"Here, let me," Isobel insisted, taking the condom from his hand and tearing the foil open.

She slid the sheath from its confines and positioned it over the aching head of his erection before deftly sliding it over his length. It took almost every ounce of his control not to lose it as, once he was protected, she slipped her hand between them and positioned him at her entrance. She gasped as he probed her swollen, slick flesh, the sound vibrating through him as he fought to prolong this moment for as long as humanly possible.

Then, so slowly that it made his body shudder with the effort, he sank within her inviting depths. Her body gloved him, fitting so perfectly that he knew he would not be able to maintain this level of control for more than mere seconds. Bliss flooded him in an instant—potent and undeniable.

He moved within her, her hips rising to meet his every thrust, each one more powerful than the last, the rising pleasure becoming more exquisitely intense with each stroke. And then, he was there—sensation pulsating through his body and catapulting him into a place he'd never experienced so deeply before. He held her firmly to him, his forehead resting on hers, their rapid breaths mingling in the minute space between them. When he made to pull away, Isobel's arms closed around him.

"I'm too heavy for you," he protested as she squeezed tight.

"I like this," she replied as if the simplicity of the words themselves were fully sufficient.

He relaxed against her, and realized that maybe they were. He'd never felt the full acceptance of himself with another in the aftermath of lovemaking before. It had always been a release, often a deeply satisfying one, but never quite this sense of physical communion. He didn't know what to think of it, so he took what was—for him—a very novel approach. He decided not to think at all. Not just yet. As his heart rate slowed, he rolled slightly to one side, pulling her along with him.

Isobel reached up a finger to trace the line of his lips, her touch leaving a tingle of longing in its wake. He gave in and leaned into her to kiss her—not a kiss with the flaming sensuality they'd shared before, but one of quiet intimacy. Of thanks. He finally forced himself to break away and moved to rid himself of the condom, returning to the bed as quickly as he could and scooping her against him. Isobel tangled her legs in his and rested her head on his chest. For all that he barely knew her it felt almost frighteningly right.

One night, he reminded himself. That was all this was. Just one night.

Three

Isobel traced a circular pattern with her index finger on Ethan's chest. She'd been stunned by the force of their lovemaking, by their connection to one another. It almost seemed a shame that she'd be moving on to her next assignment tomorrow without ever seeing Ethan again, but she would live with that. She had to. It was the way she lived her life. Always fluid, always moving. Never staying still long enough to set down roots. It suited her.

And to her surprise, so had he.

She knew deep down that tonight had not been the type of thing a man like Ethan indulged in often, if at all. It piqued her curiosity. Why had he broken with what were probably very rigid personal boundaries to bring her home and share such profound intimacy? It was tempting to believe that it was just her influence that had him throwing caution to the wind, but she sensed that there was more to it than that. Her photographer's instinct always knew when there was more at play than what could be immediately seen. Before she knew it, the question slid from her lips.

"Why me, Ethan?"

"Huh?"

He sounded sleepy, as if she'd dragged him from that in-between place in the middle of consciousness and slumber.

"What happened to you today?" she asked.

He sucked in a deep breath and his arm tightened around her. "You don't want to hear about that."

"Try me," she coaxed. "You strike me as the kind of guy who doesn't usually share what troubles you. Maybe you should try it sometime, like now, with me."

She kept drawing the circles on his chest and waited in silence for him to make up his mind. She could almost hear the cogs turning in his brain as he weighed up the pros and cons of sharing with her. It never failed to surprise Isobel that people could share the most personal experiences to-gether physically, yet reveal so little on an emotional level. Somehow it mattered to her to know why Ethan had over-stepped his boundaries with her.

"I got some news today that I hadn't anticipated," he finally disclosed.

"Bad news?"

"Yes and no."

"It upset you," she stated firmly.

"Yeah, I don't know how to deal with it."

"It must have been really bad, then."

She felt him nod. "You could say that. My dad died re-cently and I've been going over his records. I found some payments that didn't marry up with the data I had before me, so I checked with the family accountant who referred me to our lawyer. That's where I went today. Basically I discovered that my father hid the truth about our mother from my sister and me. We were told she died twenty-five years ago, but she didn't. She left us and accepted his money to stay away."

"Oh, that's awful. You must have been devastated," Isobel whispered in shock.

She knew what it was like to find out a parent had been lying to you. It was the deepest kind of betrayal.

"I don't understand why he did it and now I can't ask him, either."

Tension radiated from his body as the frustration he'd been feeling wound tight inside of him.

"Maybe he just wanted to protect you and your sister. If it happened twenty-five years ago then you can't have been all that old," she said, trying to soothe him.

"I was six, my sister only three. I would have had some understanding of his decision not to tell us then, if my father had bothered to tell me the truth later, when I was an adult. It's not as if he didn't have ample opportunity. Even after he died, there was no letter, nothing in his will to let me know the truth. If I hadn't started asking questions about the payments, I never would have known."

The bitterness in his voice hung in the air.

Isobel sighed. "It isn't easy to understand the choices our parents make." That much, she knew from personal experience. "Usually, I guess they think they're protecting us."

"Why would I need to be protected from the truth? Don't I deserve to know why he thought my sister and I would be better off without our mother in our lives?"

"Maybe it wasn't as clear-cut as that."

Ethan shook his head. "It must have been. Otherwise, he wouldn't have been able to get the rest of our family to support him in his lie. My aunt and my uncle and his wife, they all knew the truth. They've all kept the secret for all these years."

"Are they still alive?"

"Yeah, we all live on the family property. We see each other pretty much every day."

"Then maybe you can find out from them," she suggested. "Whatever the outcome, though, Ethan, there's no point in holding a grudge against a dead man. Right or wrong, your father made his decisions. They can't be undone or the past changed. The only thing you can do is move forward."

"Is that what you do?" he asked. "Move forward and not ask questions?"

She smiled and lifted her head and met his serious dark brown gaze. "Except for right now, yeah, something like that. It saves on baggage."

Ethan shook his head slightly. "I can't imagine living like that."

Isobel shrugged. "It's not for everyone. Certainly not for someone like your father, for example. For whatever reason, he kept those payments going for years, got your whole family involved, with the idea that he was protecting you and your sister. I imagine you're probably very much like he was. Strong." She coasted her fingertips over his shoulders and down his arm. "Intelligent." She ran her fingers back up his arm and lightly touched his forehead. "And protective." Her fingertips traveled back down to his chest and she rested her full palm against it. "Those are the qualities about your father you should remember him by. And how much he must have loved you."

Ethan remained silent for a while before speaking. "You have an interesting insight for someone who never met my father and who never met me before tonight."

"You think I'm being presumptuous, offering you my opinion?"

"No, not that. If anything, you probably described my

father to a tee. I suppose that coming to terms with everything, losing him as suddenly as we did, I had briefly lost sight of that. I still want to know why he never told me about our mother, though."

"Is tomorrow soon enough for that?" Isobel asked, raising onto her knees and straddling him as she'd done earlier. "Because I think, for now, it might be fun to distract you with other things."

Four

Isobel woke as the sun was beginning to cast a corona around the edges of the heavy floor-length drapes at the window. For a moment she was disoriented, but soon remembrance flooded her mind. She lay motionless next to Ethan's sleeping body, listening to his steady breathing, reveling in the warmth that radiated from him. Wow, she thought, that had been quite a night. Who would have thought that Mr. Buttoned-Up would be quite so skilled in the bedroom? She smiled to herself. It was true what they said. It was the quiet ones you had to watch.

Her body still tingled and she felt wonderfully alive. Last night had been special. Very special. She turned her head on the pillow and looked at Ethan in the half light. His beard had grown, dusting his jaw with an even darker haze than had been apparent at dinner. That, and his mussed-up hair, made him look more untamed and approachable than he'd been before. It was as if he was two people. A public, reserved Ethan and a private one. She liked that she'd gotten a chance to spend time with both.

Her fingers itched to reach out and touch him. To awaken him both mentally and physically. But caution stilled her hand. If she was going to leave, best to leave now, while he was still sleeping. That way, they could avoid the awkward goodbye that would come after she told him she'd rather not keep in touch. She wasn't prepared to invest time into any type of commitment. It wasn't her way. And this guy, well, he had commitment written all over him. In fact, she didn't doubt that she'd been an aberration for him.

She slid carefully from the bed and found her dress and shoes on the floor at the end of the bed. Her panties were a lost cause, she decided, after silently scanning the carpet for a minute. Besides, she had clean pairs in her pack. Giving a mental shrug, she held her things to her and carefully made her way to the door, thanking the efficiency of modern maintenance that the door opened and closed silently, allowing her to exit the bedroom without making a sound.

In the main room she located her pack behind the sofa where Ethan had left it last night and quickly got dressed. She'd give just about anything for a hot shower and a toothbrush right now, but she didn't want the sound of running water to wake Ethan. Now that she'd made her decision to cut and run, she didn't want anything to stand in her way. Not even the man who'd ensured she'd enjoyed what had unarguably been the best sex of her entire life.

Her inner muscles clenched on the memory of the pleasure he'd wrung from her. No hit and miss with him. She smiled. No, he was hit after hit every time. A girl could get addicted to that, could want to hang around for more of the same. She reminded herself that she wasn't the hanging-around type. Not for any reason, and certainly not for a man. She was a wanderer through and through, with little to call her own aside from what she could carry in her pack.

Ethan had talked about a family business, relatives that he worked with and spent time with every day. She couldn't imagine an existence more different from her own. No, there was no room for commitment in her life, and no place for some as impermanent as her in his.

Isobel threaded the straps of her shoes through the fingers of one hand while hoisting her pack over one shoulder with the other. She turned to blow a silent kiss in the direction of Ethan's bedroom. It had certainly been fun while it lasted.

In the elevator on the way to the ground floor, Isobel slid her sandals onto her feet and smoothed her dress, thanking the good sense she'd learned years ago to only purchase non-crush fabrics. Sometimes it cost a little more, but it was worth it when you lived a transitory life out of a backpack.

The air had a definite autumnal chill to it when she exited the massive glazed doors of the apartment building and she hesitated under the portico, deciding where she should head to next.

She really needed to find somewhere inexpensive to check into so she could shower and change and get her professional head back on her shoulders. Last night had been a sinfully satisfying deviation from her usual behavior but the sooner she put it behind her, the better. Question was, how was she to do that? She waited in the cool morning air for a few minutes and then, as luck would have it, a taxi pulled to the curb to drop off a passenger. Someone returning from overseas, judging by the amount of luggage the driver hefted from the trunk of the car. As he started to get back in, Isobel stepped forward.

"Excuse me, is there any chance you could take me to a low-price hotel near here?"

"Sure, love. Hop in."

Thanking her lucky stars, Isobel pushed her pack into the backseat and followed it onto the worn upholstery. As the car pulled away, though, she wondered what might have happened if, instead of slinking away, she'd stayed to waken Ethan. Where could they have gone from last night? That they would have made love again was in no doubt. In fact, they could have skipped the potential for morning-after awkwardness and worked their way straight through to afternoon delight.

No, she told herself sternly, forcing her head to remain resolutely facing forward. As good as their night together had been, she had to remember her motto, her very code for living. *Never look back.*

Besides, she had work to do that would have drawn her out of town soon, anyway. A job that was a cakewalk when it came to it, but that would bring in a tidy paycheck. It was these safe, easy glamour jobs that gave her some much-needed rest after a more trying assignment, and paid enough to subsidize the side of her work that was really important.

She'd allowed herself a month to get the project completed to both her and her client's satisfaction. One month to recoup funds, to rest and recharge, and then she was heading back to the African continent. Back to what she did best and what spoke to her heart. What she earned in the next few weeks would grease the palms necessary to get her exactly where she needed to be to take the pictures she needed to take.

But even as the tires on the taxi ate the kilometers putting space between her and Ethan, she still felt that tug— that desire to turn back. To explore the vulnerability that

lay beneath the face Ethan presented to the world at large.
To revel in the strength and capability he exuded. The guy
was addictive. Dangerously addictive. It was just as well
she'd never see him again because deep down she knew
he had the power to make her want to stay with him longer than a night and she couldn't do that.

No, she'd never do that.

Ethan stretched against the fine cotton of the bedsheets
and reached beside him for Isobel's sleeping form, but his
hand came up empty. In fact, the room itself held an emptiness that left him in no doubt that she'd moved on.

Conflicting thoughts plagued him as he rolled out of bed
and walked naked into the main living area of the apartment, just to confirm she had indeed gone. Relief that they
didn't have to face any stilted morning-after discussion,
tempered with a deep regret that they couldn't start the
day the way they'd finished last night, warred within him.

Relief won out. Especially in light of the discussion
they'd had after the first time they'd made love. What on
earth had possessed him to open up in such detail to an
absolute stranger? He hadn't even told his sister the news.
In fact, he didn't even know if he *would* tell her.

Wasn't it far better that Tamsyn remember their dad the
way he'd have wanted to be remembered—not as a man
who'd deliberately altered their family history without so
much as an explanation left behind when he died? Didn't
she deserve at least that? Ethan didn't even want to con-
template what it would do to Tamsyn to learn their mother
had willingly abandoned them. How it would destabilize
the world they'd grown up in.

God, it was all such a mess. No less so than it had been
yesterday but, he had to admit as he walked back into the
bedroom and headed for a shower, at least he himself felt

a little better about it. Somehow, Isobel Fyfe had woven her magic around him from the minute he'd seen her. Just that one chance glimpse of her before she entered the pub, like a butterfly alighting on a leaf, and his day had taken a decided turn for the better. He turned on the shower and stepped in before the water could come up to temperature, yet even the multijet sprays couldn't shake the lingering sensation of her touch from his body, or his mind. Somehow, she'd inveigled her way into his thoughts so thoroughly, and in so short a time, that he couldn't fully dislodge her.

She wasn't his type, he reminded himself. She was only a one-night stand, by her own choice. He hadn't kicked her out—she was the one who had left. Their night together had satisfied both of them, and then she had moved on. It was for the best. It was what he'd wanted, too, after all. The prospect of a single night of no-consequence pleasure with a stranger was the only reason he'd invited her back to the apartment. He never expected to see her again. Yet he could still remember the precise pitch of her laugh, the softness of her voice, the warmth of her breath on his skin, the texture of her tongue as it—

Ethan switched the mixer to cold. This wasn't getting him anywhere but uncomfortable. No, it was best that she'd gone as she had—leaving no trace other than the lingering scent of her fragrance on his bedsheets and the indelible imprint she'd left on his mind. The bedsheets would be taken care of by housekeeping, his mind he could take care of himself. He just needed to change his focus.

Later, as he got ready to head home, back to his work at the winery, he told himself he was succeeding. They couldn't have taken things any further than they had, even if they'd both been interested in doing so. She was completely disconnected from the things that formed the cornerstones of his world. She was a transitory creature of light and laughter—charming, but unreliable. He was stable, grounded in his work and his family. The people in his life depended on him. He needed to be able to depend on them, as well.

He'd needed distracting last night and she'd definitely been quite the distraction.

It was with a satisfied smile on his face that he let himself out of the apartment half an hour later and took the elevator to the basement-level parking. The Isobel Fyfes of this world were good for a fling, and they'd enjoyed a mutually pleasurable one at that, however, she couldn't be further from his idea of a forever woman in his life if she'd actively been trying.

No, it was women like Shanal Peat, one of his old university friends who more closely fit that bill. She was serious and clever and, with her mixed Indian and Australian heritage, exquisitely beautiful. They were already close friends. She'd be a far better life mate for a man like Ethan than Isobel could ever be, plus, with her Ph.D. in viticulture, she'd be a brilliant asset to The Masters winery and vineyard. He could see her fitting in well with his family, with her gentle, steady demeanor. She'd understand and respect the generations of tradition that went into their family vineyard, and would slide seamlessly into their lives and work with no confusion or upheaval.

It would be a mistake to even consider someone more bold, more unexpected and spontaneous. Women like that added excitement to life, but they added chaos, as well. No, a woman like Shanal was exactly what he needed. They were a melding of minds and personalities that could only succeed.

Ethan got into his 5-series BMW and headed out the basement and into the glorious sunshine of another beautiful Adelaide autumn morning. This business with his parents was just a minor glitch. He could take care of it later. And, he wagered, as long as the payments to Ellen Masters continued unabated, he had no reason to worry about her suddenly returning and reasserting her parental rights. The secret could remain a secret a while longer. There was no need for his aunts and uncle to know he was aware of the truth—or for his sister to know anything about the matter at all.

By the time he cruised through the gates of The Masters and past the cellar door tasting room and point of sale, it was late morning. He turned down the private road that led to the main house and pulled his car to a halt outside. As he got out of the car, he took a moment to breathe in the scent of the air and fill his lungs with it.

Home. There was nothing quite like it. His eyes drifted to the top of the ridge where the shell of his family's old home, Master's Rise, destroyed by bush fire more than thirty years ago, still stood. The stone-wall construction of the late-nineteenth-century building had withstood the voraciously hungry flames that had systematically consumed most of the property, and proved too solid to be economically torn down. Its profile endured as a constant reminder of what could be lost, while the lands that roamed beneath it continued as proof of what could be achieved in the face of disaster.

Ethan looked around at what his family had rebuilt in his father's lifetime. The large double-storied home that housed most of the family under its roof, the vineyards stretching across the valley and up the hill, the winery, which consumed Ethan's time and expertise and challenged him in all ways to constantly do better. Yeah, it was good to be home and even better to have this all to come home to.

A movement on the path from one of the luxury cottages, which provided accommodation for guests, caught his attention. Tamsyn, his sister, ran that side of the business, and had probably just finished the final inspection of the cabin for a guest before walking back toward the house.

"Good morning," she said with a smile as she drew nearer. She gave an exaggerated look at her watch. "Or should I say, afternoon?"

He smiled in return. "It's still morning," he confirmed.

"Did you have a good night in town?" she inquired innocently, although the sparkle in her eyes told him she was delving for more information.

"Yeah, thanks," he replied, deliberately vague.

Tamsyn sighed. "No gossip?"

"Since when have I been the subject of gossip?"

"You know what I mean," she said on a huff of disappointment. "You need to get a life, Ethan. Sometimes you're just too absorbed in this place."

He looked at her this time, really looked. There was a note in her voice that implied dissatisfaction in her world, something he'd never heard from her before.

"Is everything okay, Tam?"

She pasted on a broad smile. "Of course. Why wouldn't it be, right? By the way, are you going to be at dinner this evening? I have the new photographer for the catalog shoot arriving later this afternoon and I'd like you to meet—"

"Sure, I'll be there," he interrupted. "Same time, same place," he said with a wink.

It was a family joke. Whichever family members were in residence usually met for predinner drinks in the main salon before dining together. It was a good way to stay in touch, although he knew that some people found it a bit old-fashioned. Personally, he liked that some traditions remained the same, and there was always the option of cooking for yourself—something he was generally loath to do. It would be tough, though, facing his aunts and his uncle. Looking them in the eye and knowing they had conspired to keep a secret from Tamsyn and him for all this time. Did they not wonder, now John Masters was dead, if the truth would come out? Well, Ethan certainly wouldn't be throwing it into the conversational pot tonight. He still needed time to come to terms with it himself.

He continued. "How's the wedding business going?"

"Mine, or for here?"

As part of her work in running the accommodation side at The Masters, Tamsyn also oversaw special events—business retreats and the like. Since her engagement to Trent Mayweather just over a year ago, she had happily expanded into coordinating small, but exclusive, wedding packages at the property.

"Either. Both." Ethan shrugged.

"Fine. The latest bridezilla would seem to finally be appeased by the fact that, since harvest is well and truly under way, we will not have green vines flush with grapes for her favored photo shoot, so overall things are looking good. And since Trent and I have yet to set a date, there's no business to worry about there," she replied airily.

Still no date. Despite her determined attempt to sound flip about the issue, Ethan sensed there was an underlying hint of frustration in her voice. Before he could press her further, Tamsyn changed the subject.

"Did you manage to get everything done that you needed to in the city?"

A shadow passed over him and he suppressed a small shiver. Tam had enough on her plate right now without more stress. He was glad he'd decided not to share his father's secret with her yet.

"It's all the same old, same old."

Tamsyn began to speak but the cell phone in her hand began to chime the wedding march. "Uh-oh, bridezilla again. I need to take this. Talk later?"

Ethan gave her a nod and watched as she pasted on a smile while she answered the call and slowly walked toward the house. She did that a lot lately, he realized. Fake smiled, faked being happy. He'd put it down to grief over their father's sudden death, but he couldn't help but wonder if there wasn't more to it. Trent appeared to have offered her precious little support to date. Sure, the guy was busy at his inner-city law practice, but there were times when loved ones came first. Were things not entirely right in their relationship? He made a mental note to dig a little deeper next time he and Tam were alone together, but for now he had other demands on his time. Work demands that he should have been here earlier to attend to...if he hadn't been so willingly distracted last night.

Ethan entered the salon later that evening, satisfied he'd put in a good afternoon's work at the winery. Fermentation had begun on the first of the season's harvests and he had high hopes for the new wine. As he walked into the room, he scanned those already there. His aunt Cynthia reigned with her usual regal decorum, his uncle Edward stood head to head with his wife, Marianne, in quiet discussion.

Looking at them, no one would have suspected they'd colluded with their brother, John, to hide the truth about Ethan and Tamsyn's mother.

Still, in this family, blood ran deep and thick and, up until his death, John had been very much the patriarch whose word was final. With a little more distance from the revelation, Ethan found himself more willing to forgive his relatives for falling in line with his father's wishes. If whatever he'd decreed had been seen to be in the best interests of the family and the business, it would have been adhered to. No matter the cost.

Ethan joined his cousins, two of Edward's three adult children, Cade and Cathleen, who ran the cellar door, tasting room and café operation at the property.

"Busy day?" he asked them after he'd poured himself a glass of Shiraz.

"Busloads today," Cathleen commented ruefully. "The poor kitchen staff was flat out with washing dishes by hand after the dishwasher broke down, and there's still tomorrow's usual Sunday crowd to come. I've called in a couple of casuals to help out."

"That's good. So, are you still wanting to expand to include dinners with the café menu?" Ethan asked.

"Of course," Cade confirmed. "The figures are looking good for the expansion. Demand is already there. Besides, with Tamsyn's wedding side of things becoming more popular, it makes sense to ride on her coattails. After attending a wedding here, there've been plenty of guests who have wanted to come back for an evening meal at another time."

Ethan nodded. It was surprising how, in such a short period of time, the family business had expanded from purely being a vineyard and winery to what was now far more diverse than what their grandparents, or even their parents, had ever imagined. Cade and Cathleen's older brother, Raif, worked the viticulture side of The Masters with his father.

"Did you hear that Tamsyn managed to secure IF Photography for the new catalogs?" Cathleen interrupted his thoughts. "Our chef is beside himself with glee and can't wait for her to start."

"Tam mentioned something about a photographer," Ethan said absently. Tamsyn hadn't turned up yet tonight. He hoped she was okay.

"*Award-winning* photographer. She's from New Zealand, apparently, but travels worldwide," Cathleen corrected excitedly. "We're lucky to get her at all but to have her here for a month doing all aspects of The Masters is amazing. The new catalogs and web photos will be fantastic."

"Well, they do have great material to work with," Ethan said with a wink. "Speaking of Tam, do you know where she is tonight? I thought she'd be here by—"

A frisson of awareness traced a ghostly fingertip down the back of Ethan's neck.

"She's just arrived," Cathleen said, gesturing toward the entrance to the salon. "Oh, and look who's with her! She must be the photographer. Let's go and say hi."

Ethan stiffened and all his senses went on alert as Cade and Cathleen went over to greet the newcomers. IF Photography. *IF.* The initials trickled through his mind coming to one conclusion. Isobel Fyfe.

Surely not.

He turned and faced his sister and her guest and felt the blood drain from his head in shock as he recognized the angel-haired woman at his sister's side.

Five

Isobel saw the exact moment Ethan registered her presence and noted as, in equal measures, shock and then anger flooded his features. Tamsyn was happily oblivious to Ethan's rising fury as she introduced Isobel to Cade and Cathleen and then to the others in the room, working in a circle until they ended up in front of Ethan.

Masters. So that was his surname. A shame she hadn't paid more notice at the time, Isobel thought with an inward cringe. It would certainly have avoided this predicament. Clearly, he thought she knew, and was not happy that she'd kept their upcoming encounter a secret.

Every line in Ethan's body broadcast his displeasure at her appearance and his brows pulled together in a forbidding line.

"Ethan, this is Isobel Fyfe, the photographer I was telling you about. Isobel, this is my big brother, Ethan. Don't pay too much attention to him. His bark is always way worse than his bite."

Isobel felt her cheeks flame with color. She knew exactly what Ethan's bite was like. In fact, she still had a few faint marks on her body here and there to prove it. She extended her hand and waited for Ethan to observe the proprieties.

"Ms. Fyfe," he said stiffly, finally extending his hands and briefly clasping hers.

As brief as the contact was, she knew he felt the same flare of physical reaction she did. His eyes flamed ever so briefly before resuming their cold appraisal of her.

"Please, call me Isobel," she said with a smile that felt artificial on her lips. "I prefer not to stand on formality."

"And you must call him Ethan," Tamsyn said. "We're all on first-name terms here."

Isobel cast a look at Ethan, a little unnerved by the intensity of his glare. It made a small wave of anger rise inside her. He had no need to be so angry or distant. She hadn't kept anything from him deliberately—she honestly hadn't realized their paths would cross again. And was it so terrible that they had? Did he think she was the type to kiss and tell? It wasn't like she was about to share intimate details of his sexual prowess with the people in the room with them. Nor was she likely to bring up the matters he shared with her about his parents. His bristling attitude was offensive and she didn't hesitate to turn away from him when Tamsyn drew her attention to another part of the room.

She could feel his eyes boring in her back as they walked away and it raised her ire another notch. How dare he treat her that way? Sure, they'd neither of them expected to see one another again but she'd never have anticipated him being so...so distant. Jerk.

Unbidden, the shaded image of him over her body, slowly entering her, driving her to another glorious peak of satisfaction, speared through her mind. She drew in a sharp breath as her body gave a sudden pulse of remembered pleasure.

"Are you okay?" Tamsyn asked. "I'm sorry about Ethan. He's usually far more friendly. I think there's something bothering him at the moment and, knowing him, we won't hear about it until he's sorted it all out himself." She gave a little embarrassed laugh.

"I'm fine, really," Isobel hastened to reassure her. What had happened between her and Ethan was between the two of them only, and by the looks of things, Ethan was suffering from an overabundant dose of regret. Well, that was his problem, Isobel decided. She was here to do a job and that's exactly what she was going to do.

She focused her attention back to Tamsyn. "Tell me about your cousins—Raif, Cade and Cathleen. Am I right? Aren't those the names of the Calvert children in *Gone with the Wind?*"

Tamsyn laughed. "Yeah, Aunt Marianne is a big Margaret Mitchell fan."

All through the evening and even during dinner she could still feel Ethan watching her, but she did her best to ignore him. They were seated at opposite ends of the long and impeccably set dining table and it took next to no effort to keep her own gaze riveted to the other family members around her. She thought she had everyone pegged so far.

Cynthia was very much in charge of the household. A beautiful woman, but with a hardness about her mouth and eyes that gave fair warning that she had very high expectations of those around her. She'd make an interesting photographic study. Edward and his wife appeared to be close, and generally friendlier than Cynthia. Isobel wondered how Ethan and Tamsyn's father must have fit into all of this. She assumed he would have been the eldest of the family, much as Ethan was amongst his cousins.

The Masters family made for interesting watching, that was for sure. All attractive in their own ways, and each with very clearly defined personalities and yet close-knit at the same time. It was a fascinating dynamic from the point of view of someone who had grown up as an only child and without extended family. A long-hidden part of her felt a deep twinge of envy at the easy way they all took one another's presence in each other's lives for granted, but she suppressed it almost as swiftly as it surfaced.

Never look back.

It was later, as the evening was drawing to an end and only a few remained at the table drinking coffee and lingering over their desserts, that she proffered her thanks for the evening and rose from the table. To her surprise, Ethan rose, too.

"I'll see Isobel to her accommodation," he said firmly, his hand squeezing Tamsyn's shoulder gently and keeping her in her seat as she made to rise with them. "You go on up and have an early night."

"If you're sure?" Tamsyn said, looking up at her brother and then across at Isobel.

"I can make my own way," Isobel said quickly. "The path is well lit and it's a beautiful evening."

"I wouldn't think of letting you walk back alone on your first night," Ethan said smoothly, closing the distance between them and gesturing to the French doors that led outside to the massive wraparound decking.

Once they were a short distance from the house Ethan drew to a halt.

"What are you playing at?" he asked in a steely tone.

"Playing?"

"Why didn't you tell me last night that you were coming here?"

Isobel gave a humorless laugh. "Because I didn't know this was your home. I didn't catch your surname over the noise in the bar and I really didn't think it mattered enough to ask."

"It matters. I want you to leave. Make up some excuse in the morning and just go. I'll cover your costs."

"Wow, that's good of you, especially since you probably have no idea of what I charge," Isobel said with as much sarcasm as she could muster. "But I think you're forgetting something. I am a professional and I've entered into a contract with The Masters to provide my services. That's exactly what I'm going to do."

"I'm sure there's an out clause in there somewhere. Look, I'll even pay a premium on top of your fee."

"What makes you think I'm so desperate for money that I'd do what you're asking?"

"For goodness' sake, you live out of a backpack and, by your own admission last night, you don't *own* anything of real value. Of course you want the money."

Her pride stung at his arrogance. Was this the real Ethan Masters? How could he be so different from the man she'd spent last night with?

"Look, I'm more than happy to stay out of your way but my contract is with Tamsyn and her marketing division, and I always honor my contracts."

He took a step closer and instantly her senses were flooded with the warmth emanating from his body, and the discreet lightly wooded scent he wore. She inhaled it without thinking and her body went on full alert—her nipples tightening, her breasts feeling full and heavy and aching for his touch. Heat gathered low down in her body.

God, even at his condescending worst she was attracted to him. How pathetic was that?

"But that's part of the problem, isn't it, Isobel? You won't be able to stay out of my way—and more than that, you won't be able to stay out of Tamsyn's way."

She had been turned away from him slightly, refusing to meet his dark eyes as she stared at a point in the fragrant garden just beyond them, but her surprise at this turned her eyes back to lock with his.

"What's wrong with me interacting with Tamsyn? You're a grown man—even if she finds out that we spent the night together, why would she care?"

"I'm not worried about that, I'm worried about you sharing my confidences in you with Tamsyn."

Again she felt the stinging barbs of his words. Isobel drew in a steadying breath and faced him full on.

"Ah, so you haven't told your sister yet? Don't you think you ought to? She deserves to know."

"That's for me to decide. Look, I barely know you, I don't know if I can trust you, or if I even want to."

"Well, that's just a risk you're going to have to take, isn't it?"

She turned and stepped away, determined that was the end of their conversation, but warm fingers caught at her hand and tugged her back toward him. Fiery tendrils of desire wound their way through her body.

"I'm warning you, Isobel. I'm not a man to be tangled with. Do not disclose any of what I told you to my sister."

Isobel yanked her hand loose, absently rubbing it with her other hand in a vain attempt to wipe away the lingering sensation of his touch.

"And I'm not the kind of woman who responds well to orders," she hissed back at him. "Don't worry—I already regret meeting you. *Tangling* with you again, as you so eloquently put it, is the last thing on my mind."

She stalked away from him, her entire body vibrating with anger. How dare he treat her this way? If it wasn't such a matter of principle for her to never walk away from a job, she'd have told him exactly, and in explicit detail, where he could shove his money and his stupid family secrets. Isobel's eyes burned. To her shock she realized she was crying. She never cried. Tears of anger, that's all they were, nothing more. She swiped at the moisture on her cheeks and silently vowed not to let Ethan Masters get under her skin again for the duration of her stay here. In any way, shape or form.

Ethan watched Isobel until she reached the cottage she'd been assigned. He flinched as he heard the heavy wooden front door slam closed. It would seem he'd managed to get his point across—rather more forcefully than he'd intended. He shook his head. In his shock at seeing her here tonight, in his home, he'd allowed anger to cloud his decisions, to direct his behavior. He'd lacked his usual level of control. And it hadn't just been because he worried about her spilling secrets. No, it was because in spite of his concerns, in spite of the very real damage she could do to his family, he still couldn't stop himself from being damnably drawn to her. She did that to him.

He turned and walked slowly toward the main house. His direct approach to Isobel had been clumsy, but he still had another option up his sleeve to get her to leave. Isobel had insisted her contract was with Tamsyn—that meant Tamsyn could withdraw it. He looked up to the second-story windows that he knew were his sister's. The lights were still on. He let go a short sigh of relief. Good, he could deal with this tonight rather than wait until morning.

Ethan let himself into the house and headed for the main stairs. In no time his knuckles rapped out a gentle tattoo on Tamsyn's door.

"Ethan?" she said from inside.

"Yeah, got a minute?"

"Sure, come in."

He let himself into the room and closed the door behind him. His sister was curled up on the small sofa in front of an empty fireplace. It wouldn't be long before the small cavern would be glowing with the cheerful light of a fire as autumn slowly gave way to winter, but today its emptiness seemed sad and lonely.

"Did you see Isobel to the cottage okay?" Tamsyn asked, putting down the book she'd been reading onto a side table.

"I did, and she's what I want to talk to you about."

"Really?" An expression of interest flickered across his sister's features. "What do you want to know?"

Ethan rested one hand on the polished wooden mantel and chose his next words carefully.

"How much do you know about Isobel Fyfe?"

"What I've heard by referral mostly, and from her website. Why? Are you worried about something? Don't you think she's capable of doing the job?"

"I don't think she's right for the job, to be honest. Can we break the contract, Tam?"

Tamsyn sat upright and looked at him in surprise. "Break the contract? Why?"

"I'd rather we use someone else," he said bluntly.

"Seriously, Ethan, without a very good reason I'm not going to break the contract with Isobel. She came very highly recommended and her portfolio is extensive. We were lucky to get her as much of her work is done overseas, and she's only in Australia for a month. What have you got against her?"

"I'd prefer not to say."

This was more difficult than he'd thought. Normally, Tamsyn was only too happy to acquiesce to his suggestions but in this instance, of all instances, she'd decided to be stubborn.

"Well, like I said before, unless you can give me a good reason, she's staying."

What reason could he give his sister? That, because of his carelessness, Isobel held a secret that could rock the foundations of Tamsyn's world? That she held the key to unlocking a potential world of hurt and unanswerable questions?

Tamsyn's eyes, so like his own, bored into him as he remained silent. He saw the exact second an idea occurred to her.

"You're attracted to her, aren't you?" Tamsyn could be equally as blunt as him.

"That's not the point," he said, unable to straight out lie to her and deny her observation.

Tamsyn smiled. "What are you afraid of, Ethan? Following your heart?"

"There's no danger of my heart being involved," he said firmly. "Besides, you know I plan to marry Shanal one day."

Tamsyn snorted in an unladylike fashion. "Look, I love Shanal, she's a great friend but there's no spark between you. Why are you afraid of exploring something with someone who doesn't come in a paint-by-numbers relationship?"

Paint by numbers? Was that what she thought of his friendship with Shanal? Just because he considered a relationship between them rationally, evaluating the different traits and compatibilities they'd bring to a marriage rather than getting swept away in meaningless passion? What was wrong with that?

And as to exploring "something" with Isobel, he'd already been there. Talk about getting swept away... His fists clenched involuntarily as his body was flooded with remembrance of what they'd been doing with one another only twenty-four hours ago. He tamped the wayward sensation down by sheer force of will.

"There's no shame in leading with your head rather than your heart, Tam."

"That's not my point," Tamsyn said, getting up from the sofa and coming to stand in front of him. "You're my brother and I love you, Ethan. But sometimes you infuriate me, especially when you are hell-bent on controlling everything around you. Some things are not meant to be controlled."

"Look, I didn't come in here for a discussion about my love life. I came to talk about Isobel Fyfe's unsuitability."

To his surprise, Tamsyn laughed out loud.

"Really, Ethan? Is this a case of protesting just a bit too much? I saw the way you looked at her tonight."

"Looked at her? What do you mean?" he demanded, more than a little bit thrown by her questions.

"It's hard to describe. Half the time you looked as if you wanted to devour her. Seriously. You barely took your eyes off her all night and she was working equally as hard *not* to watch you. If I didn't know better, I'd say you two had met before or had some history together."

Ethan fought to keep his features composed. Sometimes his sister was too observant and she knew him too well.

"That's it, isn't it?" Tamsyn pressed. "You've met her before. When?"

"You're being ridiculous," he hedged. "If you're not prepared to cancel her contract then could you at least make sure you keep her out of my way as much as possible for the time she's here? For all our sakes." It wouldn't do much good if he couldn't keep her away from Tamsyn, too, but at least if Isobel wasn't around him, he might be able to think clearly and come up with a better plan.

He walked from Tamsyn's room, determined not to utter another word on the subject. But before he'd left, he'd seen the shrewdly assessing look in Tamsyn's eyes—and the light of mischief there. He groaned out loud when he got to his suite. He should have left well enough alone and not raised the subject with his sister. Now she'd be like a dog with a bone over it.

Two hours later he still couldn't sleep. Dressed only in pajama bottoms, he padded across the lushly carpeted floor to his windows and stared out in the darkness across to the cottage where Isobel was. As he stood there, a light flicked on inside the cottage. So, she couldn't sleep, either. He absently rubbed his belly, his hand stilling as he remembered her touch—her hand, her mouth, her tongue— at the very same spot last night.

Desire rolled through him and he closed his eyes briefly, seeing in his mind's eye the shimmer of her fair skin in the half light of the room, feeling its smooth softness beneath him. Feeling her.

His eyes flew open. The light at the cottage was still on. Damn. Ethan reached for the pull cord and yanked his drapes closed, but even knowing he'd blocked her from view, he couldn't help thinking that it looked like it was going to be a long night for them both.

Six

Isobel woke the next morning still furious. As if it wasn't enough that Ethan Masters had consumed her waking thoughts with his arrogance, his skillful lovemaking from the night before had infiltrated her sleep. As a result, she'd woken an aching, frustrated wreck, torn between the urge to track him down and slap him…or track him down and pounce on him. Not her best look, that was for sure, she decided as she surveyed herself in the bathroom mirror.

Thankfully, she didn't have to face anyone yet this morning. She'd asked for the time to herself, to familiarize herself with the property and the layout. To ease into the feel of the place so she could reflect its special character in the photos she was to create for their new marketing plan. She turned away from the mirror and started the shower running. During her usual jobs, showers were a rare luxury—and the one in this cabin was uncommonly nice. If only she could enjoy it without her head full of distractions. A quick wash and rinse of her hair and she was done and back out again.

Five minutes later, Isobel was dressed and busily surveying the contents of the refrigerator in the very compact yet well-appointed kitchen. They really thought of everything here, which gave her an idea. She grabbed one of her cameras and took a few quick shots of the contents of the fridge. Then, grabbing a banana, she went outside.

The land here was beautiful, especially in the early-morning light. Row upon row of grapevines and framework stretched across the land and up the hillside almost as far as she could see. And there, up on the ridge of one hill, stood a massive ruin. Her curiosity piqued, she pulled the door of the cottage closed behind her and struck out in that direction.

She'd raised a light sweat by the time she crested the hill. Ahead of her rose the remains of what must have once been a magnificent residence. Isobel spun in a slow circle. Clearly, from here, the house had overlooked the land in all directions, almost like a castle set atop a mountain. There was even a tower standing about four stories tall.

She walked closer, eyeing the red brick walls that loomed above her, the gaping holes where windows were once the eyes upon the valley below. A strange sadness settled over her. So much destruction, so much loss. Here and there plants had taken a hold in the brickwork, finding purchase in the most unlikely of places. Nature had a way of doing that, she reminded herself. It reclaimed everything if left to do so.

She raised her camera, shooting off a series of shots, fascinated by the play of light through the yawning window frames and the juxtaposition of new life and growth with what had been the complete obliteration of a wealthy home. The sound of hoofbeats and the creak of leather dragged her attention back to the here and now.

A large, dark horse cantered with incredible grace across the hard-packed ground, the man on its back no less beautiful. Her body recognized him before she could make out his face. Ethan reined in the horse a few meters in front of her.

"I didn't realize your charter included the ruin," he said stiffly, looking down the long blade of his nose at her.

"My *charter,* as you so eloquently put it, is to compile a collection of photos of the property, and specifically to create dossiers of pictures for each business center associated with The Masters. This is part of the property, is it not?"

She squinted up at him. Had he done that on purpose? Ridden toward her with the sun at his back to put her at a disadvantage?

"Part of its history, not its present." He swung one long denim-clad leg over the back of the horse and, letting go of the reins, kicked out of the other stirrup to drop, with the finesse of a large cat, to the ground. He took a few steps toward her.

"Aren't you worried he'll run away?" she asked, gesturing toward the horse.

Ethan shook his head. "He knows his place."

Isobel felt her lips pull into a smile. She had to hand it to the guy. He was nothing if not confident and completely self-assured. Her eyes raked over him, taking in the slightly mussed hair from his ride, the beat of his pulse at the open neck of his shirt, the way his cuffs were rolled up slightly exposing strong forearms. She rapidly averted her gaze before she did anything stupid, like start to send him the wrong signals.

Ethan Masters obviously knew his place, too. Master of all he surveyed. Looking out over the vineyard and the buildings below them, she had to admit that it was quite an estate that he lorded over. But that didn't mean she answered to him.

Ignoring every cell in her body, which demanded she stay within Ethan's orbit, she took a few steps away.

"I think I'll head back."

"So soon?"

There was a note to his voice that she didn't quite understand. Half snark, half enticement. He was a conundrum, all right. Last night he'd made it clear that she was persona non grata. At least as far as he was concerned. And yet, just now, he must have seen her here and had chosen to join her. He could easily have avoided talking to her.

Isobel shrugged. "I've been here awhile."

"Don't you want to hear the history behind Masters' Rise? Most do."

"I'm not most people, though, am I?"

He cocked his head slightly to one side, as if he was seeing her again but for the first time. "No, you're definitely not."

"It's not my habit to look at the past," she felt compelled to add. "I'm more about the here and now."

"An interesting trait," he commented.

"One I thought you might appreciate, given that you seem to want to forget we met before last night," she answered, the challenge clear in her voice.

"Touché," he said with a quirk of his lips. "Look, I'm sorry for how I reacted last night. It was uncalled for."

Isobel stared in surprise. An apology? From Ethan? Goodness—maybe the moon really was made of blue cheese after all.

"Apology accepted," she managed to say, biting her tongue to prevent herself from adding a smart-mouthed rejoinder.

Ethan gave a brief nod. "If you're heading back now, do you want a ride?"

"On that?" she asked.

There was little that frightened Isobel in this world, but horses were very near the top of that short list. In fact, she'd rather be sheltering under gunfire from tribal militia than climb on board that creature. No one said fear had to be rational.

"Afraid?"

There was a distinct challenge in that single word.

"Definitely," she said. "Thanks, but I'll walk."

"I won't let any harm come to you." He held out a hand. "Come on. Don't you trust me?"

She shook her head. "After last night, no. You made your feelings about me being here quite clear."

"Perhaps I'm merely being a good host."

Isobel snorted her disbelief. "Look, I said I'm happy to stay out of your way as much as I can, so how about you let me do that?"

Ethan fixed her with a hard stare, his chiseled lips set into a firm line of disapproval. Clearly, he was used to being obeyed, especially in his own domain. She held his gaze with her chin tilted up. Obedience had never been her strongest suit.

"Fine," he said after what felt like long minutes rather than seconds. "Tamsyn mentioned at breakfast that she plans to pick you up at the cottage at lunchtime for your full tour of the property today. Don't keep her waiting."

Ethan swung up onto the back of his horse and gathered the reins. Without another word he wheeled the beast around and headed back in the direction he'd arrived.

Isobel couldn't tear her eyes from the dashing figure he made on horseback. His long, powerful legs clamped to the horse's flanks, his body moving in synchronicity with the animal's gait. His fluidity and grace sent a wild spear of longing through her.

What would it have been like to double back with him? To feel the strength of his body supporting hers, to relinquish her safety to him and his ability to control the powerful animal beneath him? Isobel clenched her hands into tight fists and fought back the groan of frustration that built inside. Ethan had a powerful magnetism that pushed all her buttons every blasted time she came into contact with him. She needed to get a grip on herself or this contract would prove to be the most difficult and potentially dangerous one she'd ever embarked upon. Not physically, perhaps, but mentally—and she'd never, ever let anyone mess with her mind before.

She didn't plan to now, either.

Ethan checked the first of the ferments he had in progress and was relieved to have the distraction. What on earth had possessed him to talk to Isobel Fyfe this morning? He'd woken, determined to keep as much space between them as possible and had taken Obsidian for a much-needed dose of exercise and fresh air to clear his head. But the instant he'd seen a flash of color topped by the sun-kissed glow of blond hair, he'd headed toward the ruins. Even knowing it could only have been one person, he'd still gone there. Was he a closet masochist perhaps? he wondered scathingly as he considered his earlier actions.

She'd walked and climbed a fair distance and yet she'd looked as fresh and ready to tackle the return journey as she'd probably been when she'd started. She'd virtually glowed with health and vitality and he had to admire her fitness. He could attest personally to her physical strength, stamina and agility, and that memory hovered persistently at the back of his mind.

Relief warred with frustration at her refusal to ride back to the house with him. He wasn't used to being turned down, and for all he'd sworn he'd steer clear of her there was a part of him that still craved the warmth of her body hard against his—even if it was only on the back of a horse. He'd owed Isobel an apology; he'd given it. That was all.

Ethan shook his head and attempted to apply himself to his work. He had a meeting with Raif and Uncle Edward later today to discuss future planting programs and there was still plenty to attend to here at the winery. He was ever thankful that he had a strong team working with him. Without their hard work and support, especially through this fermentation period, he wouldn't be able to accomplish nearly as much. And he needed to accomplish something today—needed something to occupy his mind and energy so they wouldn't keep turning in the wrong direction.

He was particularly excited about the special reserve chardonnay they would soon be harvesting from The Masters reserve block. The oldest vines on the property, and the only ones to survive the fire that had decimated the house on the hill and virtually everything around it, they had been the backbone of the business as the family knew it today. There was a sense of pride and longevity in every vintage he'd been involved in and the harvest would be painstakingly handpicked before being crushed to extract the juice. The timing of the harvest was crucial to the outcome of the wine, as would be the fermentation process, but Ethan had full confidence in his team's ability to bring out the very best the crop had to offer.

He loved his work. Loved the science and the technicalities, as well as the romance and sensibilities involved in the making of the fine wines The Masters prided themselves on. And this part of the property, where the grapes reached their full potential, was his place.

A noise at the door made him stop what he was doing and turn to see who'd arrived.

"And this is the winery," Tamsyn said. "Where, according to Ethan, the magic begins, although I think Uncle Edward and Raif would have something to say about that because to them it's all about the vines."

Ethan's body went on high alert as Tamsyn and Isobel came toward him. Isobel had changed from her earlier attire and was wearing a soft floaty dress that alternately clung and flicked away around her legs. Legs he wasn't looking at, he reminded himself while dragging his eyes up her body.

"I'm showing Isobel around the property," Tamsyn said with a blithe smile, completely ignoring the daggers he was mentally throwing at her. "I thought we'd start here."

Before Ethan could respond, Tamsyn's cell phone began to trill and she excused herself to take the call.

"So this is where the magic begins, huh? With you?" Isobel said softly. "Who'd have thought?"

Ethan's eyes meshed with hers and he couldn't help thinking about the breathtaking magic they'd created together. Before he could answer, Tamsyn ended her call.

"Ethan, that was bridezilla's mom. I have to meet them at the restaurant to confirm the menus again. Looks like the apple didn't fall far from the tree with that bunch."

"Now?" he asked, struggling to keep a note of somewhat panicked displeasure from his tone.

"Sure, now. Nothing with that family is ever anything less than immediate. You can look after Isobel, right?" She turned to Isobel and gave her a quick hug. "Sorry to dump you on my brother, but if I don't get back here in the next couple of hours, I'll still see you for a drink before dinner, okay?"

And then she was gone. Leaving him alone, quite deliberately he suspected, with the one woman he would have preferred on the other side of the world.

"Look, I'll just take care of myself," Isobel began. "It's obvious you're busy."

Every cell in his body urged him to accept her offer but a perverse alter ego pushed him to reply in the negative. Did she think he couldn't control himself around her, couldn't be the flawless host and tour guide the situation required him to be? She would learn that there was little he could not do, once he set his mind to it.

"I can spare a few minutes to show you around."

"Look, only if you're sure it's no bother."

"Come on," he said, gesturing for her to follow.

"Why do I get the impression you've neglected to say 'Let's get this over with' at the end of that?"

There was a barely suppressed bubble of laughter at the back of her voice and he felt his lips tug reluctantly into a wry smile in response. "I didn't say that." Though apparently, it was completely obvious that that was what he'd been thinking.

She laughed out loud at his dry response. "Look, why don't we start as if we have never met before."

Ethan looked at her askance. "You have to be kidding, right?"

Even now her light scent filled his nostrils. He could still vividly remember the feel of her body against his, the taste of her skin, the sensation of joining with her in the most intimate of possible ways. No, there was no way on this earth that he was capable of pretending they'd never met before, never shared the closeness and familiarity with one another's bodies that they'd experienced.

"Yeah, okay, you're right. It was worth a shot." She looked around the area they were in, taking in the large tanks and barrels that lined the walls. "This really is where it happens, isn't it? Can you walk me through what has to take place to get to this point and what it is that you do here?"

"I thought you were a photographer, not a wannabe winemaker."

Isobel shrugged. "I like to understand my subjects before I begin to work. Makes it easier to know what is important and what isn't."

Ethan gave her an assessing look, taken aback by how genuinely interested she appeared. He launched into a description of the coordination of tasks that were required between the vineyard and the winery and was challenged by the astute questions she asked in a bid for more information. By the time he was leading her through the building to the main entrance, a couple of hours had flown by.

She was surprisingly good company, though all along his body had been buoyed by a buzz of latent attraction that simmered beneath the surface. He'd tried to avoid physical contact, but on those few occasions their hands had brushed as they walked along, he'd been shocked by the flare of hunger and desire that had flashed through him.

Their attraction was dangerously addictive, her proximity here at The Masters all too enticingly near. He had to create some distance or the next few weeks would be absolute hell.

He was surprised to see Tamsyn walking toward the winery as he and Isobel left the building.

"Meeting go okay?" he asked as his sister drew nearer.

"Well, we have a consensus—for today, at least," Tamsyn said with a weary smile.

His sister looked from him to Isobel and back again. He could see the light of an unasked question clear in her eyes and it forced him into making a decision.

"Now that you're back to take care of Ms. Fyfe, I'm off to see Shanal."

"Shanal? Today?"

He didn't answer Tamsyn directly but turned instead to Isobel. "Let me know if you need more information and when you plan to start shooting."

"Sure, thanks for your time."

She sounded polite, professional and as far removed from the lover whose skin he'd explored thoroughly with both his hands and his mouth as it was possible to be. And yet, despite all that, he still felt that zing of awareness when she held out her hand to shake his. The instant his hand enveloped hers he wanted to tug her toward him, wrap her in his arms and kiss her like he'd been aching to do since last night.

As if her hand was suddenly and unbearably hot, he let her go, gave Tamsyn a nod and turned back to the winery. As delectable as Isobel Fyfe's company had been, he wasn't going to go there again. He'd have to be wary around her, especially given her growing friendship with Tamsyn. Could he trust her with what she knew? Could he be certain that she wouldn't take it upon herself to share with his sister the information he wanted to keep only to himself?

Only time would tell, he thought as he lifted his phone to his ear, the auto dial already punching through to Shanal Peat's mobile. There was no way he could know for sure, unless he was prepared to spend day in and day out at Isobel's side—and right now, as disconcerting as the thought had been, and as emphatic as he'd been about keeping some distance between them, it also held tantalizing appeal.

Seven

Isobel looked around the gathering. Friday night looked to be friends' night at The Masters, and the swell of people stretched across the back lawn and wide veranda of the main house looked as if they were well used to the company and the surroundings. One arrival had interested her the most. The woman was an exotic beauty with mixed Indian and Australian heritage that made Isobel's fingers itch to reach for her camera and capture the play of late-afternoon light across Shanal Peat's exquisite features.

She looked around for Ethan, expecting to see him here already.

"Looking for my brother?" Tamsyn asked from beside her.

"No, not really," Isobel protested but even she knew the conviction in her voice was weak.

"He's still at the winery, although I'm sure when he hears that Shanal is here, he'll be over. This is usually his most antisocial time of the year so I'm surprised he invited her today." Tamsyn gave Isobel an assessing look even as she hung on the arm of a tall, leanly built man with sandy hair and blue eyes. "Unless he thinks he needs the added protection, that is."

"Not from me, that's for certain," Isobel said firmly.

All week Tamsyn had been passing remarks about her brother and Isobel that had been laden with innuendo, and all week Isobel had been deflecting them as carefully as she could. It didn't help that every time she'd caught a glimpse of the man in question she'd felt her heart rate speed up while a flush of heat, and something more, spread through her body. Each member of the Masters family was charming and attractive, certainly more so than any one family deserved or ought to be, but Ethan seemed to be the only one who hit her hot button.

"Have you met my fiancé yet?" Tamsyn asked. "Trent works for a law firm in the city—too hard, I might add. Trent, this is Isobel Fyfe. She's the photographer I was telling you about. Isobel, Trent Mayweather."

"Pleased to meet you," Isobel said, extending her hand.

She was surprised when Trent only gripped the tip of her fingers and gave her a halfhearted shake. The action rankled with her and made her feel as if she was being treated as undeserving of the full force of his attention. Swiftly, she pushed her negative thoughts aside. The guy was probably only being polite and didn't want to inflict a bone crusher on her. Besides, he was Tamsyn's fiancé and the other woman was very clearly in love with the man at her side. There must be more to him than she was seeing at the moment. Maybe she'd just caught him at the tail end of a bad day.

"And you," he said in a voice as smooth as his *GQ* attire

and expertly styled hair. "I followed your blog while you were in Africa last month. It's great work you do there."

The guy jumped in her estimation.

"Thanks. I do what I can to raise public awareness. I'm planning to head back after this assignment."

"But weren't you—"

"Invited to leave?" Isobel said with a broad smile. "Yes, but I have my methods. I'm confident I can get back and finish what I'd set out to do."

Trent nodded. "I admire your tenacity. I don't think I'd be as brave."

"Actually, bravery doesn't really enter into it," she replied. "I'm sure you have situations in your work where you're not prepared to back down, no matter the incentive to do so."

"You're right," he conceded. "Although the danger levels are perhaps a little less obvious in the Supreme Court."

Isobel laughed at his dry observation but the mirth dried in her throat as she caught sight of Ethan arriving and making a beeline directly for the beautiful Shanal Peat. As she watched, the other woman's sea-green eyes lit up at the new arrival and her mobile lips curved into a smile of welcome. Isobel couldn't ignore the stab of envy that pierced her as Ethan smiled with genuine warmth at Shanal and bent to kiss those lips. She turned her back on the happy reunion and focused anew on something Trent was saying. The last thing she wanted to do was be a voyeur…the second to last thing she wanted was to admit to herself why it bothered her so much to see Ethan up close and personal with another woman.

She'd seen very little of him this week. She'd heard he'd been busy with the ferments and coordinating the cellar work, plus a Shiraz harvest from a vineyard outside the home estate, and he hadn't even made it to dinner each

evening. In fact, she'd heard more than enough about his
day-to-day activities from Tamsyn whenever the opportunity arose. Now, finally in the same room with him again,
every cell in her body urged her to turn around, to drink
in the sight of him, to try and quell the yearning desire
that simmered in her body and colored every moment of
every day she was here.

Sure, he was overbearing and a bit on the authoritative
side. In most guys that was just too much. But in Ethan,
especially here, in his home patch, it was simply who he
was—like it or not. Each family member had their own
area of expertise, was in charge of their own minibusiness
within the whole that was The Masters, yet all deferred to
Ethan in their own way. Clearly, with the death of his father, he'd become the head of the family and now, having
seen the family, she realized what a massive responsibility lay on his broad shoulders. It explained a lot about his
attitude. Growing up he must have always known he'd be
in charge one day. He was the type to relish that responsibility rather than shirk or shy away from it. And from the
looks of things, he'd taken his duty to protect the family
very seriously—especially when it came to protecting his
sister from the risk of getting hurt.

Tamsyn and Trent made their excuses to Isobel and
drifted away to welcome another newcomer, and Isobel
gave in to her need to turn around. For a moment she felt
as if she was adrift as Ethan was not in her immediate line
of sight. But then she caught the sound of his voice, his
laughter, and tracked him down.

Her insides melted at the sound of his laugh. It was rich
and full and unabashed in its joy. Again, that pang of envy
speared her as she realized that it was Shanal who was the
cause of his mirth. It seemed she was the only one here

who was capable of lightening his dark countenance and showing another side to this multifaceted man.

It was a good thing she was only here for another few weeks, Isobel thought with a small shiver that was in direct contrast to the warmth thrown out by several gas heaters positioned around the property. Any more of this torment and she'd be a blithering wreck by the time she left. She didn't belong here, with this well-established family and their well-established life. Nothing drove that point home like seeing the kind of woman that Ethan Masters so clearly wanted by his side. Everything about her, from her polished appearance to her quiet, flawless manners, to her easy and clearly well-established familiarity with Ethan's family members was in direct contrast with Isobel.

It was rare that Isobel found herself wanting. She'd never lacked for confidence before, but somehow, in this crowd, she realized that despite all her protestations to the contrary, some things had definitely been missing from her life, and this full sense of family and belonging were among them.

Ethan looked up from his conversation with Shanal and found Isobel looking directly at them. Looking, but not seeing. Her eyes were unfocused, her expression empty of her usual vivacity. Briefly, he wondered what was wrong, before something Shanal said dragged his attention back again. But it wasn't long before his eyes lifted again, searching the gathering for Isobel's cap of light blond hair.

He saw her over by the table on the veranda that was now groaning with food. She had a plate but even from this distance he could see she barely had anything on it. His protective instincts rose to the fore.

"Um, Ethan? Are you still listening to me?" Shanal asked with a smile on her face.

He looked at her, struck anew by the perfect symmetry of her face and her exotic coloring. She had to be the most beautiful woman he knew, and probably the most intelligent at the same time. And yet… His gaze flicked to Isobel before he forced himself to respond to his guest.

"I'm sorry. It's been a busy few days," he said with an apologetic smile.

"And going to get busier, too, I imagine," she replied, laying a hand on his arm to show she accepted his apology. "Which reminds me, I can't stay too late tonight. I need to check on some data I'm collating on the new strain of organic seed stock."

"We'd better hit the buffet then. We can't let you go home hungry."

They walked arm in arm to the veranda and Ethan was struck by how comfortable he felt with Shanal. After all, they'd known each other since their first week at university, had even shared an apartment together for a while. The ease he felt in her company made him sure about his decision to court her and hopefully, eventually, marry her. Although that ease also made him wonder about the lack of chemistry between them. They were a pair of healthy adults in the prime of their lives. Shouldn't there be something there?

He mentally shrugged the question away. There'd be time enough for that in the future. For now he was content to know that being with Shanal didn't leave him constantly on edge, or worse, constantly in a state of arousal that shattered his legendary concentration and focus and made him crave things that had no place in his life. Things? No, not things—a person. More specifically, Isobel Fyfe.

She was at the end of the veranda, a pashmina slung with casual elegance around her shoulders, while she talked to Zac Peters, Tamsyn's assistant and the brainchild for the marketing side of The Masters. Isobel listened intently to something Zac said, and he wondered what it was that held her attention so keenly. It was probably the most still he'd ever seen her and the fall of her straight hair almost completely shielded her face, hiding its mobile expressiveness and adding to the impression of stillness. As he looked, he remembered how that hair was soft and silky and felt like a million dollars as it stroked over his skin. He uttered an involuntary groan.

"You okay?" Shanal asked, her brow creased with concern.

"I'm fine," he hastened to assure her, but he was anything but.

Just like that, Isobel had woven her way past his defenses again. The woman was addictive and it seemed the harder he tried to resist her allure, the more he was drawn to her. Maybe that was it. Maybe he just needed to get her out of his system. He'd always sneered when he'd heard people tell of that before, but now he had an inkling as to how they felt. The compulsion to follow through on his thoughts was like a match to dry straw.

He shepherded Shanal to the opposite end of the veranda, where Isobel wouldn't be in his line of sight and gave his attention to the woman he, in all honesty, was most relaxed with. They were friends, good friends, and it was time to see if they could move their friendship up to the next level. It was about an hour later that Shanal looked at her watch.

"I'd better be on my way. Thank you so much for including me this evening. It's been lovely. I always enjoy your company."

"As I do yours," Ethan said, injecting his voice with more feeling than usual. He laid a hand at the small of Shanal's back. "Here, let me see you to your car."

They walked around the side of the house to the main driveway, which was lined with visitors' cars. He stopped by Shanal's practical silver compact. Imported, stylish and elegant, the car was like her in many ways. Chic but not fussy. Attractive but not over the top. She unlocked the doors with a press of her remote and Ethan reached to open her door for her. Before she could get in, however, he gathered her closer and leaned down to kiss her. The press of their lips was fleeting, pleasant but certainly not ground shaking, and it was over almost before it had begun with Shanal being the first to pull away.

"Thanks again for tonight," she said, ducking her head as she got into the car. "I had a really lovely time."

"Me, too," Ethan said. "How about dinner later next week?"

"Sure. I'm not certain how my diary is looking but give me a call, okay?"

And then she was gone. As he watched her car wind along the driveway and toward the main road he wondered if he was indeed doing the right thing by deciding to shift the course of their friendship. He mulled the question over as he walked back to the gathering. Isobel was the first person he saw as he rounded the side of the house and that zing of awareness poured through his veins.

How was it that he could feel more for a woman like Isobel Fyfe than for Shanal, who he'd known for almost half of his life? For the rest of the get-together the answer eluded him. Still, it kept tickling at the back of his mind as he went through the motions of circulating through the guests he hadn't spoken with yet and spending a little time with each family member to catch up on their days.

It was nearing midnight when the last of the guests had finally driven off. He knew he should go up to bed, tomorrow was going to be another demanding day. Instead, he found his feet were tracking quietly along the path toward Isobel's cottage. He hadn't seen her leave, but he'd heard from Tamsyn that she'd helped with clearing things away to the kitchen before slipping off after saying good-night. Had she been avoiding him? Probably, and with good reason if she'd been suffering the same form of physical discomfort as he had these past few days. Or maybe she was taking him at his word. Staying away from him exactly as he'd asked. Asked? Who was he kidding?

It was sheer madness going to see her now, but it was something he knew he had to do. Perhaps if he confronted the pull drawing him to her, he could lay the demons of his attraction to her to rest once and for all. A voice inside him laughed. Who was he kidding? He wanted her like he'd wanted no other woman ever before. Desire drummed in his blood, a constant reminder of what they'd once shared. What he wanted to share with her again. Anonymous, meaningless release. But could it be that still? She was no longer the complete stranger she'd been the evening they'd met.

Before he knew it he was at the entrance to her cottage, his hand poised and ready to knock. He could leave now. She'd never know he was here. If he did, there'd be no recriminations come morning. No regrets.

He knocked at the door.

Eight

Ethan filled the doorway, framed in the soft light that bathed the front entrance.

"Ethan? What—?"

Isobel never got to finish her question. Her answer, such as it was, was immediate in the envelopment of his arms, and the searing, questing fierceness of his kiss. Her arms instinctively reached up, her hands linking at the back of his neck and holding him to her. Her feet arching onto tiptoes so she could meet him on a more level ground. Her body aligning with his, softness against muscle. And it felt so good.

She hadn't realized until right this moment just how much she'd craved him. Wanted his strength, desired his touch, needed his possession.

Dimly, Isobel was aware of being buoyed backward, of the solid thud of the wooden door closing behind Ethan's back, but then her senses filled once more with him—

gloriously, excitedly overflowing with anticipation and eagerness.

Their lips were still joined, their tongues engaged in a sensual dance of remembrance.

He dragged his mouth away, resting his forehead against her own, his breathing ragged and raw.

"Tell me you don't want this and I'll go."

She bracketed his face with her hands and looked deep into his dark brown eyes, eyes that glowed with passion and need.

"I want you," she said softly.

"Thank you." He sighed.

Isobel couldn't help but smile a small private smile. Even in this he couldn't help but be straitlaced and proper. But she knew there were two distinct sides to Ethan Masters. There was the leader and family chieftain, and then there was the lover—it was the lover who'd come to her tonight. The lover who would stoke her internal fires until she was raging with heat, until she'd explode like a supernova burning bright in a distant sky.

Ethan's hands shoved at the waist of her pajama bottoms, making the cotton drawstring pants drop to her feet. His palms cupped her buttocks, pulling her firmly against him, against the hardness that showed her more than words could ever say, what effect she had on him.

She felt her body quicken instantly and she pulled his shirt free of his trousers and yanked his buttons open, heedless to the damage she wrought in her quest to feel his skin beneath her hands, her lips, her tongue.

He smelled divine, and she inhaled deeply, drawing in the scent of his skin and storing it away in her memory because she knew this—his presence, his overwhelming need for her—was an irregularity in his world. She'd take what she could get and she would cherish it to carry with her when she left again.

Ethan's hands moved slowly up her body, dragging the tank top she'd paired with her pajama pants up over her body as he went, exposing her to his hungry gaze. Her nipples grew tight and her breasts felt full and aching—wanting his touch above all else. His fingers softly skimmed their roundness, barely touching her yet igniting a line of fire that shot straight to her core, making her inner muscles clench on a wave of sensation.

She pushed at his shirt with her hands, dragging it off him and dropping it to the floor, then pressed herself into the hard plane of his chest. The ache, rather than being relieved, intensified into a raw demand that had dwelt just below the surface this entire past week. Patience, never her strongest point, deserted her completely. She grabbed for his belt, tugging it loose and unfastening his trousers with surprising finesse. She shoved at his pants and slipped her hand inside the waistband of his boxer briefs, pulling the fabric away and letting the hard length of his desire spring against her palm. Her fingers closed around him and she felt him shudder. She loved the feel of him, the texture of his skin, the engorged strength and leashed power, the silken head. She stroked his length and felt him shudder again.

His fingers closed around hers.

"Not yet, I'm too close, too desperate for you to touch me like that right now," he said in a strained voice.

"I like desperate," she whispered in response and clenched him that little bit tighter.

He drew in a sharp breath. "Soon," he said roughly. "Very soon."

Ethan guided her hand away from him and caught her mouth in a kiss that claimed her totally. His hands skimmed up the length of her back, sending thrills of delight running through her. His thigh pressed between her legs, affording a brief respite to the longing that gathered at the apex of her thighs, but she knew it wouldn't be enough for long.

She ground against him, seeking more pressure, seeking release. The muscles of his thigh beneath her were so firm, the hairs on his leg abrading the insides of her legs in a tantalizing contrast to the smoothness of her own.

"Okay, you win," Ethan groaned, pulling away from her and spinning her around. "Hold on to the back of the sofa," he instructed roughly.

She felt him shift behind her and bend to retrieve something from his trouser pocket. And then she felt the warm, blunt probe of his erection between her legs. She arched her back downward, raising her hips and spreading her legs that little more. His hands, warm and smooth and strong, were at her hips. She pushed back and felt his tip ease inside her.

It felt so good, but it wasn't enough. She needed him all—all the way. Finally, he thrust against her, stretching and filling her so deeply it all but took her breath away. And then he began to move, and the pressure inside her built higher. She wanted to draw out each acute delight but her body, and his, had other ideas. Her climax rushed upon her, making her legs shake and her inner muscles spasm in tight coils of ecstasy over and over, forcing her to cry out loud, lost in the web of sensation that caught her in its thrall.

She felt Ethan stiffen, his hips pressed hard against her, his body jerking as his own climax took him. His fingers were still tight on her hips—she'd probably have marks there tomorrow but she didn't care. How could she when they were so good together, so incendiary?

His grip softened, his palms once more skimming her heated flesh, stroking her, soothing her. He lowered himself over her back and pressed a kiss against her nape, which sent a corresponding shiver the length of her spine and made her insides tighten once more.

"I can't stay away from you," he said softly against her shoulder. "I've tried and I just can't do it."

Her heart contracted in response to the helplessness in his voice. She felt the same way but she knew it was a fleeting thing they shared. Isobel understood fleeting. She also knew that when something was short-lived it paid to grab it with both hands to make the most of it, and worry about the consequences later.

"Then don't try," she answered, her voice shaking with the aftermath of what they'd just shared.

"But why you? Why now?" he asked.

"Does it matter?" She sighed softly. "Let's just be together, for now."

"I can do that," he answered, kissing her nape again as he carefully withdrew from her body.

She straightened and forced herself to turn around, almost afraid to see what might be in his eyes when she met them.

"Come on," she said, holding out her hand. "Come to bed with me."

He stood still as a statue, and equally as beautiful, before taking her hand in silent acquiescence. They left their clothing where it lay, scattered on the sitting room floor, and walked together to her bedroom. The king-size bed was already rumpled, evidence of how much she'd already tossed and turned in the short time she'd been in bed before Ethan's knock had propelled her to the door. Isobel pulled back the sheets and climbed onto the bed, pulling Ethan after her.

She understood how much it had cost him to come to her tonight. He'd been aloof toward her all week, and she could see why. She could understand the level of responsibility he bore on his shoulders and why it was so important to him to live up to his family's expectations. A life like the Masters family enjoyed was so far from what she was used to, but it didn't mean she had no empathy for Ethan as the new head of what was arguably a dynasty.

For a man with his pride, to crumble and come to her door as he had tonight, he had to be at war within himself. And she knew all about the ravages of war. How it displaced families, how it destroyed livelihoods and both past and present. War, whether physical or mental, always exacted a price. The question was would this be at his cost, or hers?

Isobel pushed Ethan down against the bed, her hands gently roaming the curves and valleys of his body, coaxing a response from him that wasn't driven from a place of anger or fear...or of loathing. Because that was what she was frightened of. That he might loathe her or at least loathe what this attraction between them was doing to him. That it was making him lose precious control.

This was all about giving that control back to him. Because the more comfortable he felt with the draw that existed between them, the more likely it was that he'd indulge himself in exploring it for as long as she stayed at The Masters.

She peppered a line of kisses along his collarbone then down the center of his chest. His arms came up around her, his hands drifting up and down the line of her spine. Isobel felt her body respond in degrees. The shimmering heat of desire kept building and building within her as she stoked the same heat within him. By the time she reached for the side pocket of her pack, which she kept beside the bed, she was more than ready to feel the heavy weight of his body within hers.

Ethan barely said a word, watching her with eyes that glittered like chips of dark volcanic glass, as she extracted a condom and slowly, carefully, smoothed it over the straining length of his flesh. She positioned herself above him and held him in one hand, guiding him to the secret part of her body that ached for his possession. He rose up as she sank onto him, her body stretching to accommodate him, her eyes fluttered closed as a sigh of gratification eased from her at the rightness of this union between their bodies.

His hands gripped her hips, holding her steady when she wanted to rock against him. Her eyes flicked open, locking with his. Only then did he loosen his hold on her and allow her to move. She moaned at that first movement, at the sensations that spread out through her body, at the intensity of the connection between them as they continued to look directly into one another's eyes. Time blurred as she rocked against him, her movements deliberate and slow, until she could barely take it any longer. Beads of perspiration dotted her face, her body, matching the sheen across his as they remained locked together in a sensual wave of motion. A wave that built and built, taking her closer and closer to the edge.

Ethan suddenly shifted, holding her hips and maintaining their union even as he slid her beneath him and settled between her legs. He kept up their momentum, driving her to even greater heights before slowing down again. Just when she thought she was incapable of feeling any more, he upped the tempo. In seconds she was spiraling high, higher than she'd ever been as wave after building wave of pleasure resonated through her body. As her body clenched around him, she felt Ethan stiffen before he plunged into her, again and again until a shout clawed its way from deep in his throat and he shuddered against her.

He rolled to the side, taking her with him, his breathing ragged, his eyes now closed, his pulse beating like a crazy thing at the base of his throat. She leaned forward and kissed him, right there, at that exact spot that evidenced the passion they'd just shared. His skin was hot, slick and slightly salty. She stroked her hand across his chest in a lazy sweep, not wanting for a second to lose that link they'd so tenuously established.

Ethan's eyes opened, and one of his hands closed around hers, holding it firmly against his chest.

"Thank you," he said, his voice a low rumble.

"Thank you?"

"For not telling me to get the hell out of here."

She smiled. "What, and miss all this?" She squeezed her internal muscles, teasing him in voice and deed.

Some of the tension that had begun to appear on his face eased away.

He shook his head slightly. "Don't you take anything seriously?"

"I take my work seriously," she replied. "But everything else, well, that's fluid."

"What's that like?" he asked, releasing her hand and reaching out to twist a length of her hair around his finger.

"It's freedom. Unless it impacts directly on my work, I don't have to worry about what other people think, or say, or do. I look after myself and I like it that way."

"No plans to ever settle down in one place?"

She shook her head emphatically. "Definitely not. I've moved around for most of my life. I couldn't imagine doing it differently, or why I'd want to."

He relaxed a little more and she wondered for a second if he'd been worried that now they'd made love again that she might begin to put demands upon him, expect more than just the amazing sex they shared.

A fleeting pang of regret pierced her chest but she pushed it aside. She didn't do long term. She just didn't. This, whatever they had, was just fine by her. For however long they had it. Now that Ethan had climbed down off his high horse, maybe they could just enjoy each other for the time she was here.

"Is that why you chose photography as your career?" he asked, continuing to twirl her hair between his fingers.

"It's certainly flexible, but that isn't why I do it. It chose me, I suppose. When my dad and I left New Zealand, and started traveling, one of his friends gave me an old SLR camera. I played around with it—discovered I had a knack for composition. It wasn't long before I became fascinated with the play of light and darkness on life."

"That sounds deep," Ethan commented with a smile.

"I don't spend all my life doing catalog work, you know." She laughed lightly.

"So what do you do the rest of the time?"

The laughter fled from inside her as she recalled her last photo assignment in Africa. Recalled the heat, the smells, the poverty. The destitution and helplessness of the people being rousted out of their homes and livings by a despotic and avaricious leader. And how, even in that desolation, there was still hope. Hope for something better, for someone or some nation to help. That was Isobel's mission. To show the world the people who needed help. To bring that desperation into more privileged peoples' and their governments' consciousness. To help, somehow, and give those struggling people some hope.

"I take photos of people. Families, mostly."

She worked hard to keep her voice light. There was a time and a place for discussing what she did and that wasn't here or right now. It was why she kept a very successful blog running on her visits to areas like the one she'd just been expelled from and why, when she was away from those areas, she lived her life to the fullest, with color, with joy.

"What, like mall photographers? Grumpy babies and toddlers?"

"Not quite," Isobel amended, weighing up whether or not to go deeper into what she did with Ethan.

The decision was taken from her hands when he let her hair go and rose from the bed.

"I'll get rid of this and then get going," he said, referring to the used condom.

"You don't want to stay?"

She wasn't upset that he planned to leave her now that his passion for her had been sated. Or at least that's what she told herself.

"I have an early start tomorrow. I don't want to disturb you. Besides, I don't think it's a good idea if we make a habit of this."

His emotional shutters were back down. She could see it as plain as day on his face, and for some stupid reason it hurt her deep inside. What had she been hoping for? A declaration of his feelings for her? A promise to make every night as spectacular as this one had been? She gave herself a mental shake. That wasn't what she wanted.

Liar, a voice in the back of her mind whispered piercingly through her consciousness.

She shoved the thought back just as swiftly as it came. As he headed to the bathroom to clean up, she rolled out of bed and walked naked into the living room to pick up Ethan's clothes, as well as drag her pajamas back over her body.

He came out of the bathroom and uttered his thanks as

she silently handed him his things. He gave her a brief, chaste kiss once he was dressed, and then he was gone. Isobel turned off the lights behind her as she went back to bed and curled into a ball where he'd lain. Telling herself she was all sorts of pathetic for wishing him back here at her side even as she tried not to inhale the faint traces of his scent on the pillow where his head had lain only minutes before.

It seemed that from the moment she'd met Ethan Masters her life had been thrown into a state of heightened awareness and confusion. Despite his being the antithesis to the way she lived her life, she remained inexorably drawn to him. *It's just the sex,* she told herself. And yes, it was great sex. Off-the-scale sex. Better than she'd ever had in her entire life sex. But they were two very different people.

She was transient, lived her life out of a backpack and traveled wherever whim took her. He was established, had generations of history behind him and backing him from sunup to sundown. He was grounded in the earth here as much as those vineyards she'd walked through several times this past week. Perhaps even more so.

He was a commitment kind of guy. A guy who looked great with a woman like Shanal Peat on his arm and in his life. Try as she might, Isobel couldn't quell the fierce sense of possessiveness that swept through her. She didn't want to think about Ethan with Shanal, or with any woman, for that matter. But, she reminded herself firmly, she was only here for, at most, three more weeks—whereas Ethan would be here for the rest of his life.

Forever—it wasn't the kind of thing she could commit to, nor wanted to, she told herself as she rolled to her other side. She dragged the bedcovers over her now-chilled body and told herself that the bed didn't feel half-empty without Ethan lying by her side.

Nine

Whatever he'd been thinking by going to Isobel on Friday night, it had been the wrong thing to do, Ethan decided as he roamed the winery late on Sunday.

Everyone had gone to bed, leaving him alone with his thoughts and his work. This was his favorite stage of production, and he took his work very seriously—checking and rechecking everything. Overseeing whatever he'd delegated so thoroughly, he may as well have done it all himself. Tam teased him about being a control freak but he felt no shame in wanting to ensure that The Masters label maintained its hard-won profile in the marketplace.

Yet tonight was different. He struggled to concentrate on his tasks, his mind constantly sliding back in time to Friday. To the expression on Isobel's face when she'd opened her door to him. To her easy acceptance of what he'd been there for. To the feel of her limbs wrapped tight around his.

Ethan pushed a trembling hand through his hair and tried to shake the images of Isobel's long back, her tapered waist, and her rounded buttocks from his mind. She hadn't hesitated when he'd turned her around, hadn't balked when he'd driven into her body like a crazy man. She'd accepted everything, and then taken him to her bed where she'd given to him all over again.

Then, when he'd so abruptly left her, she hadn't so much as batted an eyelid. Not a single plea to him to remain had passed her lips, although he knew he'd have been welcome.

In fact, the lure of her warm and accepting body had been strong. Too strong. He'd known it would have been all too easy to stay in her bed, in her arms, all night long. He already felt too vulnerable—too exposed in his endless desire for her. Sleeping beside her would only let her further behind his defenses. She read him far too well as it was. And she'd already proven she could manipulate him with ease.

Oh, sure, their pleasure had been mutual, but in hindsight, Ethan could see that she'd been the one in charge all along, no matter what he'd thought at the time. The realization was an eye opener. He was used to taking charge, to being the boss, and she'd turned the tables on him without him even noticing.

And here she was, still stuck firmly in his mind. He'd even had lunch today with Shanal. That had been far less promising than he'd hoped. They'd walked the botanical gardens at Mt. Lofty before heading out to a nearby café, and despite his best efforts, there'd been no zing when he'd taken her hand, no excitement when he'd embraced her after returning her to her home. He knew she'd felt the same way. She'd presented her cheek for a kiss to avoid kissing him on the lips.

It left him feeling out of sorts. Not irritated, exactly,

but something close to that. He just couldn't understand it. He and Shanal were perfect for each other. Always had been. And they knew each other so well—were comfortable together. So why was there no spark?

And, more important, why had he spent half the time with Shanal wondering what Isobel was up to today? He'd seen her drive off with Cade earlier on and had felt a surge of jealousy so strong it had left a very nasty taste in his mouth. He didn't do jealousy and he had no right to, either. After all, hadn't *he* been out with Shanal at the very same time?

He and Isobel had slept together. Twice. That was all. He had no claim over her. If she wanted to she could sleep with all the men in his family and he had no rights to stop her.

His head began to pound and an irrational sense of possessiveness clawed at his gut. He shook his head. This was ridiculous. Even here, in his sanctuary—the winery, the one place where he could always find solace in his work—she still invaded his thoughts.

The sound of a car driving slowly along the drive toward the main house caught his attention. He looked outside his window and saw Cade's car turn up the small driveway that led to Isobel's cottage. It seemed to Ethan that it lingered there an inordinately long time before swinging around and heading back to the main house.

Ethan tried desperately to ignore the not so subtle urging in the back of his mind. The one that told him to go to Isobel. To find out for himself what she'd been up to with his cousin all day. Before he was even aware of it he was turning off the lights at the winery and locking the door behind him, his feet treading the pathway to her cottage as they had only two nights ago.

Through the cottage window he could see her seated at the dining table, her laptop in front of her and a slideshow of photos up on the screen. He hesitated in the darkness, feeling like some creepy voyeur as he took in the delicate line of her neck as she bent over a notebook and scribbled something into its pages.

Damn, he'd thought not seeing her for the past couple of days would have taken some of the sharpness of the ragged edges that had remained after he'd left her bed.

He must have made a sound because she dropped her pen and whipped her head around, her eyes searching the darkness where he stood. Her actions served as the catalyst to make him move forward, to knock gently at her door. Isobel swung the door open and eyed him carefully.

"You're starting to make this a habit, aren't you?"

"May I come in?"

He didn't even fully understand why he was here. All he knew was that he'd felt compelled to come. Now that she was in front of him, he barely knew what to say. His body, on the other hand, had its own agenda. Already he could feel the slow, steady drumbeat of desire through his blood.

She stepped aside and gestured for him to come in. "Can I offer you a drink? A glass of wine or something?"

"Sure," he said, looking at the table where she had a glass of red wine sitting next to her laptop. "Whatever you're having will be fine."

"Are you sure?" Her eyes lit with that habitual spark of waywardness that seemed to linger around her like an aura. "It's not one of yours."

"Tastes like vinegar, does it?" he answered mockingly in return.

"It's actually very good, in my opinion. Mind you, I'm no connoisseur."

Ethan walked over and picked up the bottle, recognizing the New Zealand wine label instantly. "You're right.

Vinegar should never even be mentioned in the same room as this."

Isobel brought him a glass and he poured the ruby liquid into the wide bowl.

"I guess you didn't come here to discuss wine," Isobel said, picking up her own glass and taking a sip.

For a second, Ethan was mesmerized by the tip of her tongue as she ran it along her bottom lip, but then he brought his attention very firmly back to her eyes. There was a challenge in them. One he recognized and to which he instantly felt an answering call.

"No, I didn't. How was your day?"

His question clearly startled her and for a second or two she didn't answer. Eventually, she took a breath and let it out slowly before speaking.

"It was good. And yours? How was your lunch with Shanal?"

"How did you know about that?"

"Was it supposed to be a secret? Cade and I saw you two walking at the botanical gardens. We didn't stop to say hi because he was taking me into Adelaide for the rest of the day."

Ethan felt the obscure urge to apologize for taking Shanal out, but that was ridiculous. He barely knew Isobel. They'd only been acquainted for a handful of days—and their paths would only continue to cross for a few weeks longer before she left The Masters—and him—behind. If he chose to devote his afternoon to a woman who actually intended to stick around, then what right would she have to complain?

"We had a nice afternoon," he settled on saying. "How about you?"

A smile poked at the corners of Isobel's lips. "Cade took me to the apartment."

"He what?"

A gurgle of laughter bubbled from Isobel's mouth. "I thought you'd react like that."

"I'm not reacting," Ethan denied emphatically, tamping down the raw urge to hunt down his younger cousin right here and right now and warn him off Isobel for good.

"He offered me lunch, that's all. He's very good in the kitchen, you know."

Ethan nodded, feeling relief ease through his veins to chase away the irrational urges that had flared so suddenly.

"We're lucky his loyalty to The Masters keeps him here. He's been headhunted by several hotel chains so far, as well as some of the more high-profile restaurants in Sydney and Melbourne."

"It's not stifling him to stay here?" Isobel asked, rolling the rim of her glass across her full lower lip.

Ethan tore his gaze from her mouth. "Stifling him? What makes you say that?"

"You know, keeping him here, working at the café and tasting room instead of letting him stretch his wings elsewhere."

"No one is forcing him to stay, Isobel. We're not quite that feudal."

"Not quite," she agreed. "But you can't deny that he'd do well if he did leave."

"Of course not, but why should he? He's in charge of his own world here. He works with people he knows and trusts—people who care about him and not just about the product he churns out. He's never expressed any desire to be anywhere else."

"Or maybe, because of the expectation to remain here, he's never felt he could."

Ethan narrowed his eyes and looked at her sharply. "Did he ask you to say something to me?"

"No, not at all." Isobel waved a hand in denial. "But he's so talented and still so young. It seems a shame for him to molder away here when the world is, quite literally, his oyster."

"Is that what you think we do here? Molder?"

"Perhaps that wasn't the right word to use," she said quickly. "But you have to admit, it's unusual for one family to stay together like this."

"Unusual, maybe. But not stifling—supportive. We all have a vested interest in how well things go here."

"You more than most."

"What makes you say that?"

Isobel smiled again, the expression making her features lighten from the seriousness of just a moment ago.

"You, of all people, have to ask me that?"

She leaned against the back of the sofa where he'd taken her so urgently two days ago. For the life of him he couldn't get the picture of her out of his mind. His groin ached at the memory. He fisted his empty hand and shoved it in his trouser pocket. It didn't help. Even taking a scouring pad to his memory wouldn't help, he admitted to himself.

Isobel continued when he didn't respond. "It's very clear that the mantle of responsibility here begins and ends with you."

"We all have our part to play," Ethan hedged, oddly unwilling to admit to her that his was the primary role here.

"I'm not used to that. To a setup like you have where all of you are linked by family and work. I suppose I've been on my own for so long that I find it hard to imagine how it could work all together the way you do."

"I guess we're lucky. The business has grown with our strengths. With Cade and Cathleen, for example, they've developed an entirely new side of The Masters, one that complements all the other aspects of our family business, but also one we'd never have considered if they hadn't chosen cuisine and hospitality as part of their studies."

Isobel didn't seem quite ready to agree with him, but at least she didn't seem to wish to argue the point. Instead, she reached for the wine bottle on the table and refilled their glasses.

"Why don't we sit down," she said, putting the bottle on the small coffee table between the sofa and the lazy chair that formed the lounge area of the cottage.

Ethan chose the chair while Isobel curled up on the sofa.

"How are the photos coming along?" Ethan asked, gesturing with his wineglass to the laptop on the dining table.

"Eager to get rid of me?"

"That's not what I said," he answered smoothly, but her response forced him to consider it.

Was he keen for her to leave? Most definitely yes…and then again, no. He didn't like how out of control she made him feel. But then, he didn't like the thought of saying a final goodbye to the passion she stirred in him, either.

"You're still worried about me spilling the beans to Tamsyn about your mother, aren't you?" she asked, cutting straight to the original source of his unease. He did still worry about that. He believed that Isobel liked Tamsyn, that she wouldn't reveal the secret deliberately out of spite. But on the other hand, she seemed uncomfortable with the entrenched structure of their family. As independent as she was herself, Isobel might not believe that he had the right to make the decision to keep the information from his sister, just to protect her.

"It's not your information to share."

"She deserves to know, Ethan." Isobel's voice dropped to a lower pitch, all humor gone.

"Let me be the judge of that."

"I would, but—"

Ethan cut her off. "It's none of your business, Isobel. Leave it alone, okay?"

"It might not have anything to do with me, but it *is* Tamsyn's business. Even you have to accept that."

"Not knowing it hasn't done her any harm for the past twenty-five years. She's managed just fine with my dad and me and our extended family around her. She's not some wounded dove that needs you to campaign on her behalf. She's a strong, beautiful and intelligent woman. Her life doesn't need to be cluttered with questions about a woman who apparently walked away from us both without a backward glance or a second thought. What on earth could knowing she's still alive bring to enrich Tam's life now?"

Isobel took a sip of her wine before answering. "The truth, maybe? Answers as to why she left, why she didn't come back, why she never tried to stay in touch? Have you ever considered that maybe there's more to the story than you know, even now?"

"No." His response was emphatic. "I haven't. Nor do I care to consider it. And as far as Tamsyn is concerned, our mother no longer exists. For now, I'm happy to keep it that way."

"You're wrong, Ethan. You owe it to Tamsyn to let her make up her own mind, make her own choices regarding your mother."

She just wouldn't let it go, would she? Ethan cursed silently. This isn't what he came here for. Hell, he didn't even know himself why he'd sought Isobel's company again but it sure hadn't been for an argument.

"Why are you so hell-bent on making me change my mind?" he asked abruptly.

"Families shouldn't keep secrets," she replied emphatically. "At least not from one another."

A hint of pain showed on her face and his protective instincts flared to the forefront of his mind. What, or more important, *who* had put that sorrow in her soft blue eyes? A parent? A sibling? He had to ask.

"Who kept a secret from you?"

She took her time before answering, and the sudden gleam of moisture in her eyes took him completely by surprise.

"My mother. My father. They conspired to keep mum's illness from me. She suffered from a rare and fatal lung disease, but they never told me once they found out she was sick. She was always just tired or having a bad day. They sheltered me so thoroughly that by the time she was seriously ill, I still barely knew it. Worse, they never gave me a chance to understand *why* she was always unwell."

"How old were you when she died?" he asked softly.

Isobel swiped impatiently at her eyes with one hand and frowned slightly, as if she couldn't bear to show him this weakness. When she continued, her voice was hard, harder than he'd ever heard it and his heart ached a little for the pain she was shielding behind her obvious anger.

"Sixteen. I'd only learned the truth a few months prior. I felt so stupid, as if I'd been deliberately oblivious to her illness. But they never let me understand it. Mum developed complications right at the end. I was only allowed to visit her once in hospital but even then they withheld the truth from me, leading me to believe she'd get well again and come home."

"They were trying to protect you," Ethan said, trying to allay some of her anger and frustration.

"They were keeping a secret from me. Do you honestly think it was fair of them to keep me in the dark like that? I wasn't an idiot, nor was I an infant. I should have had time to understand what her illness could do to her, been given a chance to truly cherish the time we had together.

I never even got to say goodbye to her. Dad arranged for her to be buried without a funeral, without a celebration of her life or the woman she was, or anything."

Tears ran unchecked down Isobel's cheeks now and her voice shook as she continued. "The morning after she passed away, he woke me up and told me she was gone. Then he instructed me to pack a bag with no more than what I could comfortably carry. We went to the airport and that's the last time I saw home. We traveled together until Dad died about four years later. He never really got over Mum's death and I always felt as if he was running away from facing a life without her right up until he passed away."

"Isobel, I'm so sorry you went through that. But Tamsyn's and my situation is different. We're adults now. We've grown up believing one thing all this time. I don't even know what to do with the information about our mother. How can I expect Tamsyn to shoulder that, too?"

"You have to at least give her a chance," Isobel insisted, getting up and finding a paper towel in the kitchenette to dry her tears with. "Like you said, she's an adult. She's quite capable of reaching her own decisions about what to do with the knowledge that your father lied to you both all this time. Is that why you don't want her to know? You don't want her to remember your father any differently than she does now?"

"Maybe," he admitted carefully, surprised at her perceptiveness.

"It won't make her love him any less, you know." Isobel sat back down on the sofa and pulled her knees up under her chin. "For all that my parents kept such an important secret from me, I still love them deep in my heart—I always will. I just wish they'd trusted me with the truth. I was a young adult, but they never respected me enough to share their fears with them. Sheltering me from it all wasn't the best thing for me and it's not the best thing for Tamsyn, either. This is something the two of you should be sharing. You need each other now more than ever."

"I don't agree, but—" he held up a hand when Isobel made to protest once more "—I will give it some more thought. Either way, I need to know I can rely on you to keep the information to yourself. I should never have told you in the first place…."

"But you never expected to see me again. Nor I, you." Isobel sighed. "You know, my mother always loved the poetry of Charles Péguy. Her favorite opening line was '*The faith that I love best, says God, is hope.*' It's what keeps me going—*hope.* Hope that something better, brighter, happier—*anything*—is just around the next corner. I am still angry with my parents for so many reasons for what they did, what I feel as if they stole from me—the chance to make the most of every second with my mother rather than being a bratty teenager. The chance to prepare for a life without her rather than have it thrust upon me. The chance to say goodbye to her and tell her how much I loved her—but I still have hope. Not for a chance to make things right with my parents, obviously. That ship has long since sailed. But I can make a difference for other people. Give them hope, y'know? And you and Tamsyn have that, too. You have a fresh chance with your mother, if you'll only allow yourselves."

"No." His response was absolute. "I don't believe in second chances. I am really very sorry for what you went through, Isobel, but your circumstances are vastly different from ours. And I think, on that note, I should go. We're never going to agree on this issue. Thanks for the wine."

He stood to leave, surprised that Isobel seemingly had

no more to say on the subject. At least until she saw him to the door.

"Trust Tamsyn," she urged as he walked away into the chilled night air. "Trust *her* to know what's the right thing to do about your mother."

"Why can't you just trust me to know what's best for my sister!" he snapped, and turned sharply on his heel to stride away into the darkness.

He simmered with anger all the way back to the house where, unable to help himself, he stood at his window staring down at Isobel's cottage—watching as, one by one, the lights went out, leaving the dwelling in darkness. Why the hell had he gone there? It certainly hadn't been with the intention of arguing about Tamsyn. So what had led him there? Had he wanted to warn her off Cade? Or was it simply to stamp his own possession upon her? Or maybe even to root out the source of his fascination with her so that he could attempt to control it, to control his reaction to her.

Whichever way, he'd failed.

Ten

"These are fabulous!" Tamsyn squealed, her face brightening. "Have you shown Cade and Cathleen?"

"Not yet. I've got an appointment to see them and their restaurant staff later this afternoon."

Isobel leaned back in the chair at Tamsyn's office desk, and watched the slideshow of shots she'd done to date for The Masters new catalog as they slipped across her computer screen. She couldn't help but feel an immense sense of pride in the quality of the work she'd done here. Despite Ethan's remark about mall photos and grumpy babies and toddlers, she felt she did her best work featuring people, and she'd tried to incorporate that here within the guidelines set by Tamsyn and the marketing team.

Even the shots of Raif and his father, tending vines in the distance in what were indisputably her best landscape shots ever, still lent that personal family touch. The body language between the men spoke volumes as to their relationship and how close they were, how much respect they tendered for one another. Of course a lot of the art of that was lost on most people, but it still gladdened her heart to see that she'd captured it, even if from a distance.

Had Ethan and his father been like that? she wondered.

"I love that one." Tamsyn interrupted her reveries. "I know it's the vineyard and all that and the way the sun's dropping over the hills looks fantastic, but I really see Raif and Uncle Edward in that shot. Can we crop it around them more?"

"Sure," Isobel agreed and hit the necessary keys. "Like this?"

"Yeah. Any chance I could have a print of that? I reckon Uncle Edward and Aunt Marianne would love it."

"No problem. I'll put the image on a CD for you and you can have it printed any way you want it." To Isobel's surprise, a look of sadness washed across Tamsyn's face. "Tam? Are you okay?"

Tamsyn gave her a watery smile. "Just missing my dad, I guess."

"That's only natural."

"His death was so sudden, it took all of us by surprise. And now it's just me and Ethan, I feel like I need to hold on to something, you know? We've lost that connection in our lives," she said, gesturing to the cropped photo on the screen. "I don't want to lose it completely by forgetting a thing about Dad. I've tried to talk to Ethan but he won't even discuss him at all. It's like now he's gone, for Ethan, he's really gone. End of story, move on. Dad was the same way, when it came to our mom. I was so little when she died that I barely have any memories of her at all. And now we've lost them both, I…I just wish I had more of them to hold on to."

Tears spilled over her lower lashes and traced silver

streaks down Tamsyn's face. Isobel pushed out of her chair and pulled the other woman into her arms, rocking her silently. She felt Tamsyn's grief like a sword in her gut. It didn't need to be this way. It was wrong of Ethan to withhold the information about their mother. Totally and utterly wrong.

Tamsyn spoke through her tears. "I don't understand the way Ethan's dealing with it. Family means so much to him. But Ethan's just moved on from Dad's death so quickly. I miss Dad, but I don't think my brother does at all. I just don't understand how he can pretend losing our father is nothing to be upset about."

"Everyone grieves differently," Isobel murmured, biting back the words she really wanted to share with Tamsyn.

"I know, and I've read about the different stages of grief. To be honest, I think Ethan is locked in anger—he's mad at Dad for something. What, I don't know. Whether it's the fact that he died so unexpectedly or something else… he just won't talk about any of it with me."

"All you can do is keep trying. He's not the kind of guy who shares his feelings easily, is he?"

A strangled laugh fell from Tamsyn's mouth. "No, he's not. He's always been very staunch, even when we were kids. Some people think he's unsympathetic, but I think it just comes down to the way he shoulders responsibility. He was always the ringleader when we were growing up, and he seemed to think that meant that he wasn't allowed to ever get scared or upset. He wanted to be like Dad— and Dad was always steady and in control. But now he's gone even beyond that. It's as if he's not allowing himself to care at all. He's gotten more distant with our aunts and uncle…and with me. I just wish I knew why."

"You miss your brother—the way he was before your father died," Isobel said with sudden clarity.

"Yes, it's exactly that. We grew up without a mother, we've lost Dad. I feel like I'm losing my brother, too."

"Talk to him," Isobel urged, letting Tamsyn go and grabbing a box of tissues off a nearby shelf. "Make him listen to you. He loves you."

"I know." Tamsyn blew her nose, then turned away from Isobel and wrapped her arms around her body as if shielding herself from her grief. "I just feel like I'm stuck on the outside, y'know? As if I'm on the outside of my own life, looking in like some kid with their face pressed on the glass at Haigh's Chocolates."

"Oh, yeah, that place on the corner of Rundle and King William? I am so that kid!" Isobel laughed at Tamsyn's analogy and tried to lighten the mood, but even so she could still feel her friend's pain emanating off her in waves.

"I think we're all that kid." Tamsyn smiled through her tears. "I love Ethan dearly. He's my rock, and always has been, but he's so determined to be strong for me that he won't let me in. He won't show me what he's really feeling when all I want is to be able to share our grief and help each other work through it."

"Can you talk to Trent about it? After all, you are going to be married to him. He should be helping you through this, too."

An expression Isobel couldn't quite put her finger on appeared in Tamsyn's eyes.

"We're both always so busy with work that we barely see each other. Then, when we do manage to coordinate our schedules and get together, I can see he's stressed with the demands of his job and I really don't want to burden him with anything else."

Just privately, Isobel thought that to be pretty unfair. If you couldn't unload to your partner, who the heck else could you unload to?

Tamsyn sighed and sank into a chair. "I just feel so alone sometimes. I always used to be able to talk to Ethan about virtually anything, and now I really feel like he's holding something back from me."

"He is," Isobel blurted before she could give a second's thought to the ramifications of what she'd begun.

"He what? What do you mean?" Tamsyn asked, her face creased in confusion.

Isobel took in a deep breath. Too late to take back those two insignificant words now. In for a penny, in for a pound, she decided. "He is holding something back from you. You need to ask him about it."

"What? What is it, Isobel? And how come you know about it, if it's such a big secret?"

Oh, God, Isobel thought, she'd really opened a can of worms now. "When I came here that first night, it wasn't the first time I'd met Ethan."

"I knew it!" Tamsyn said. "I knew there was something between you two. I could feel it. He's usually so polite and accommodating when we have a guest and he was so not that way with you. So come on, give up the details."

Isobel cringed inwardly but there was no way she could fudge the truth. Tamsyn deserved that, and more.

"We actually met, by chance, the night before. We, uh, we were intimate with one another."

Tamsyn's eyebrows shot toward her hairline. "You guys had a one-night stand? But Ethan never—"

"Nor do I, but we did. I also never expected to see him again, so coming here and being brought face-to-face like that was a little disconcerting for us both."

The other woman looked at her, assessing what she'd said and narrowing her eyes slightly before speaking. "That's not all, is it? That's not what Ethan's holding back from me."

Isobel closed the short distance between them and squatted on her haunches in front of Tamsyn, reaching for her hands and holding them firmly. "No, it isn't. Ethan confided something in me, something I have no right to tell you but it's something you most definitely deserve to know. Since it appears he has no intention of sharing it with you—and since it's obviously creating a rift between you—I'm going to tell you what he told me."

Tamsyn paled. "It's got to be something awful. Do I really want to know?"

"Maybe not. I know your brother thinks you don't. He's trying to shelter you, keep you from getting hurt. But you need to know, Tam. You deserve the chance to decide how you want to handle this yourself." She squeezed Tamsyn's hands, then spilled the truth.

"Your mother is still alive. Your father hid the truth from you all these years. Ethan only found out that Friday he came to the city. If he's angry at your father, that's why. He's had to battle with the discovery on his own."

For a few moments, Tamsyn was stunned silent. When she finally spoke, Isobel was surprised at the anger in her voice. "He didn't have to, not on his own. Never on his own. He could have had me, if he'd been willing to trust me." Tamsyn's pain was evident in every word she uttered.

"He's your big brother. He just wanted to protect you."

"Oh, don't go making excuses for him." Tamsyn pulled free from Isobel's clasp and stood abruptly, her movement sending her chair skidding backward on the polished wooden floor. "In case either of you hadn't noticed, I'm a grown woman. He had no right to keep that information from me. Neither of you did."

Before Isobel could utter another word, in her own defense or otherwise, Tamsyn was gone, the door slamming behind her. Isobel sat down in the chair that Tamsyn had so rapidly vacated. Her hands shook and her stomach churned uncomfortably. Ethan would be livid. He'd never understand why she'd found it necessary to impart the news he'd been so determined to keep to himself.

A tremor rocked her body at the enormity of what she'd set in motion. What on earth had she done?

Eleven

Ethan left the winery with thunder in his face and murder on his mind. Okay, so maybe murder was taking things just a little too far, but Isobel Fyfe had definitely over-stepped the mark. They'd only discussed this very thing last night—he'd reiterated his stance on the matter and yet she'd gone behind his back and told Tamsyn about their mother.

His ears still rang with Tamsyn's vitriolic verbal attack from only moments ago. She'd accused him of all manner of things, including treating her like a child and of push-ing her away. He hadn't known what to say. She'd been so angry he decided that it probably didn't matter what he said—nothing would diffuse the situation.

Damn Isobel for sharing news that wasn't hers to tell.

His footsteps echoed sharply on the flagstone path. Iso-bel had better be at her cottage because what he had to say to her right now did not need an audience and, the way he felt, he wasn't going to hold back even if she was with someone else. Rage roiled inside him as he lifted his fist to hammer on her wooden door which, to his surprise, opened before he could make the first strike.

"I've been expecting you," Isobel said calmly. "Please, come in."

Ethan let his arm drop uselessly to his side. She was expecting him. Well, wasn't that nice?

Isobel turned away from him and moved into the sitting room area, gesturing for him to take a seat.

"I'd rather stand. This won't take long. I've just been with Tamsyn, although I guess you already knew that."

An intense haze of anger dried the words in his throat and he fought to swallow it down. Ethan's fists clenched at his sides and he slowly and deliberately unfurled his fingers, one by one, as he fought to control his fury.

"Why?" he said, when he was finally able to get the growl out of his voice. "Why did you do it?"

To his annoyance, Isobel looked cool and composed.

"Because someone had to and you wouldn't."

"You had no right."

"It's not about my rights—it's about Tamsyn's rights. She deserved to know."

Ethan huffed out a hard breath. "What? Deserved to know that our mother was apparently an alcoholic? One who drove away from here, filled to the gills with wine and with both of us in the car, on her way to meet her lover? A car that she crashed, injuring both of us but allowing her to walk away unscathed—and never come back for us? Do you think Tamsyn is really better off knowing all that?"

He put up a hand as Isobel made to speak. "Don't say a word. You've said more than enough already. You didn't have the full story and you didn't respect my right to withhold it from Tamsyn. I believe now that our father was right to keep the truth from us. We didn't both need to have our childhood memories of our mother tarnished. But now you've taken that choice away from me with your interference."

"Horrible or not, I still believe Tamsyn deserved to know. You might not have wanted to face up to the truth, but she at least had to be given the chance to know what happened and decide for herself how she feels about it."

Isobel stood her ground. Her posture straight and stiff, her blue eyes blazing. She wasn't going to back down and admit she'd been in the wrong and knowing that just spiked his ire even more.

"You don't know any of us well enough to have made that judgment call." Despite the fire raging in his veins his voice was cold and hard. "You're not part of our family, you don't know what we've been through. We were better off without our mother, that much is clear. Now that you've told Tamsyn she's still alive, she has some hare-brained idea that she needs to find her."

"As I would myself, if I had that chance, which is ex-actly *why* I told Tamsyn. You grew up with your father as your mentor. Who did Tamsyn have?"

"She had all of us—the whole family. We've always been here for each other. Why would she need some drunk who didn't care enough about us to stay? Who actually took money in exchange for agreeing to abandon her chil-dren?" he answered scathingly. "Your meddling has cre-ated a far bigger problem than having grown up without a mother. Didn't you stop to think beyond the actual words you said? Did the ramifications of Tamsyn knowing only the smallest amount of information not occur to you?"

"She's upset, of course—"

"Upset? *Upset?*" Ethan pushed a hand through his hair in frustration. "Of course she's upset, but worse, she feels abandoned now on top of everything else. And she wants to know why. She's a determined young woman, Isobel. She won't rest until she knows the full truth behind what happened and, dammit, she doesn't need that cluttering up her life right now."

Isobel eyed him carefully. "She doesn't? Or *you* don't? Be honest with yourself, Ethan. You don't need this as a complication in your life. You were quite happy to just trawl on in your own private kingdom, maintaining the status quo. Don't you remember your mother? Don't you remember the good times with her? Tamsyn was too young for any of that but now she still has a chance to learn about her and, if she's lucky, to forge a relationship with her. Yet you still think you had the right to stand in her way of happiness."

"*What* happiness? Our mother abandoned us. Do you think she really wants Tamsyn to walk back into her life now? What happens when Tamsyn tracks her down and gets rejected—when instead of barely remembering a mother who died, she gets to have crystal-clear memories of her mother telling her to her face that she doesn't want her?"

He was viciously pleased to see Isobel flinch at that, but she still didn't back down. "You can't know that will happen. And even if it does, all you can do is be there for her. Tell her the whole truth, and then help her deal with it. Let her help *you* deal with it. You can't protect her by shutting her out. She feels like an outsider in her own home. Did you know that?"

Ethan felt her words suck the anger out from deep inside him, leaving behind a void of darkness and hurt. He shook his head abruptly.

"I suppose she told you that during your little heart-to-heart?" he bit out.

"She did. That's why I told her about your mother. Once everything's out in the open, you won't have to exclude her anymore. She can finally understand what's going on."

Silence stretched out between them until Ethan groaned. "I wish I'd never met you."

He watched the impact of his words upon her dispassionately, noted the tightening of her lips, the paleness that replaced the natural warmth in her cheeks.

"It was inevitable, Ethan—Tamsyn finding out about your mother. It was going to happen eventually."

He shook his head. "I want you to leave."

"I told you before and I'll tell you again. My contract isn't with you. I'm not going until my job is done."

"If you had any decency, you'd go."

"It's because of my integrity that I'm staying. Besides, Tamsyn needs someone in her corner right now who's willing to be honest with her. I will not desert her."

Ethan stared hard into her eyes. She didn't so much as blink, meeting his gaze in a full-on challenge.

"Just stay out of my way," he growled.

"That's going to be hard to do," Isobel said. "We have the wine-tasting shoot this week. Can we at least be civil to one another?"

"Civil, you say? I don't feel terribly civil right now. I can arrange for one of the others to be there in my stead."

She shook her head. "No, that won't do. The focus of the new brochures is the Masters family ethos. As head winemaker and new head of the family, you have to be involved."

To his surprise, Isobel stepped closer and laid one hand on his chest. "You're a good man, Ethan Masters. I know you love Tamsyn, I know you wanted to do what you thought was best for her."

"And yet you still went ahead and told her anyway.

We'll never be able to go back, Tamsyn and I. Nothing will ever be the same."

"Change can be a good thing."

Isobel's hand dropped away from him and, as much as he hated to admit it, he felt its loss immediately. He didn't want to be that weak—to allow her to affect him this way. His response, when it came, was sharp and clear.

"I hope for your sake it is. You say that Tamsyn is your friend and that you wanted to help her, so if this ends up blowing up in our faces, with our mother leaving Tamsyn feeling even more rejected and betrayed, then you 'helped' her right into a whole new world of heartbreak. A world *I* tried to protect her from ever entering."

Before she could respond, he spun on his heel and stalked back out of the cottage. The fury that had driven him there had abated but it had been replaced by a cold, hard anger that sat like a leaden ball in his gut.

"Well, that went well," Isobel said to the empty room after Ethan had left.

She sank down onto the sofa and hugged her arms around her. She'd known he'd be angry but she'd expected a full-on explosion of it—not the intensely controlled version Ethan had brought to her just now. It made her begin to wonder if Ethan had come to terms with the news about Ellen Masters himself. As she turned the thought over in her mind, it occurred to her that he probably hadn't even had time to properly grieve his father's death, either.

Being as controlled as he was—as responsible and conservative as he was—he had to be undergoing a massive internal struggle with himself. Her heart ached for him. She knew what that struggle felt like, should—in an ideal world—be able to help him with this. But their entire relationship, if you could call it such a thing, had been flashes of passion interspersed with flashes of disagreement. It was the original push-me-pull-you type of attraction she'd never understood in others. Didn't understand in herself now, either, to be honest.

Isobel looked across the room and out the picture window that faced the vineyard. The Masters was all about stability, longevity and growth. All of which formed strong foundations in their family. She'd undermined that stability by taking it upon herself to tell Tamsyn what she had today.

She still believed she'd been right to do it—but at what cost to everyone else? Ethan was right that Tamsyn would be very vulnerable when she confronted her mother. If the meeting went badly and the rift was still in place between her and her brother, would she even be willing to turn to her family for comfort? The thought of that, more than anything, sat very heavy in her heart right now.

She couldn't regret what she'd done. But she could ache, with all her heart, over the pain it had caused for both Ethan and Tamsyn.

The next few days proved busy, a fact for which she was grateful. Tamsyn appeared to be none the worse for the revelation about her mother, although Isobel noted that from time to time her attention would wander, her expression become pensive. Personally, Isobel felt that Trent should be very strongly supporting Tamsyn right now but he remained as scarce as he'd been through the duration of her stay to date. When Isobel pressed Tamsyn about this, her friend merely brushed her concern aside, saying he was busy in the city and that she was okay.

When the morning of the wine-tasting shoot dawned, Isobel rose early, her stomach tied in knots. She scowled at her reflection as she brushed her teeth at the bathroom mirror, reminding herself she was a professional and would continue to behave that way no matter how distant or rude Ethan might be.

Ethan. God, the very thought of him sent a spear of longing through her body, making every sense come alive. She had it bad, but infatuation was like that. They'd barely seen each other since he'd confronted her here at the cottage, but even if they hadn't had their falling-out, she doubted she would have gotten much of his time. He was incredibly busy at the winery, pulling long hours with his team as the harvest from their reserve block arrived. New barrels had been brought in and even though Isobel had taken shots of the entire process, Ethan had kept his distance from her.

Today, though, it would be only the two of them. The new brochure would feature each family member in their role at the vineyard. The photo of Raif and his father, Edward, working in such obvious unity had been the family's pick for the vineyard part of the operation. Tamsyn in her office, her wall planner filled behind her, a phone to her ear and her day planner in her hand, had been designated for the accommodation and events along with a surprisingly poignant photo Isobel had taken of the bride and groom during bridezilla's special day last weekend. Cade and Cathleen together with the chef at the restaurant had photographed well in a lighthearted moment that had been an absolute joy to capture. Now it was Ethan's turn.

Isobel checked the smaller daypack she carried with her when she worked, making sure her camera batteries were fully charged and that she had additional memory cards if she needed them. Ethan was delightfully photogenic, she'd discovered in the surreptitious shots she'd taken of him to date. The camera loved the sculpted lines of his face and the way the light fell upon his bone structure. An all-too-familiar ache throbbed low in her belly, forcing her to remind herself that for today, he was only a subject. One to be captured in the course of his work—that was all.

Ethan was prepared and waiting for her at the winery when she arrived. She checked her watch quickly—no, she wasn't late and yet he had that look about him as if he'd been waiting for her for some time. She cast her eye across the setting he'd created—the bentwood chairs set at a crisp-white-linen-covered round table with a row of barrels behind them and the handcrafted stone walls visible as a backdrop. The lighting was to be augmented with strategically placed spotlights that Isobel had hired specifically for this shoot, and she could see them standing off to one side.

"Good morning," Ethan said as she drew closer.

Isobel felt an indefinable frisson ripple down her spine. So he was going for civilized today. She could live with that.

"Good morning. Thank you for setting up in advance today."

He nodded in acknowledgment. "Do you need a hand with the spots?"

Isobel considered the lighting in the area. It was dim, but had a distinct ambience that lent itself well to the solemnity of the process she knew was about to be unveiled to her camera. If she made the right adjustments it was possible she might not need the spotlights after all.

"I think I'll leave them for now," she said. "If you could sit there, at the table for a moment, I'll do a few test shots and see."

Ethan did as she bid without comment. Isobel moved around him, her camera poised and ready for action. The minute she caught him in her viewfinder, her stomach clenched. He was so incredibly beautiful in the most masculine kind of way. A persistent buzz of awareness set up deep inside her but she fought to ignore it. Taking a step back, she scrolled through the photos she'd just taken.

"Stay where you are," she instructed. "We're going to need additional light after all."

She fussed with the spots, taking more shots, until with a grunt of satisfaction, she knew she had the right juxta-position of light and shadow.

"Okay, we're ready to roll," she said, lifting her camera to her eye again. "Now, just start talking and leading me through the wine-tasting process. Use two glasses on the table, as if you have company."

She waited for Ethan to move. He appeared to hesitate, as if to say something, but then he reached for the gold-labeled Shiraz on the table. Instinctively, Isobel began to shoot.

"Wine tasting is an adventure that engages your senses," Ethan started, his voice deep and smooth and sending a thrill of delight through Isobel that she couldn't ignore. "It's more than just taste, although taste is vitally impor-tant and highly individual. It also involves you visually, engages your olfactory senses and plays on your emotions and memories at the same time."

Isobel's finger worked the shutter button unconsciously as Ethan opened the wine and gently poured a sample into each of two empty glasses on the table. His voice provided a background commentary that stroked her senses to boil-ing point, making it more and more difficult with each shot to keep her focus on her subject and not on what his pas-sion for his subject was, in kind, doing to her.

Ethan lifted one of the glasses from the table, angling the bowl slightly away from him, and began explaining about color and tone. Isobel was so caught up in his words that she forgot she was supposed to be merely a silent ob-server, and found herself speaking up.

"To be honest," Isobel interjected, "My wine expertise has always come down to what I like the taste of and how much I like that taste. I've never really stopped to consider color or density."

Ethan turned and gave her a smile that just about made her toes curl. Clearly, in this moment, his animosity had been forgotten. "Then you're seriously missing out. Put the camera down and come here. Try it."

"But I thought you only had an hour for me today."

He shrugged. "So I'll have to make up time somewhere else. This is important. The better you understand the method, the better the photos will be, right?"

Isobel didn't answer, she merely placed her camera down on the table and sat opposite Ethan. She felt absurdly pleased when he gave her a nod of approval.

"Let's see if we can't instill a better appreciation of the process of tasting wine, hmm?" he said.

"You make it sound like a ritual," she commented, picking up her glass and doing as he'd done earlier, tilting it and studying the color and clarity with the same absorption she usually reserved only for her proofs.

"It is, in a way. And there's nothing wrong in making a ceremony out of it, in showing our appreciation for the work that's gone into bringing this bottle to the table all the way from the vine."

Ethan's enthusiasm for his subject shone through in his every gesture and every word. If at all possible, it made him even more attractive to her, and as he continued to lead her through the formalities of using her senses to see, smell and taste the wine he'd chosen for the shoot she felt herself falling for him just that bit more. Ethan the vintner was a far cry from Ethan the authoritative brother and family head. He was just as deliberate and in control, but it felt easier and more natural to let him take the lead in this arena where he was so clearly an expert…and where he was using his expertise to enhance the pleasure she'd find in the experience. As she tasted her wine and allowed the carefully formulated final product roll around in her mouth, she wondered briefly what it would be like to see him year-round—to observe him work through every step of his magical process, turning harvested fruit into a sensation of aromas and flavors that gave her a new appreciation for his art.

See him year-round? What on earth was she thinking? She was transient and she liked it that way. Seeing a man like Ethan Masters year-round would mean staying in his world, because he certainly wasn't the kind of man to uproot himself to live in hers. A man like him had roots that went deeper in the soil at The Masters than those of the vines that striated the fields around them. He wouldn't accept anything less than a permanent, lifelong commitment.

She didn't do permanent. Had never wanted to.

A shocking afterthought penetrated deep into her heart. Until now, perhaps.

Twelve

To give herself some distance from her thoughts, Isobel deliberately set her glass down on the pristine white cloth and reached for her camera again. As she did so, a drop of wine from the rim of her glass tracked down the outside of the bowl and along the stem, spreading onto the base until it leaked into the finely woven linen, leaving a stain.

As she had with her presence here.

Ethan liked everything neat and organized, with every piece tucked into place. Isobel brought mess and chaos with her everywhere she went. She'd brought it to Ethan's life. The thought came to her sharp and swift, and it hurt. She still believed she'd done the right thing by sharing with Tamsyn the information. But only now did she fully appreciate the repercussions of what she'd done. Only now, when she really considered what it might be like to be part of his family, did she think of the damage she might have done to all of them by opening the door between Tamsyn and the secret the rest of her family had made the decision to keep.

This family, these people, they were intertwined with one another just as much as the vines were on the frames they grew along. Each dependent on the other for its success, its support. And she'd potentially undermined that.

It just went to show that she was better off on her own. Whenever she spent time with a strong family or community, it only went to prove to her that she had no idea how to belong. No idea how to be anything other than alone.

"I'm sorry, Ethan," she blurted.

"For the spot on the cloth? Don't worry. We've seen far worse."

"No." She shook her head. "Not that. I mean for telling Tamsyn. I know you had your reasons for keeping the news about your mother to yourself. Whether I agreed with them or not I shouldn't have interfered."

Ethan sighed and rose from the table. "No, you shouldn't have interfered, but I won't accept your apology, either."

He wouldn't? A sudden spurt of anger flared and, just as quickly, extinguished inside of her. He wouldn't. No, of course not. She was the outsider here. The interloper who'd well and truly set a cat among the pigeons.

"That's okay, I understand," she managed to say through lips that felt as thick and unresponsive as rubber. "Look, I think I have everything I need here today. Let me run these through my computer and I'll forward you a selection to choose from for your brochure."

"Isobel, wait."

His voice was a command, not a request. It was so like him, she thought with a rueful twinge of recognition.

"You want me to take some more shots?"

"No." He brushed her question aside with an impatient movement of his hand.

A hand that had done exquisite things to her body. A hand that had left her panting and demanding more—which was exactly what he'd given. A tiny shudder rippled through her. This was torture. Very different from what had been threatened toward her before she'd vacated the country she'd last been in, but equally as devastating emotionally.

She stood silently, awaiting his next move and wishing he would get to whatever it was that he wanted to say. Once he was done, maybe he'd finally let her go to gather her scattered nerves back to some semblance of order again. But his words, when they came, knocked the air straight out of her lungs.

"I owe *you* an apology."

She didn't know what to say, how to act. She let instinct take over.

"No, you don't. I was in the wrong. I acted without really thinking it through."

He mustered a half smile. "I can't say I'm thrilled with the way you went about it, but you were still right. If anyone deserved the full story about our parents it was Tamsyn. I should have told her from the start, when I'd found the discrepancy in my father's personal accounts. If not then, certainly when I found out that our mother was still living."

"I…I don't know what to say."

It was a new sensation for Isobel. Normally she had no trouble blurting out whatever came next in her mind. But this? An apology from this incredibly strong and proud man? She knew how hard it must have been for him to back down like this.

"Then don't say anything. Just listen. Tamsyn and I had a long talk last night. She's still mad at me, and rightly so, but I accept that I was being overprotective. I do still try to shelter her—she *is* my little sister, after all, and I doubt my need to shield her from things will ever go away entirely. But she's an adult—one who had every right, just as you said, to know what I knew. We've discussed it all. Our memories of our mother, the little we got out of our father, the information the solicitor gave me—everything."

"I'm glad you guys could sort it out," Isobel said, gathering her things together to hide her awkwardness.

To her surprise, his hands closed around hers, halting her in her actions. How on earth had he moved so fast? He drew her round to face him.

"Isobel, I am sorry for the way I spoke to you. I've been angry since the day I met you—struggling to come to terms with my father's death, with my additional responsibilities here, with the awful truth he kept from Tam and me all those years. I began to associate you with that emotion, and it wasn't fair." His mouth quirked into a crooked smile, one that made her heart somersault in her chest before he continued. "I'm not proud to admit it, but I needed you that first night to take me away from all of that—to wipe things from my mind. By the morning, when you'd gone, I felt as though I had it all under control again. Then, when you turned up here, it just brought my vulnerability back to me. Being weak isn't something that sits comfortably on my shoulders."

"Believe me, whatever pleasure or escape you got from us being together, I got that, too."

"Escape? What do you need to escape from, Isobel?"

He lifted a hand to move a strand of hair from where it had fallen across her cheek. His touch sent an instant line of fire searing across her skin.

For a minute she thought of the atrocities she'd so recently left behind her. The ones she still felt a moral burden to bring to public awareness through her blog and, with luck, more gallery showings worldwide. This world here at The Masters was so far removed from the day-to-day existence she'd come to accept as normal that, by contrast, it was almost a fantasy come true.

But whose fantasy? She hadn't stood still long enough in the past ten years to even begin to remember what it was like to be rooted in one place. To call somewhere home. And she didn't want to, she reminded herself with a hard mental shake. No matter how compelling the impetus to do otherwise.

"Isobel?" Ethan prompted.

She shook her head. "Nothing. Just...nothing."

"Am I forgiven?" he asked, his dark eyes boring into hers as if willing it to be so.

"Of course," she answered as lightly as she could manage. "But you must forgive me, too."

"Done," he agreed.

Isobel pulled her hands from his and stepped back. "Right, now that's settled, I'd better get back to work."

She felt flustered, his behavior today surprising her more than she cared to admit—showing a side of him that she hadn't envisioned.

"Don't let me hold you back," Ethan replied, turning to the table and recapping the wine bottle. "Here, take this back to your cottage and when you try it, think about what we went over."

Isobel very much doubted she'd ever be able to think about anything or anyone else when she touched wine again, but she accepted the bottle and then collected her camera bag and left the winery. Outside the autumn sunshine was clear and bright, quite a contrast to the controlled environment she'd just left and, she realized, a perfect analogy for her and Ethan. His world was controlled by season and longevity, security and routine. Her world was full of light and air and impermanence. They didn't belong together. Aside from a physical synchronicity that transcended all others, they were complete and utter opposites.

But if that was the case, why did it hurt so much to think about leaving here, leaving him?

Ethan returned from dinner with Shanal feeling completely out of sorts. Despite his overtures, she'd shown no interest in developing their relationship any further than their existing friendship. He'd seeded their conversation with hints about her hopes for the future, her dreams. Marriage hadn't figured in there at all. And then there'd been the lack of physical contact or even chemistry between them. Sure, they'd talked long into the evening about their work, but he knew that if a marriage between them was to work, they needed more. They needed some compatibility beyond inquiring minds and similar interests.

Yet every time he thought about compatibility, a different face swam into view. A face framed with sun-kissed blond hair. A face with blue eyes, not green. He'd felt better for apologizing to Isobel and hoped the truce between them would dull the edge of the wild infatuation that had plagued him from the moment he'd first seen her. He'd sworn to himself he'd keep his hands off her from now on. It was too dangerously addictive being around her.

Fortunately, creating distance between them at The Masters had proven quite straightforward as she threw herself into finishing the assignment. They'd crossed paths only briefly since she'd done the tasting shoot, acknowledging one another's presence with little more than a nod or a wave in passing. Their dealings were now confined to email as he'd approved her selection of proofs to be dealt with by their marketing department.

He knew she'd be leaving soon, very soon. It was a

relief to know he didn't have to spend every waking minute wondering if he'd see her or catch a reminder of her scent.

Ethan garaged his car and made his way up to his bedroom, crossing the floor swiftly to draw his drapes closed. As he did each night, however, he paused at the window. His eyes were inexorably drawn to Isobel's cottage. The interior lights burned until late every night. Either she was a complete night owl or she had about as much trouble sleeping as he did. He closed the drapes with a sharp snap and got ready for bed, forcing his thoughts to turn to Shanal Peat again.

What was it about the two of them that didn't spark? he wondered as he lay in the dark. He'd thought it would be so simple. Well, he'd make it work somehow. He just had to. He had the future of his entire family network to consider and ensuring its stability was one of his many responsibilities. Someone like Shanal was perfect.

And if he told himself often enough, he might just believe it.

But as the hours ticked over and sleep remained elusive, he found his thoughts straying in a different direction. One that lay only a couple of hundred meters from him right now. One that was completely wrong for him and his plans for the future on so many levels he shouldn't even be thinking of her at all.

Ethan rolled over and focused on making his body relax, emptying his mind, breathing deep—and then starting with his toes and working up his body, clenching and releasing muscles until he all but melted into the surface of his mattress. Then an image of Isobel flicked into his mind again. Just like that he was taut as a bow once more. Taut and aching and thinking all kinds of inappropriate thoughts for a man who was attempting to woo a different woman altogether.

What kind of man did that make him? Certainly not one he was proud to be. All his life he'd striven for excellence, worked tirelessly for his family's and, more important, his father's respect. And he'd earned it. He'd basked in their pleasure in his achievements, at first academically and then later on with the wines he'd produced to many international accolades.

He'd done it all for them but he'd done it for himself, too. He enjoyed the ride, the challenges, the success. Why couldn't he succeed at this? Why did his friendship with Shanal lack the vital catalyst that pushed a relationship past amity and into passion?

And why couldn't he get his mind off a woman who was wrong for him in every way? She was a free spirit, while he was bound by a hundred different ties. He thrived on responsibility and commitment while she ran the other way. He wanted to spend his life at The Masters, contributing to his family's legacy, while by all indications, she couldn't get away fast enough. And yet somehow, Isobel challenged him on every level—mentally and physically. He didn't want to want her like this but she was now embedded in his psyche.

He got out of bed with a frustrated growl and went through to his bathroom for a glass of water. Something, he hoped, that would slake the thirst that made him crave so much more than a long draw of cool liquid.

She'd be leaving The Masters soon, probably even leaving Australia, and that was a very good thing, he told his hazy reflection in the moonlit en suite. A very good thing, indeed.

But the thought of never seeing her again made his body ache and turned his mind to the two nights they'd shared. He wanted more. He wanted her. He wanted that sensation of having his senses scattered to the wind, he wanted to take risks and do crazy things with her. He wanted, even for only that briefest moment, to be wonderfully and truly happy again. To forget the responsibilities and pressures that confined him and to give himself over fully to the moment.

He wanted Isobel Fyfe.

Thirteen

"Ethan, you have to go to the awards ceremony. You can't possibly think of sending someone else."

Tamsyn had been reminding him of the upcoming wine awards ceremony for days now and he'd been ignoring each reminder deliberately. He knew he had an amazing team but he also hated to leave the property at this stage of the winemaking process. The reserve chardonnay was about to head into its secondary fermentation and bulk aging in oak barrels, while the Shiraz was already into its malo-lactic fermentation stage.

Sure, he could delegate a lot of the testing that needed to take place at this point—it was how he'd been trained by his father and how his father had been trained before him, after all. If you didn't share and, in some cases, relinquish responsibility, no one learned anything of real value along the way. The family often teased him about the strangle-hold he kept on operations and his pedantic methods, but they worked. After all, wasn't that why The Masters was up for this most recent award in the first place? Quality was everything.

"Ethan? Are you even listening to me?" Tamsyn persisted.

"Of course I'm listening to you. Will you come with me?"

"I wish I could, you know that. But this weekend is bridezilla's parents' surprise anniversary and vow renewal service." His sister pulled a face that left no doubt as to how eager she was to see the back of the coming weekend. "Why don't you take someone else?"

"Hmm, I wonder if Shanal is free?" he pondered out loud.

"Shanal? I was thinking more along the lines of Isobel." Tamsyn gave him a pointed look.

"Isobel?" His senses went on high alert at the very thought of her.

"Why not? Maybe she could take some photos, as well. Marketing will be able to use them, if not in the new brochure then certainly for other publicity releases for the vintage. I can check with her if you like."

Ethan stroked his chin thoughtfully. If he took Isobel, he knew the awards ceremony would be very much the last thing on his mind. "Let me check with Shanal first."

"Really? Ethan, she's lovely and she's a wonderful friend but why are you doing this?"

"What are you talking about?"

"Why are you ignoring what you could have with Isobel to chase after Shanal, who we both know you don't care about in that way?"

"Tamsyn—" he started to protest but his sister cut him off.

"No, don't fob me off. We've learned the hard way how

precious things are in life. How special relationships can be. I know you like Shanal, and she's lovely, but she's your friend, not your lover. You can't create what isn't there. With Isobel I know you have that special something. Can't you just give it a try?"

"Look, you're on the wrong track. Isobel and I... We're not suited. It wouldn't work out in the long term."

"Damn the long term!" Tamsyn's outburst startled him. "What about how she makes you *feel?* Think about it, Ethan. Life isn't just a series of processes season in and season out. Sometimes you have to roll with change, exercise your senses, allow yourself to take a walk on the wild side. Do what feels right in the moment instead of sticking to the plan come what may."

There were tears in his sister's eyes. "What's going on, Tamsyn? This is about more than who I invite to the awards, isn't it?"

"Of course it is. I don't know about you, but I don't feel like I can just trot along on my merry little life path the way I used to anymore. Things have changed. We need to learn to change with them. Since Dad died I've been thinking a lot about my life and my future. I don't know if I want the same things anymore. I don't think, if you're really honest with me and with yourself, you do, either. And I have questions that I no longer have the answers for. Don't you? Don't you want to know more about Mum, about why she left, about why she stayed away? About why Dad never spoke about her again or let her see us?

"Things have changed now that I know she's alive. I can't pretend everything's the same and just trundle along as if all is business as usual. I don't feel as if I can move forward again until I know the answers to those questions. They're important to me. You should be considering what's really important to you, too."

She turned and left his office before he could reply, tension radiating from her body in waves. It upset him to see her like this. Tamsyn was usually so centered, so level. Always the one to smooth troubled waters and to make sure that everyone was happy. Their father had called her "his biddable child" because she'd always do whatever was expected of her with a smile on her face. He knew she'd still deliver on everything that was expected of her, but at what cost to herself?

Damn, he wished she was still his baby sister that he could still guard against the things that would upset her, but he'd accepted he could no longer do that. She was an adult and had long since earned the right to stand on her own two feet. All he could do was make certain she knew she had his backing if she needed it, as he had hers. Which brought him back to what she'd said just now. About considering what was important to him.

The Masters, most definitely, and everyone associated with it—but even as he thought it, his mind drifted to a slender waif of a woman. One with lightly tanned skin, clear blue eyes and hair the color of sunshine after a spring rain.

He was on his feet and heading out of his office before he could double think this. Tamsyn was right. His time with Isobel was short. He needed to make the most of it.

And he wouldn't let himself think about how soon it would come to an end.

"Are you sure this is a good idea?" Isobel asked as she tightened the straps on her pack.

"No."

Ethan's reply was succinct and made her look up and do a double take at the expression on his face.

"I thought we weren't going to—"

"We weren't."

"But we're—"

"We are."

"Okay." She breathed out on a long breath and lifted her pack to walk out of the cottage toward Ethan's car. "Are we staying in the apartment again?"

His lips firmed as if he was weighing up his response. "Yes, unless you'd rather stay at a hotel?"

"No, I'd rather be at the apartment. I liked it there," she answered with a smile that felt both slightly shy and unashamedly bold at the same time.

He was different today. In fact, he'd been different from the moment he'd asked her if she'd like to be his plus one at the awards evening. She'd basically wrapped up all her work at The Masters, with the exception of a shoot of Cade's latest dessert creation, which Cathleen had insisted on including in their feature. Theoretically, she was a free spirit once again. Free to travel whenever and wherever she wanted to.

The human rights issues were calling her again. The idyll here in South Australia had been an opportunity to recharge her batteries but she needed to get back to work—real work—very soon.

She had to be honest with herself, though. There had been a very definite hold on her here. A hold which began and ended with the man walking at her side—the man who set her senses alight with no more than a glance. The prospect of even just one more night with him made her senses vibrate with a keenness she knew she ought to control better, but for the life of her, simply didn't want to.

The ride into Adelaide was smooth and swift and Isobel found herself looking for specific landmarks on the way through. Landmarks that led them closer to the apartment.

Ethan spoke only occasionally on the journey into the city but he seemed relaxed, happy even.

When he pulled into the underground parking at the apartment tower and rolled the car into its space, he suddenly reached across the compartment and took her hand.

"We've got time. Come on."

"Time? For what?" She felt the beginnings of a smile tug at her lips.

"You'll see." He smiled back and let her hand go, reaching across her to open her car door. "Come on. Let's not waste a second."

This side of Ethan was different from the ones she'd seen before. He was more carefree. And the expression on his face, all heat and intent, was making her stomach somersault in anticipation of what he had in mind. Ethan was out of the car and grabbing their things from the trunk before she had even unclipped her seat belt.

"Come on, lazybones," he chided playfully. "Let's go."

She did as he said, catching up with him as he began to walk toward the elevator without so much as a glance back at her. He hit the remote lock and she heard the car's electronic system engage just as she caught up to him.

The ride up in the elevator was mercifully swift. Isobel's skin felt tight, too tight for her body, and the light abrasion of her clothing reminded her with every step of the featherlight touch of Ethan's fingertips upon her. By the time the doors opened in the foyer of the apartment she thought she might explode with the tension that gripped her.

Ethan stepped out of the elevator and dropped their bags on the floor with one movement, then reached for her in another. She was plastered against his body before her thoughts could catch up with her actions. His erection pressed hard against her, his mouth lowered and caressed hers softly before taking her lips in a kiss that all but blew her mind.

She reached up and hooked her arms around the back of his neck, her fingers tangling in the short strands of his hair and pulling him toward her. She couldn't get close enough, taste him enough. She swept her tongue gently over his lower lip before catching it lightly between her teeth, suckling against the soft flesh before releasing him again. He shuddered against her, grinding his hips against hers, sliding his thigh between her jean-clad legs and hitching her up slightly.

Instinctively, her pelvis tilted and she felt the jolt of energy that radiated from her core. She moaned aloud only to have the sound snatched from her mouth as he kissed her again, this time deeper, harder, stronger than before. His hands slid down her body, cupping her buttocks and lifting her higher. She hitched her legs around his waist, holding on to him for dear life as he began to walk them both down the hall, never taking his lips from her for one second.

Finally, blissfully, she felt a bed at her back. She reached for the fastening of his jeans, her fingers shaking as she undid the metal buttons and shoved the denim off his hips and down the top of his thighs. He did the same, albeit with a little more finesse—taking her G-string briefs with her jeans and hooking off her slip-on shoes in a modicum of movement.

Isobel reached for him, her fingers closing around his length through his boxer briefs, stroking him through the cotton, reaching lower to cup his balls and squeeze lightly as he dragged a condom from the bedside cabinet. He was sheathed in seconds, sliding inside her in less.

Their tempo was frantic, her heart beating so fast in her chest she thought she might expire. At last, with a deep

thrust, Ethan pushed her body over the edge of desperation and into a realm of feeling so rich and so divine she
felt tears slip from the corners of her eyes. He collapsed
against her, shoving her deep into the mattress as his body
pulsed with his own release.

She lay beneath him, relishing the weight of his body
pinning her to the bed, still enraptured by the heights of
responsiveness he drew from her body. She wrapped her
arms tight around his waist, not wanting this moment,
this closeness to end. Ethan nuzzled her neck, nipping her
skin lightly and sending another ripple coursing through
to her core. She clenched her inner muscles tight around
him, and felt an answering reaction in his own body, that
involuntary throb of sensation.

"Let's blow off this thing tonight and just stay here," he
said against her throat. "I have tortured myself with denial
of you for far too long. Let's not waste another minute."

She laughed, tempted to agree to his outrageous sug-
gestion, but the accolade he was nominated for tonight was
major industry recognition. She wanted to see him win,
wanted to share in his success.

"We have the rest of the night after the dinner and
awards."

"No, it's not enough," he said, pressing a line of kisses
around the neckline of her blouse. "It'll never be enough."

"What if I promise that if you win, I'll…"

She whispered something in his ear.

"Only if I win?"

"Well, maybe if you don't win, too, but only if we go
and I get those photos Tamsyn insisted on."

He groaned and rested his forehead on hers. "You drive
a hard bargain, but okay. I agree. Let's go shower."

He withdrew from her body and stood up, grabbing her
hands and pulling her up with him. She laughed again as

he kicked off his shoes and the jeans that had settled at his ankles. She felt so relaxed, so unbelievably happy.

So very much in love.

Fourteen

No. She couldn't be. Not in love. She'd never loved a man, not like this. The realization was exhilarating and terrifying in equal measure. No, cancel that, she thought. It was quite simply terrifying. She didn't love. Love meant attachment. Love meant being with someone forever. She didn't do forever. She did change—a kaleidoscope of people, places, lives.

But this feeling, this overwhelming reaction that filled her heart and her mind—it was different from anything else she'd ever felt before. It exhilarated her, but it terrified her at the same time.

Emotionally numb, Isobel allowed Ethan to lead her to the bathroom where he led them into a massive multihead shower and began to soap up her body. The slick feel of his lathered hands on her skin was a welcome distraction to the shattered thoughts that splintered through her mind. She grabbed a metaphorical hold of the desire that began to grow within her, allowing Ethan's touch to stoke that fire so that it consumed all thought of anything else. When he knelt before her, placing his lips and mouth at her core, doing unspeakably creative things to her with his tongue, she let herself ride the waves until he coaxed her over the edge and into oblivion, leaving her shaking and weak, barely able to stand—definitely unable to think.

The rest of the evening passed in a blur. She knew she did the right things, went through the right motions, took the right photos, but inside she was still in shock. How had she allowed him under her radar? How had he inveigled his way into her heart?

In the aftermath of her mother's death and her father's quest to run from his grief for the rest of his life, Isobel had sworn she would never let anyone matter that much to her. She never wanted another soul to have that power to inflict hurt or sorrow on her life. She never wanted to be dependent on another for her happiness.

The way she chose to live was her protection. Looking at her world through a lens, but not necessarily being involved on a deeper scale with it. Oh, sure, she knew people argued that if she didn't empathize with her subjects, or at the very least feel some sense of responsibility toward them, that she wouldn't enjoy the success she'd had to date, and they weren't wrong. She let herself feel, let herself care, but never let herself get truly attached.

Isobel watched Ethan across the table where they'd been seated upon arrival at the awards ceremony. He looked up for a moment, as if aware of her gaze, and gave her a small secret smile. The look in his eyes made her breath catch in her throat. As he held her gaze she felt her nipples tighten beneath the dress she wore, one that Tamsyn had loaned her and which made her eyes look bluer than blue and her skin become almost luminescent. She smiled in return. It was all she was capable of here in this room filled with people and noise and the clatter of cutlery on fine china. But when she got Ethan alone, oh, yes, then she'd show him exactly what that look did to her, and she'd do it to him, too.

She noted the exact second her intent reflected in her eyes, the flare of acceptance, of challenge, in his own. His smile deepened and she felt as if time stood still as he made his excuses to the people he was talking with and rose from the table. He was at her side in a moment, his warm hand on her bare shoulder.

"Had enough for tonight?" he asked as he bent down slightly, his breath warm in her ear and sending a thrill of excitement through her.

"Not nearly enough," she replied, reaching for the small beaded bag Tamsyn had also loaned her and rising as he pulled out her chair.

"Let's not waste another second, then, hmmm?" he said as he tucked her hand in the crook of his elbow.

They were delayed a few times by people wanting to congratulate Ethan on his latest gold medal success, but the accolades appeared to wash over him. Tension radiated from his body, transferring itself to her in waves.

As the valet brought Ethan's car around the front of the reception center she asked him, "Did you enjoy yourself this evening?"

"Not as much as I enjoyed thinking about the rest of tonight with you."

She laughed, the sound a gurgle of joy and surprise. The comment was so unlike the taciturn Ethan she'd come to know. She liked this side of him, too. In fact, she liked pretty much everything about him and she couldn't wait to show him just how much.

"What about you?" he asked. "Did you have a good time?"

She cocked her head a little, considering his question carefully. "It was good to see you get the recognition you deserve. There were a lot of envious people in the room there tonight. I'd say you could pick your price if you ever wanted to work for another winery pretty much anywhere in the world."

"I wouldn't do that. I'd never leave The Masters."

His answer was straight to the point, like him. She hadn't realized it until he'd said it that she'd been subconsciously asking a question of him—wondering if he'd ever be willing to set off somewhere new, start fresh without the weight of ties and family obligations. He'd given her the answer she expected. It still gave her a pang of regret. No matter the attraction between them, no matter her new-found feelings for Ethan, she was not the woman for him. He needed someone as committed to The Masters as he was himself. Perhaps even more so, as that woman would need to be committed wholly to him also to fully understand why it was so important for him to continue the traditions of generations of Masterses on South Australian soil.

Isobel was not that person, and acknowledging that blunt truth set up an ache deep inside that she knew would take a long time to ignore. Being busy with her work would be a most excellent way to hurry the process, but in the meantime, she at least had tonight, and maybe another week as she finalized things with Tamsyn and the marketing team over the publicity shots.

When they returned to the apartment, Isobel found herself wanting to prolong every moment with Ethan, to tuck away memories to take out and savor another day. When he suggested a nightcap, she agreed, and they sat in the massive lounge room, overlooking the lights that sparkled in the distance while sipping an aged tawny port.

She kicked off her shoes and pulled her feet up onto the sofa where they sat. When Ethan reached for one foot and began to absently massage it she all but melted under his touch. He turned every part of her body into an erogenous zone. She could only hope she could do the same for him.

And later, in the bedroom, she did her very best so that when they collapsed, exhausted, on their tangled sheets, she felt certain that he'd be as unlikely to forget her as she would to ever, ever forget him.

The persistent buzz of his cell phone vibrating dragged Ethan from a deeply satisfying sleep. He reached for the bedside cabinet and grabbed the phone, sliding from the bed even as he answered it and heading out of the bedroom so he wouldn't disturb Isobel.

"Ethan, it's Rob."

Rob, one of the winemakers who formed an integral part of his team at The Masters, spoke before Ethan could even identify himself. His stomach dropped as he registered the concern in his colleague's voice.

"What is it?" he demanded, knowing Rob wouldn't be calling him this early in the morning unless there was a serious problem.

"It's not good."

Ethan's brows drew together as he listened. Somehow, someone had put the reserve chardonnay in the wrong tank, inadvertently blending it with a lesser quality wine. By the time he ended the call, Ethan felt sick to his stomach. This was a monumental error that should never have happened. He should have been there—he should have stayed at home and remained focused on his work. He shouldn't have gone to the awards ceremony. He hadn't needed the accolade to know what he did was good—he knew what he did was good because he paid attention, because he obsessively kept an eye on progress, because he remained in control.

But he'd relinquished control and look what had happened. Oh, sure, they'd make a good wine in the long run with careful blending and fining. But it wouldn't be produced under the renowned The Masters reserve label—the label he personally undertook to ensure was consistently world class.

"Ethan?" Isobel's voice came from behind him. "Is everything okay?"

He felt every muscle in his body weaken at the sound of her voice. And therein lay the chink in his armor. His weakness.

Isobel.

He turned to face her. Her cheek had a slight mark on it from where she'd lain on the sheets, and her hair was rumpled, her eyes still heavy lidded with sleep. It didn't matter how she looked, how she dressed—or undressed, for that matter—she tempted him every single time. And it had to stop. It had to end, here and now. Tamsyn was wrong. It wasn't worth it to live in the moment—no matter how good the moment might be—if it put everything else at risk.

"No, everything's not okay. There's been a mistake at the winery, one that wouldn't have happened if I had stayed where I should have been all along."

"Oh, no," she cried sympathetically. "Can it be rectified?"

He shrugged. "We'll have to wait and see. The wine itself won't be of the standard or quality it was designated to be. The waste is epic."

Frustration and anger with himself pulled his thoughts

this way and that. A growing cycle wasted. He could only imagine what Raif would say when he heard the news. Raif had built his home within sight of the small vineyard that had escaped the bush fires that had nearly destroyed their family's livelihood so many years ago. He had taken over the nurturing and care of the old vines, and was as vigilant over and proud of his grapes as Ethan was about what he did with their fruit. His cousin would be equally devastated at the news.

"What happened?" Isobel asked, breaking into his thoughts.

"What should never have happened. Two wines were mixed that shouldn't have been, and it's my fault."

"Ethan, you weren't there. You can't blame yourself."

Isobel put a hand on his arm but he shook it off.

"Can't I?" he asked, futile rage beginning to build inside him. "I *should* have been there."

"You have to be able to delegate sometimes, surely."

"And if this is what I can expect when I do?" His mind raced with thoughts of things he should have done, checks he should have put into place to keep something like this from occurring. "The final responsibility rests with me. I am the family head, not anyone else."

"Ethan—"

"No, Isobel. Nothing you say changes anything. When my father died, I took over his obligations. All of them."

"But you had to be here last night," she persisted. "You owed it to yourself, to this brand you speak of and to your family to front up for the award."

"Owed it to myself?" He shook his head slowly. "I didn't come because I wanted to receive the award in person. I could have sent anyone else from The Masters. They could have damn well posted the thing to me in the mail! No, I came because I wanted to be with you. I don't focus when I'm with you.

"I can't trust myself when I'm with you, Isobel. I can't trust myself to be who I'm meant to be—who I was brought up to become. Until I met you nothing and no one could distract me from my work. I believed…I believed I could have both, at least for a little while. I knew you'd be leaving soon, but I thought that while we were here, that we could…that I could… But I can't, don't you see? I can't have you in my life and be good at what I do at the same time. My work has to come first. I owe that to my family, to my father. My work is what will *last*—" *after you go away,* he continued silently in his thoughts.

"And that's why I can't see you anymore."

Isobel staggered back in shock, her face ashen. But he didn't hold back. He couldn't. He took a deep breath.

"I don't want you to come back to The Masters with me. You can stay here as long as you need to. I'll get the building concierge to key your fingerprint into the biometric reader. You can communicate with Tamsyn via the phone and the internet, but I think it's better if we end this here and now. You've finished the job you came here to do. Dragging it out won't do either one of us any good."

"Do you really think sending me off will make things better? Hiding from your feelings won't make them go away. You have to be stronger than that."

"What? Like my father was strong? Like my mother leaving him didn't change him? He could have gone after her, you know. But he chose to stay—to focus on his family, to focus on the winery. It's what I have to do, too." He held up a hand as she started to protest. "No, please. Hear me out on this, Isobel. This thing we have together, it consumes me. I lose control when I'm with you—my temper, my passion, my joy. Everything. I can't allow myself to be that man.

"I'm going to get dressed and head home. I'll leave it to you as to what you do next, but please, don't come back to the winery."

"Ethan, please, think about this some more before you go. I know you're upset. I know what's happened with the wine is a big deal, but it's happened. Can't you just let it go? Move on?"

He ignored the wobble in her voice and reached deep for what he had to say next.

"I am moving on, Isobel. We're too different to make a relationship between us work. One of us will always end up hurt as a result. It's what happened to my parents, and I won't have it happen to me, too. My mother was…like you. A free spirit. And when she couldn't take being tied down anymore, she decided to leave my father. Take Tamsyn and me and leave him. Pull us from our birthright and our father. No wonder he paid her to stay away after that."

He rubbed his eyes with one hand and fought to push back the overwhelming sense of bleakness that now threatened to swamp him. "You and I, we have no future together. You go wherever the wind takes you, but I stay here. 'Here' is all I've got. And I can't let my feelings for you distract me from that. Which is why I can't have you around."

Isobel stared at him in disbelief. She swallowed against the emotion burning in her throat, determined she wouldn't show him for even so much as one second how much his words just now had hurt her.

"Fine. I won't return to The Masters. I'm just about finished up, anyway. I can complete any last-minute things via email with Tamsyn."

To her surprise her voice was steady and sure, as sure as her determination to refuse to show Ethan just how deep his words had cut her and how much she'd found herself wishing he'd asked her to stay.

Thank God she hadn't told him that she loved him. That would be the ultimate irony, the ultimate weakness. She, who'd never wanted to stay or settle with any one person, and especially not to fall in love, was head over heels with a man who, it appeared, was willing to toss her aside, anyway.

"Thank you for not making this awkward," he said, his voice devoid of expression.

She looked at him, struggled to believe this was the same man who'd laughed with her last night, who'd loved with her in the darkness. The man who'd stolen her heart.

Her lips twisted in an ironic smile. "I'll go now. Just give me a few minutes to get my things together. Good luck with your work. I really do hope you'll be happy. You deserve to be happy, Ethan. Remember that."

Somehow she found the strength to turn away from him without touching him, to make her way to the bathroom where she showered quickly and dressed in her standard uniform of jeans and a shirt then, without checking to see if he was still in the main living area waiting for her, she hefted her pack onto her shoulders and let herself out the second entrance they'd used last night.

She had her pack, and her health and a sizeable check on its way to fatten her bank account soon. Those were all the things she'd ever needed to get by. They were all she'd need now. They'd have to be…because the chance of having anything else was now over.

Fifteen

Isobel was at the airport waiting for her flight to Singapore. From there she was heading back to Africa and it couldn't be soon enough, she decided. Her cell phone began to vibrate in her pocket and she slid it out to check the caller ID. Tamsyn. She sighed. Every instinct told her to ignore the call, to keep things purely to email between them. Too much could be read into tone of voice and she didn't want anyone to know what an idiot she'd been to fall in love with Ethan Masters, especially not his sister.

But Tamsyn had been her friend, as well. She owed it to her to speak to her directly. Isobel thumbed the pad of her phone, answering the call.

"Isobel? Are you okay?"

"I'm fine, Tamsyn. Just got a heads-up on my next project and I needed to take advantage of it. I'm sorry not to have been able to say goodbye in person."

"Really? Is that why you're leaving so soon? Ethan came

back here like a bear with a sore head. I know he's upset about the reserve but I thought... Well, never mind what I thought. I'm sorry, too."

Silence stretched out between them for a moment or two. Isobel forced herself to speak.

"Look, they'll be calling my flight soon. I have to go. Thanks for everything, Tam, and you take care, okay? I'll email you."

"Yeah, sure. Look, I wanted to let you know that I've decided to try and find my mother, to at least find out where she is."

"Are you sure that's wise? You might end up opening a whole can of worms you're not ready for."

"I know," Tamsyn agreed. "That's why I'm not rushing into anything. It's not as if I don't have enough other stuff to keep me busy, anyway. But I need to know more about her."

"I understand, but be very careful about what you decide to do once you do have the information you're looking for. Promise me? Things may not always turn out the way you hope they will."

Tamsyn gave a short, dry laugh. "Is that the voice of experience talking now, Isobel?"

Isobel closed her eyes for a moment, shutting out the busyness of the terminal building and focusing on her friend's voice, on imagining her in her office, overlooking the property and the people who worked there.

"Yeah, maybe," she admitted.

"You can always come back, Isobel."

"No, I can't," she said softly. "I never look back."

"Are you sure you can't make an exception this time?"

"No exceptions, Tam. I'm sorry. Look, it's been wonderful getting to know you. I meant it about staying in touch, okay? And let me know how things are going with your search for your mother."

"Sure, I will. Take care, Isobel. I'll miss you."

"I'll miss you, too."

Isobel disconnected the call, not wanting to actually say goodbye, not wanting to hear it in return. Because that would make her leaving all the more final.

Ethan looked at Shanal across the intimate dining table at the select restaurant he'd chosen to bring her to tonight. The past couple of weeks had been difficult. Coming to grips with the accident at the winery was one thing; getting used to the fact that Isobel was no longer nearby was something else entirely. He gave himself a mental shake. Dwelling on the past was not going to consolidate his future, a future he hoped would include the woman seated across from him.

Shanal's pale green eyes glittered in the soft lighting in the dining room. Her long, black hair was a glossy fall down her back. She was beautiful, intelligent, warm and friendly. Everything he wanted in a life mate—especially when he factored in her steady and reliable nature.

The waiter brought their coffee and withdrew, reminding Ethan that the evening was drawing to a close and he had yet to broach the subject of marriage with Shanal. He drew in a deep breath and let it out slowly before reaching across the small table to take Shanal's hand.

She looked up at him, startled by his action.

"Shanal, do you often think about the future?"

She gave him a nervous smile. "The future? Of course I do. All the time, actually."

"So do I," Ethan said with more confidence. "And I think we make a good pair, don't you?"

"Ethan, I—"

He rushed on, interrupting her. "We should get married. We're great friends already. We have the same interests, the same wants. We would be great together."

To his absolute shock, Shanal burst out laughing.

"What?" he asked, more than a bit put out by her re-action.

"Oh, Ethan. Surely you're not serious?"

He thought for a moment of the ring set with diamonds and an unusual pale green amethyst he had stowed in his pocket. One he'd chosen for its uniqueness and because it reminded him of the exact color of Shanal's eyes. "Why wouldn't I be serious about it?"

"Because you're in love with someone else. Besides, I'm not *in* love with you and, call me old-fashioned, but I think love is definitely a prerequisite for a long and happy marriage, don't you?"

"But I do love you," he protested, even as his gut clenched.

"Sure, and I love you, too, but not *that* way." She tugged her hand free. "Ethan, we're great friends and I hope we'll always share that special relationship no matter where we are or what we're doing. When you started asking me out, I was willing to try to see if there could be something more between us. I thought you'd realized, as I did, that there couldn't—and that that was why I hadn't heard from you for the past few weeks. When you rang to ask me out to-night, I was expecting you to admit the truth—that we're better off as friends."

"Are we?"

"Of course we are. It's not just that you're not in love with me. It's that you *are* in love with Isobel. Even a blind man could see that. You're crazy not to grasp what the two of you could have and hold tight. You owe it to yourself, and to her, to keep it safe forever because a love like that doesn't come along in every lifetime."

"Isobel?"

Shanal huffed a sigh of frustration. "You know, for an intelligent man, you can be hopelessly dense sometimes. Yes, Isobel. Tell me, how did you feel the first time you ever saw her?"

"Like I'd suddenly found light in a dark place."

She smiled. "Exactly. And what did you do?"

"I followed her."

"And then?" she prompted.

Ethan felt heat rise into his cheeks. He wasn't about to share with Shanal what had happened next. She obviously noted the high color in his face.

"See what I mean? When has anyone ever made you feel like she did, behave like you did together? It was way more than infatuation or lust, Ethan. Don't forget, I know you well. I knew you had some crazy bee in your bonnet about us, but when I saw you with Isobel I wondered if you weren't fighting against her just a little too hard."

She lifted her coffee cup and took a sip and eyed him over the china rim. "Seriously, what are you afraid of? You have the chance to have the kind of forever love that many people can only dream of. I envy you that because that's the kind of love I want from the man I marry, if I ever marry. And you can be certain I'm not prepared to settle for less than that, ever."

"Are you sure, Shanal? We could be a great partnership." He had to try, just one more time, because what she was suggesting was impossible and scary all at the same time.

"I'm one hundred percent certain. Now, enjoy your coffee and take me home and we can put this behind us and get back to normal again."

By the time he arrived home and went upstairs to his room, he felt shattered. Building up to tonight had taken more out of him than he'd expected and, oddly, he now even felt some relief that Shanal had turned him down. It seemed she knew him better than he knew himself, he thought with a rueful smile as he unknotted his tie and threw it at an easy chair in the corner of his room.

His attention was dragged to the open drapes at his window, to the darkness beyond that served as a reminder of the empty cottage where Isobel had stayed. Where they'd made love. A fist clenched tight in his gut. He'd sent her away and she'd gone, willingly. On to the next thing, the next adventure, the next job, the next man.

The thought made him feel physically ill and he snapped his drapes closed with a decisive flick. Shanal could say what she liked about him and Isobel having a special connection. The truth was, she'd had one foot out the door from the moment she arrived at The Masters. Sending her away had shortened her stay, but nothing he could have done would have made her stay for good.

A knock at his door made him turn around.

"It's only me," Tamsyn said through the door. "Can I come in?"

"Sure," he said, pulling the door open. "What's up?"

"I just wanted to see if congratulations were in order."

"Me and Shanal? No. She turned me down."

"Oh, thank God!"

Ethan looked at his sister in shock. "You think we would have been such a bad match?"

"No, not that, but you wouldn't have been happy. Not really happy like you deserve."

Her words echoed the ones Isobel had parted from him with. "I'll never know now, will I?" he said flippantly.

"You will if you do something about Isobel."

"Like what?"

"Like tell her how you really feel."

It seemed everyone knew him better than he knew himself. Strangely, the thought didn't rankle as he thought it might.

"What's the point? My life is here, and she'd never want to settle down."

"You could try asking her, you know."

"Asking her to give up her whole life? Her work? Her plans?"

"Ask her if she'd be willing to try. There's a chance you could reach a compromise, if you're willing to work for one. I've never known you to turn away from something just because it would be hard work. Usually you take that sort of thing as a challenge. What do you have to lose by asking?"

"And what if I'm afraid to? Have you ever considered that?"

"You, Ethan? Afraid?" Tamsyn looked stunned, as if the idea had never occurred to her. She pressed her lips together, her expression showing she was thinking hard. "Okay, I get that you'd be careful—you're not the sort to rush into anything—but afraid? Why?"

Ethan sat down on one of the easy chairs positioned in front of the stone fireplace in his room and motioned for his sister to do the same. "We haven't exactly had the best examples set for us, have we? Aunt Cynthia and Uncle Charles split up and put their kids through hell. Dad let us think that Mum was dead all this time—and she was so eager to get away from him that she did nothing to show us otherwise. Even Uncle Edward and Aunt Marianne haven't always been smooth sailing."

"No, but that doesn't mean we can't make a success of things ourselves. If all people ever looked at through history was failure, without changing something to do it better, then humankind would cease to exist."

He smiled at her words. She was right. But that was what he'd done already—tried to improve on the past, to fix mistakes and avoid the same pitfalls.

"I have done it differently than Mum and Dad. I've been careful. I haven't led with my heart."

"Sure, but at the cost of all else," Tamsyn protested. "You try to wrap everything around you in cotton wool. You don't take risks, you only bet on a sure thing and you're so protective of me and the family it's almost suffocating."

Suffocating? Is that what she thought? A flare of frustration warred with sadness that she felt that way. He felt obligated to respond.

"When Mum died, or at least when we were led to believe she had, I felt as if the cornerstone of my world had crumbled away. Dad was always so busy here that she was our real compass. You're probably too young to remember the way she was with us. One time, I remember she was dressed up for a ladies' tea somewhere. But when she heard we were off to the creek with some of the other cousins, she kicked off her high heels, threw on a pair of flip-flops and came with us. Just like that. She was always there for us and then all of a sudden she wasn't.

"In the hospital, after the accident, Dad told me to be his little man, to look after you, and I did. Maybe I took that a little too far."

"Don't be too hard on yourself," Tamsyn said softly. "You're a great big brother and I know how lucky I've been. But I am a grown-up now. Don't take this the wrong way, but when I need your help, I will ask for it. You don't need to make my decisions for me anymore."

Ethan accepted the truth of her words, even though a

part of him still struggled to let go. It was going to take some rethinking on his part, but he'd get there. Looking out for his family was firmly entrenched in him, but he'd try to be less smothering, more accepting of everyone's right to make their own decisions. And that began right now with Tamsyn and their mother.

"You want to find her, don't you?"

"I need to," she answered simply.

He sighed softly. "Then I'll do whatever I can to help you."

"Thank you. And I'll do whatever I can to help you, too."

He smiled at her earnestness. Deep down she was still his baby sister, still seeking his approval, still eager to please.

"Help me?" he asked, not entirely sure what she was angling at.

"With Isobel. With getting her back." He started to protest, but she held up a hand to cut him off. "If you're going to let me make my own decisions, then you definitely have to let Isobel make hers, as well. At least tell her how you feel. Then let her take it from there."

"I don't even know where to begin," he answered in all honesty. "Our chemistry aside, I hardly know anything about her except she's good at what she does and she travels a lot."

"Start with her blog, 'IF Only.' You'll understand what's important to her. The rest will come." Tamsyn rose from her chair and bent to kiss Ethan on the cheek. "You'll do what's right. You always do. G'night."

He raised a hand in acknowledgment as she left the room and closed the door behind her. He was alone with his thoughts. Thoughts he hadn't wanted to believe or acknowledge. But he couldn't ignore them now. He'd been trying so hard to do the right thing, to be the right man, and in doing so he'd probably lost the best thing that had ever happened to him in his entire life.

He didn't know if he could convince her to give a relationship between them a chance, but he had to try. Somehow, he had to get Isobel back.

Sixteen

Ethan's eyes burned the next morning. He'd been up until the small hours reading Isobel's blog and experiencing a welling sense of shame in the way he'd treated her. He'd thought her careless, bohemian, incapable of commitment—yet she was so much more than any of those things. She was always on the go, without any of the attachments he cherished, but she used her freedom to help people, and make a difference in so many lives.

His conscience still stung with embarrassment when he thought about the throwaway comment he'd made to her one day about taking mall photos of grumpy babies and toddlers. The photos she'd put up on the internet, the devastation and poverty, the homeless children and uprooted families—they were so powerful and moving. She'd walked in the shadow of those people, some still proud and fighting for what they believed in, others beaten and bowed. Yet every person she'd featured had been treated with a dignity and respect he hadn't even had the grace to afford Isobel herself.

They said the bigger you were the harder the fall. Well, he'd fallen—hard. His arrogance and presumption left a bitter echo in his mind, one he was determined to rinse out and to never, ever allow back into his thinking again.

While the photos Isobel had taken were shocking and carried a powerful message—sometimes of hope, other times of despair—it was her commentary that showed how clever and insightful she was and how deeply she respected her subjects. It was easy to see how committed she was to highlighting their plight and the need to effect change in their world.

He particularly admired the series she'd done just before coming to Australia—one that had focused on the infants and small children struggling to survive in a refugee camp on the border of two war-torn countries. And here he was, still fuming about the loss of a tank of wine. He had been such a fool. Guilt riddled his conscience. Had he bothered, even just once, to try and truly understand what mattered to Isobel? He knew she loved her work, but he'd never made even a fraction of the effort to understand her commitment to photography that she'd made to understand his passion for wine. He only hoped that he could have another chance to put things right between them.

After he finished work that day, Ethan checked her blog again, rereading some of the entries Isobel had made before she'd come to The Masters. In them he noticed an undercurrent of concern that she might not be able to complete the task she'd set herself. One entry finished with a brief comment stating she'd been cordially invited to leave the country and to avoid any further confrontations. She'd done exactly that. The way she'd worded it, he could almost hear her breezy tone downplaying the seriousness of the event. Reading between the lines, however, it sounded as if she'd narrowly avoided imprisonment for her activities.

Ethan scrolled through the blog until he reached her most recent entry. In it she talked about the hiatus she'd enjoyed in South Australia and she'd used a picture she'd obviously taken while exploring the ruins up on the hill. She'd then expanded a little on returning to the refugee camps to complete what she'd started earlier. Her commentary sent him on a web search and what he found made his blood run cold. No matter how lightly she worded it, Isobel was investigating illegal border crossings and the people who facilitated them. What she was doing was a clear breach of media regulations.

A sick feeling of dread swept through him as he considered the circumstances surrounding her departure from the warring nation the last time she'd visited, and the likelihood of her coming to harm if she ever returned. He checked the date of her most recent blog entry. Just over two weeks ago. Nothing since. It wasn't like her. Given the example of her many previous trips away, she usually posted at least once, sometimes twice a week. Maybe he'd missed something. He refreshed the page. Nothing.

He opened another window on his computer, his fingers rapping against the keys until he found what he was searching for. Bile rose in his throat as he read the news report stating a female international photographer had been detained by military forces on behalf of the government on a charge of media infringement. The dates matched. The location matched. It had to be Isobel.

Isobel squatted on her haunches, her back against the filthy wall behind her. She was equally filthy, her skin crawling, her hair matted and dull, her stomach an aching pit alternately craving food then griping painfully over the weevil-filled slop she and the other prisoners were sporadically given. She'd begun to lose track of time and she knew that was a bad thing. Without the progression of days and nights, weeks, this entire nightmare would fade into a blur and she was afraid she'd disappear into the overcrowded numbers of people being detained on a variety of charges—some valid, many not so valid.

A commotion at the entrance to the cell she shared with twenty-seven other women failed to even attract her attention until she felt hands pulling at her, dragging her forward.

"They want you, miss," one of her cell mates hissed at her under her breath. "Go, now, before they come in and get you."

Isobel staggered to her feet, her breath catching as her circulation restored and painful pins and needles flooded her lower limbs.

"Isobel Fyfe?" a uniformed guard barked at her with narrowed eyes.

She nodded. "Yes, that's me."

"This way."

The cell door clanged closed behind her as she followed the guard down the narrow cell-lined corridor. Shouts and cries from other prisoners followed her.

"What's happening? Why have you called me?" she asked, but the guard continued to walk ahead, eventually slowing to open a door.

When she didn't enter immediately, he grabbed her shoulder and pushed her through, shutting and locking the door behind her—exchanging one form of imprisonment for another. She wheeled around, banging her hands on the solid wood, shouting for an explanation, but none was forthcoming. It could have been ten minutes later, it could have been an hour, but eventually the door reopened to reveal an older man in a suit, his skin so pale it was obvious he was not a resident here.

"Miss Fyfe, I'm glad we found you. Let me introduce myself. Colin James. I'm with the New Zealand Embassy. We've secured your release."

"My release?" She barely believed her ears. "But how did you know I was here?"

"Let's just say you have friends with influence. Besides, the important thing is you're being discharged, so let's not go into the legalities, shall we? I think we'd be best advised to make haste before they change their minds."

She didn't argue, but one thing still worried her. "The man who was with me, is he—"

The look on Mr. James's face told her everything. "I'm sorry m'dear."

A swell of grief threatened to overwhelm her, but she fought it back. There'd be time to give in to her sorrow when she was away from here. Away and safe. She was so lucky that she had someone, somewhere, who could advocate for her. Her guide had not been so fortunate and he'd paid the ultimate price. She'd find some way to get money to his family and she'd try, somehow, to get them away from here. It was the very least she could do. She swallowed against the lump in her throat before getting her thoughts back in order.

"My things, my cameras?"

"Forfeit, I'm afraid."

"Everything? Even my clothing?"

"I understand your pack was confiscated along with everything inside and whatever you had in your possession at the time of your arrest. We have negotiated the return of your passport on condition you understand that should you ever set foot here again, you will be arrested on sight. You have been classified an enemy of the current regime and I cannot advise you strongly enough that it is in your best interests that once you're out of here, you stay away."

She nodded. Three weeks in prison had been an eye-opening experience. She'd always imagined that, should the situation arise, she'd be prepared for anything. But she couldn't have been more wrong. She was as committed to her work as ever, but now that she was intimately acquainted with the consequences, she could never be as blasé about the risks as she'd been in the past. Maybe the time had come to learn to be more careful, more meticulous in her planning, more cautious in choosing her targets. If she'd been less reckless, she might have been able to avoid imprisonment altogether. It was an experience she never wanted to repeat.

The only thing that had kept her sane had been thinking about The Masters. About the long, rolling lines of grapevines, about the silhouetted ruin on the hill reminding everyone that even in adversity, life could begin anew. About Ethan. Again, tears burned in the back of her throat and she fought to control the trembling that shook her body.

"I understand. We should go then. Thank you."

Her things she could replace and although the memory cards and her recent photos were a loss, they were nothing compared to the forfeit of a human life. She had been so lucky to be travelling on a New Zealand passport. She was so relieved that, even though she hadn't set foot in the country of her birth since she and her father had left ten years ago, she still had the benefit of a government division that had fought for her release.

It wasn't until she was in Johannesburg, awaiting her flight to Singapore, that she finally began to feel safe again—although even once she was airborne, she couldn't relax enough to sleep. She was foggy with exhaustion as she transited in Singapore, checking into an airport hotel for one night before catching a flight to Auckland, New Zealand. It was time to go home. Time to reassess her life, her priorities.

She still felt sick to her soul that she'd been responsible for the death of her guide. Logically, she knew that it hadn't been her who had pulled the trigger on the man, but he had been in the wrong place at the wrong time because of her. She'd have to institute some new precautions during her assignments going forward—not just for her sake, but for the sake of those with her.

Isobel took out a short-term lease on a furnished inner-city apartment on her arrival in Auckland, and spent the next month recovering her strength. She still woke screaming in the night, clawing at the monsters that weren't there and filled with the terror of her arrest and subsequent incarceration. Some days she was fine, ready to pick up her new cameras and to start all over again. Other days, she did nothing more than ride back and forth on the ferry between Devonport and Auckland city center, lost in her thoughts and the changing faces and accents that surrounded her.

She was grieving, she rationalized on her better days. For her guide, for the people whose lives she'd failed to make a positive difference in, for herself and the life she'd so guilelessly accepted as her right, for the love she'd borne for a man who couldn't possibly ever love her in return, and for the mother she'd never had a proper chance to say goodbye to.

She'd spent so much of her life running, avoiding attachment by staying on the go. It wasn't until she'd been literally unable to move, locked up in a jail cell that she was forced to truly examine her life. She wasn't happy with all that she'd found. It was time to stop running from herself—to accept her past, and come to terms with what she wanted for her future.

She'd been home about six weeks before she finally discovered exactly where her mother had been buried. She rode a series of buses out to the graveyard on the outskirts of the sprawling city. The weathered, small, wooden cross was little reminder of all that her mother had been and all they'd left behind when Isobel and her father had left New Zealand. She sank to her knees beside the marker. Her mother had deserved more than this. Her memory deserved more than this. Running away from the reality of his wife's death might have been her father's way of dealing with things, but it hadn't been fair to the woman who'd loved him to leave her behind without a suitable memorial to mark her passing.

Isobel lost track of time there, kneeling in the grass alone with her thoughts and memories. She was stiff and cold when she finally rose and left the graveyard. But even though she'd grown uncomfortable physically, she felt more at peace than she had in a very long time. Later, back at her apartment, she opened her new laptop and searched for monumental masons. Now she was home it was time to do right by her mother and really put her to rest. That started with a suitably inscribed headstone. One with her mother's favorite line of poetry forever linked with her name.

While on her laptop, Isobel checked the online storage cache of her work. Despite patchy internet connections, she'd managed to upload most of her pictures except the shots she'd taken on the day she was arrested. Her hand trembled as it hovered over the mouse pad and she had to dig deep for the courage to open the album, to look again into the eyes of the man who'd given his life in her service and in the service of his people.

She scrolled through the album, tears running unchecked down her cheeks, her stomach tied in knots. When she was done, she signed in to her blog and wrote and wrote and wrote some more, until her heart ached a little less and her eyes burned, dry now and scratchy and sore.

Then, finally, she slept.

Isobel was pushing breakfast around her plate at a small café the next day when she checked her blog. A small cry of amazement passed her lips when she saw the outpouring of support for her post, support with offers both financial and physical to help wherever and however people could. And there, buried amongst them all, was a comment from Tamsyn, together with a request for Isobel to message her privately.

She leaned back in her chair, and debated whether she should just let that part of her life go, put it behind her. Never look back, she reminded herself. It had been her modus operandi for so long, it went against everything she'd schooled herself to be to get in touch with Tamsyn now. After all she'd been through, the life her friend led seemed ever more distant than it had before. Maybe it was time to make a clean break after all.

Coward, her conscience chided her. Self-preservation, she silently argued back. She had no desire to hear about Ethan's marriage plans with Shanal, and if she contacted Tamsyn she had no doubt her friend would feel obliged to bring her up-to-date. It plagued her the rest of the day, until she caught sight of a society column in an online paper. Tamsyn's name was mentioned. Apparently, she was visiting with her cousin and his wife in Auckland.

Before Isobel could overthink things, she fired an email off to her friend and, to her surprise, a reply lobbed straight back in, suggesting they meet for lunch the next day. Isobel was shocked to realize that this would be her first social interaction with another human being since she'd left

Africa. She'd become so introspective, so reclusive, since her imprisonment and release. It was time to rectify that.

Seeing Tamsyn in the hotel lobby where they'd agreed to meet, Isobel was hard-pressed not to fly across the polished tile floors and launch herself into her friend's arms. She hadn't allowed herself to realize just how much she'd missed Tamsyn until now, when they stood here face-to-face.

"Oh, my God, Isobel, you've lost so much weight. Are you okay?" The words tumbled from Tamsyn's lips as she reached for Isobel and hugged her tight. "You're all skin and bone. C'mon, let's hit the restaurant. You definitely need feeding up. My treat."

Once they were seated, Tamsyn leaned forward and reached for Isobel's hand.

"Tell me," she urged. "Are you okay? Really okay? I read your blog post. It must have been wretched."

Isobel gave her a weak smile. "That's one word for it, yeah."

"I'm so relieved you're safely home. So, tell me what you've been doing since you've been back."

Isobel shrugged. "Nothing. I've sorted out a headstone for my mother's grave and that's about it. I can't seem to get motivated to work or to do anything about showing any of my work. I just feel so directionless."

"You've been through a lot," Tamsyn sympathized. "You'll come right with time."

"But will I? Most days I don't even feel like picking up a camera again. Photography has been my life for so long, I'm terrified at the thought that I'm never going to be able to do it again. I really believed coming back to New Zealand would help, that it would make me feel as if I'd come full circle, ready to start the next stage of my life. But it's all I can do to even get out of bed each day."

Tamsyn picked up a teaspoon and absently stirred her coffee, the look of concern on her face almost Isobel's undoing. She'd managed to stay strong for a couple of days now but faced with her friend's worry on her behalf, she felt the all-too-familiar tears rise near the surface again.

"Listen to me. I haven't even asked how you're doing," Isobel said, struggling to pull herself together.

"I'm fine, but I'm worried about you, Isobel. You don't look or sound like yourself. I know you've been through a harrowing experience, and that it takes time to recover from something like that, if you even can fully recover from what you went through. But the Isobel I know wouldn't let anything or anyone strip the light out of her life."

"You're right. I've let them win," Isobel said bleakly. "I need to fight back."

"Or maybe you need to take a few steps back. Regroup, regain your strength. Have you thought about why you're having so much trouble?"

"Not really," she admitted helplessly.

"Maybe you should. And maybe you should think about whether part of this languor you're suffering from isn't because you're missing Ethan."

That really made her sit up straight. "Ethan? Why would I be fretting over him? He was the one who told me to leave. I was too much of a distraction, apparently. And I was keeping him from his work."

Tamsyn laughed. "Is that what he told you? Seriously? Did you never stop to consider that maybe he was scared? Scared to love you? You're so different yet so perfect for one another. The perfect complement."

"Not as perfect as Shanal, apparently. How are their

wedding plans coming along?" Try as she might, Isobel couldn't quite keep a touch of snark out of her tone.

"They're not. He isn't marrying Shanal. They're great friends but totally unsuited for anything else, and they know it. You know, you should think really hard about where you go next, Isobel. Look deep inside and follow your heart."

"I've always followed my heart. It's what I've made my reputation doing."

Tamsyn waved aside her words as if they were of no consequence. "I'm not talking about causes. There's a difference between following a cause that's close to your heart and true love. Think about it, Isobel. True love can move mountains…and governments."

Isobel jolted at Tamsyn's last words. Governments? Was Tamsyn suggesting what she thought she was suggesting? The New Zealand embassy representative *had* mentioned she had friends with influence, and she'd struggled to think who they could have been. The only way to find out was to ask outright, but her mouth struggled to form the words. Eventually, though, she managed to speak.

"Was Ethan behind my release?"

"Look, he made me swear not to tell a soul what he did but since you've put two and two together, I'm not going to lie to you."

Tamsyn went on to give Isobel the full story about how Ethan had pulled every last favor he'd been owed, contacted every friend in high places in Australia and New Zealand, as well as every government contact he'd ever made, and hounded them to pull the necessary strings to see to it that Isobel was released.

Isobel didn't know what to think, what to feel. It was an emotional slap upside the head that she hadn't been expecting.

"He loves you, Isobel, and I know you love him, too. He can be overbearing, but it's all right sometimes, isn't it? It's how he found you, and got you home safe. I know wanderlust is your middle name but can't you find some way to make it work between you? From what I can tell, you're both miserable apart."

"We weren't all that happy together. We were too busy fighting." Isobel attempted to reason but was rewarded with a look of irritation from Tamsyn that made her firmly shut her mouth.

"If you weren't happy it's because you were both fighting what, deep down inside, you both wanted all along. For goodness' sake, Isobel—don't you want to be happy?"

"Of course I do, and I am…mostly."

Tamsyn groaned aloud, earning them a strange look from the couple at the table next to them.

"I swear, Isobel, the pair of you are enough to wear out the patience of a saint. Seriously. Look, don't make any decisions here and now. Think about what I've said and ask yourself, deep down, what's most important. I've done my part."

"Thank you," Isobel said, reaching to squeeze her friend's hand. "I don't deserve you."

"Of course you do, and more. So grab it, Isobel. You came close to losing your life without ever really living it. Don't you owe it to yourself to at least try?"

About to argue that she'd lived her life more fully than most, Isobel hesitated. She knew what Tamsyn was talking about. For all she'd done, for all her travels, she'd never risked her heart. She'd never, not once, taken that leap of faith and put her happiness in the hands of another person. But could she? Could she trust another person so much, so deeply, and put her carefully constructed world at the mercy of another?

There was only one way to find out.

Seventeen

Ethan looked out his office window as the shiny red hatchback pulled up outside the winery. He didn't recognize the car and, to his knowledge, they weren't expecting anyone today. His heart skidded across a few beats when he recognized the slender blond-haired woman who got out from the driver's side.

Isobel? What on earth…?

Before he realized it, he was out of his chair and headed outside. He had to be mistaken, surely. But no, the woman standing opposite him was indeed Isobel, albeit a pale, hollowed-out version of the bright butterfly he remembered. Every male protective instinct welled to instant life inside of him and he fought the urge to sweep her up in his arms and make everything better in her world once more.

His eyes raked over her, taking in the fact she'd lost weight, noting the lack of health in her skin and the missing gleam in her hair. She was a shell of who she used to be, but at least she was still alive, he reassured himself. He had that to take pleasure in at the very least. And she was here.

"Is it true?" she said abruptly, her voice a rasp on the chill winter air. "Are you responsible for my freedom?"

It was a loaded question, one with multiple answers if you examined the various layers of what freedom was. Ethan opted for the simplest of them all.

"Yes."

"How?"

"I called in some favors," he said, downplaying the many phone calls and emails he'd made and sent once he figured out that Isobel had been arrested.

"They must have been some favors," she commented.

He had no answer for that. How could he tell her that he'd been prepared to move heaven and earth to ensure her safety? He only wished he could have been there himself when she was freed, to shepherd her safely home. But the idea had been impossible. For one thing, he hadn't wanted her to know that he'd been involved. He hadn't wanted her to feel indebted to him. Instead, he'd reminded himself daily of the old saying, "If you love something, set it free. If it was yours, it will come back to you. If it doesn't, it was never meant to be."

He had all but given up hope of seeing her again, but here she was.

"Why, Ethan? Why did you do that for me?" she asked, her hands clenched in tight balls at her sides.

"Look, why don't we go inside the house and talk. It's cold out and I swear your lips are turning bluer by the minute."

She let him take her elbow and guide her to the main house. He was relieved that, aside from the handful of staff he could hear at the back of the house, none of the family was home. He settled Isobel on a sofa in the small sitting room that Tamsyn liked to use when she was home, and added an extra log of wood to the fire. He hadn't been kidding about Isobel turning blue out there. She was so cold, she was shivering.

Ethan sat next to her and, taking her hands, chafed them together between his larger, warmer ones. Finally, the shivering stopped.

"Sorry I'm being such a wimp," she said.

"You're not a wimp. Here, I'll go and organize some tea for us. You stay by the fire until I'm back."

He was gone a bare five minutes but every second felt like forever. When he carried the tray through to the sitting room, he almost expected to discover that she'd been a figment of his imagination all along. But to his relief, she remained on the sofa where he'd seated her. He poured a mug of tea and added the small dash of milk he knew she preferred before handing her the mug.

"Thanks," she said, wrapping her fingers around the ceramic cup and lifting it to her mouth to sip at its contents. "So tell me, Ethan, why did you work so hard for my release?"

"Tamsyn told you, didn't she? I asked her—"

"I made her. I needed to know. It's why I'm here."

Ethan felt his body sag, the tension escaping him as quickly as it had arisen. It wasn't love that had brought her here—just gratitude. "All this way just to say thank you? There was no need. I just want you to be happy and safe, Isobel. Isn't that enough?"

"But why is that so important to you?"

She wasn't going to let go until he told her the full truth. Ethan looked her square in the eye and hoped she'd be strong enough for the truth.

"Because I love you, Isobel Fyfe. I would move mountains for you if it was necessary."

Twin spots of color highlighted her cheeks, but she said nothing. Then, to his shock, her face crumpled, her eyes welled with tears and she began to cry—huge wrenching sobs that racked her body. Ethan took the mug from her hands before she could spill hot tea on her legs, then pulled her into his arms, holding her frail frame against him as if he could absorb her sorrow and make everything better again. He wished it could be so easy. Instead, he just had to wait while she cried it out. And hold her, just hold her, and thank God she was safe.

Eventually, her sobs quieted and she pulled back a little. "I'm sorry," she said, swiping at the moisture on her face. "I haven't been the same since…"

He wasn't surprised. He'd heard little about her ordeal in Africa but reading between the lines of her latest blog entry, it hadn't been pleasant.

"It's okay," he hastened to reassure her. "You're safe now. You're here, with me."

"And you love me?"

Her voice was tiny, as if she hardly dared believe the words she'd just said. He put everything into his response. All the fear, all the worry, all the relief when he'd heard she'd been released.

"I love you with all my heart."

A tremor ran through her and she lifted her tear-stained face, her watery gaze meeting his. "No one has ever loved me like that before."

"You've never let anyone close enough to love you, have you?" Ethan asked with unerring accuracy. "Will you let me into your heart, Isobel? Will you let me love you?"

"I want to."

She was still scared, still wary. Ethan knew what he had to do next.

"It's safe to let go, Isobel. Safe to love me back if that's what you want to do, and I hope you do. But if you don't, that's okay, too. I could live with that, provided I know you're okay and that you're happy. It took a lot for me to realize it, but you're the most important thing in my whole world. I'm here for you, always.

"I know how important your work is to you and I'm embarrassed that I never considered the importance of what you do and how vital it is to you. How good you are at what you do. I understand that now. I know you need to travel and I know you can't be tied down to any one place or any one person but, if you'll only let me, I will support you in whatever you want to do provided that, from time to time, you come back to me."

Isobel heard the words coming from Ethan's lips. Just simple words but filled with so much meaning. They both terrified her and yet gave her hope, healing that place inside of her that had felt empty and barren for so long.

She looked at him with new eyes. He loved her. It was a gift beyond compare. And even though he loved her, he still anticipated nothing from her in return, except perhaps her love. There were no demands, no expectations. With him she'd be as free to do whatever she wanted, be whomever she wanted, as she'd been all her life.

Maybe this was the true meaning of love, after all. This freedom, the give and take. The all-consuming devotion of her parents for one another had excluded her on so many levels and had left her father a damaged and broken man. One who'd remained on the run from his own feelings, his own grief, until his breaking heart had eventually given out on him and taken him at a time of his life when he should still have been in his prime.

Could she believe that with Ethan she could have a true partnership? One with give and take on both sides? He was willing to do so much to be the man she needed him to be. Could she be the woman *he* needed? She wanted the answer to be yes. She had no doubt that he was that man for her. Not a doubt in the world. It was more than she'd ever dreamed of having, this opportunity, this gift. With his love in her life she would have more freedom than she could ever believe possible—the freedom to love unconditionally.

But only if she had the strength to reach out and grab it.

Not so very long ago she'd have run from this chance at happiness—hell, she *had* run rather than stay and fight for it, even after she knew how she felt about him. And look where that had landed her.

She entangled her fingers with Ethan's and dragged his hands to her lips, pressing a kiss to his knuckles.

"Thank you," she said. "Thank you for being you, for loving me, for freeing me."

"Oh, Isobel, you're easy to love."

"But why me? Why now? When I left, you were so adamant we were wrong together."

Ethan sighed and bowed his head for a minute. When he lifted it again he had a look of shame on his face.

"I was wrong. I was scared. It's no excuse, I know. I couldn't handle the weight of my own feelings for you so I pushed you away. It was stupid. No, *I* was stupid. I pushed you away and I nearly lost you for good. I don't know if I'm ever going to be able to forgive myself for that."

"I would have gone, anyway. I had my own mission."

"I know, and I wouldn't have stood in your way, but

I may have been able to do something sooner when you were taken into custody."

"You did enough. I'm here, aren't I?"

"You are. I'd like to believe it's for good, but I know I can't expect that of you. But I do want you to know that you will always have a place here with me, whenever you want it. I meant that, Isobel. Whenever, however—you call the shots. I'm yours."

Isobel felt her heart fill at his words. They still had so much to work through but here he was, this proud man, offering her his world.

"I never thought I'd ever want to spend forever with one person, or to have one home base for the rest of my life. I've been traveling for so long now that it's become second nature."

"Maybe sometimes I can come with you."

"I'd like that." She smiled and cupped his face. "I'd like that a lot. And when you can't, I think I'll like coming home to you."

She leaned down and kissed him, savoring the sensation of his lips against hers, of how right it felt to be with him again. When she broke the kiss, she snuggled against him, and they half sat half lay on the sofa in front of the fireplace together, wrapped in one another's arms and their own thoughts. Eventually, Isobel knew she had to tell Ethan how she really felt, about why she'd come back here to The Masters.

"I knew I loved you when I left. It terrified me, in fact. Even though I wanted you to ask me to stay, I think I would have left, anyway." His arms tightened around her but he remained silent and she was grateful for the mental space, the opportunity to regroup her thoughts and deliver them to him as he deserved. "I realize now that it's actually safe to love someone else, to trust them with your heart. No, let me get that right. It's safe for me to love *you*. I know you have the capacity to hurt me, to crush me if you really wanted to, but I also know you couldn't do what you did for me and be someone who would deliberately hurt me at the same time.

"I really struggled with knowing I loved you, but when I was stuck in that prison, in a cell with a couple of dozen other women, each of whom had so much less than me, it was thinking of you, of here, that kept me from losing my mind." She reached up and pushed her fingers through his hair, loving the fact she could do this, that she could feel him with her on so many levels. "Before I left I worried that I didn't fit in here, with you in your home and in your family and in your world. But knowing that you love me makes me understand that I belong with you—that I can finally put down roots, as long as you're with me, too."

"If you'll let me, I will always be with you, Isobel. I don't want to ever let you go again, although I know you'll need to for your work. I can handle waiting for you wherever you go if I know you'll be coming back. Wherever I am will always be your home, too."

"I know that now. I guess I was on the run from commitment because I was just too afraid to trust in anyone else. I told you about my parents, about how they kept my mother's illness from me and about how my dad uprooted me when she died. I never made peace with that and I never, ever wanted to give anyone the capacity to hurt me the way my dad hurt once Mum was gone. It wasn't just them. I saw it over and over again in many of my subjects overseas. For me, it became the face of love, and it wasn't something I was prepared to try—not when it came at such an incredibly high cost."

Ethan sighed and rubbed his hand across her back. "I know what you mean. As much as I loved my father, he was a distant man. He didn't give love easily unless he felt you'd earned it. Maybe that's what drove my mother into another man's arms. Who knows. But despite his distance, I'm sure he loved her in his own way. Sadly, for them, it wasn't enough.

"I spent too many years of my life emulating his example. I don't want to do that anymore. I need to learn to bend and flow a bit more, to share responsibility and to let other people into my life, and particularly into my heart."

Isobel looked up at him. Beneath her ear she heard his heart beat steadily and filled with warmth at the knowledge that it beat for her. "People like me?"

"Definitely you, Isobel. Always you."

He closed his arms tight around her, holding her as if he'd never let her go, and for the first time in her life Isobel didn't feel restrained.

"I thought I'd lose myself if I loved someone like I love you," she said. "But it isn't about losing me at all—it's about filling that part of me that wasn't whole to begin with. You are that person for me, Ethan. I feel whole when I'm with you. I'm only half a person when we're apart. I had to go away to understand that."

Ethan pressed a kiss to her forehead. "If that's the case, then the past couple of months have been worth the agony of waiting to find out if you were ever coming back to me."

"I will always come back to you," she vowed fervently. "But one day, not too far away, I think I'll be ready to settle down, to live a quieter life. One where we can have a family of our own, where we can plan our future together."

"I look forward to that day," Ethan replied. "And in the

meantime, let me show you just how glad I am to know we have that to look forward to."

And he did. All. Night. Long.

* * * * *

"You were...extraordinary. As I knew you would be."

His heartfelt compliment made her blush and filled her with unexpected pleasure. She shouldn't be happy that he was so impressed with her performance tonight. She should be annoyed. Sorry that she'd helped to bolster his or Ashdown Abbey's reputation in any way.

But she was pleased. Both that she'd maintained her ruse as a personal assistant, and that she'd done well enough to earn Nigel's praise.

She was candid enough with herself to admit that the last didn't have as much to do with his standing as her "boss" as with him as a man.

"Thank you," she murmured, her throat surprisingly tight and slightly raw.

"No," he replied, once again brushing the back of his hand along her cheek. "Thank you."

And then, before she realized what he was about to do, he leaned in...

Dear Reader,

Want to know a secret? I'm a huge fan of television shows like *Project Runway, Fashion Star* and *24 Hour Catwalk*. It's not the competition itself that interests me nearly as much as the creativity and construction behind the designs that eventually walk the runway.

So when my editor and I began discussing ideas for a new Mills & Boon® Desire™ miniseries, PROJECT: PASSION leaped into my head. I just loved the idea of playing off *Project Runway* for titles, and creating characters and a world that revolves around high fashion. Plus, it seemed like the perfect excuse to watch *Project Runway* marathons and call it "research."

I can only hope you'll love the Zaccaro sisters as much as I do. Lily Zaccaro—eldest sister and founder of Zaccaro Fashions—kicks off PROJECT: PASSION with *Project: Runaway Heiress*. She's as protective of her business as she is of her sisters, so when someone steals her designs, her first instinct is to find out who and why. Even if her suspicions lead her straight into the arms of handsome, mouthwatering Nigel Statham, the British CEO of a rival label.

Enjoy!

Heidi Betts

HeidiBetts.com

PROJECT:
RUNAWAY HEIRESS

BY
HEIDI BETTS

MILLS & BOON

Published in Great Britain 2013
by Mills & Boon, an imprint of Harlequin (UK) Limited,
Eton House, 18-24 Paradise Road, Richmond, Surrey TW9 1SR

© Heidi Betts 2013

ISBN: 978 0 263 90474 1
ebook ISBN: 978 1 472 00605 9

51-0513

An avid romance reader since junior high, *USA TODAY* bestselling author **Heidi Betts** knew early on that she wanted to write these wonderful stories of love and adventure. It wasn't until her freshman year of college, however, when she spent the entire night before finals reading a romance novel instead of studying, that she decided to take the road less traveled and follow her dream.

Soon after Heidi joined Romance Writers of America, her writing began to garner attention, including placing in the esteemed Golden Heart competition three years in a row. The recipient of numerous awards and stellar reviews, Heidi's books combine believable characters with compelling plotlines, and are consistently described as "delightful," "sizzling" and "wonderfully witty."

For news, fun and information about upcoming books, be sure to visit Heidi online at HeidiBetts.com.

A huge American thank you
to UK reader Amanda Jane Ward, who read much of
this story and troubleshot details for me all the way to
the end to help ensure that my British hero came across
as authentic and, well, you know…British.

Any mistakes are my own—
due entirely, I'm sure, to the fact that Jason Statham
still refuses to accept my phone calls.

Thank you, Manda! If I couldn't use Jason for my
research, you were definitely the next best thing. ;)

One

Impossible. This was impossible.

Lily Zaccaro maximized her browser window, leaning in even more closely to study the photo on her laptop screen. With angry taps at the keyboard, she minimized that window and opened another.

Dammit.

Screen after screen, window after window, her blood pressure continued to climb.

More angry keystrokes set the printer kicking out each and every picture. Or as she was starting to think of them: The Evidence.

Pulling the full-color photos from the paper tray, she carried them to one of the long, wide, currently empty cutting tables and laid them out side by side, row by row.

Inside her chest, her heart was pounding as though she'd just run a seven-minute mile. Right there, before her very eyes, was proof that someone was stealing her designs.

How had this happened?

She tapped her foot in agitation, twisted the oversize dinner ring on her right middle finger, even rubbed her eyes and blinked before studying the pictures again.

The fabric choices were different, of course, as were some of the lines and cuts, making them just distinctive enough not to be carbon copies. But there was no mistaking *her* original sketches in the competing designs.

To reassure herself she wasn't imagining things or going completely crazy, Lily moved to one of the hip-high file cabinet drawers where she kept all of her records and design sketches. Old, new, implemented and scratched. Riffling through them, she found the portfolio she was looking for, dragged it out and carried it back to the table.

One after another, she drew out the sketches she'd been working on last spring. The very ones they'd been prepared to work with, manufacture and put out for the following fall's line.

After a short game of mix-and-match, she had each sketch placed beside its counterpart from her rival. The similarities made her ill, almost literally sick to her stomach.

She leaned against the edge of the table while the images swam in front of her eyes, sending a dizzying array of colors and charcoal lines into the mix of emotions that were already leaving her light-headed and nauseated.

How could this happen? she wondered again. How could this possibly have happened?

Wracking her brain, she tried to think of who else might have seen her sketches while she was working. How many people had been in and out of this studio? There couldn't have been that many.

Zoe and Juliet, of course, but she trusted them with her life. She and her sisters shared this work space. The three of them rented the entire New York apartment building, using one of the lofts as a shared living space and the other as a work space for their company, Zaccaro Fashions.

Although there were times when they got on each other's nerves or their work schedules overlapped, their partnership was actually working out surprisingly well. And Lily showed her sisters all of her design ideas, sometimes even soliciting their opinions, the same as they shared their thoughts and sketches with her.

But neither of them—not even slightly flighty party girl, Zoe—would ever steal or sell her designs or betray her in any way. Of that, she was absolutely, one hundred percent certain.

So who else could it have been? They occasionally had others over to the studio, but not very often. Most times when they had business to conduct, they did it at Zaccaro Fashions, their official, public location in Manhattan's Fashion District, where they had more sewing machines set up, with employees to produce items on a larger, faster scale; offices for each of the sisters; and a small boutique set up out front. Something they hoped to expand upon very soon.

Of course, *that* particular dream would be nearly impossible to realize if their creations continued to get stolen and put on the market before they could release them.

She collected all of the papers from the cutting table, being sure to keep each of the printed pictures with its corresponding sketch. Then she began to pace, worrying a thumbnail between her teeth and wearing out the soles of her one-of-a-kind Zoe-designed pumps while she wondered what to do next.

What *could* she do?

If she had any idea who was responsible for this, then she might know what to do. Bludgeoning them with a sharp object or having them drawn and quartered in the middle of Times Square sounded infinitely satisfying. But even going to the police would work for her, as long as the theft and replication of her clothes stopped, and the culprit was punished or fired or chased out of town by a mob of angry fashion designers wielding very sharp scissors.

Without a clue of who was behind this, though, she didn't even know where to begin. Wasn't sure she had any options at all.

Her sisters might have some suggestions, but she *so* didn't want to involve them in this.

She'd been the one to go to design school, then ask their parents for a loan to start her own business. Because—even though they were quite wealthy and had offered to simply *give* her the money, since she was already in line for a substantial inheritance—she'd wanted to do this herself, to build something rather than having it handed to her.

She'd been the one to come to New York and struggle to make a name for herself, Zoe and Juliet following along later. Zoe had been interested in the New York party scene more than anything else, and Juliet had quit her job as a moderately successful, fledgling real-estate agent back in Connecticut to join Lily's company.

Without a doubt, they had both added exponentially to Zaccaro Fashions. Lily's clothing designs were fabulous, of course, but Zoe's shoes and Juliet's handbags and accessories were what truly made the Zaccaro label a well-rounded and successful collection.

Accessories like that tended to be where the most money was made, too. Women loved to find not only a new outfit, but all the bells and whistles to go with it. The fact that they could walk into Zaccaro Fashions and walk back out with everything necessary to dress themselves up from head to toe in a single shopping bag was what had customers coming back time and time again. And recommending the store to their friends. Thank God.

But it wasn't her sisters' designs being ripped off, her sisters' stakes in the business being threatened, and she didn't want them to worry—about her or the security of their own futures.

No, she needed to handle this on her own. At least until she had a better idea of what was going on.

Returning to the laptop, she hopped up on the nearest stool and straightened her skirt, tucking her feet beneath her on one of the lower rungs. Her fingers hesitated over the keys, then she just started tapping, not sure she was doing the right thing, but deciding to follow her gut.

Two minutes later, she had the phone number of a corporate-investigation firm uptown, and five minutes after that, she had an appointment for the following week with their top investigator. She wasn't certain yet *exactly* what she would ask him to do, but once he heard her dilemma, maybe he would have some ideas.

Then she continued searching online, deciding to dig up everything she could on her newest, scheming rival, Ashdown Abbey.

The London-based clothing company had been founded more than a hundred years ago by Arthur Statham. Their fashions ranged from sportswear to business attire and had been featured in any number of magazines, from *Seventeen* to *Vogue*. They owned fifty stores worldwide, earning over ten million dollars in revenue annually.

So why in heaven's name would they need to steal ideas from her?

Zaccaro Fashions was still in its infancy, earning barely enough to cover the overhead, make monthly payments to Lily's parents toward the loan and allow Juliet, Zoe and herself to continue living comfortably in the loft and working in the adjoining studio. Ashdown Abbey might as well have been the Hope Diamond sitting beside a chunk of cubic zirconium in comparison.

The hijacked fashions in question had originated from

Ashdown Abbey's Los Angeles branch, so she dug a little deeper into that particular division. According to the company's website, it was run by Nigel Statham, CEO and direct descendant of Arthur Statham himself.

But the Los Angeles offices had only been open for a year and a half and were apparently working somewhat independently of the rest of the British company, putting out a couple of exclusive lines and holding their own runway shows geared more toward an American—and specifically Hollywood—customer base.

Which meant it wasn't all of Ashdown Abbey out to ruin Lily's life, just the Los Angeles faction.

Lily narrowed her eyes, leaning closer to the laptop screen and focusing on a photo of Nigel Statham. Public Enemy Number One.

He was a good-looking man, she'd give him that much. Grudgingly. Short, light brown hair with a bit of curl at the ends. High cheekbones and a strong jaw. Lips that were full, but not too full. And eyes that looked to be a deep shade of green, though that was difficult to tell from a picture on the internet.

She wanted to despise him on sight, but in one photo, he was smiling. A sexy, charming smile that went all the way to his eyes and threatened to turn her knees to jelly.

Of course, she was sitting and she was made of sterner stuff than that, so *that* wasn't going to happen. But at first glance, she certainly wouldn't have pegged him as a thief.

She continued to scroll through pictures and articles and company information, but much of it was for the U.K. division and the other European stores. The Los Angeles branch still seemed to be finding its footing and working to establish itself as a British clothing company on American soil.

Deciding there wasn't much more she could do until she met with the investigator except seethe in silence, Lily began to close up shop. She checked her watch. She was supposed to meet her sisters for dinner in twenty minutes, anyway.

But as she was shutting down browser windows, something caught her eye. A page filled with "job opportunities at Ashdown Abbey—U.S.A." She'd been perusing the list just to get a better idea of how the company operated.

Now, though, she expanded the window, clicked on the link for "more information" and hit Print.

It was crazy, what she was suddenly thinking. Worse yet that she was contemplating actually going through with it.

Her sisters would try to talk her out of it for sure, if she even mentioned the possibility. The investigator would undoubtedly warn her against it, then likely try to convince her to let *him* handle it at—what?—one hundred...two hundred and fifty...five hundred dollars an hour.

It would be so much easier for her to slip in and poke around herself. She knew the design world inside and out, so she would certainly fit in. And if she made herself sound smart and qualified enough, surely she would be a shoo-in.

A tiny shiver of anxiety rolled down her spine. Okay, so it was dangerous. A lot could go wrong, and she probably stood to get herself into a heap of trouble if anyone—or the *wrong* someone, at any rate—found out.

But it was too good an opportunity to pass up. Almost as though she was meant to go through with this, fate bending its bony finger to point the way. Otherwise, what were the chances *this* particular position would open up just when she most needed the inside scoop on Ashdown Abbey?

No, she had to do this. She had to find out what was going on, *how* it had happened and get it to stop. And going to work for Ashdown Abbey seemed like a good way to do exactly that.

Not just good—perfect.

Because Nigel Statham needed a personal assistant, and she was just the right woman for the job.

Two

Nigel Statham muttered an unflattering curse, slapping the company's quarterly financial report down on top of his father's latest missive. The one that made him feel like a child in short trousers being scolded for some minor transgression or another.

Handwritten on personal stationery and posted all the way from England—because that's how his parents had always done it, and email was too commonplace for their refined breeding—the letter outlined the U.S. division's disappointing returns and Nigel's failure to make it yet another jewel in the Ashdown Abbey crown since he'd been appointed CEO eighteen months ago.

Disappointment clung to the words as though his father was standing in the room, delivering them face-to-face: hands behind his back, bushy white brows drawn down in a frown of displeasure. Just like when he'd been a boy.

His parents had always expected perfection—an aim he

had fallen short of time and time again. But he hardly thought a year and a half was long enough to ascertain the success or failure of a new branch of the business in an entirely new country when it had taken nearly a century for Ashdown Abbey to reach its current level of success in the U.K. alone.

He thought perhaps his father's expectations for this new venture had been set a bit too high. But try telling the senior Statham that.

With a sigh, Nigel leaned back and wondered how long he could put off responding to the letter before his father sent a second. Or worse yet, decided to fly all the way to Los Angeles to check in on his son in person.

Another day, certainly. Especially since he was currently dreading the job of training a brand-new personal assistant.

He'd been through three so far. Three attractive but very young ladies who had been competent enough but hardly dedicated.

The problem with hiring personal assistants in the heart of Los Angeles, he decided, was that they tended to be either aspiring actresses who grew bored easily or quit as soon as they landed a part in a hand-lotion commercial; or they were aspiring fashion designers who grew bored when they didn't make it to the top with their own line in under six months.

And each time one of them moved on, he had to start all over training a new girl. It was enough to make him consider hiring an assistant to be on hand to train his next assistant.

Human resources had hired the latest in his stead, then sent him a memo with her name and a bit of background information, both personal and professional. It probably wasn't even worth remembering the woman's name, but then he'd never been *that* kind of boss.

Before he had the chance to review her résumé once more, there was a tap on his office door. Less than half a second later, it swung open and his new assistant—he deduced she was his new assistant, at any rate—strode across the carpeted floor.

She was prettier than her photo depicted. Her hair teetered somewhere between light brown and dark blond, pulled back in a loose but smoothly twisted bun at the back of her head. Her face was lightly made up, the lines classic and delicate, almost Romanesque.

A pair of dark-rimmed, oval-lensed glasses sat perched high on her nose. Small gold hoops graced her earlobes. She wore a simple white blouse tucked into the waistband of a black pencil skirt that hit midcalf, concealing three-quarters of what he suspected could prove to be extraordinary legs. And on her feet, a pair of patent-leather pumps, color-blocked in black and white with three-inch heels.

Being in fashion, he took note more than he might have otherwise. But as a man, there were certain aspects of her appearance he would have noticed regardless.

Like her alabaster skin or the way her breasts pressed against the front of her shirt. The bronze-kiss shade of her lips and rose-red tips of her perfectly manicured nails.

"Mr. Statham," she said in a voice that matched the rest of the package. "I'm Lillian, your new personal assistant. Here's your coffee and this morning's mail."

She set the steaming mug stamped with the Ashdown Abbey logo on the leather coaster on his desk. It looked as though she'd added a touch of cream, just the way he liked it.

She placed the pile of envelopes directly in front of him, and he flipped through, noticing that it seemed to be all business correspondence, no fluff to waste his time sorting out.

As first impressions went, she was making a rather positive one.

"Is there anything else I can get you?"

"No, thank you," he replied slowly.

With a nod, she turned on her heel and started back toward the door.

"Lillian." He stopped her just before she reached the doorway.

Spine straight, she returned her attention to him. "Yes, sir?"

"Are those Ashdown Abbey designs you're wearing?" he asked. "The blouse and skirt?"

She offered him a small smile. "Of course."

He considered that for a moment, almost afraid to believe that his luck in the personal-assistant department might actually be changing for the better.

Clearing his throat, he said carefully, "You wouldn't happen to be an actress, would you?" He resisted the urge to use the term *aspiring,* but only barely.

A slight frown drew her light brows together. "No, sir."

"What about modeling? Any interest in that?"

That question brought out a short chuckle. "Definitely not."

He thought back to some of the bullet points from her résumé. She hadn't simply wandered in from the street, that was for certain. Her background was in both business *and* design, with a degree in the former and a few very strong courses in the latter.

On paper she was rather ideal, but he knew as well as anyone that everybody became a bit of a fiction writer when it came to cooking up a résumé.

"And your interest in the fashion industry is…" He trailed off, leaving her to fill in the blank on her own.

For the blink of an eye, she seemed to consider what response he might be looking for. Then she replied in a firm tone, "Strictly business. And the opportunity to get my hands on fresh designs sooner than the rest of the world. I'm a bit of a clotheshorse, I'm afraid." She ended with a guileless half grin that brought out the tiniest hint of dimple in the center of her right cheek.

Almost in spite of himself, he caught his own lips turning upward. "Well, then, you've certainly come to the right place. Employees get a discount at our company store, you know."

"Yes, I know," she said slowly, and he could have sworn he saw a sparkle of devilment in her eye.

"Excellent," he murmured, feeling better about her employment already.

He hadn't exactly seen her in action, but she had, as they say, passed the first hurdle. At the very least, she hadn't walked in with a wide smile and an IQ equal to her age.

"If you haven't already, please familiarize yourself with my daily schedule and appointments for the week. There may be a few meetings and events to which I'll need you to accompany me, so watch for those notations. And be sure to review the schedule frequently, as I tend to change or update it regularly and without warning."

Picking up his coffee, he took a sip, surprised to find it quite tasty. Almost the exact ratio of cream to coffee that he preferred.

"Yes, sir. Not a problem."

"Thank you. That will be all for now," he told her.

Once again, she turned for the door. And once again, he stopped her just before she stepped out of his office.

"Oh, and, Lillian?"

"Yes, sir?" she intoned, tipping her head in his direction.

"Excellent coffee. I hope you can make an equally satisfying cup of tea."

"I'll certainly try."

With that, she closed the door behind her, leaving Nigel with a strangely unexpected smile on his face.

As soon as the door to Nigel Statham's stately, expansive office clicked shut and she was alone—blessedly, blissfully alone—Lily rushed on weak legs to the plush office chair behind her large, executive secretary's desk and dropped into it like a sack of lead.

She was shaking from head to toe, her heart both racing and pounding at the same time. It felt as though an angry gorilla was trapped inside her chest, rattling her rib cage to get out.

And her stomach…her stomach was pitching and rolling so badly, she thought she must surely know how it felt to be on a ship that was going down in a storm-tossed sea. If she *didn't* lose her quickly scarfed-down breakfast in the next ten seconds, it would be a miracle.

To keep that from happening, she leaned forward, tucking her head over her knees. Over them, because it was nearly impossible to get between them in the slim, tailored skirt she'd chosen for her first day of working undercover and with a false identity.

Lillian. *Blech.* It was the best name she'd been able to come up with that she thought she would answer to naturally, the blending of her first and middle names—Lily and Ann.

And as a last name, she'd gone with something simple and also easily identifiable, at least to her. George—what she and her sisters had called their first pet. A lazy, good-natured basset hound their father had found wandering around the parking lot where he worked.

Her mother had been furious right up until the moment she'd realized George woofed at the top of his lungs the minute anyone stepped foot on their property. From that point on, he'd been her "very best guard dog" and had gotten his own place setting of people food on the floor beside the dining-room table whenever they sat down to eat.

So Lillian George it was. Even though being referred to as Lillian made her feel like a matronly, middle-aged librarian.

Then again, she sort of looked like a librarian.

Her usual style, and definitely her own designs, leaned very strongly toward the bright, bold and carefree. She loved color and prints, anything vibrant and flirty and fun.

But for her position at Ashdown Abbey, she'd needed to be much more prim and proper. Not to mention doing as much as she could to disguise her identity and avoid being recognized or linked in any way to Zaccaro Fashions.

She could only hope that the change of name and switch to a wardrobe drawn entirely from Ashdown Abbey's own line of business attire, coupled with the glasses and darkening of her normally light blond hair would be enough to keep anyone at the company from figuring out who she really was.

It helped, too, that Zaccaro Fashions was only moderately successful. She and her sisters weren't exactly media darlings. They'd been photographed here or there, appeared in magazines or society pages upon occasion, but mostly in relation to their father and their family's monetary worth. But she would be surprised if most people—even those familiar with the industry—would recognize any one of them if they passed on the street. Although Zoe was doing her level best to change that by going out on the town and getting caught behaving badly on a more and more regular basis.

After a couple of minutes, Lily's pulse, the spinning of her head and the lurching in her stomach all began to slow. She'd made it this far. She'd made it past human resources with her creatively worded but fairly accurate résumé and her apparently not-so-rusty-after-all interview skills. Then she'd stood in front of corporate CEO Nigel Statham himself without being found out or dragged away in handcuffs.

He also hadn't followed her out of his office, shaking a finger at her deceit, or instructed security to meet her at her desk. Everything was quiet, calm, completely normal, as far as she could tell.

Ashdown Abbey certainly didn't have the hum of voices

and sewing machines in the background the way the Zaccaro Fashions offices did. But, then, Zaccaro Fashions wasn't a major, multimillion-dollar operation the way Ashdown Abbey was, either. They hadn't yet reached the point where their corporate offices and manufacturing area were two separate entities.

Frankly, Lily thought she could use the mechanical buzz of a sewing machine or her sisters' laughter as she worked with her cell phone pressed to her ear right about now. Sometimes silence was entirely overrated. Times like these, when all she could hear was her own rapid breathing and the panicked voices in her head telling her she was crazy and sure to get caught.

To keep those voices from getting any louder and leading her in the wrong direction, she started to recite one of the simple, meaningless poems she'd been forced to memorize in grade school, then slowly sat up.

Tiny stars flashed in front of her eyes, but only for a second. She blinked and they were gone, leaving her with clear vision and a clear—or clearer, anyway—head.

Nigel Statham believed she was his new personal assistant, so maybe she should go back to acting like one.

Rolling her chair up to the desk, she pulled out her computer's keyboard and mouse, and started clicking away. She'd familiarized herself with the computer's operating system just a bit before going into Nigel's office, but was sure there was much more to learn.

His daily schedule, for instance. Something she was apparently going to have to stay on top of or risk not knowing what she was supposed to be doing from one hour to the next.

She felt a small stab of guilt as she bypassed the email program, wondering if her sisters had found her note yet and honored her wishes by *not* telling anyone about her sudden disappearance or trying to track her down themselves.

She'd told them she had some personal business to attend to. Something she couldn't discuss just yet, but needed some time away to deal with. She assured them she would be fine and wasn't in any danger, and asked them to trust her to get in touch as soon as she could.

She didn't want them to worry about her, but she wasn't ready to tell them what was really going on, either. One day... one day she would fill them in on everything. She would tell them the entire story over a bottle of wine, and chances were they would have a good laugh about it.

But not until it was resolved and there was a happily-ever-after to report. When the threat to their company was gone and there were no fears or rumors left to spread like wildfire if anyone else got wind of it.

Before she left, she'd also met with Reid McCormack of McCormack Investigations about running comprehensive background checks on everyone under Zaccaro Fashions' employ. Lily honestly didn't believe he would find anything incriminating, but better safe than sorry.

And she'd informed him that she would be out of town for a while, so she would call in weekly for updates. It seemed easier than having him leave messages at the apartment, where her sisters might overhear or access them, or having him call her on her cell phone at an inconvenient moment while she was still in Los Angeles.

Frankly, she hoped he never had anything negative to report, or that if he did, it would turn out to be completely unrelated to Zaccaro Fashions—an employee with an unpaid speeding ticket or college-age drunk-and-disorderly charges that had eventually been dropped.

But until her first scheduled check-in, she needed all of her energy and brain power focused on her new job and attempts at stealth investigations.

Studying Nigel's schedule for the day, she was somewhat

relieved to see that it didn't seem to be a—quote, unquote—
heavy day for him. It looked as though he would be in his
office most of the time. He had a lunch appointment and
a conference call in the afternoon, but nothing so far that
would require her to go out with him—and hope not to be
recognized or to do something she wasn't ready or properly
trained for.

She glanced at the schedule for the rest of the week, making a mental note to check again in a couple of hours. Just
to be safe until it all became second nature to her for as long
as she was here.

She took a few minutes to investigate some of the other
programs and files on the system, but hoped she wouldn't
be expected to do too much with them too soon. Either that,
or that the company provided tutorials for the seriously lost
and computer illiterate.

What she did understand, though, was design. She knew
the vocabulary, the process and what was needed to go from
point A to point B. So she did recognize and know how to
use some of the items already installed on the PA's computer.

The question was: Could she use them to access the information she needed to track down the design thief?

Maybe yes, maybe no. It depended on whether or not Nigel
knew about the thefts.

Was he involved? she wondered.

Had he sent a mole from Ashdown Abbey into her company? Or maybe on a less despicable level, had he recognized
her designs within his company's latest collection and ignored
them? Looked the other way because it was easier and could
advance Ashdown Abbey's sales and brand recognition?

A part of her hoped not. She didn't want to think that there
were business executives out there who would stoop to such
levels just to get ahead. Not when they had a bevy of talented designers on staff already and didn't *need* to stoop to

those levels. Or that someone so handsome, with that deep, toe-curling British accent, could be capable of something so heinous. Although more attractive people had been guilty of much worse, she was sure.

It happened every day, and she wasn't naive enough to believe that just because a man was sinfully attractive and already a millionaire he wouldn't steal from someone else to make another million or two.

Not that any of her designs had earned a million dollars yet, Lily thought wryly, but the potential was there. If she could keep other companies and designers from scooping her.

Tapping a few keys, she brought up what she could find on the California Collection—the Ashdown Abbey collection that included so many of her own works, only with minor detail alterations and in entirely different textiles. Just the thought sent her blood pressure climbing all over again.

A few clicks of the mouse and the entire portfolio was on the screen in front of her, scrolling in a slow left-to-right slideshow. The flowy, lightweight summer looks were lovely. Not as beautiful as *Lily's* designs would have been, if she'd had the chance to release them, of course, but they were quite impressive.

She studied each one for as long as she could, taking in the cuts and lines. The collection mostly consisted of dresses, perfect for California's year-round sunny and warm weather. Short one-pieces, a couple of maxi dresses, and even some two-piece garments consisting of a top and skirt or a top and linen slacks.

Not all of them were drawn directly from Lily's proposed sketches. Small comfort. And it might actually work against her if she ever tried to prove larceny in a court of law.

A good defense attorney could argue that there might be *similarities* between the Ashdown Abbey and Zaccaro Fashions designs, but since the Ashdown Abbey line also included designs *without* similarities, it was obviously a mere case of creative serendipity.

Hmph.

Closing down the slideshow, Lily dug around in the other documents within the file folder. She found another graphics slideshow, this time the sketches for the final pieces that made up the California Collection.

They were full color and digital, done on one of the many art and design computer programs that were becoming more and more popular. Even Lily had one of them on her tablet, but she still preferred pencil and paper, charcoal and a sketch pad, and actual fabric swatches pinned to her hand-drawn designs over filling in small squares of space with predetermined colors or material samples on a digitized screen.

But what caught her attention with these designs wasn't *how* they were done, it was the fact that they were signed. Ashdown Abbey apparently had design teams on the payroll rather than one designer in charge of his or her own collection.

Moving from the graphics files to the text files, she found a list of the California Collection's entire design team, complete with job titles and past projects they'd worked on for Ashdown Abbey. A jolt of adrenaline zipped through her, and she hurried to send the list to the printer.

The zip-zip of the machine filled the quiet of the cavernous outer office. It rang all the louder in her ears for the fact that she didn't want to get caught.

When a buzz interrupted the sound of the printer, Lily jumped. Then she looked around, searching for the source of the noise. Finally, she realized it was coming from the phone, one of the lights on the multiline panel blinking in time with the call of the intercom.

Chest tight, she took a deep breath and pressed the button for Nigel Statham's direct line.

"Yes, sir?" she answered.

"Could I see you for a moment?"

The abrupt request was followed by total silence, and she realized he'd hung up without waiting for a reply.

Grabbing the list of designers from the printer tray, she folded it over and over into a small square and stuffed it into the front pocket of her skirt. Patting the spot to make sure it was well concealed, she strode to the door of Nigel's office, unsure of what she would encounter on the other side. She didn't even know if she should bring a pad and pencil with her to take notes.

What did personal assistants automatically pick up when summoned by the boss? Paper and pen? A more modern electronic tablet? She hadn't even had a chance to poke around and find out what was provided for Nigel Statham's executive secretary.

So she walked in empty-handed after giving one quick tap on the door to announce her arrival.

Nigel turned from typing something into his own computer to jot a note on the papers in front of him before lifting his attention to Lily. She stood just behind one of the guest chairs, awaiting his every request.

"What are you doing for dinner this evening?" he asked.

The question was so far from anything she might have expected him to say, her mind went blank. She was quite sure her face did, too.

"I'll take that to mean you don't have plans," he remarked.

When she still didn't respond, he continued, "I'm having dinner with a potential designer and thought you might like to join us. Having you there will help to keep things on a business track, as well as better familiarize you with your position."

For lack of anything more inspired to say, she replied with a simple, "All right."

Nigel gave an almost imperceptible nod. "I'll be leaving

from the office, but you're welcome to go home and change, or take a bit of a rest, if you like. I'll come round for you at eight. Be sure to leave your address before you finish for the day."

He returned his attention to his work, giving Lily the impression that plans for the evening had been decided and she'd been dismissed.

"Yes, sir," she said, because she thought it was respectful and some sort of acquiescence was needed. Then she tacked on a short "Thank you" for good measure before hurrying back out to the reception area.

Taking a seat behind her desk, she tried to decide how she felt about this latest turn of events.

On the one hand, she already had a list of designers for the Ashdown Abbey collection based on her work. She considered that quite a coup for her first day in the enemy's camp.

On the other, her most fervent prayer had been merely to get through the day without being found out. She'd never imagined she would be asked to put in extra time outside the office. Especially not *alone* with the boss.

Of course, she wouldn't really be *alone* with him. It was a business dinner, so at least one other person would be there. But it was still an after-hours situation in much-too-close proximity to the man who held her future in his hands.

Her professional future and possibly her very freedom.

Because if he ever learned who she really was and why she was working incognito within his company, she'd likely find herself behind bars. No amount of crying "he was mean to me first" would save her then.

Three

At five minutes to eight, Lily was still racing around her apartment, trying to be ready before Nigel arrived.

It didn't help that she'd just moved in and had brought very little with her from New York. Or that this was supposed to be merely a place to sleep. Nothing fancy. Nothing expensive—at least by Los Angeles standards. Simply somewhere to rest and hunker down with her suspicions and evidence while she worked days at Ashdown Abbey.

Never had she imagined that her boss—CEO of the entire company—would decide to "drop by" and pick her up for dinner.

And then there was the fact that she hadn't planned for after-hours job requirements. Once she'd arrived, she'd filled her closet with Ashdown Abbey business attire, not only to fit in, but to subconsciously give Nigel Statham and everyone else the impression that she absolutely belonged there. But she hadn't purchased a single item for an evening out.

Granted, she could probably get away with wearing the
same skirt and blouse that she'd worn that day. If she was attending this meal as Nigel's personal assistant, then it couldn't
hurt for her to look like one.

But she suspected Nigel's choice of restaurant might be of
the highly upscale variety, and she didn't want to stand out.
Or worse, blend in with the servers.

So she'd done the best she could with what her limited
current wardrobe had to offer.

Another black skirt, shorter this time, with a sexy—but
not too sexy—slit up the back. A sheer, nearly diaphanous
sapphire-blue blouse that she'd intended to wear as a shell
over a more modest chemise top. Now, though, she wore it
over only a bra.

She'd checked and double-checked in the mirror to be sure
the effect wasn't trashy. Thankfully, the bra was barely visible, even though in certain light, flashes of skin could be
seen beneath the top.

To dazzle it up even more, she added sparkling chande-
lier earrings, a matching *Y* necklace, and open-toed four-
inch heels that—now that she was wearing them—might be
a bit too suggestive for nine-to-five. They were more than
appropriate for a night out on the town, though, professional
or otherwise.

She threw a few items like her wallet, a lipstick, keys and
her cell phone—just in case—in a small, plain-black clutch,
and *finally* thought she was ready enough to jump when Nigel
arrived.

She'd just taken a deep, stabilizing breath and was contemplating one last visit to the restroom when the doorbell rang.

Whatever calm she'd managed to find with that long inha-
lation evaporated at the shrill, mechanical sound, and a lump
of dread began to grow in the pit of her stomach.

Fingers curled around her purse, she swallowed hard and

moved to the door. Because she didn't want Nigel peeking inside and seeing that there were no personal touches to the apartment to affirm her claims of having lived in the city for several years, she opened it only a crack, using her body to block his view.

As quickly and smoothly as she could, she slipped out into the hallway, pulling the door closed and locked behind her. Leaning back, she used the doorjamb to prop herself up, feeling suddenly overwhelmed and overly scrutinized.

Nigel's hazel eyes studied her from head to toe. He was standing so close, she could see the specks of green dotting his irises and smell his spicy-with-a-hint-of-citrus cologne.

She inhaled, drawing the scent deeper into her lungs, then realized what she was doing and stopped, holding her breath in hopes that he wouldn't notice her small indiscretion.

It was not a good idea to start thinking her boss smelled good. She already found him attractive, simply because he was. Anyone, female or male, would have to agree based on his physical attributes alone. Much the way everyone knew the sky was blue, a handsome man was a handsome man.

That didn't mean she should be building on that initial assessment by adding "smells really good" to the tally.

He was a good-looking man with exceptional taste in cologne, that's all. Lily hoped that others might consider her on the pretty side with good taste in perfume, as well. Especially after how much time she'd put into her appearance tonight.

Nigel—her boss, her attractive and well-scented *boss*—returned his gaze to her face.

"You look lovely," he commented. "Ready to go?"

"Yes."

To her surprise, he offered his arm. There was nothing romantic in the gesture, only politeness. After a short hesitation, she slipped her hand around his elbow and let him lead her down the well-lit, utilitarian hallway of the apartment building.

Would an American man have acted so gentlemanly, or was it just Nigel's British upbringing? Whatever the case, she liked it. Maybe a little too much.

They walked down the three short flights of stairs rather than waiting for the elevator. Outside, the early evening air was fresh and cool, but not cold. A long, silver Bentley Mulsanne waited at the curb, and Nigel opened the rear door, holding it while she got in.

She'd intended to slide across so he could climb in behind her, but there was a rather large console turned down between the two rear seats, as well as fold-out trays on the back of the front seats. The one on his side was down, with an open laptop resting on it.

While she was still marveling at the awesome interior of the luxury vehicle, Nigel opened the door opposite hers and took his place, quickly closing the computer and tray.

"Sorry about that," he said, moving the laptop out of the way on the floor beside his briefcase.

When she didn't respond—she was apparently sitting there frozen, like a raccoon caught rummaging through household garbage—he returned the center console to its upright position, then leaned past her to pluck the seat belt, stretch it across her motionless form and click it into place.

As he stretched to reach, his arm brushed her waist, terribly close to the underside of her breasts. A shiver of something very un-employee-like skated through her, warming places that had no business growing warm. She swallowed and tried to remain very still until the sensation passed.

Nigel, of course, had no idea of the response he'd caused by such an innocent action. And with luck, he never would.

Licking her lips, she tamped down on whatever was rolling around under her skin and made sure her lips were turned up in at least an imitation of a smile.

"Thank you," she said, tugging at the safety belt to show that she was, indeed, alive and well and capable of simple human functions. "It looks like you're working overtime," she added, relieved that her voice continued to sound steady and normal.

He leaned back in the seat, running his hands along his thighs and letting out a breath as he relaxed a fraction. "There doesn't seem to be overtime with this position. It's round-the-clock."

Lily certainly knew what he meant by that. She'd worked twenty-four/seven to establish the Zaccaro label. Then when her sisters had joined in, the three of them had given all they had to get the company truly up and running.

Even now that they had their boutique open and were producing items on more than a one-off basis, life was no less stressful or busy. They'd simply exchanged one set of problems for another. And having an office-slash-studio at home only kept the work closer at hand.

"For tonight's dinner," Nigel began in that accent that would be charming even if the looks and personality didn't match—at least to her unaccustomed American ears, "we're meeting with a designer who's looking to move from Vincenze to a higher position at Ashdown Abbey."

Lily's eyes widened a second before she schooled her expression. Vincenze was a huge, multimillion-dollar design enterprise. A household name and very big deal. If she wasn't busy running her own fashion-design business, she would have been ecstatic over the possibility of going to work for them.

Yet tonight they were meeting with someone who wanted to *leave* Vincenze for Ashdown Abbey.

Which wasn't to say Ashdown Abbey was a lesser label.

Far from it. If anything, Ashdown Abbey and Vincenze were similar when it came to levels of success. But their design aesthetics were entirely different, and it would definitely take some doing—at least in her experience—for a designer to go from one to the other without traversing a sharp learning curve.

Fighting to keep her mind on the job she was *supposed* to be doing rather than the one that came more naturally to her, Lily said, "I'm not sure exactly what my role is this evening."

"Just listen," he replied casually. "It will be a good way for you to learn the ropes, so to speak."

He turned a little more in her direction and offered a warm smile. "Frankly, I asked you to join me so I wouldn't have to be alone with this fellow. These so-called business dinners can sometimes drone on, especially if the potential employee attempts to regale me with a long list of his or her talents and abilities."

Lily returned his grin. She knew what he meant; the fashion industry was filled with big mouths and bigger egos. She liked to think she wasn't one of them, but there was a certain amount of self-aggrandizing required to promote oneself and one's line.

"Maybe we should work out a signal and some prearranged topics of discussion," she offered. "That way if things get out of hand and your eyes begin to glaze over, you can give me a sign and I'll launch into a speech about global warming or some such."

Nigel's smile widened, showing a row of straight, sparkling-white teeth. "Global warming?" he asked, the amusement evident in his tone.

"It's a very important issue," she said, adopting a prim-and-proper expression. "I'm sure I could fill a good hour or two on the subject, if necessary."

He nodded a few times, very slowly and thoughtfully, his

lips twitching with suppressed humor. "That could certainly prove useful."

"I thought so," she agreed.

"What would you suggest we use as a signal?"

She thought about it for a minute. "You could tug at your earlobe," she said. "Or kick me under the table. Or perhaps we could have a code word."

"A code word," he repeated, one brow lifting with interest. "This is all starting to sound very…double-oh-seven-ish."

Appropriate, she supposed, since he reminded her a little of James Bond. It was the accent, she was sure. Her stomach tightened briefly.

Feigning a nonchalant attitude she didn't entirely feel, she shrugged. "Spies are good at what they do for a reason. But if you'd prefer to be trapped for hours by a potential employee you can't get away from, be my guest."

Silence filled the rear of the car, only the sound of the tires rotating beneath them audible as the seconds ticked by and Lily's anxiety grew.

She might have overstepped her bounds. After all, she'd only been in this man's employ for twelve hours. That might have been a bit too early to start voicing her opinions and telling him what to do.

Worse, she probably shouldn't have jumped on his mention of James Bond movies and followed the spy thread. Because technically, *she* was a spy within his organization, and she didn't want him spending too much time wondering how she knew so much about the business of espionage.

"I definitely agree that an escape plan is in order," Nigel said, finally breaking the nerve-inducing quiet. "How would it be if I inquired about your headache from earlier? You can say that it's come back and you'd really like to get home so you can rest."

"All right." It sounded as good as anything else they might

come up with, and she certainly knew more about headaches than she did about global warming.

"And if *you* grow bored," he continued, "you can ask me if I'd like another martini. I'll decline and say that we should get going, as I have an early appointment in the morning, anyway."

"Will you be drinking martinis?" she asked.

"Tonight, I will," he said, a spark of mischief lighting his eyes. "It will bolster our story, if we make an excuse to leave the restaurant early."

"We haven't even arrived at dinner yet, and already we're thinking of ways to get away as soon as we've finished eating," she remarked.

"That's because it's a boring, uptight business dinner. If this were a dinner date, I would already be considering options for drawing things out. Excuses to keep you there well past dessert."

Lily's heart skipped a beat, her palms growing damp even as a wave of unexpected heat washed over her. That was not the sort of thing she expected to hear from her boss. It didn't *feel* like a benign, employer-to-employee comment, either. It felt much too…suggestive.

And on top of that, she was suddenly picturing it: a dinner date with Nigel rather than a business dinner. Sitting across from him at a candlelit table for two. Leaning into each other as they spoke in soft tones. Flirting, teasing, building toward something much more serious and intimate.

The warmth grew, spreading through her body like a fever. And when she imagined him reaching out, touching her hand where it rested on the pristine white linen of the tablecloth, she nearly jumped, it seemed so real.

Thankfully, Nigel didn't notice because the car was slowing, and he was busy readjusting his tie and cuff links.

Lily licked her lips and smoothed her hands over her own

blouse and skirt, making sure she was as well put together as he was.

When the car came to a complete stop, he looked at her again and offered an encouraging half smile. "Ready?" he asked.

She nodded just as Nigel's door was opened from the outside. He stepped out, then turned and reached back for her.

Purse in hand, she slid across the wide seat and let Nigel take her arm as she stepped out. His driver nodded politely before closing the door and moving back around the hood of the car to the driver's seat.

Looking around, Lily realized they were standing outside of Trattoria. She wasn't from Los Angeles, but even she recognized the name of the elegant five-star restaurant. To her knowledge, the waiting list for reservations was three to four months long.

Unless, she supposed, you were someone like Nigel. The Statham name—and bank account—carried a lot of weight. Not only in L.A. or England, either, but likely anywhere in the world.

She was no stranger to fine dining, of course. She'd grown up at country clubs and taken international vacations with her parents. She even knew a few world-renowned master chefs and restaurateurs personally.

But she wasn't with her family now, and hadn't lived that way for several years; she'd been too busy working her fingers to the bone and building her own company the old-fashioned way.

She was also supposed to be from more of a blue-collar upbringing, not a secret, runaway heiress. Which meant she shouldn't be familiar with seven-course meals, real silverware or places like this, where appetizers started at fifty dollars a plate.

The good news was that she wouldn't embarrass herself

by not knowing which fork to use. The bad news was that she needed to act awed and out of her element enough not to draw suspicion. From anyone, but especially Nigel.

Passing beneath the dark green awning lined with sparkling lights, he led her past potted topiaries and through the wide French doors at the restaurant's entrance.

A tuxedoed maître d' met them immediately, and as soon as Nigel gave his name, they were led across the main dining area, weaving around tables filled with other well-dressed customers who were talking and laughing and seemed to be thoroughly enjoying their expensive meals.

At the rear of the restaurant, the maître d' paused, waving to a medium-size table set for four where another man was already seated.

Rounding the table, Nigel held a chair out for her while the other man rose. He was young—mid to late twenties, Lily would guess—with dark hair and an expensive suit. Most likely a Vincenze, even one of his own designs, since that's where he was currently working.

"Mr. Statham," the designer greeted Nigel, holding out his hand.

Nigel waited until she was seated to reach across the table and shake.

"Thank you for meeting with me."

Nigel inclined his head and introduced them. "Lillian, this is Harrison Klein. Mr. Klein, this is my assistant, Lillian George."

"Pleased to meet you," Harrison said, taking her hand next.

When they were all seated, a waiter brought leather-bound menus and took their drink orders. True to his word, Nigel ordered a dry martini. He even made a point of asking for it "shaken, not stirred," then turned to her with a humorous and entirely too distracting wink.

Soon after they placed the rest of their orders, their salads and entrées arrived, and they made general small talk while they ate. Nigel asked questions about Klein's schooling and experience and his time at Vincenze.

It was odd to be sitting at a table with another designer and the CEO of one of the biggest labels in the United Kingdom—and soon possibly the United States—without adding to the discussion. So many times, she had to bite her tongue to keep from asking questions of her own or inserting her two cents here and there into the conversation.

In order to avoid saying something she shouldn't, she stayed busy sipping her wine, toying with the stem of her glass, studying the lines of each of their outfits. Mentally she deconstructed them, laying out patterns, cutting material and sewing them back up.

Finally, they were finished with their meals and the table was cleared. Nigel declined the dessert menu for all of them, but asked for coffee.

And then he held out a hand to the other man. "Your portfolio?"

Harrison's Adam's apple bobbed as he swallowed nervously, but he leaned over and retrieved his portfolio from the floor beside his chair. He passed it to Nigel, then sat back and waited quietly.

Lily found her pulse kicking up just a fraction. This was such an important, nerve-racking moment for any designer. She still wondered why someone who already had a job at a successful design corporation would be interested in moving.

She had gone an entirely different route, striking out on her own to establish a personal label and company instead of taking a job elsewhere and working her way up the ladder.

In a lot of ways, that would have been easier. It might have taken her longer to form her own label and have her own storefront, but she certainly would have learned from the best and maybe avoided some of the pitfalls she'd encountered while barreling ahead with her one-woman—and then three-woman, thank goodness—show.

The tension at the table thickened as Nigel studied the portfolio carefully, page by page. Sitting beside him, Lily could see each design clearly, and couldn't resist drinking them in.

After several long minutes, Nigel closed the portfolio and passed it back. "Very nice, Harrison, thank you."

From the other man's expression, Lily could tell he'd been hoping for a far more exuberant response. She almost felt sorry for him.

"We'd best call it an evening," Nigel continued, "but we have your résumé and contact information, and will be in touch."

Klein's face fell, but he recovered quickly. "I appreciate that. Thank you very much," he said, holding out his hand.

The two men shook, putting a clear end to the dinner meeting. But Lily couldn't resist tossing in a quick, "Are you sure you wouldn't like another martini?"

Nigel raised a brow in her direction, one corner of his mouth twitching in mirth.

"No, thank you. I've had quite enough to drink. I think it would be best if we call it a night, especially considering our early morning meetings."

Biting back her personal amusement, she nodded. The three of them rose, said their goodbyes and headed out of the restaurant. It took a few minutes for Nigel's car to arrive, but they were silent until they were closed inside and the vehicle was slowly moving again.

"So," Nigel began, shifting on the wide leather seat to face her more fully. "What did you think?"

Somewhat startled by the question, Lily swallowed. "About what?"

"Klein," he intoned. "The interview. His designs."

What a loaded set of questions, she thought. She had opinions, to be sure. But as his personal assistant, should she be spouting them off? And what if she said too much, revealed herself as being too knowledgeable for such a low-level position?

"It's all right. You can speak freely," he said, almost as though he'd read her mind. "I want your honest opinion. It doesn't mean I'll listen, but I'm curious all the same. And it won't have an impact on your position at Ashdown Abbey one way or the other, I promise."

Hoping he was as good as his word, she gave a gentle shrug. "He's talented, that's for certain."

"But..."

"No buts," she corrected quickly. "He's clearly very talented."

Nigel kept his gaze locked on her, laser eyes drilling into her like those of a practiced interrogator.

"Fine," she breathed on a soft sigh. "He's very talented, *but*...I don't think his designs are at all suitable for Ashdown Abbey."

"Why not?" he asked in a low voice.

"Ashdown Abbey is known for its high-end business attire, even though you've recently branched out into casual and sportswear. But Klein's aesthetic leans more toward urban hip. I can see why he's done well at Vincenze—they've got a strong market in New York and Los Angeles with urban street and activewear. But Ashdown Abbey is a British company, known for clothes that are a bit more professional and clean-cut."

She paused for a moment, wondering if she'd said too much or maybe overstepped her bounds.

"Unless you're planning to move in that direction," she added, just to be safe.

Long seconds ticked by while Nigel simply stared at her,

not a single thought readable on his face. Then one side of his mouth lifted, the hazel-green of his eyes growing brighter.

"No, we have no plans to move in that direction for the time being," he agreed. "Your assessment is spot-on, you know. Exactly what I was thinking while I flipped through his designs."

For a moment, Lily sat in stunned silence, both surprised and delighted by his reaction. She so easily could have screwed up.

With a long mental sigh of relief, she reminded herself that she was supposed to be poised and self-assured. She'd lobbied for the job as his PA by making it clear she knew her stuff. As long as she didn't let anything slip about her true identity or reason for being there, why shouldn't she let a little of her background show?

"Maybe you'll be glad you hired me, after all," she quipped.

He gave her a look. A sharp, penetrating look that nearly made her shrink back inside her shell of insecurity.

And then he spoke, his deep voice and spine-tingling accent almost making her melt into the seams of the supple leather seat.

"I think I already am."

Four

Though she insisted it wasn't necessary, Nigel walked Lillian to the front door of her flat. It was the least he could do after eating up her evening with Ashdown Abbey business.

He hadn't actually needed her to accompany him to the restaurant this evening. Past personal assistants had certainly attended business functions such as that, but most had taken place during normal working hours. He'd never before requested that his assistant go to dinner with him—even a business dinner.

He wasn't entirely sure why he'd made the request of Lillian. Perhaps he'd hoped to test her mettle because she was so new on the job. They'd had a mere handful of hours together at the office, during which she'd impressed him very much. But he'd wanted to see her outside of the office, in a more critical corporate situation, to see how she handled herself in the real world, when faced with real Ashdown Abbey business associates.

But that was only what he was telling himself. Or what he'd tell others, should he be asked.

The truth lay somewhere closer to him simply not being ready to say goodbye to her company just yet.

She was quite attractive. Something he probably shouldn't have noticed…but then, he was human and male, and it was rather difficult to miss.

The package she put together intrigued him, and he'd decided to find a way to study her a bit more closely and for a while longer.

Coercing her into going to dinner with him might not have been the wisest decision he'd ever made as an employer toward an employee, but it had been quite enlightening.

Lillian George, it turned out, was not only beautiful but smart, as well. In the car, she'd been witty and charming. Though she'd started out nervous—at least by his impression—she'd quickly loosened up and even begun to tease him with her notion of creating a plan for their escape from a boring dinner meeting.

Then, at dinner itself, she'd been nearly the perfect companion. Quiet and unassuming, yet brilliant at making small talk and knowing when to speak and when to remain silent. Definitely an excellent performance from his personal assistant.

Not for the first time, though, he wondered what she might be like over a dinner that had nothing to do with business.

His mind shouldn't be wandering in that direction, he knew, but once the thought filled his head, he couldn't seem to be rid of it. It would have been nice to focus his full attention on her throughout the meal, and to feel the same from her. To talk about something other than Ashdown Abbey and potential new designs or designers, and to chat about the personal instead of business.

How long had it been since he'd taken a woman to dinner or out on the town?

Not since Caroline, for certain.

And a beautiful woman who had nothing to do with his family's company...?

Well, Caroline definitely didn't qualify there. She hadn't been involved with Ashdown Abbey when they'd first met, but she *had* been an American model eager to sleep her way to the lead in their runway shows and ad campaigns—preferably in the U.K. so that she could go "international."

And the random models he was often seen with at fashion-industry functions simply didn't count.

But then, neither did tonight. Not really. Though a part of him wished it could.

They made their way down the narrow hall of her building, coming to a stop in front of the door to her flat. She fit her key into the lock and turned it, but didn't open the door. Instead, she turned back round to face him, the knob still in her hand, one arm twisted behind her.

"Thank you," she said softly. "I had a very nice time tonight."

"Even though I forced you to come along as part of your role as my assistant?" he couldn't help but inquire.

She smiled gently at him. "Even though. I appreciated the chance to sit in on one of your meetings. I know how important something like that is. And I appreciate that you let me voice my opinion on Harrison Klein's work. You certainly didn't have to ask when I've only been working for you a single day."

"That's *why* I asked," he told her. "I wanted to know what you were made of, and that seemed a fast way to find out."

"So I passed your little test?" she asked, tipping her head slightly to one side.

"With flying colors," he said without hesitation.

"I guess that means I still have a job and should go ahead and show up in the morning."

"Most definitely. Keep up the good work, and I may just promote you to VP of the company."

"I'm sure the current vice president would be delighted to hear that."

Nigel shrugged. "Eh. It's my uncle. But he's a grumpy old sod and should probably be retiring soon, anyway."

Lillian laughed, the sound light with only a hint of nerves.

Were they the nerves of an executive secretary having a frank discussion with her new boss? Or of a woman standing much too close to a man in an empty hallway?

Knowing he was skating dangerously near the line that separated personal from professional, Nigel straightened and cleared his throat.

"Well," he murmured. "I should let you go inside and get to bed, since I know you have to be at work early tomorrow. Thank you again for your company this evening."

"Thank you for a delicious meal. It was a treat to be able to sit at Trattoria and order more than tap water with a slice of lemon."

He chuckled at that. It hadn't occurred to him that his restaurant of choice might be that far out of the realm of normalcy for Lillian. But now that he thought about it, Trattoria was almost certainly too pricey for an assistant's salary. Even an executive assistant's.

"I'm glad you enjoyed it. Good night, then."

Placing his hands on her upper arms, he leaned in and pressed a quick kiss to her cheek. Quick and entirely innocent…but one he found himself wishing could be longer and much *less* innocent.

Juliet Zaccaro paced the length of the living room in the loft apartment she shared with her two sisters.

"I don't know what you're so worried about," her youngest sister, Zoe, said from where she sat in the corner of the sofa.

She was curled up, nonchalant and bored. More concerned with her latest manicure than their middle sister's well-being.

"How can you say that?" Juliet all but snapped. "Lily has been missing for a week."

"She left a note," Zoe returned. "She told us not to worry about her, and not to look for her. Obviously, she knows what she's doing and needs some time away."

Zoe might have been speaking the truth, but that didn't mean Juliet had to like it. Or agree.

"I don't care," she said, crossing her arms beneath her breasts and pausing in her pacing to tap her foot angrily. "This isn't like her. What if something is wrong?"

"If something was wrong, Lily would tell us," was Zoe's bored and yet utterly confident reply. "She's never exactly been shy about asking for help before."

Juliet's brows pulled together in a frown. She really hated it when Zoe—the youngest, flightiest, most self-absorbed of the Zaccaro sisters—was also the sensible one.

"Well, it can't hurt to look for her. *Ask* her face-to-face if everything is okay."

Absently, she twisted the gold-and-diamond engagement ring on her left ring finger around and around. Where in heaven's name could Lily have gone? *Why* would she run off like this? It wasn't in her sister's nature at all to disappear without a word…or to disappear after leaving only a brief, cryptic note.

Juliet might have been the oldest of the Zaccaro girls and stereotypically the responsible one, taking her role as big sister seriously, but Lily was no empty-headed blonde slacker. She'd started her own fashion line that had evolved into her own company. She'd been successful enough and dogged enough to bring Juliet and Zoe in as partners to help her run the company with her.

These were not the actions of someone who would wake up one morning and decide she wanted to be a beachcomber instead. Not when there was so much going on at Zaccaro Fashions right now, so many balls in the air that Lily was juggling almost single-handedly.

Juliet and Zoe helped where they could, but…well, Zoe tended to be easily distracted, and they never knew if she would show up clearheaded and raring to go or call from Las Vegas to say she'd met a guy and would be back in a couple of weeks.

And Juliet was nearly ready to yank her hair out. In addition to overseeing handbag and accessory design for Zaccaro Fashions, she had her wedding to plan. And her moody, sometimes demanding fiancé to keep happy… She hadn't told her sister yet, but Paul had begun pressuring her—strongly—to move back to Connecticut after their honeymoon. He'd seemed fine with her life in New York when he'd proposed. She'd been here more than a year already, and he'd acted as though he was supportive of her new career direction and would be more than willing to move down to be closer to her.

Then she'd said yes, accepted his proposal and things had slowly started to change. It bothered her. Concerned her, even. But the date had been set, the venue reserved, a caterer hired, flowers chosen… How could she back out now just because her feet were getting a little chilly?

As she kept telling herself, multiple times a day, it would pass. Dragging her thoughts back to the matter at hand, she stalked across the hardwood floor to the kitchen island and slid open the drawer where they kept everyday odds and ends. Pencils and pens, paper clips, a pair of scissors and the thick borough of Manhattan phone directory.

She pulled it out and flipped to the yellow, paid-advertisement section, looking for listings for private detectives or investigators or whatever they were called. Maybe one of them could figure out what had happened to Lily, because she was sure staggering around in the dark. She had no idea where to begin looking for her sister, or even who to call to ask about her possible whereabouts.

As she got closer to the *P*s, the directory fell open, and she noticed a stiff business card stuck between the tissue-thin pages. Plucking it out, she turned it over and read the black print on a plain white background.

McCormack Investigations
Corporate. Private.

She had no idea where the card had come from, but judging by the corresponding ad on the page in front of her, it was probably one of the numbers she'd have called, anyway.

Taking the card with her, she marched back across the living room, casting an annoyed glance at Zoe, whose attention had been drawn to the latest issue of *Elle*.

"I'll be in my room," Juliet muttered through her teeth.

Tipping her head over the back of the sofa, Zoe watched her go. With an exaggerated sigh, she closed the magazine and tossed it on the coffee table.

"Okay. I think I'll go over to the studio to work for a while. Let me know if you want to go out for dinner."

Even if they made plans, chances were Zoe would change her mind and zip off to some club at the last minute, leaving Juliet to her own devices.

She waited until Zoe was gone and she was alone to pull out her cell phone and dial the number for McCormack Investigations. It took her a few minutes to convince the receptionist that her problem was a serious one and that time was of the essence, though she didn't go into a lot of detail.

The woman collected her name and contact information, promising to pass her message along and get back to her as soon as possible.

Juliet would have preferred being put on the phone with one of the company's investigators immediately or being told she could come in first thing in the morning to meet with someone in person. But she knew her dilemma wasn't exactly an emergency—at least not yet.

And please, God, don't let it become one. The idea of something happening to her sister made Juliet's blood run cold.

So she agreed to stay by the phone and told herself not to panic, not to let her imagination race out of control.

She should go over to the studio with Zoe and try to get some work done. Keep her mind off Lily and the phone in her hand that refused to ring, even after five whole minutes of waiting.

Instead, she resumed pacing a path through the middle of the living-room area. Which was much easier without Zoe in the way, distracting her with her sensible arguments and assurances that Lily was just fine.

Step. Step. Step.

Tick. Tick. Tick.

Turn.

Step. Step. Step.

Tick. Tick. Tick.

Five minutes turned into ten. Ten into twenty.

She stopped. Worried her thumbnail. Tapped her foot. Went back to pacing.

At thirty minutes and counting, she let out a huff of breath and dropped into the center of the sofa, the cushion wheezing at the sudden addition of her weight.

When her cell phone pealed, she jumped and let out a startled yip. She'd been concentrating so hard on making the stupid thing ring that when it finally did, it scared the bejesus out of her.

Heart pounding for more reasons than one, she brought it to her ear and whispered, "Hello?"

"Ms. Zaccaro?"

"Yes."

"This is Reid McCormack from McCormack Investigations. I have here that your sister is missing and you'd like help tracking her down."

"Yes," she said again.

"You understand, don't you, that she's an adult and is allowed to leave town without telling anyone where she's going," the man on the other end of the line intoned.

Through gritted teeth, Juliet responded, "Yes."

"And if she left a note...she did leave a note, correct?"

Hoping she didn't end up with a cracked molar after this conversation, she ground out yet another, "Yes."

"If she left a note, then she really can't be considered missing. The police would tell you to wait and hope you hear from her. And that you can't file a missing-persons report unless there are actual signs of foul play."

Feeling deflated and more frustrated than ever, Juliet dropped her head and murmured a dejected, "I understand."

A beat passed before Reid McCormack spoke again.

"So why don't you come by tomorrow around 11:00 a.m.? I can't promise anything. I may not even be able to look for your sister. But we'll talk. All right?"

His low-timbred, slowly spoken words had Juliet's head shooting up so fast, it left her dizzy.

Had she heard him correctly? Clearing her throat, she swallowed and forced out the only thing she could think of. "What?"

"Come by tomorrow," he repeated as patiently as a parent spoon-feeding a child, "and we'll talk."

"All right. Thank you." She hopped to her feet in excitement, though she knew perfectly well he couldn't see her.

"See you tomorrow, then," he murmured before they said their goodbyes and hung up.

Juliet slapped her phone down on the low coffee table, then headed back to her room. What did one wear to a meeting with a private investigator?

The only detectives she could picture were the television and pulp-fiction type—*Magnum, P.I.,* Sam Spade, *Columbo.* But somehow she couldn't imagine showing up in a hibiscus-covered blouse or '30s-style dress and wide-brim hat.

Thanks to her role at Zaccaro Fashions, her closet was bursting at the seams with clothes to choose from. Surely she could put something together by tomorrow morning.

As she fingered through hangers and studied her shoe choices, she found herself pushing aside Mr. McCormack's assertion that he might not be able to help her find Lily, letting herself believe that he not only could, but *would*.

Five

Lily arrived at Ashdown Abbey bright and early the next morning—but not without a struggle. She'd only gotten about four hours of sleep before her alarm had rudely awakened her and forced her back into the land of the living.

Gulping down her third cup of coffee since reaching the office, Lily sat at her desk and prayed she would be able to hold her composure when Nigel stepped off the elevator.

After saying good-night and slipping into her apartment, she'd gone to the bedroom and changed into a pair of simple cotton pajamas, then returned to the living room with all of the printouts and information she'd managed to sneak out of Ashdown Abbey earlier.

Her movements had been so calm and deliberate. Robotic. Because underneath it all, she was a beehive of confusing thoughts and conflicting emotions.

She was *not* in Los Angeles to have her hormones go haywire just because she was in close proximity to a handsome, charming Brit. He was supposed to be her *enemy,* for heaven's sake.

But her hormones *were* going wild, distracting her and throwing her off her well-planned-out path.

Not just because Nigel was an attractive man. She'd met handsome men before. Met them, worked with them, dated and even slept with a few.

Good looks were nice, but she wasn't so weak that they could push her over the edge into total stupidity. Nor could a thick British accent, no matter how toe-curling it might be.

No, there was something else about Nigel that had her pulse thrumming and her head spinning like a kaleidoscope.

She actually kind of liked him so far, despite her preconceived notions of who Nigel Statham must be—a rich, entitled CEO, not above stealing another designer's ideas to advance his own agenda.

But would a rich, entitled thief ask her opinion on something as important as hiring choices and then actually *listen* to her answer? Would he compliment her on her insight and walk her to her door at the end of the evening?

The worst part, though, was the kiss. A simple kiss on the cheek, not much different than she'd received a thousand times from older acquaintances, uncles, even her own father.

Then again, it was *so* not like a kiss from her father. Light and on the cheek, yes. To anyone who might have been watching, it would have seemed to be exactly what it was—a polite, friendly good-night kiss. A thanks-for-a-nice-evening, take-care, sleep-tight kiss from one friend to another. Or in this case, a man to a woman he'd only recently met.

But Lily knew differently. Or at least she *felt* differently. Never before had a simple kiss on the cheek caused her temperature to rise. Her heartbeat to kick into a gallop. Her stomach to launch into a series of somersaults that would put an Olympic gymnast to shame.

And that was all at only the first touch of his lips on her skin.

She'd expected him to pull away almost immediately. A quick peck, that's all. It was almost what she'd hoped for, because then her vitals would return to normal.

For some reason, though, he'd lingered. Not long enough for the moment to become awkward, but certainly long enough for everything in her to turn warm and liquid, and for her chest to tighten as she held her breath.

One-one thousand.

Two-one thousand.

Three-one thousand.

She'd begun to count silently, the way she and her sisters had when they were young, playing hide-and-seek. Until she worried that lack of oxygen might start to make her light-headed.

And then he'd pulled away. Straightening to his full height, and gazing at her with an intensity that sent a shiver down her spine.

Murmuring another quick, mumbled goodbye, he'd turned on his heel and marched away.

He'd gone, but the aftereffects of the kiss had remained. Through the rest of the night and into this morning.

She could swear she still felt the brush of his mouth against her cheek even now.

And wasn't that going to be a terrific way to go through the day? Imagining ghost lips dancing along her skin. Wondering if the look she'd seen in Nigel's eyes just before he'd walked away had been desire...or distaste.

Taking another long swig of coffee, she let the strong, hot brew slide down her throat and trickle into her system. A caffeine IV would be better. Then again, so would a nice shot of vodka. Or maybe a splash of whiskey to make the coffee both smoother and more potent.

Fingers flexing around the ceramic mug, Lily told herself to stop being so flighty. She wasn't here—in Los Angeles or at Ashdown Abbey—to daydream or wax poetic. And she certainly needed to get her act together before Nigel arrived.

Thoughts of that stupid kiss and what it might or might not mean had kept her up half the night. They didn't need to distract her all day, too. Especially since she had much more important things to focus on.

One was pretending to be the perfect personal assistant for Nigel.

The other was digging and snooping to see what else she could find concerning her stolen designs.

She'd gone through the California Collection design print-outs as much as she could last night before finally succumbing to exhaustion and crawling into bed, but she could barely remember a thing about them now. A second and possibly even third run-through was definitely called for. Of course, she couldn't do that until tonight when she was home and alone again.

A few yards down the hall, she heard the hum of the elevator and the whoosh of the doors as they opened and closed. Rushing to set aside her coffee, Lily took a deep breath, straightened in her chair, and started typing nothing in particular in an effort to look busy.

Nigel spotted Lillian the minute he stepped off the lift onto his office floor. If it was possible, she looked even more lovely today than she had last evening, and she'd looked quite stunning then.

Perhaps because he'd always had a bit of a soft spot for the "sexy librarian" type. Her hair was pulled back in a sexy bun, bookish, dark-rimmed glasses resting on the bridge of her nose. Her jewelry was understated. She wore a red blouse that

opened at the throat to reveal just enough pale flesh and shadowed cleavage to make a man's libido sit up and take notice.

She was seated behind her desk, so he couldn't tell what
she was wearing from the waist down. What he imagined,
though, was tight and formfitting, showing off her legs and
posterior to perfection. On top of that, he imagined her perch-
ing on the edge of the desk, legs crossed, shoe dangling from
the toe of one foot, nibbling seductively on the end of her pen.

Oh, yes—naughty librarian, indeed. Or more to the point,
naughty secretary. Which was the thought that had plagued
him all through last night.

An affair with his secretary was not only bad form, but an
extremely bad idea in general. As was allowing himself to be
distracted by ungentlemanly and very un-bosslike thoughts
about her.

He'd spent an inordinate amount of time unable to sleep,
kept awake by memories of their dinner together and that kiss
at her door just before saying their good-nights.

For a kiss akin to one he might give his mother or a be-
loved aunt, it had rocked him back on his heels and made him
sorry he had to walk away.

Worse, though, was that the thought of that one simple kiss
on the cheek had snowballed into a thousand other thoughts
and images he had no business thinking.

Lillian perched on the edge of her desk, shoe dangling
from her toes was only the first of many. The wee hours of
the night had also been filled with more erotic fantasies.

Pressing Lillian up against the door to her flat and kissing her for real. On the mouth, with lips and tongue and un-
bridled passion.

Walking her backward into her flat and taking her on whatever surface they bumped into first. Table, counter, sofa, coffee table…even the floor itself.

Bringing her home with him and making love to her in his

own bed. On satin sheets, with moonlight streaming across their naked bodies and bringing out the highlights in her dark blond hair.

The one that was bound to cause him the most trouble, however, was of watching her saunter into his office under the pretense of work, only to have him strip her of those sexy schoolmarm eyeglasses, pull the pins from her upswept hair and shag her brains out in the middle of his desk.

It was the single, red-hot thought spiraling through his mind and making it decidedly uncomfortable to walk the remaining distance to his office. She lifted her head as he approached, and he hoped to heaven she didn't notice the state of his arousal behind the zip of his otherwise pressed and pristine trousers.

"Good morning," she greeted him.

If her smile seemed a bit stiff or falsely bright, he pretended not to notice. She wasn't the only one feeling awkward and uncomfortable over whatever had passed between them last night.

"Good morning," he returned without inflection, studiously avoiding eye contact while he reached for the morning's post on the corner of her desk and flipped through.

"Coffee?" she asked.

"No, thank you."

Her smile slipped, uncertainty skating like clouds across the sky-blue of her eyes.

Nigel blew out a breath. He was being a bleeding sod, and he knew it. It wasn't her fault that he'd gotten very little sleep and woken up about ten feet to the left of the wrong side of the bed.

"I would love a cup of tea, though," he said in a much kinder voice.

She nodded quickly and rose, going around him and her

desk to the small pantry that was tucked away at the far side of the reception area.

He watched her cross the expanse, her long legs eating up the space in record time. The slant of her three-inch, open-toed shoes made those legs look even longer, more taut. And her skirt—which turned out to be short and black—encased her buttocks like a second skin.

Not exactly conducive to quelling his arousal. The only thing that might help with that was distance. And possibly being struck blind.

Since the latter wasn't likely to occur in the next few minutes, he opted for the former. Taking the stack of envelopes with him, he moved into his office and took a seat behind his desk.

He'd just logged on to check his email when Lillian appeared carrying a full tea service—the one he'd ordered when he'd first come to work in the States, but hadn't seen hide nor hair of since. When he'd requested a cup of tea from his previous assistants, they'd all brought him a big, clunky ceramic mug with a nondescript tea bag bobbing in a pool of lukewarm water.

Nigel sat back, waiting while she set the tray on the edge of his desk and proceeded to pour already steeped tea from a china pot into a china cup. Through a stainless-steel strainer and complete with matching saucer, no less.

"This is a surprise," he said.

She raised her head, meeting his gaze. The question was there in her eyes.

"I was expecting something much simpler," he explained. "Aren't you Americans fond of tea that comes in bags?"

"We are," she answered. "Very. Probably because it's a lot easier than all of this." She waved a hand to encompass the tray and its accoutrements. "But I've heard you Brits are much more particular about your tea. And that you don't think we Americans could brew a decent cup to save our lives."

His lips quirked with the urge to grin. "We sound like a demanding lot with sticks up our bums."

Lillian chuckled, returning her attention to the tea service. "You said it, I didn't," she replied, handing him the cup and saucer.

"To be safe, I went online and researched how to make a cup of *true* English tea. I make absolutely no promises that I've done it right, but I do hope you'll at least give me points for trying."

Gesturing to the other items on the tray, she said, "Milk, sugar and lemon."

The real thing, he noticed. Milk—not cream, which so many Americans assumed should be added just because they used it in their coffee—the sugar cubed and the lemon cut into wedges.

"I wasn't sure which, if any, you preferred."

"If this tastes as good as it looks, I may even give you a bonus," he told her. "For future reference, though, I take it black, so all the rest isn't really necessary."

She blinked, looking at him as though he'd said he wasn't actually British, it was all just a cruel hoax.

"Then *why* do you have a full tea service in the kitchenette? I bought all of this specifically so you could have tea just the way you like it and wouldn't be disappointed."

He bit back a grin, but had the dignity to flush at her chastisement. "Truthfully, it came that way, as a set. My mother has used a full tea service from the time I was a lad, so I suppose it never occurred to me that I really only needed the pot, cups and saucers."

With a huff, she dropped into one of the soft leather chairs opposite his desk and crossed one leg over the other. Her skirt shifted, revealing inches more of stocking-clad skin that he shouldn't be staring at. But he couldn't seem to drag his gaze away until he'd looked his fill.

Licking suddenly dry lips, he swallowed and drew his attention—reluctantly—to her face.

"I apologize for misleading you."

"But I worked really hard on getting this right, and now I find out I could have just dropped a tea bag into a cup of hot water and been done with it," she said, still sounding put out.

He inclined his head, acknowledging her upset. "I understand. My fault entirely. Feel free to do exactly that from now on. It may not be my preference, but it's no less than I deserve."

She studied him for a moment, blue eyes locked on his. Then she leaned back, almost deflating into her chair.

"You're not what I expected, you know," she said finally, surprising him with her boldness.

He cocked a brow. "Oh? How so?"

"I thought you would be a bit more demanding. Dictatorial, even. Like that chef on the cooking show who yells all the time and calls the contestants names."

Nigel couldn't help but chuckle. He knew exactly who she was talking about. "Actually, I believe he's Scottish, not British. And I don't recall ever calling anyone a donkey, no matter how angry I might have been."

"Good thing," she replied matter-of-factly. "I don't think you'd appreciate my reaction if you used a term like that with me."

"I can imagine." He could, and it wasn't pretty. Of course, he'd never been one to get red in the face and start slinging invectives when he lost his temper, so she had nothing to worry about on that score.

"You're not at all what I expected, either," he confessed.

He regretted the words as soon as they passed his lips. It

was a bit too much sharing for their short acquaintance, not to mention entirely out of character for him.

Of course, she'd heard him, so it wasn't as though he could pretend he hadn't said it.

She tipped her head to one side, glancing at him curiously. "You mean you thought I'd be quieter, more tractable, eager to please."

Nigel chuckled aloud at that description. Despite the fact that she had, indeed, seemed eager to please her new boss in the two days she'd been in his employ, something told him that wasn't entirely usual for her, and that the rest didn't suit her by half.

Quiet? Not if by that she meant meek.

Tractable? He couldn't imagine any such thing.

"No," he answered, giving his head a rather decisive shake. "Not at all. Given the past assistants I've had here in the U.S., I was expecting you to be…a few biscuits short of a tin, if you understand my meaning."

"You're in the habit of hiring mentally unstable personal assistants?" she teased, brow raised.

"Not unstable, thank goodness," he responded, "but young, and not a lot going on above the neck, other than good grooming and dreams of becoming either a supermodel or the next fashion designer to become an overnight success. Not only could they not make a decent cup of tea, but they couldn't keep their minds on their responsibilities long enough to accomplish what they'd actually been hired to do."

She thought about that for a moment, then inclined her head and her gaze toward the cup still resting on the desk in front of him.

"You haven't even tasted the tea yet. How do you know *I* can make a decent cup?"

He didn't bother to answer, simply lifted the cup to his mouth and took a long, hearty swallow. Setting the cup back down, he said, "Excellent. It would have been better if I'd started drinking it while it was still piping hot, but really—quite excellent."

"Well, you have only yourself to blame for that, don't you?" she quipped.

Without a hint of remorse or fear of speaking in such a manner to her employer. And not just any employer, but the CEO of the whole bloody company.

Why did that amuse him so damn much? Amuse, as well as arouse.

The sight of her, the thought of her, the knowledge that she would be seated just outside his office door for eight hours each day, was enough to send his blood to the boiling point.

Even now, he wanted to stand up, round his desk, lean down and kiss her just for the hell of it.

Well, for the hell of it, and also to discover if she tasted as good as he thought she would. That was something he suddenly wanted to know. Very, very badly.

In an attempt to cool the heat rising in his body and bringing small beads of perspiration to dot his brow, he raised the tea back to his lips and drained the cup dry. It didn't cool him off as much as he'd hoped.

"So," he commented to fill the increasingly awkward silence. "You can make a fine cup of tea, and you know your way about the design business—at least judging by last night's conversation. I think it's safe to say you've already surpassed the skills of all of my other assistants here in the States put together."

"I'll take that as a compliment," she replied, giving him a bright smile that Nigel believed could only be genuine.

So he responded with one of his own. "As you should. It was intended as one."

"I can expect that bonus to be reflected in my first pay-check, then?"

She made it a question. Loaded and dangerous.

Narrowing his eyes, he answered carefully. "We'll see. Keep up the good work, and I'll have no problem rewarding your efforts monetarily. But you've only been here two days. I need to see you in action awhile longer than that before I make any promises."

She shrugged one slim shoulder. "Can't blame a girl for trying."

With a laugh, Nigel emptied the rest of the tea into his cup, then sat back, linking his hands in front of him. "Certainly not. And you may just earn yourself some extra perks yet. Especially if you bring me another pot of tea before running down to the fourth floor to see how things are going. We've got a special runway show coming up in two weeks, and I want to be sure we're on track."

Lillian sat up in a suddenly more serious, alert manner. "I'll be happy to, but isn't that something you should do yourself? I'm not sure I'll know enough to judge how well things are going."

"You'll do fine," Nigel assured her. "The head of the design team should be able to tell you what's been done so far and what still needs to be taken care of. Then you can report to me, and if I think anything is out of sorts, I'll go down and put the fear of unemployment into them."

"Very stealthy of you," she said. Then, taking a deep breath, she pushed to her feet. "I'll do my best. It will be fun to visit the design-room floor. I've never been on one before."

Her gaze darted away and she shifted from one leg to the other. Peculiar, to say the least.

Ignoring the odd behavior, Nigel said, "Take your time down there. It really is quite fascinating to watch the designers work."

She nodded, collecting the china cup from the center of

the desk and adding it to the other items on the tea-service tray. Gathering it all, she headed for the door.

"Tea first," she said over her shoulder, "then I'll go down and spy on your happy little elves."

He watched her disappear out into the reception area, enjoying the sway of her hips and straight line of her back. It wasn't until he heard her returning with a second cup of tea several minutes later that he realized he hadn't moved a muscle since she'd walked away.

Which was not a good sign. Not good at all.

Six

Lily knew better than to make rash judgments about people. First impressions often made you think somebody was wonderful, friendly, trustworthy…and then later you discovered they were none of those things. Other times, the opposite was true. You met someone and didn't care for them at all, only to discover hidden aspects of their personality later that caused you to end up becoming close friends.

So the fact that she was finding Nigel Statham more handsome, more charming and more enticing the longer she knew him—even after only two short days—could go either way. She'd started out certain he was a thief with questionable business ethics. Could she have been completely and totally wrong about that? Or was she letting his intense good looks and honeyed accent blind her to the truth?

She'd expected to come to Los Angeles, go to work for the big, bad CEO of the U.S. branch of his family's company and immediately begin finding evidence to shore up her arguments about his involvement in the theft of her designs.

Instead, she'd found nothing. None of her poking around in his files—or his former personal assistants' files, at any rate—had turned up a single thing or question mark. If anything, she was less convinced of his involvement.

But the theft *had* occurred, so there had to be evidence somewhere. A thread she could find, pick at and follow back to its source.

The elevator she was riding down to the fourth floor stopped with a small jolt and she straightened, pushing away from the rear wall where she'd been leaning to wait for the doors to open.

She'd lied to Nigel when she'd told him she'd never visited a design-room floor before. Sometimes she felt as though she lived on one, especially when she and both of her sisters were in their home studio together, all working in tandem.

Which was probably why she was so looking forward to visiting the one here. Not only was she curious to see how things worked at a company of this size, but it would be comforting to be back in the thick of the creative side of the fashion business again. Even temporarily.

As she stepped off the elevator, the click of her heels on the slick polished floor mixed with the sound of voices and the hum of sewing machines. Not a dozen running all at once, but one here, one there, being used as needed, much the way they were in her shop.

She loved it. A noise that would probably grate on anyone else's nerves after a while soothed hers and helped her to take her first deep, comfortable breath since leaving New York.

She was smiling as she made her way down the main hall. This floor was made up of large, open-area rooms filled with long tables, dress forms, sewing equipment and plenty of fabrics and supplies. And most of the rooms she passed had their doors open so she could see the people working inside. Design teams, most likely, each assigned a different look or aspect of whatever collection they were currently putting together.

What Lily wouldn't give for this kind of setup. Not only the work space—which was like comparing a football field to a foosball table—but the employees. Extra creative minds, extra hands, twice or probably even quadruple the work accomplished in half the time.

Of course, in order to put something like this into effect, she would also need a lot more money. And that would mean either asking her parents for another, more substantial loan, or winning the lottery.

But a girl could dream, couldn't she? And one day, Zaccaro Fashions *would* be this big, this efficient. They would be a huge, world-renowned brand name in their own right, and she wouldn't need her future inheritance to make it happen.

She wanted to stop at each doorway and take a good, long peek inside. She wanted to know what everyone was making, see their work, listen in on their conversations. Especially since it was possible they were once again ripping off her designs.

There wasn't a lot of time for poking around, though. She was supposed to find a man named Michael Franklin, the head designer for this particular collection, and get a progress report for Nigel.

Despite his comment that she should take her time, she didn't trust him not to come looking for her. He was a big, corporate bigwig who didn't even make his own coffee or tea. What were the chances he could get through an hour or two without needing her for something?

And he was quite obviously a man who expected his assistant to come running the minute he called...even if she was three floors away. So the less time she spent away from her desk the better, at least until she'd been at the company a little longer and had a better handle on his routine.

Strolling down the hall, she took in the activities of each room peripherally as she passed, heading straight for the office at the end, where Nigel had told her she would most likely find Mr. Franklin. Or at least it was a place to start.

"Office" was a bit of a misnomer. It was actually a glass-fronted version of the other design areas, but in addition to equipment and a cutting table that doubled as a sketching and design surface, there was a cluttered desk and file cabinets.

Mr. Franklin's name was etched on the closed door, but no one was inside. Chewing the inside of her lip for a second, she tapped her foot and tried to decide what to do next. Her only option, she supposed, was to go back the way she'd come and pop her head into each room after all. Surely someone would have an idea of where she could find Mr. Franklin.

She was spinning on her heel to do just that when she nearly ran into another woman coming toward her.

"Oh, I'm so sorry."

Their simultaneous apologies were followed by amused chuckles.

"Sorry about that," the woman said again. "I saw you standing outside Mr. Franklin's office and was just coming to ask if I could help you with anything."

"I'm looking for Mr. Franklin, actually," Lily said. And then she stopped, tipping her head and narrowing her eyes as she concentrated more intently on the other woman.

"Wait a minute. Don't I know you?" She wracked her brain, positive the young woman looked familiar.

"Oh, my gosh," she exclaimed as it finally came to her. "You're Bella, aren't you? I'm sorry, I can't think of your last name off the top of my head, but you're Zoe's friend, aren't you? Her roommate from college."

"It's Landry," the other woman, who was a petite brunette,

supplied. And then she widened her cornflower-blue eyes. "Do you mean Zoe Zaccaro?"

Lily nodded.

"I haven't seen Zoe in ages, but we definitely spent our college years together. How do you know her?"

"I'm Lily, Zoe's sister. We met briefly the last time you visited Zoe in New York."

She wasn't surprised at Bella's lack of recognition. Normally, she and her sisters looked enough alike—with their long, blond hair and similar facial features—that they were often mistaken for one another. But with her hair both darkened and pulled up in an out-of-character twist, and unfamiliar glasses perched on the bridge of her nose, she'd done a pretty good job of muting all of the things that made her stand out as a Zaccaro by looks alone.

Not to mention that she hadn't seen Bella in years—and had only met her a couple of times before that, when they had visited Zoe on campus or Zoe had brought Bella home with her for the odd holiday break.

"Oh, yes. Wow, small world. It's great to see you again. And how is Zoe?" Bella asked.

"Great," Lily told her. "Same as usual."

They both laughed at that, aware of exactly what Zoe's "usual" was.

"So what are you doing here?" Bella wanted to know.

The question stopped Lily cold, slapping the smile right off her face. Uh-oh. Until then, she'd forgotten she was supposed to be keeping a low profile and *definitely* remaining anonymous to everyone who worked at Ashdown Abbey. She had forgotten while exchanging pleasantries with a friend of her sister's whom she'd run into out of the blue.

Mind racing, she tried to figure out how to cover her mistake and come up with a plausible reason for her presence here in Los Angeles.

"The three of us are, um…taking a little time off from designing, working to establish the store and brand as they are now. So while Zoe and Juliet are running things back home, I decided to come out here and intern with Ashdown Abbey for a while."

That sounded okay, didn't it? She very pointedly didn't mention that she was working as the big kahuna's assistant. And she hoped Bella didn't find out, because then she would have to explain why she was going by a different name and pray they never ran into one another while Nigel was around.

"Cool," Bella replied, apparently accepting Lily's explanation at face value.

"How about you?" Lily asked, eager to turn the younger woman's attention away from her and on to something, anything else.

"Oh, I'm, um…" Bella stammered, glancing down at the toes of her pointy, leopard-print shoes before returning her gaze to Lily, but not quite meeting her eyes. "I'm an associate designer for the company," she said finally. "I've been here for almost three years now."

"That's wonderful," Lily told her, meaning it. She didn't know Bella well, wasn't even sure how long she and Zoe had been friends, but she'd never heard her sister speak a bad word about her, and she seemed perfectly nice.

"You're working on the latest collection, then?" she asked, nodding her head to indicate all of the fourth-floor workrooms.

Bella gave a jerky nod, her gaze skating away again for the briefest of moments. "I don't really have much to do with it. I'm just sort of a cog in the wheel, doing a little here and a little there. Whatever needs to be done."

"Hey, you have to start somewhere," Lily said with a pleasant smile, knowing the truth of that better than anyone. "I'm sure it will be great. All of Ashdown Abbey's designs are exceptional. You should be proud to be a part of it."

That was true, too, even if it pained her to say so. Especially since she was still smarting from their use of *her* great designs for their California Collection.

She thought about trying to wheedle information from Bella—about the California Collection, or Nigel, or maybe just Ashdown Abbey itself. It was possible she knew something important without even being aware of it. But after blurting out her real identity when she was supposed to be undercover, she was afraid of coming across as too curious and giving herself away even further, so she kept her mouth shut. She could always come back later to pick Bella's brain if she needed to.

It also crossed her mind that—being a friend of Zoe's and having been in their studio in the past—Bella might have had something to do with the theft of her designs. She didn't want to believe that a friend of her sister's—especially one who'd roomed with Zoe for four years straight—would do such a thing, but made a mental note to look into it anyway. At least cursorily, just in case.

"Do you know where Mr. Franklin is?" she asked instead of beginning an impromptu interrogation right there in the hallway.

Bella glanced back over her shoulder. "Um…he should be here somewhere. Try workroom B. He's been working pretty closely with that team this week."

"Great, thank you."

"Do you want me to take you?" Bella offered, finally making eye contact.

"No, thanks. I can find it, and I'm sure you have work to do," Lily said. "It was nice to see you, though. I'll tell Zoe you said hi."

After saying their goodbyes, Bella headed in one direction

while Lily retraced her path toward the elevator. She went more slowly this time, figuring she had a valid excuse for poking her head into each room to see who was there and what was going on. So what if workroom B was one of the last rooms she'd pass?

She caught glimpses of the color palette and fabrics that were being used for this particular collection, as well as a few of the designs themselves being pieced together on dress forms. Lily liked what she saw, and so far, at least, she hadn't spotted anything that set off alarm bells in her head. Nothing that looked eerily similar to her own design aesthetic.

It was a relief, but also a touch disappointing, since it got her no closer to finding out how her designs had been stolen in the first place.

Since she didn't see anyone in the other workrooms who seemed to be in charge, she decided to wait until she reached workroom B to ask after Mr. Franklin. She could always backtrack later if she needed to.

Reaching workroom B, she stepped inside, taking in the two women bent over a cutting table, heads together in discussion, and another woman over by a dress form, talking with a short, squat man while they fingered pieces of a pattern already attached to the form, moving them around and trying to decide on the best placement.

She might have been jumping to conclusions, but Lily assumed the man was Mr. Franklin. Sidling just a few feet more into the room, she leaned against one of the cutting tables and studied some of the patterns and sketches laid out there while she waited for them to conclude their business so she could get Nigel's update and report back to him before he sent out a search party.

The next week went by in such a blur, Lily could barely keep up. Nigel kept her running, skipping and hopping nearly twenty-four/seven.

Even once she clocked out and dragged herself to her home away from home, she had enough energy only to wash her face, change into pajamas and fall into bed for as much sleep as she could manage before the alarm went off and demanded she start all over again. Which left very little time for snooping and research.

She was gaining a whole new respect for secretaries, receptionists and personal assistants, to be sure.

And even though she was often left scrambling or faking her way through certain tasks, Nigel seemed pleased with her performance. So she supposed if the "design thing"—as her father sometimes called it—didn't work out, she could always fall back on this.

But she wasn't here to work hard and see that Ashdown Abbey's CEO looked good so the company could advance. She was here to save and avenge *her* company, and she was becoming increasingly frustrated with her inability to do that.

More determined than ever to find a moment or two to poke around for her own benefit, Lily stalked out of the elevator first thing that Monday morning and went straight to her desk. She'd arrived a tad early, and with luck, Nigel would run late this morning so she could dig into the California Collection files without fear of getting caught.

There had to be something somewhere that would lead her to the culprit she sought. She was especially interested in finding the original sketches that the California Collection was based off of. They should give her more of an indication of what inspired the collection than the later, more cleaned-up versions she'd already printed. They might even give her some hint of how someone got ahold of her designs in the first place to mimic them.

Of course, her lack of progress with her private little investigation wasn't the only dilemma she was facing. She also had a real private investigator breathing down her neck.

Reid McCormack had called to ask where she was and what she was up to. She'd found the question and his tone of voice peculiar, since he was the one who was supposed to be working for her.

But while she'd hired him to see what he could find out about Ashdown Abbey's theft of Zaccaro Fashions' designs from his vantage point in New York, she hadn't told him that she was planning to head for Los Angeles to do a bit of investigating on her own. She doubted he would approve, and suspected he would only try to talk her out of it.

She was right about the disapproval part. He'd been as livid as a person could be over the phone when it wasn't his place to tell her what to do—or what not to do—and he knew it.

He'd wanted to know *exactly* where she was and *exactly* what she was doing. Then when she'd refused to tell him, he'd informed her that "whatever she was up to," she obviously wasn't doing a very good job of it because her sister—Juliet—had just come to his office asking him to track her down.

Lily had gotten the feeling he was more put out at having to lie to one sister because the other was already a client than anything else. And maybe that he'd been blindsided, not even knowing client number one had hied off on her own until potential client number two came along wanting her sister treated like a missing person.

Though she'd hoped Juliet and Zoe would trust her to go off on her own for a while without needing specifics, she apparently hadn't done as efficient a job as she'd thought of making excuses, assuring her sisters she was fine and would return home soon.

It had taken a long time and quite a bit of verbal tap dancing to finally convince Mr. McCormack to pretend to take Juliet's case. Lily offered to compensate him for his time on both issues, if he didn't feel comfortable taking money from Juliet for doing nothing and lying to her to boot. And it was only until she could figure out what to say to her sisters that wouldn't send them into a tailspin. She promised to call Juliet herself as soon as she could so her family wouldn't continue to think she was missing or in trouble.

It went against McCormack's personal code of ethics, she could tell. She could almost imagine him grinding his teeth, flexing his fingers over and over again, and generally fighting the urge to reach through the phone line to strangle her.

Eventually, though...*eventually*, he agreed. About as enthusiastically as one might say, "Oh, yes—please give me a root canal without anesthetic!"

So now that was hanging over her head, as well. She hated thinking that her sisters were worried about her, especially when she'd left a note with the sole purpose of making sure they didn't.

But if she called to reassure them again and let them know everything was okay, they—namely Juliet—would want to know where she was and what was going on. They would be more curious and demanding than ever. And she had no idea what to tell them.

With a sigh, she dropped down into the chair at her desk and punched the power button on the computer. While it was booting up, she stowed her purse and tried to figure out where to begin. The sooner she could get this mess cleaned up and the mystery solved, the sooner she could go home and tell her sisters everything.

She tapped at the keyboard, searching folder and file names, looking specifically for anything related to the California Collection while keeping one eye on the elevator down the hall.

Though she wasn't sure it would lead anywhere, she discovered a folder that seemed to have all kinds of documents in it related to the California Collection. As quickly as she could, she slipped a blank flash drive into the USB port and hit Copy.

The file had just finished loading, and she was dropping the flash drive into her purse, when the door to Nigel's office opened directly behind her.

Her heart stopped. Literally screeched to a halt inside her chest as a lump of pure panic formed in her throat.

"Good. You're here," Nigel murmured at her back.

She knew she should respond, at least turn around and face him, but she felt glued in place, as frozen as an ice cube.

Thankfully, rather than getting upset or reprimanding her for her seeming lack of respect, he came to the edge of her desk. When the dark blue pinstripe of his dress slacks came into her peripheral vision, she finally managed to swallow, turn her head and lift her gaze to that of her boss.

As always, the sight of him made her mouth go dry. She'd thought that after working with him for a while, getting used to his quiet confidence and startling good looks, it would get easier to be around him. That she would suffer less and less of a lurch to her solar plexus each time they came in contact—which was more often, even, than she caught her own reflection in the restroom mirror.

Heart beating again—though not in any pattern a cardiologist would approve of—she licked her lips and made herself meet his eyes.

"Good morning," she said, glad her voice sounded almost human. "I didn't think you were in yet."

Understatement. She'd been watching the elevator like a mouse on the lookout for the cat of the house. Meanwhile, he'd been in his office the entire time. If he'd been a cat and she a mouse, she was pretty sure she'd be lunch by now.

"I was waiting for you to arrive," he said by way of answer.

Pushing aside a few items on the corner of her desk, he sat

down, letting one leg dangle. A nicely muscled leg, encased in fabric that tightened across his upper thigh.

Once again dragging her gaze to his face, she tried to take slow, shallow breaths until her internal temperature stopped climbing toward heatstroke levels.

"We need to talk about next week's show," he continued.

"All right." He'd sent her down to speak with Michael Franklin several more times, but to the best of her knowledge, everything was still running smoothly and on schedule.

"As you know, the show is in Miami."

She had known that, though she hadn't paid much attention one way or the other to the show's location.

"I have to be there, of course," he said in that slow, calm British way of his. Whatever point he was trying to make, he was taking his time getting there.

"The runway show itself is for charity, but buyers for many of our biggest accounts will be there, and we'll be taking orders for the designs throughout the event."

She nodded in understanding.

"I was hoping you might be willing to go along, as well."

Lily's eyes widened and she sat back in her seat, more than a little surprised by the request. They'd been discussing the show on and off since her arrival, but he'd never once hinted that he might want her to travel across the country with him.

"Do your personal assistants normally travel with you for this sort of thing?" she wanted to know.

He inclined his head. "Quite often."

"Then you're *telling* me I'll be going along, not asking if I'd like to," she said, making it more of a statement than a question.

"Not at all," he replied quickly, shifting on the corner of her desk. "I'd very much like you to accompany me, and it will be work-related, but I'll certainly understand if you have other plans."

She thought about it, trying to weigh the pros and cons and mentally map out the best plan of action where her true purpose for working at Ashdown Abbey was concerned.

On the one hand, she would probably make more progress and have more privacy to really dig around if she stayed behind while Nigel flew to Miami.

On the other, she *really* wanted to go. The idea of traveling with Nigel—no doubt first-class all the way—was intriguing enough. But the true thrill would be the up-close-and-personal experience of a live show with numerous famous designers sending their latest creations down the runway.

She could really benefit from watching how the organizers pulled it together and getting to see how such a large-scale event worked behind the scenes. Watching the clothes walk down the runway on professional and likely very sought-after supermodels. Rubbing elbows with some of the biggest names in the business—designers, buyers and the media alike. People who might one day take an interest in her own designs and help Zaccaro Fashions go national and then international.

Granted, she wouldn't be able to let any of them know who she really was or talk up her own work, but still… The contacts she might make, even under the guise of acting as Nigel's personal assistant, could serve her well down the road.

"It will be an overnight stay," Nigel added, breaking into her thoughts to give her even more to consider. "Through the weekend, actually. We'd fly out Thursday and return late Sunday night."

It was a substantial amount of time to be away from the Ashdown Abbey offices and attempt to carry out her pretense in public, but was she really going to say no? Pass up such an amazing opportunity? She would never be able to live with herself if she did, despite the fact that it would set back her "investigation" by that much longer.

"I'd love to go," she said after a minute of deep thought,

relieved when the words came out normally instead of sounding like those of a kid standing outside a bouncy castle.

"Brilliant," he exclaimed, slapping the palms of his hands against the tops of both thighs.

Then he rose and headed back toward his office. "You can check my schedule for the specific itinerary and the promotional materials for the show to get an idea of what you might like to pack. We'll work out the rest of the details later."

With that, he disappeared behind the solid wooden door separating their two work areas, leaving her alone once again.

Knowing he was there meant she couldn't risk doing any more snooping. Especially since she'd learned the scary way that he could pop out at any moment rather than relying on the phone or intercom to address her.

She should have been annoyed, but was suddenly too excited. Now she had Miami to look forward to.

It was a detour, and would definitely put her behind on the whole find-the-thief-and-get-the-heck-back-to-New York thing. But it was *Miami*, for heaven's sake.

Not just Miami the city. She'd been there several times before, as well as Key West and one ill-fated trip to Daytona Beach that her parents still didn't know about. And with luck, they never, ever would.

No, it was Miami during the event of the season—at least one of them, as far as the fashion world was concerned. A number of labels, not just Ashdown Abbey, would be flaunting their latest designs during what had become a very high-profile annual show.

The show itself—Fashion for a Cause—raised money for a different charity each year. This time, it was for a children's hospital. But the one-of-a-kind fashions that were shown at the event were then mass-produced and began to show up in retail outlets across the country and even around the world, depending on orders received during and soon after their debuts at the show.

Lily and her sisters were nowhere near the level one needed to achieve to participate in this type of event. She'd never even attended, though it had always been a distant, hopeful dream.

Now she had the chance to go. Not just as a member of the audience twelve rows back, but as Nigel Statham's girl Friday.

It was kind of a thrill. One that could quickly turn into a nightmare, if her true identity was discovered, but she was pretty sure it was worth the risk. Even after bumping into Bella Landry, no one had looked at her differently or started asking pointed questions about her presence, so she still seemed to be safe.

In fact, during a bit of digging into Bella's association with Ashdown Abbey, she'd actually learned that the young woman had just requested a bit of personal time from work. Lily intended to look into that, see if there was any more to it than sick days or a short vacation, but hadn't yet had the chance.

But with luck, her obscurity at the company would continue.

And she was almost giddy with anticipation about the charity show, so…yeah, she was going to take the chance. Wear giant sunglasses, introduce herself under her assumed name and hope for the best.

Too excited to simply sit there, she accessed Nigel's daily schedule and zipped ahead to the dates of the Miami trip. It looked as though they would be gone four days and three nights. Flying on the corporate jet. Staying in the luxury suites of the Royal Crown Hotel, one of the most expensive hotel chains on the East Coast.

As excited as she was about the runway show itself, she wondered if there would be time to slip away for a massage and spa treatment. Lord knew the amenities at the Royal Crown had to be amazing.

Like any good PA, she needed to start making a list. Of everything she would need to pack for herself, but also whatever business-related items she—or more specifically, Nigel— might need.

Clothing-wise, she knew she should continue wearing garments exclusively from the Ashdown Abbey lines. But even though they did some very nice summer and activewear pieces, nothing that she'd seen so far was as ideal for the sun and surf atmosphere of Miami as her own designs.

Her lightweight fabrics, bright colors and floral prints would be perfect, absolutely perfect for such a trip. And she had several just-perfect pieces with her in California.

The question was: Did she have the courage to take them along and wear them in front of Nigel? Would he notice they weren't from the Ashdown Abbey collections and wonder about her sudden switch? Or would he write it off as simply a female thing, knowing that women tended to have over-stuffed closets filled with every type of clothing for every type of occasion and very few were loyal to only one designer or label? If it looked good, fit well and—with luck—was on sale, a woman would buy it.

She sighed. It wasn't easy pretending to be a serious, buttoned-down executive secretary when all she wanted to do was rush home, kick off her shoes and blazer, let down her hair and run around packing sundresses and sandals for Miami as though it was a beach vacation rather than a short but significant business excursion.

Seven

The flight from Los Angeles to Miami was as long as it had ever been, but it passed by so smoothly, Lily couldn't have said whether it took three hours or thirty.

Nigel's—or rather, Ashdown Abbey's—corporate jet was incredible. She'd been on a Jet Stream before, but traveling with Nigel as his personal assistant was quite different from traveling with her parents and sisters for a business-slash-pleasure trip. Especially since that had been years ago, when she was much younger and harder to keep in her seat.

This time around, she was mature enough to appreciate the soft-as-butter leather seats, the interior that looked more like a *House Beautiful* living room than the inside of an airplane and the single flight attendant who appeared when she was needed, but was otherwise neither seen nor heard.

A car was waiting for them when they landed. The driver stood outside, ready to collect their bags and load them into the trunk after holding the rear door while they climbed inside the perfectly air-conditioned vehicle. Given Miami's balmy heat, Lily was grateful for the convenience.

Despite her continued misgivings, she'd opted for many of her own clothes for this particular excursion. She'd packed a couple of dark, formfitting suits, just in case, but had filled her luggage mostly with her own summer-inspired creations. Sleeveless maxi dresses that were feminine but elegant enough for the occasion, and a couple of linen skirts with light, flowy tops.

So far, Nigel didn't seem to mind her change of wardrobe, even though she'd been wearing a much darker, more subdued outfit the last time he'd seen her, and now she was sunflower bright in a short yellow dress and strappy cloth espadrilles.

The truth was, she felt much more like herself dressed this way. But since she needed to remember she wasn't *supposed* to be herself around Nigel Statham, that doing so could very well pose a problem.

She would have to be careful of what she said and how she acted—around everyone, not just Nigel—no matter what she was wearing.

When they arrived at the hotel, the driver pulled to a stop beneath the portico, then hurried around to open Nigel's door. Nigel stepped out and turned back to reach a hand in toward her.

Lily slid across the seat, putting her fingers in his as she climbed out, careful not to flash too much thigh as her dress rode up a few perilous inches.

The second they touched, a wave of heat washed over her, making the breath stutter in her chest just a bit. She tried to tell herself it was the heavy humidity hitting her as she stepped out of the air-conditioned interior of the car, but she didn't think that was true.

She'd been struck by too many unexpected hot flashes or zaps of electricity in his presence to believe they were geographical or weather-related. After all, she'd first noticed her reactions to his proximity in his office, and there had certainly been no natural humidity or direct sunlight beaming down on her there.

Avoiding Nigel's gaze in case he'd noticed the hitch in her breath, she moved away from the car while the driver and a bellman unloaded their luggage and stacked it on a waiting cart. When they finished, Nigel tipped the driver, then placed a hand at the small of her back as they followed the hotel employee inside.

Nigel had already given the bellman his name so that as they passed the registration desk, key cards were ready. All the bellman had to do was collect them, then lead the way directly to the bank of elevators that would take them to the presidential suites.

Before they'd left Los Angeles, Lily had told Nigel that just because he was staying in a luxury suite didn't mean she needed to. She could just as easily stay in a regular room, or perhaps a lower-level suite, then meet up with him whenever necessary.

Nigel wouldn't hear of it, however. He insisted that it would be more convenient to have her right next door. And besides, the reservations had already been made; no sense bothering with them now.

So even though she still thought it was an unnecessary expense, she was kind of looking forward to having an entire presidential suite to herself. It would be almost like having the entire loft back in New York to herself, which almost never happened.

The elevator carried them slowly upward, the doors opening with a quiet whoosh. The bellman stepped out with the rolling luggage cart and led them down the carpeted hallway.

At the end of it, he paused, slipped a key card into the coded lock, and let them into what was, indeed, a luxury suite.

The carpeting beneath their feet was thick and off-white, the furniture plush and chosen to match. French doors lined one entire length of the main room—facing the ocean, of course.

The view, even from across the room, was magnificent. Lily couldn't wait to get to her own suite so she could walk out onto the balcony and enjoy the soft breeze and salty sea air.

Remaining near the open door, Lily watched the bellman pull bags from the cart. When he reached for hers, though, she stepped forward and stopped him.

"Oh, no," she told him. "Those are mine. They go in my room."

The young man paused, hand still on the handle of her overnight bag. "Would you like me to carry them into the bedroom for you?" he asked, sounding slightly confused.

"No," she tried to clarify. "I'm staying in another suite. Next door, I believe."

Letting go of the bag, he checked the small paper envelope in his hand that had held the key card. "I'm sorry, ma'am, but I was only given the key to one room. Could your room be under another name?"

That drew her up short. Turning to Nigel, she cast him a questioning glance. His face was as blank as a sheet of paper.

Sensing the confusion in the room, the young man cleared his throat. "Let me call down to the front desk. I'm sure there was simply an oversight. We'll get it straightened out right away."

Crossing the room, he picked up the phone resting on the credenza beside a huge vase of freshly cut flowers. He spoke in low tones to whoever picked up on the other end.

A moment later, he hung up and turned back to them, his expression saying clearly that they weren't going to like whatever it was he had to say.

Lily's stomach tightened as she waited.

"I'm sorry, but the front desk only has one reservation under Mr. Statham's name, and none for you."

Lily exchanged another confused glance with Nigel. He shrugged a shoulder beneath the tailored lines of his charcoal suit coat.

"So we'll get a second room now. It's not a problem."

The bellman winced, and Lily knew what was coming even before he took a fortifying breath to speak. The fact that he refused to look either of them in the eye was another clear sign of impending doom.

"Unfortunately, we're fully booked. With the Fashion for a Cause event in town, just about all of the higher-end hotels are. I'm very sorry."

For several beats, no one in the room said a word, or moved a muscle for that matter. The bellman looked nervous. Nigel looked undecided. And Lily was pretty sure she looked plain old put-out.

But whatever mistake or misunderstanding had taken place, it certainly wasn't the poor hotel employee's fault.

With a sigh, Lily said, "It's all right. This suite is big enough for a family of twelve. I'm sure the two of us will be able to make do." She ended with what she hoped was a reassuring smile.

The bellman's chest dropped as he blew out a breath of relief. He thanked her profusely and finished taking their luggage off the cart, which he then rolled to the door.

Nigel followed behind, handing him what she hoped was a generous tip—hazard pay, and for nearly being sent into a panic attack—before he disappeared into the hallway.

"I'm sorry," Nigel said, strolling back to the center of the sitting area and stopping just a yard or so in front of her. "There must have been some sort of mix-up."

"I'd say so."

"My assistant normally makes these reservations for me."

She lifted a brow, silently asking if he seriously intended to blame this situation on her.

He almost—almost—cracked a smile.

"I don't usually invite my assistants to join me for these things, however, so when I asked you along, I apparently forgot to tell you we'd need to book a second room."

"Apparently," she replied drily.

Then, without another word, she turned and crossed to the large mahogany desk set against the far wall. Pulling open drawers, she found the phone book and started flipping through.

"What are you doing?" Nigel asked, moving a few feet closer.

"Looking for another hotel. A less ritzy one that might have a room available."

Reaching the desk, he leaned back against the corner nearest where she was standing, crossing his arms over his chest. "Why?"

She shot him a castigating glance. "I'm going to need somewhere to sleep. And as we've established, you only reserved one room, and this hotel is full up."

"I thought you said the suite was large enough for the both of us."

Lily kept her attention glued to the phone book, pretending her stomach hadn't just done a peculiar little somersault. In a low tone, she murmured, "I lied."

"Don't be silly," he said after a moment of tense silence.

Though she kept her gaze strictly on the yellow pages of the directory, his long, masculine fingers suddenly came into view, grasping the book at its center and plucking it from her hold.

Setting it flat on the desk behind him, he remained where he was, one palm flat on the phone book to hold it in place and stop her from snatching it back.

"There's no need for you to stay elsewhere when there's plenty of room here. Besides, as I told you before, having you at another hotel, possibly all the way across town, won't exactly be conducive to business. What if I need you for something?"

She narrowed her gaze, mimicking his earlier posture by folding her arms beneath her breasts and hitching back on one hip.

"You can call and I'll come over. I'm sure that all of the hotels in this area have working phone lines and taxis that travel in between," she told him flatly.

The specks of green in his hazel eyes flashed briefly, and Lily thought perhaps she'd gone too far. She was supposed to be his beck-and-call girl, after all, and should probably keep her sarcasm to a minimum.

"I'm afraid that's simply unacceptable," he told her, his already noticeable accent growing even thicker and more pronounced. "I don't pay you to show up when you can, I pay you to be there when I need you."

Score one for the prim-and-proper Brit, she thought.

Licking her lips, she said, "How much do you think you'll need me?" No sarcasm this time, just a straight-out question. "I was under the impression this trip would be on the light side, as far as work was concerned."

"Still," he responded without really addressing her question, "it would be better for us to stay in close proximity, just in case. Having you one door over would have been fine, but no farther than that."

Pushing away from the desk, he offered her an encouraging smile. "Don't worry, we'll make it work."

He returned to the pile of their combined luggage in the center of the room. Picking up his briefcase in one hand, laptop case in the other, he moved them to the coffee table in front of the sofa. It matched the eggshell hue of the carpet almost perfectly.

"I don't suppose this presidential suite has two bedrooms," she remarked, relaxing enough to take a few steps in his direction.

She kept her arms across her chest, though. Not tightly, but because she knew if she let her arms fall to her sides, she would only end up fidgeting.

Resigning herself to staying in the same suite as her boss was one thing. Staying in the same suite with this man, who just happened to be her temporary boss, but who also caused her mouth to go dry and other places to grow damp, was something else entirely. It made her nerves jump and dance beneath her skin.

"I don't believe so, though you're welcome to check."

More because it gave her a chance to put a little space between Nigel and herself than because she thought there was an actual chance at success, she strolled away to explore the rest of the suite.

For the most part, it had everything: a rather large kitchenette; dining and sitting areas; an entertainment area complete with television, DVD player, stereo and even a Wii; an officelike work area; and a balcony. There was a small bathroom in the main portion of the suite, but she assumed the bedroom had one of its own, as well.

And then there was the bedroom itself. Unless it somehow broke off into two separate sleeping quarters past the single doorway, there was only one. One spacious, beautiful, far-too-intimate bedroom.

Stepping over the threshold, she took in the totality of the room in a single glance. The enormous bed—a queen size, at least, but she suspected king—with the woven bamboo headboard. A low, matching bureau with an oval, almost seashell-shaped mirror attached. The small table and chair over by the sliding glass door leading to the balcony. And the open doorway that led to the master bath.

She'd been right about that, too. Apparently sparing no expense, the hotel had put in marble flooring, marble vanity, marble shower enclosure and marble tub surround. The bathtub and shower were also separate—one sunken, with jets that made her want to strip and climb in for a long, hot soak that very minute; the other the size of a compact car with an etched-glass enclosure and half a dozen nozzles arranged on the other three sides to send water spraying in all the right places.

Without a doubt, Nigel would be paying thousands of dollars a night for so many of these amazing amenities. And Lily was beginning to think they might just be worth it.

But the question remained—where was she supposed to sleep?

Nigel watched Lillian as she prowled around the suite, investigating the layout. He was afraid she would be disappointed by what she found—namely a single bed in a single bedroom off the main sitting area.

She stood in the doorway, studying the room. He tried to decipher her thought process by her body language—the line of her spine, set of her shoulders, the movements of her hands and fingers dangling at her sides. Unfortunately, she was giving nothing away.

After several long minutes, she turned back around. For a second, she stared at him, looking none too pleased. But then her gaze floated past him and her chest fell as she expelled a breath.

"I guess I can sleep on the sofa," she said, giving him a wide berth as she walked past him. "With luck, maybe it pulls out."

The sofa was long enough for a body to stretch out upon,

but didn't look comfortable enough that anyone would want to. Still, she started removing the cushions one by one, feeling around for a handle that would turn it into her bed for the night.

Nigel opened his mouth to stop her before the first cushion was even taken off, but found himself distracted by the sight of her shapely rear as she leaned over. He'd noticed her change in wardrobe this morning when he'd picked her up for their flight—from the dark, Ashdown Abbey business attire she'd been wearing around the office to a much lighter, brighter dress of unknown origins—but hadn't truly appreciated her current clothing choice until just now.

When she didn't find what she was looking for, she straightened with a huff, putting her hands on her hips. He could have gone on admiring the view all afternoon, but finally took pity on her.

"Nonsense," he said, causing her to spin around, cushions still askew. "There's no need for you to stay on the sofa."

She quirked a brow. "Do you expect me to sleep on the floor, then?"

He gave a snort of laughter. "Certainly not."

The quirked brow lowered as she narrowed both eyes, her mouth flattening into an angry slash. "If you say the bed is big enough for both of us," she all but growled, "I will not be responsible for my actions."

Her frown deepened when he chuckled at her obvious irritation.

"What kind of employer do you think I am?" he couldn't help but tease.

She didn't respond, simply waited, her expression still one of a woman who'd just unwittingly sucked on a lemon.

Crossing the space between them, he cupped her shoulders, giving her an encouraging "buck up" shake before letting his palms slide down her bare arms.

"Surely this suite is spacious enough for the two of us to manage without getting under each other's skin. And we can ask that a cot be brought up before nightfall, set it up out here. I'll use it," he added. "You can stay in the bedroom."

Some of the temper leached out of her features, softening the lines around her mouth and eyes.

"I can't make you do that. This is your suite. You should be able to enjoy the bed."

He had half a mind to inform her that he'd enjoy it best if she joined him there. He hadn't even seen the bed in question yet, but he'd stayed in enough luxury suites to have a pretty good idea of just how expansive and inviting it would be.

Surely enough room for two to sleep comfortably. And more than enough room for them to do much more than that.

Though he knew it was a bad idea all around, he indulged himself for a moment in fantasies of having her naked and in his arms. Of rolling around on slick satin sheets with her. Of having her beneath him, above him, plastered to him by their own perspiration and mutual passion.

His errant thoughts alone caused tiny beads of sweat to break out along his brow and upper lip. He could only imagine the physiological response he might suffer from full-on body-to-body contact of a carnal nature with her.

Which was a problem. A rather large, obvious problem, if she'd cared to glance down and notice as much. Thankfully, she didn't.

But hadn't he sat down just last week and given himself a stern talking-to? Hadn't he learned his lesson with Caroline?

Lessons, plural, he reminded himself now. Thanks to his ill-fated affair with Caroline, he'd learned not to get involved with women who were even loosely involved in the fashion industry, and certainly not one with whom he worked. His own personal assistant would be even worse.

He'd also learned that it was probably wise to avoid any

sort of romantic attachment to American women altogether. Especially when he was trying to get Ashdown Abbey firmly established here in the States. And when his father was breathing down his neck about the delay in that success.

For those reasons and probably hundreds more, Lillian needed to remain off-limits. He couldn't deny that he would enjoy a quick, lusty romp with her. No warm-blooded male could without being accused of lying through his teeth.

But better to lie on a too-short, too-narrow cot in the middle of the sitting room, picturing Lillian on the other side of the bedroom door, than to make one of the biggest mistakes of his life.

No amount of pleasure was worth the destruction crossing that line could bring. Or so he tried to convince himself.

"It's no problem, truly," he told her, wanting to move things away from the hazardous territory his thoughts were treading upon.

Not giving her a chance to protest further, he grabbed her bags and carted them into the other room, setting them at the foot of the bed. When he turned, she was behind him, watching his every move.

"Go ahead and unpack, settle in. I'll call down for a cot and ask them to have it delivered by nightfall. In the meantime, I have a business dinner at seven o'clock with the head of one of our most important accounts. I'd like you to come along, if you're feeling up to it."

After a short pause in which she didn't respond, he added, "I'll understand if you're tired from the flight and would prefer to stay in."

"No," she responded quickly, straightening in the doorway. "I'd love to go."

He gave a sharp nod. "Excellent. I'll leave you to freshen up and get ready. We'll leave in an hour, if that's all right."

"Of course."

They both started forward at the same time, she toward her luggage and he toward the bedroom door. Their arms brushed as they passed one another, a jolt of electricity, awareness, summer heat pouring through him. It made him catch his breath, swallow hard and wonder if she was suffering the same disturbing effect…or if he was the only one doomed to spend the weekend drenched in sexual frustrations thicker than the Miami heat.

Eight

Dinner their first night in Miami. Breakfast in the room—but set out so beautifully and served so elegantly that they might as well have been at a five-star restaurant. A business luncheon. And then, the evening before the Saturday morning fashion show, a cocktail party where a handful of those involved in the show—designers, buyers, planners, executives—could rub elbows and size up the competition in a friendly, noncompetitive atmosphere.

Lily had known the schedule ahead of time, but hadn't realized how busy or rushed it would actually be.

True to his word, Nigel slept on a cot in the middle of the sitting room of the luxury suite. The roll-away bed looked completely out of place and—to Lily, at least—flashed like a giant neon sign that spelled G-U-I-L-T every time she laid eyes on it.

She didn't have any other ideas or a better solution to their awkward one bed/two bodies predicament, but it still wasn't right that she'd kicked him out of the bedroom of his very own suite.

Guiltiness aside, however, she had to admit she was more than a little relieved to have a door to close and a separate room to escape to each time they returned from yet another business-related outing.

She didn't fear for her safety, exactly—at least not physically. She feared for her sanity and her best intentions.

The longer she was with Nigel, the more she admired him. The more attractive she found him. The more often she caught herself zoning out to simply stare at him, admiring the line of his jaw, the slight bow of his mouth, the way his lips quirked when he was amused or his brows rose when he was curious or intrigued.

What sent her skittering into the bedroom so often under one flimsy excuse or another, though, was the problem she was having regulating her temperature. Oh, how she wished she could blame it on the Florida heat and humidity. Such a nice, handy reason for the hot flashes that kept assailing her at the most inconvenient moments.

But it was hard to point fingers at the weather when the worst of her symptoms seemed to hit mostly indoors, when they were surrounded by comfortable-verging-on-chilly air conditioning.

Which led her to only one terrifying conclusion: it wasn't her current location causing her so many problems...it was Nigel himself.

It was her body, her hormones, her apparently too-long-dormant, ready-to-party-like-it-was-1999 libido kicking up and screaming for attention.

Why couldn't her sex drive have come out of hibernation while she was still in New York? There were men there. Handsome, funny, available men. Or so she'd been led to believe by her sister, who seemed to find a different one to go home with every other night.

But seriously, how hard would it have been to—in crude terms—get laid before flying to Los Angeles, where she was pretending to be someone else entirely? Why had she been living practically like a nun the past several months, only to meet Nigel and have her inner pole dancer wake up wanting to shake her moneymaker?

Oh, yes, she was in trouble. Pretending to be a mild-mannered personal assistant by day, tossing and turning and fighting the urge to throw open the door and invite Nigel to join her in the big lonely bed by night.

That was why she made herself scarce at every opportunity. That was why she turned the lock on the bedroom door each night before she climbed into the king-size bed.

Not to keep him out, but to keep herself in.

But with every tick of the clock, every sleepless hour that passed, Lily was losing the battle. The thoughts that spiraled through her head made her hot and restless and frustrated.

Then she would wake up still tired and out of sorts, doing her best to get her errant emotions under control while she dressed and got ready. Thinking she was back to normal and fully prepared to face Nigel again, she would open the bedroom door…and find him standing there, looking like the answer to the prayers of single women around the world. Or he would turn at the sound of the door opening and her heart would screech to a stop, leaving her chest empty and her throat burning.

She was amazed she managed to stumble her way through the day without doing something truly embarrassing like drooling, weeping or collapsing at his feet in a puddle of needy, pathetic female.

Nigel never showed signs of suspecting her inner turmoil,

so she must have been doing a decent job of hiding it. Thank goodness.

Now here she was, holed up once again in the suite bedroom that had caused all of her problems to begin with. And Nigel was out there, once again, waiting for her.

They had time yet before they needed to leave for the pre-show cocktail party, but as cowardly as she knew it was, she couldn't bring herself to spend their in-between time out in the main sitting area.

She'd tried, early on in their stay. They'd talked business, and Nigel had filled her in on what to expect from the weekend and various events they would be attending. But the longer they talked, the more they ran out of things to say, and the more awkward the lengthy pauses became.

Awkward and...tension-filled. As though the air was slowly being sucked out of the room, replaced by a growing electrical current. It would cause her chest to grow tighter by degrees and goose bumps to break out along her skin.

So over and over again, she retreated to the bedroom and relative safety.

She wondered if Nigel was beginning to get suspicious. But even more, she wondered if he felt any of the sizzling awareness, the building attraction that assailed her every time they were alone together.

A part of her hoped he did. After all, she shouldn't be the only one suffering and running for cover like a nervous squirrel.

A bigger part of her, though, hoped that he didn't. Uncontrollable lust and a passionate fling with the man who was supposed to be her boss but was really a possible archnemesis was something she so sincerely didn't need.

It would be much better to suffer in silence, even if her continued run-and-hide routine was becoming increasingly difficult to pull off, while he remained completely oblivious.

At least tonight they would be surrounded by other people. The party would keep them busy, talking and shaking hands, drinking and nibbling on hors d'oeuvres. By the time it was all over with and they made their way back to the hotel, they would both be exhausted and more than ready to go their separate ways for a good night's sleep. Or as many hours as they could squeeze in before having to get up and go to the fashion show, anyway.

She was walking around in one of the hotel's soft, fluffy terry-cloth robes, fresh from the shower and lining up her underthings before beginning to dress, when there was a light tap at the door. Her heart lurched, mouth going dry, because she knew it could only be Nigel.

Swallowing hard, she took a deep breath and tiptoed over, checking the front of her robe to be sure she wasn't flashing too much bare skin before pulling the door open a crack.

As expected, Nigel stood on the other side. He was still dressed in the clothes he'd been wearing all day, but had removed the suit jacket and tie and opened the first few buttons of his dress shirt, giving her a rather mouthwatering peek at the smooth chest beneath.

Through the crack of the door, he looked at her, his gaze starting at her still-damp hair and skating down the line of her terry-wrapped body to the tips of her painted toes, then back up. His eyes glittered as they met hers, sending ripples of desire to every dark nook and cranny of her being.

Her pulse kicked up and she tried to swallow again, but found that both her throat and her lungs refused to function.

Thankfully, he saved her from choking on her own words and sounding like a strangled crow by filling the uncomfortable silence and speaking first.

"Lillian," he began. "Sorry to disturb you, but I have a small request."

He sounded so serious, she immediately straightened,

shifting from vulnerable woman getting dressed to personal assistant on the alert in the blink of an eye.

"Of course," she responded. "What do you need?"

"Would it be too much to ask that you wear something special this evening?"

Her brow rose. Images of lacy teddies and garter belts with silken stockings filled her head. Surely he couldn't mean *that* sort of "special."

From out of nowhere, around the other side of the door-jamb, he revealed a long, hunter green garment bag with the Ashdown Abbey logo embroidered in the upper right-hand corner.

"This is one of the gowns from the line we'll be showing tomorrow. I was hoping I could talk you into wearing it to-night as a bit of a sneak peek for our competition."

He shot her a lopsided grin, accompanied by a wicked wink, and she couldn't help smiling in return.

"I'll be happy to try," she told him, reaching toward the top of the garment bag where he held it by a thick, satin-wrapped hanger. "But I'm not exactly a supermodel. It may not fit."

His gaze flitted down her fluffy white form once again, as though he could see straight through the robe to the body beneath.

"I think you'll be fine. We don't design for stick-thin women to begin with, even when it comes to runway shows, and this dress in particular is a very accommodating design."

"All right," she said with a small nod.

She'd brought one of her own elegant maxi dresses with her that would have been perfectly acceptable for a cocktail party, but she had to admit she was curious to see what Nigel wanted her to wear. And it was more than a little flattering to be asked to model one of Ashdown Abbey's brand-new, as-yet-unseen designs in front of other designers and associ-ates for the first time.

She would rather be showing off her *own* creations, of course, but since she wouldn't be able to reveal that they were her designs, anyway…well, beggars couldn't be choosers.

Still standing there, dress in hand, bedroom door open, she wasn't quite sure what else to say. It didn't seem right to simply slam the door in Nigel's face, even though she was eager to peel open the garment bag and see what lay inside.

Finally, he said, "I'll give you a few minutes. Let me know if you have any problems."

With that, he took a step back, but seemed reluctant to move away. And she was equally reluctant to close the door, shutting herself in again. But they did have a party to get to.

"I'll only be a few minutes," she murmured.

"Take your time. The limo won't be here to pick us up for an hour yet."

She disappeared back inside her luxurious little Girl Cave as he turned and headed off to get ready himself. Hanging the garment bag on the open armoire door, she slid the center zipper all the way down and peeled back the sides.

It was almost like scratching a lottery ticket. She held her breath, slowly revealing the gown beneath.

As lottery tickets *and* designer gowns went, it was a winner. Stunning. Gorgeous. Awe-inspiring. And for her, just a bit envy inducing.

The sheer, champagne-colored chiffon shimmered in the light and with every movement, no matter how slight.

The ruched bodice ran at an angle to the single beaded shoulder strap, about two inches wide, leaving the other shoulder entirely bare. A wide swath of the same jewels from the shoulder made up a belted waistline of sorts.

From the waist down, the chiffon flowed in angled layers over the same-colored charmeuse all the way to what she assumed would be the floor once she put it on.

Suddenly, she was both excited and nervous at the pros-

pect of modeling it. Not surprisingly, the dress was beautiful. But she hadn't worn anything this fancy in a very, very
long time. And now, not only was she being asked to dress
up like she was attending a royal wedding, but she would be
expected to "sell" another designer's work.

Knowing she didn't have a choice, she hurried back to the
bathroom to finish with her hair and makeup, then returned
to the main room and shrugged out of the terry-cloth robe.
Even though she'd planned for a cocktail party and packed
accordingly, the underthings she'd brought didn't quite suit
the gown she would now be wearing.

If Nigel had shown her the dress ahead of time, she probably would have taken a quick shopping trip for something
a bit sexier. Stockings instead of nylons, perhaps, and a bra
and panty set the same color as the gown.

Luckily, some of the bras and panties she had with her were
pale enough not to be seen through the champagne material.
And though the bra wasn't strapless, the straps were able to
be rearranged or removed completely. She would just have
to hope it stayed up and in place all night.

Moments later, she was reaching for the gown, turning it
around and searching for the narrow hidden zipper that ran
the length of the back. Time to see if the design was as for-
giving as Nigel claimed.

Stepping into the pool of material, she drew it up and
slipped the single strap over her left shoulder. The bodice
settled over her breasts and the cups of her bra, the rest of the
gown falling into place from her midriff down.

Reaching around, she clutched the two sides of the dress
at the back in one hand and held them together. The fit might
be snug, but she thought it would work. Especially if she held
her stomach in most of the time.

She looked okay, too, judging by her reflection in the bureau mirror. Provided the dress stayed in one piece once she got it zipped up. Which she couldn't quite manage on her own.

Butterflies unfurling at the base of her belly, she moved to the bedroom door and opened it, slowly and quietly. Venturing into the other room, she glanced around, searching for Nigel. She might not *want* to ask for his help, but she kind of needed it.

But the sitting room was empty.

Still holding the gown closed behind her with one hand, she strolled farther into the room, checking the balcony and wondering if he'd left the suite entirely for some reason.

Then she heard a click and turned just as he stepped out of the guest bath looking like a million bucks. Maybe one point eight.

He was wearing a tuxedo. Just a plain black tuxedo, the same as men had been wearing for decades.

And yet Lily would be willing to bet he looked better in it than any other man in the history of tuxedos. The word *scrumptious* came to mind. As well as *delectable* and—as Zoe might say—*hunkalicious.*

The midnight-black jacket and slacks fit him like a glove. If they hadn't been tailored specifically for him, it was the finest bit of off-the-rack sewing she'd ever seen.

His sandy-brown hair was combed back, slightly wavy, but every strand in place.

And the tie at his throat…well, there was something about that tight, classic bow and the gold cuff links at his wrists that made her want to drop her arm, let the gown drop to the floor, and stalk forward to start peeling him out of his own uptight party wear.

The thought stopped her cold. Made her give herself a mental shake and stern reminder that lusting after the boss was a bad, bad idea.

Of course, on the heels of that came the notion that she

wouldn't mind being a bad girl. Just for a little while. And only with Nigel.

His mind may have been wandering down the same wicked path, because his eyes snapped with flecks of green fire the minute he saw her. His gaze raked her from head to toe, and she could have sworn a tiny muscle flexed along his jaw.

She drew a deep breath, which caused the bodice of the not-yet-zipped dress to slide down a notch. Pinning it in place with her only remaining free hand, she cleared her throat and smiled weakly.

"I need a little help," she murmured.

He raised a brow, his attention still glued to her lower-than-intended décolletage.

By way of explanation, she turned, giving him her back and showing the long, open rear of the gown.

She felt rather than saw him move behind her and grasp the small tab of the zipper near the base of her spine. In a slow, gentle glide, he pulled it up.

When it was high enough, she dropped the arm that had been holding the two sides together and moved it instead to her nape, where she brushed aside her loose hair. The back of the dress only reached her shoulder blades, but better safe than sorry.

As he reached the top of the zipper, his knuckles brushed her bare skin, sending shivers rippling across her body in every direction. She braced herself and tried not to let that shiver show, but she felt it all the way to her toes.

Long seconds ticked by while she stood unmoving, not blinking, not even daring to breathe. And then Nigel stepped back, his hands falling away from her bare flesh.

Relief washed through her…but so did regret.

"There," he said, the single word coming out somewhat gruff.

Lily let go of her hair and turned again to face him. This time, his gaze seemed to be taking in the detail of the gown.

"Lovely," he told her with a nod of approval. "As I knew it would be."

Lifting his eyes to hers, he asked, "What do you think?"

"It's beautiful," she answered honestly, smoothing a hand over the front of the dress and then fluffing it a bit to show the ethereal layering of the skirt. It flowed and fell like angels' wings, almost as though it wasn't there at all.

"And how does it feel?" Nigel wanted to know. "Comfortable enough to wear for the evening?"

"I think so," she told him. It was rather nice of him to ask. Most employers—most men, for that matter—wouldn't bother.

"I'll need to find some jewelry and shoes that go with the dress," she added, "but it fits better than I would have expected."

"Ah," he said, holding up his index finger and offering a crooked grin. "I believe I can help with that."

Leading her over to the sofa in the middle of the room, he began opening boxes that had been stacked across its narrow length and pulling out bits of tissue paper from around whatever the boxes held.

"I had them send over some of the footwear for tomorrow's show. All of the shoes for the line are similar in style, and we always make sure to have extras on hand, but I wasn't sure of your size."

He stepped back, gesturing for her to take a look, pick out whatever she needed. Brushing past him in her bare feet, she peeked and found an array of gorgeous, very expensive footwear.

They were, indeed, all very similar, making her even more curious to see the entire line. She wanted to know what designs Ashdown Abbey had created to go with all of these shoes...or vice versa, actually.

Checking sizes, she chose a pair of strappy gold open-toed heels and balanced on the arm of the sofa to slip them on. Even before she stood up again and glanced down to see how they looked with the dress and her painted nails peeping out, she knew they would be perfect with the gown.

Lifting her head, she found Nigel's eyes on her. Intense. Blazing. The air caught in her lungs and refused to budge.

Seconds ticked by, then minutes. Finally, he cleared his throat and reached for something else amidst the boxes and loose tissue paper.

"This should complete the look nicely," he said, flipping open the lid of a large, flat, velvet-lined box.

Inside was a breathtaking necklace and earring set. Champagne diamonds in exquisite gold settings. And if they were real—which something told her they were—they had to be worth a small fortune.

Plucking the earrings from their bed of black velvet, he dropped them into her palm. Then he removed the necklace and stepped around her to stand at her back.

Lifting the sweep of loose, wavy curls she'd worked so hard on, she waited for him to finish with the fastener before dropping her hair and pressing her fingers to her throat to touch and straighten the main pendant and surrounding web of gems.

"This is a lot of expensive fashion. Are you sure you trust me to wear it out of the suite?" she asked somewhat shakily, only half teasing.

"You aren't planning to run off with it all at the stroke of midnight, are you? Like Cinderella," he teased in return.

She certainly felt like Cinderella. A young woman pretending to be someone other than who she really was, dressed to the nines to attend a grand ball with a man who definitely qualified as a Prince Charming.

She only hoped her true identity didn't become known as the clock struck midnight, as he said. That might possibly be worse than running off with thousands, maybe hundreds of thousands of dollars' worth of Ashdown Abbey property.

Since she had no intention of doing the latter, she knew she was safe on that count. It was the former she needed to worry about. But with luck, it wouldn't be an issue tonight or at any time on this trip.

She hoped not once they returned to Los Angeles, either, but one thing at a time. First she needed to get through this evening. Then tomorrow's fashion show…then the remainder of their short stay in Miami…then their return to Los Angeles… She would deal with the rest after that.

"I'm no Cinderella," she said by way of answer.

"No," Nigel responded.

The single word came out short and clipped, drawing her attention to his face and the hard glint of his hazel eyes.

"Cinderella could never look so lovely in this gown or these jewels," he added more softly.

Lily's heart stuttered in her chest. Okay, that was definitely more than a simple compliment. That was…a come-on. A warning. A promise of things to come.

She knew now, without a shadow of a doubt, that Nigel felt at least a fraction of the attraction to her that she felt toward him. The lust she'd been feeling, the shocks of static electricity whenever they were in the same room together, were *not* one-sided.

Which was good. It was nice to know she wasn't going crazy or nursing an awkward schoolgirl crush on the captain of the football team whom she would never in a million years have a shot with.

But it was bad, too. Because while she might be able to

keep a lid on her own out-of-control emotions and baser instincts, she couldn't be sure that lid wouldn't come flying off
in the face of his pent-up passions if he decided to point them
in her direction and throw caution to the wind.

Already her mouth was growing dry, her hands damp. Her
pulse had kicked up to a near-arrhythmia pace. And every
other portion of her body was heating at an alarming rate,
sending a flush of inappropriate longing across her face and
her upper body.

If Nigel noticed her state of distress, he didn't comment.
Instead, he held an arm out, offering his elbow.

"Shall we?"

Saved by the RSVP and waiting limousine, she thought,
releasing a small, relieved breath.

"Yes, thank you," she replied, wrapping her hand around
his firm forearm.

They glided to the door so smoothly their movements
might have been choreographed. If they could keep up such
astounding synchronicity, Lily thought they might, just *might,*
be able to pull this off.

Not only her pretense of being someone she wasn't, but of
hiding the sexual tension that—to her mind, at least—rolled
off the pair of them in waves.

But while the outside world was likely to see merely a
very handsome, rich and successful businessman escorting
his fair-to-middling female assistant to an industry function,
she was almost painfully conscious of the heat from Nigel's
body burning through the fabric of his tuxedo jacket to all
but scorch her fingertips. Of the rapid beat of her heart behind the bodice of her borrowed gown. Of every second that
ticked by when she could think of nothing but being alone
with Nigel in a very naked, nonprofessional capacity.

Nine

Hours later, the noise and crowd of the cocktail party behind them, Lily sat beside Nigel in the rear of the limo as it carried them back to the Royal Crown. Her eyes were closed, her head resting against the plush leather seat. To say she was tired would be a tremendous understatement.

As though reading her mind, Nigel's knuckles brushed her cheek, tucking a strand of hair behind her ear.

"Tired?" he asked.

His touch was featherlight and possibly one-hundred-percent innocent, but still it had her sucking in a breath and fighting to maintain her equilibrium.

Rolling her head to the side, she forced her eyes open, braced for the impact of meeting his gaze. It still hit her like a steamroller.

Knowing she wouldn't be able to form coherent words to respond to his query, she merely nodded.

One corner of his mouth tipped up in an understanding

smile. "You were incredible tonight," he told her in a soft voice that washed over her like warm honey.

"You look amazing," he continued. "Better than any model we could have hired to showcase this design. And the way you are with people…you're a natural. You had everyone at the party eating out of your hand. The men especially. Well, the straight ones, at any rate," he added with a teasing wink.

Despite her weariness, she couldn't help but return his grin of amusement. "I'm glad you approve. I don't mind telling you I was nervous about tonight. I didn't want to embarrass you *or* do anything in this beautiful gown to put a damper on tomorrow's show."

"Not possible," he said with a sharp shake of his head. "You were…extraordinary. As I knew you would be."

His heartfelt compliment made her blush and filled her with unexpected pleasure. She shouldn't be happy that he was so impressed with her performance tonight. She should be annoyed. Sorry that she'd helped to bolster his or Ashdown Abbey's reputation in any way.

But she *was* pleased. Both that she'd maintained her ruse as a personal assistant, and that she'd done well enough to earn Nigel's praise.

She was candid enough with herself to admit that the last didn't have as much to do with his standing as her "boss" as with him as a man.

"Thank you," she murmured, her throat surprisingly tight and slightly raw.

"No," he replied, once again brushing the back of his hand along her cheek. "Thank *you*."

And then, before she realized what he was about to do, he leaned in, pressing his mouth to hers.

For a moment, she remained lax, too stunned to move or respond. But his lips were so soft and inviting, and she'd been imagining what it would be like to kiss him for so long…

With a low mewl of longing, she shifted into his arms, bringing her own up to grasp his shoulders. She opened to him, letting her lips part, her body melt against his and everything in her turn liquid.

Nigel groaned, pulling her to him with even more force, his wide palm cupping the base of her spine while his tongue traced the line of her mouth, then delved inside at her clear invitation.

The world fell away while they ate at each other, devoured each other, groped each other like a couple of randy teenagers.

A million reasons why they shouldn't be doing this clamored through her head. But those doubts and fears were little more than a low-level hum behind the loud roar of desire, yearning, need.

Despite the regrets she might suffer later, right now she didn't care. She couldn't remember ever being kissed this way, ever wanting a man as much as she wanted Nigel Statham.

He was danger and sex and exotic intrigue on two legs, with a bone-tingling British accent to boot. How women didn't adhere themselves to him like dryer lint throughout the day she didn't know.

How amazing was it, then, that he seemed to be attracted to her? Seemed to want her?

Maybe he put the moves on all of his personal assistants. Maybe one of his goals while he was in the United States was to shag, as he might say, as many American girls as possible.

If that was the case, she expected to be really annoyed later on. At the moment, however, she was more than willing to be just another notch on this handsome Brit's bedpost.

While one hand kneaded the small of her back, his other swept up to the bodice of the couture gown, cupping her breast, stroking through the material. Despite the thick ruching and bra beneath, her nipples beaded, drawing a moan of desire from deep in her throat.

Nigel answered with a groan of his own, increasing the pressure of his mouth against her lips. There was barely a breath of air between them, but even that was too much. And as he thrust his tongue around hers over and over, she met him with equal ferocity, sucking, licking, drinking him in.

He smelled of the most wonderful cologne. Something fresh and clean, with a hint of spice. Whatever the brand, she was sure it was expensive. And worth every penny, since it made her want to lick him from clavicle to calf, inhale him in one shuddering gulp, absorb him into her own skin like sunshine on a warm summer day.

But if he smelled good, he tasted even better. Warm and rich, like the wine he'd been sipping all evening at the party, with a hint of the whiskey he'd downed toward the end. She didn't even particularly care for whiskey, but if it meant drinking it from his lips and the tip of his tongue, she could easily drown in the stuff on a regular basis.

Nigel's hand was trailing down her side, sweeping the curve of her breast, her waist, her hip and slowly inching the long skirt of the dress upward when the limousine came to a smooth but noticeable halt. A second later, the driver's side door opened and Nigel pulled back with a fiercely muttered, "Bollocks."

Quickly, before the fog of passion had even begun to clear from her brain, he straightened her gown and the lines of his own tuxedo, taking a moment to swipe lipstick from both her mouth and his just as the lock on the rear door of the limo clicked.

By the time the door swung all the way open to reveal the driver standing there waiting for them, everything looked completely normal. Professional, even. Nigel and Lily were sitting at least a foot apart, canted away from each other on the wide bench seat, as though they hadn't even been speaking, let alone groping one another like horny octopi.

Without a word, Nigel exited the car, then helped her out.

Nigel thanked the driver, passed him a generous tip and escorted Lily into the main entrance of the hotel. They passed through the lobby, her heels clicking on the marble floor until they reached the elevators. Inside, they were silent, facing the doors and standing inches apart, even though they were alone in the confined space.

When they reached their floor, Nigel gestured for her to step out ahead of him, then took her elbow as they moved quietly down the carpeted hallway. The perfect gentleman. The perfectly polite employer with no lascivious thoughts whatsoever about the assistant who was staying in his suite with him.

With some distance now from that amazing kiss in the limousine, Lily wasn't sure what to think or how to feel.

Did she want to pick up where they'd left off as soon as they got into the suite? A shiver assaulted her at the very thought.

Or did she want to put the kiss behind her? Chalk it up to the heat of the moment and go their separate ways once they got inside? That thought made her a little sad, which surprised her.

Reaching the door, she waited for Nigel to slide the key card through the lock and decided to play it by ear.

If he began to ravish her the minute the door closed behind them, she would go limp and let it happen. No doubt enjoying every step of the way.

If he returned to his usual quiet and respectfully reserved self, not coming anywhere near her again…she would do the same. It might even be for the best, regardless of how much she would mourn the loss of his lips, the taste of him on the tip of her tongue.

As she entered the suite ahead of him, her heartbeat picked up, the tempo echoing in her ears as her anticipation grew. But he didn't grab her the second the door closed behind them, didn't push her against the wall and begin the ravishment she'd been fantasizing about. They stepped into the sitting room. Perfectly polite. Perfectly civilized.

The sound of Nigel clearing his throat made her jump. She turned slowly to face him, disappointed when she didn't find him stalking toward her, desire burning in his hazel-green eyes.

"I feel as though I should apologize for what happened in the car," he murmured in a low, slow tone of voice.

Her heart plummeted. Well, she supposed that answered the question of what he thought about the kiss, didn't it? She tried not to be offended—hadn't she already admitted to herself that fooling around with her boss-slash-possible enemy was a bad idea?—but couldn't help being slightly hurt. After all, to her, the kiss had been one step away from spontaneous combustion.

"But quite frankly," he continued when she didn't respond, "I'm not that sorry."

Her eyes widened, locking with his. What she saw there was the same passion she'd experienced in the limo. The same need, the same longing…but banked to a slow burn rather than a blazing inferno.

"Which makes what I have to ask next rather awkward."

Lily swallowed, the blood in her veins going thick and hot.

"Would you mind stepping out of your gown?"

She blinked. That wasn't so bad. A little odd, yes, but only because she would have expected him to be closer when he made the request. Maybe whisper it in her ear or want to strip it from her body himself.

But if watching her disrobe was part of his fantasy, she could certainly comply.

And then he went and ruined whatever small thread of fantasy had been forming in *her* head.

"The dress and shoes need to be returned before tomorrow's show."

"Oh." Yes, of course. The fashion show. She was walking around in one of its borrowed designs.

"Sure," she said, fumbling for both words and clear thoughts. "Just…give me a minute."

Feeling unsure and uncoordinated, she turned toward the bedroom and crossed the distance with as much dignity as she could muster while kicking herself for being seven kinds of fool.

Closing the door behind her, she moved robotically, removing the necklace, earrings, bracelet and ring, and setting them on top of the bureau. Then she toed off the strappy ice-pick heels. And though she nearly dislocated her shoulder doing it, she managed to grasp the tab of the gown's zipper at her back and tug it all the way down. Stepping out of the dress, she returned it to its satin hanger inside the garment bag, then zipped that closed.

Since she couldn't go back out to the rest of the suite in her underwear, she covered herself with the same fluffy hotel robe as earlier, which she'd left lying at the foot of the bed.

Gathering all of Nigel's borrowed items, she strode back into the sitting room. He was standing exactly where she'd left him, but she refused to meet his gaze. She'd had quite enough humiliation and emotional up-and-down, back-and-forth for one night, thank you very much.

Walking to the sofa, she draped the garment bag over the arm, dropped the shoes back in their tissue-paper-lined box, and laid the collection of pricey jewelry on the low coffee table.

"There you go," she told him, her tone clipped, even to her own ears. And still she wouldn't look at him. "Thank you again for letting me wear them tonight. It was a privilege."

Truth. It *had* been a privilege…right up until the moment it became pain.

With that, she turned and marched back to the bedroom, spine straight, head held high. She remained that way until after she'd closed and locked the door. Until she'd shed the robe and her underthings, leaving them in a pile on the bathroom floor. Until she'd stepped into the hot spray of the shower, letting the sharp beads of water pummel her, pound her, drown her in mindless sensation.

Only then did she let go of her rigid control, let oxygen back into her lungs and the hurt into her soul.

Only then did she crumble.

Well, that didn't go quite as he'd planned. And he felt like a total prat.

The kiss in the limousine had been anything but forgettable. There had been moments when he'd thought he might implode from the sensations that assailed him at the mere touch of Lillian's lips against his own.

It had taken every ounce of self-control he possessed to pull away from her when the car stopped, and to get them both set to rights before their driver came around to open his door and got more than an eyeful. Thank goodness he'd retained enough of his senses to even notice the slowing of the vehicle.

The walk into the hotel and ride up in the lift had been another agonizing test of his control. He'd wanted nothing more than to turn on her once the doors slid closed, press her up against the wall, and continue from where they'd left off. Kissing, caressing, fogging the glass…or in this case, the mirrored walls.

Every step down the narrow pathway to their suite, he'd imagined what he would do to her as soon as they were shut safely inside. Alone and away from prying eyes.

But he couldn't very well pounce on her the minute the

door swung shut, could he? She might have thought him a sex-crazed maniac. Or worse, believed that whether or not she acquiesced might impact her job.

Nigel muttered a colorful oath. The *last* thing he needed was a sexual-harassment complaint brought against him or the company.

But more than that, he didn't want to be *that* fellow—the one who flirted with his secretary, made her believe that there might be recompense if she went along with his advances... and the unemployment line if she didn't.

And he *never* wanted Lillian to think that of him. Professional status and reputation be damned. His attraction to her was genuine—if ill conceived—and he wanted her to know that. He wanted her to be genuinely attracted to him, as well. Where was the fun in any of this if she wasn't?

He'd thought he was being witty and smooth by asking her to remove the dress for tomorrow's show. True, he did need to get it back so that it would be ready and waiting for its respective model by morning.

Inside his addled and obviously not very intelligent mind, however, he'd imagined her slinking out of the dress and shoes—either right there in front of him or in the privacy of the bedroom—and then him suavely murmuring that *now that she was naked, how would she feel about picking up where they'd left off?*

It had all sounded so bloody brilliant as he'd played it out over and over in his head. And then somehow he'd mucked it up. He'd said the wrong thing or said it the wrong way.

Something had gone cockeyed, because Lillian's face had transformed from soft and mistily content to shocked and hurt.

He'd missed the chance to apologize and set the matter straight before she disappeared into the bedroom. Then when she'd come out, he'd been too gobsmacked and tongue-tied by his own stupidity to rectify the situation before she ran off again.

Bloody hell. What was it about this woman that turned him into a complete wanker?

Regardless, he had to fix it. He might not be spending the rest of the evening exactly as he'd hoped—naked and writhing around with Lillian on that king-size bed he had yet to sleep in—but he couldn't let her storm off thinking he was a git. That the kiss they'd shared meant nothing or that getting Ashdown Abbey's dress back safe and sound was more important to him than what was blooming to life between them.

Long minutes passed while he tried to decide how to go about cleaning up the mess he'd made. The clock on the mantel counted them down, grating on his nerves even as he paced in time with the steady *tick-tick-tick* of the second hand going round.

After wearing a path in front of the sofa, he moved closer to the bedroom door. He could hear the faint sound of water running and assumed she was taking a shower.

The thought of her stripped bare, standing beneath the steaming jets, made it increasingly hard to concentrate. It made other things hard, as well. Especially when he pictured her working up a lather of soap and rubbing it all along her body. Stroking, smoothing, scrubbing. First her arms, then her breasts and torso and...lower.

A thin line of perspiration broke out along his upper lip and his muscles went tense. He'd never known that the act of getting clean could be so dirty. And he very much wanted to walk in there to assist with both.

Chances were he'd get his face slapped for his trouble. He had to *talk* to her first. Work on seducing her back into the shower second.

The water shut off suddenly. And he strained to listen for

movement on the other side of the door while bracing himself with both hands against the jamb on this one.

He didn't want to frighten her, and chances were he was the last person she wanted to see right now, but he needed to talk to her.

Waiting a few minutes until he thought she would be finished in the bathroom but not yet climbing into bed, he tapped lightly on the door.

His palms were damp. His chest was actually tight with anxiety.

This wasn't like him at all. He hadn't been riddled with nerves about facing a girl since... Had he ever been? At university he'd even been a bit of a ladies' man, if he said so himself.

And now he was sweating like David Beckham after a particularly rigorous football match at just the prospect of confronting Lillian once again. Especially when he knew it would mostly involve groveling and apologizing and begging her not to continue believing he was a total squit.

When long moments passed without her opening the door, he began to suspect she was avoiding him. Not that he blamed her. But he knew she was in there, knew she'd heard his knock and knew she couldn't possibly be asleep yet.

He cocked a brow. Well, now he was growing somewhat annoyed.

He knocked again, louder this time. If need be, he would go in there with or without her invitation—after all, it was his suite, and he'd been generous up to now allowing her to have the spacious bedroom and master bath all to herself. Though he'd much prefer she open the door voluntarily so he wouldn't have to add overbearing bullying to his list of crimes tonight.

Just when he was about to try the door himself, he heard a small snick and the knob began to turn. The door opened only a crack, the light from the sitting room illuminating just one eye and a narrow portion of Lillian's face. The rest was left in shadow by the darkness of the bedroom beyond.

"Yes?"

Her voice was low, flat and far from friendly when she said it.

"I'm sorry to disturb you," he began.

Which was so very close to simply *I'm sorry,* yet he managed to skirt a straight-out apology. Brilliant.

"Could I speak to you for a moment?" he tried again, still taking the coward's way out.

"It's late," she told him, keeping the door open no more than a single inch. "I'm tired. We can talk in the morning."

And with that, she closed the door. Soundly, firmly and with a clicking lock of finality.

Bugger. Nigel barely resisted the urge to smack his fist against the solid door frame.

Well, he'd mucked that up good and proper, hadn't he? Damn it all. The bloody dress that had started this debacle was on its way back to join the rest of the collection and await tomorrow's fashion show, while he was still trying to find a way to mop up the mess he'd made.

He took a deep breath, as frustrated with Lillian's refusal to speak to him as with his own bungled efforts.

Enough of this. It was going to be dealt with right here, right now and that was the end of it.

Raising his hand, he knocked again, hard enough that she couldn't help but hear the summons and know he meant business.

"Go away, Mr. Statham."

Oh, so it was back to Mr. Statham, was it? When she'd just begun to call him Nigel.

There was only one thing to be done about that.

Leaning close to the door, he lowered his voice and ordered, "Open this door, Lillian."

He could have sworn he heard a snort of derision, followed by a mumbled, "I don't think so."

His jaw locked, teeth grinding together until he thought they might snap.

Slowly, carefully, enunciating every word, he bit out, "Open this door, Lillian, right now."

He paused, listening for movement, but heard none. "You have until the count of three," he told her, sounding like every angry father in every movie he'd ever seen, "or I'll kick it in."

In truth, he wasn't certain he *could* kick the door in. He prided himself on staying in shape, playing at least a game or two of squash per week, in addition to his regular exercise routine. But nothing in his past led him to believe he would have either the strength or the martial-arts-like coordination necessary to actually break down a door.

And then there was the sturdiness of the door itself. Not to mention the lock, which—hotel quality or not—might just prove to be un-break-down-able. He rather hoped he didn't have to find out.

Stepping backward, he took a deep breath, steeled himself and got ready to follow through on his promise.

And then there came a click. And the muted turn of the knob.

He watched as the brass-plated handle inched around, letting the air seep from his lungs on a slow exhale and the tension leach from his tendons.

Once again, she opened the door only a crack, but at least this time it was a couple of inches instead of only one. Popping her head out, dark blond hair still damp from her shower, she glared at him.

"Are you threatening me?" she asked, eyes crackling like lapis. "Because that smacks of a threat. Or possibly even harassment. I've got a phone in here with 9-1-1 on speed dial, and I'm not afraid to use it."

Nigel sighed, resisting the urge to rub a hand over his face in frustration. With her. With himself.

"Just a moment of your time," he said. "Please."

When she didn't immediately slam the door in his face, he soldiered on.

"I wanted to apologize for earlier."

Her lashes fluttered as she narrowed her eyes a pinch, but he ignored the warning. With luck she would hear him out and stop shooting daggers.

"It wasn't my intention to offend you by asking you to remove the dress so it could be returned for the show tomorrow. In retrospect, I might have worded my request a bit differently."

He watched her arch a brow, her grip on the edge of the door loosening slightly. She even let it drift open another fraction of an inch.

"For instance, I should have said that the sooner we got the dress off you and headed back for the show, the sooner we could return to what we were doing in the car. Or better yet, I should have ripped the dress off you as soon as we stepped into the suite and said to hell with the show. So we'd be short a look and a model would be sent home in tears…it would have been worth it to avoid hurting your feelings, as I obviously did. And to be making love to you right now instead of standing here having this conversation, hoping you won't slam the door in my face. Again."

There, he'd said it. It had pained him, especially in the region of his pride, which seemed to currently be residing near his solar plexus, making it feel as though a very heavy anvil were pressing down on his diaphragm.

Now to see if it had any impact on Lillian whatsoever, or if she would, indeed, slam the door in his face for a second time. He watched her carefully, trying to judge her response from the one eye, one cheek and half of her mouth that were visible.

Her lashes fluttered, and her tongue darted out to lick those lips nervously.

And then the door began to creak open—so slowly, he thought he might be imagining things.

But the door did open, all the way. And she stepped out, into the light of the sitting room. Behind her, he could see that one of the lamps beside the king-size bed was lit, but it wasn't bright enough to fill the entire room.

She was wearing one of the hotel robes, covered from neck to ankle by thick, white terry cloth. She should have looked shapeless and unattractive, but instead she looked adorable. Her hair hung past her shoulders in damp, wavy strands, her flesh pink from its recent scrubbing.

With the belt pulled tight, he could easily make out her feminine curves. The flare of her hips, the dip of her waist, the swell of her breasts. A V of skin and very slight shadow of cleavage were visible in the open neckline of the robe, making him want to linger, stare, nudge the soft lapels apart to reveal even more.

He was on extremely thin ice with her already, however, and didn't think it wise to press his luck. No matter how loudly his libido might be clamoring for him to do just that... and more.

Threading her arms across her chest, she watched him warily.

"So you don't...regret what happened in the limo?" she asked quietly.

Nigel's heart gave a thump of encouragement. If she was asking, that meant she'd been thinking about it. Thinking and worrying.

Taking a cautious step forward, he flexed his fingers to keep from reaching for her. But he answered clearly, honestly, consequences be damned.

"Not even if you call the authorities, as you threatened.

Or file a sexual-harassment complaint at Ashdown Abbey, as you have every right to do."

She seemed to consider that for a moment, and then the stiffness began to disappear from her rigid stance. Her expression lightened, her arms loosening to drop to her sides.

Taking a deep breath that lifted the front of the robe in a way that shouldn't have been seductive but was, she let it out on a long sigh.

"This is a bad idea," she murmured, letting her gaze skitter to the side so that he wasn't certain if she was speaking to him or more to herself.

"I'm working for you," she continued. "You could fire me or use me because I'm in your employ. Things could get ugly."

Nigel's shoulders fell almost imperceptibly, and he felt as though his entire bone structure slumped inside his skin. She was right, of course, but that wasn't at all the reaction he'd been hoping for.

"True," he acquiesced, albeit grudgingly. "Though I'm *not* using you, and I would never fire you over something… personal. Something that I would be equally responsible for and took equal part in."

Her eyes locked on his. "You're that noble, are you?"

His chin went up, every ounce of the pride and dignity driven into him from birth coming to the fore. "Yes. I am."

It was her turn to slump as she let out a breath. "I was afraid of that," she said, sounding almost resigned.

And then her voice dropped, but he had no trouble hearing her. No trouble making out both the words and the meaning.

"I'm not sorry, either. About what happened in the limo."

Ten

Lily knew she *should* be sorry about what had happened in the limo. She should also have graciously accepted Nigel's apology without saying anything more, then turned and locked herself back in the bedroom.

Oh, how smart that would have been.

Oh, how she wished she had that much strength of will.

But no matter how hurt and offended she'd been by Nigel's actions concerning the dress, she hadn't been able to stop thinking about *that kiss* the entire time she'd been in the shower. Even through her tears and ragged breathing, her body had hummed with unspent passion. With need and longing and plain old *want*.

Her thoughts had swirled with *what-if*s. What if they hadn't been interrupted by their arrival at the hotel? What if she hadn't been wearing one of the designs for tomorrow's fashion show? What if he'd kissed her in the elevator, then pounced on her like a cat on a mouse the minute they'd reached the room?

What if everything from the past forty minutes had happened far differently and they were in bed right now? Making love. Exploring each other to their hearts' content. Scratching the itch that had plagued her since the first moment she'd met him.

She shouldn't want any of that. She should be smart enough or even angry enough at his possible involvement in the theft of her designs to slam the door on all of it. To man up and stop letting her hormones do her thinking for her.

But she couldn't. Or at least none of her attempts so far had been successful.

So she was giving up. If you couldn't beat 'em, join 'em, right?

She knew now that Nigel was just as attracted to her as she was to him. That what she'd felt in the limo when they kissed hadn't been one-sided. And she just wanted to throw caution to the wind, to be with a man who made her toes curl and her insides feel like molten lava.

And so what if she did? Nigel didn't know who she really was, and she wasn't going to be around that much longer. A few weeks, maybe a month more. Just until she solved her mystery and could return home with information that would save and vindicate her company.

Nigel never even needed to know her true identity. She'd done a fairly good job as his personal assistant so far, if she did say so herself. And knowing it wasn't permanent employment, that he wasn't going to be her boss forever, made it even easier to justify a hot, steamy fling. She could let her hair down, have a good time, and walk away with no consequences. With a quick letter of resignation and excuse about getting another job elsewhere—preferably far away, but without hinting at her true residence in New York—she could wipe the slate clean.

So this was almost like a freebie. Casual, no-strings vacation sex.

Considering how long it had been for her, how long since she'd had a date or sex—casual or otherwise—all she could think was *yes, please.*

Which was why she'd come clean and told him that she didn't regret what had taken place between them after the party, either. She'd wanted him to tear her dress off her body and take her up against the nearest wall of the suite the minute they'd set foot inside.

Well, maybe not that dress, but *a* dress.

And she didn't want to spend the rest of the night alone in that immense bed, tossing and turning and unfulfilled.

Watching his eyes go dark and glinting at her softly spoken admission, she took a deep breath and decided to press on, letting him know in no uncertain terms *exactly* what she meant.

"As much as I enjoyed modeling one of Ashdown Abbey's newest designs, I wish I hadn't been wearing that dress tonight. Because I would have enjoyed having you rip my clothes off the second we walked through the door."

His eyes darkened even more, his jaw tightening until a muscle ticked near his ear.

"Be very certain of what you're saying, Lillian," he grated, the words sounding as though they were being dragged from the depths of his soul. "Because once we begin, there will be no stopping. No more noble gentleman. No more polite facade."

Shivers rocked her nerve endings at what he left unspoken. That once they stopped dancing around their need for each other, once they dropped all pretenses and got down to business, it would be raw, primal, unapologetic S-E-X.

Swallowing hard, she took a single step forward. Determined. Ready.

"I understand," she told him. "And I'm not slamming the door in your face."

Heat exploded across Nigel's face. Lighting up his eyes like emeralds, rolling off his body in waves and battering her like a storm front.

He closed the distance between them without a word, moving in almost a blur of motion. One minute he was over there, the next he was grabbing her by the arms and yanking her to him with such force, her feet nearly left the ground.

His mouth crashed down on hers, twining, mating, devouring. She met him kiss for kiss, thrust for thrust.

He tasted just as he had in the limo—only better, because this time she knew it wasn't a one-time-only, heat-of-the-moment thing. This time she knew he wanted her, she wanted him, and they were going all the way to the finish line, consequences be damned.

Her hands climbed the outside length of his arms to clutch his shoulders. They were broad and strong and welcoming. She kneaded them for a moment before trailing her fingers around to the front of his shirt.

She didn't need to open her eyes or look at what she was doing to loosen the knot in his tie, unbutton his collar, then open the entire front of his starched white and pleated tuxedo shirt. He groaned as she touched his bare chest, and she was close to groaning with him.

The pads of her fingers dusted across hard and flat pectorals, tickled by just a sprinkling of crisp hair. Blast-furnace heat radiated from his skin and seeped into hers.

Pushing the sides of his shirt and jacket apart, she continued to explore, to study the contours of his body as though she were reading Braille. Then she ventured down to the waist of his pants.

Her nails raked his stomach and he sucked in a breath. Though her own breathing was none too steady and she was

gasping for air from their long, tortuous kiss, Lily grinned at
the feel of his abdomen going rigid at her touch. She trailed
her fingers through the path of hair leading down the center
and disappearing into his slacks.

With a groan, he took her mouth again, cupping the back
of her head with both hands, stabbing his fingers through her
hair and against her scalp to anchor her in place.

She was only too happy to be there, to have him desperate
for her, out of control, ravishing her. She only wished they'd
started earlier instead of wasting all that time on arguments,
hurt feelings, uncertainty and explanations.

Finding his belt buckle, she worked it free, pulled the two
ends apart and dragged the long strip of leather through its
loops in one fierce yank. It hit the floor with a thud a second
before she went for the closure of his pants.

She could feel the heat of him, the hard, swollen length
pressing against the back of her hand through his fly. She
took a moment to run her knuckles up and down along the
prominent bulge, making Nigel moan and nip her lower lip
with his teeth.

She smiled against his mouth, then let out a low moan of
her own when his hands slid down either side of her spine to
her bottom, squeezing roughly and tugging her even more
firmly against his blatant arousal.

Squirming in his grip, she rubbed all along the front of him
while at the same time wiggling her fingers between them to
undo the top of his pants and slowly ease down the zipper.

He let her work. Let her get as far as dipping her fingertips beneath the waistband of his briefs before lifting his lips
from the pulse of her throat, setting her half a step away, and
tearing at the belt of her robe. It took him a moment to deal
with the knot, which got stuck from all his tugging. But then
it was loose, the edges of the robe falling open and catching

at the bends of her arms when he pushed the plush material over her shoulders.

She was naked beneath, her flesh flushed pink now from passion rather than the steam of her shower. When the cool air of the suite hit her bare skin, she shivered. But she didn't try to pull her robe back up for warmth or try to cover her nudity. Not with Nigel standing there, staring at her as though she was the most delectable morsel ever created.

Not when she'd been dreaming about this moment for far too long. Wanted it far too much to hide.

So she stood there. Half-naked. Half shivering, both from the cool interior and the need coursing through her veins. And she let him look his fill.

Of course, while he was looking at her, she was returning the favor, taking in his surprisingly tanned skin against the backdrop of the white shirt and black tuxedo. His amazingly muscular and well-formed physique. He could have been a model posing for some sexy cologne ad—and raking in the dough when women everywhere flocked to buy whatever he was selling.

Though it felt like minutes, she was sure it only took a few seconds for them both to drink each other in, then lose all patience for the five or six inches that separated them. Nigel's hazel-green eyes glittered, reflecting the same desire she knew filled her own.

Lowering his head, his eyes grew hooded, and he made a feral sound deep in his throat before stalking toward her. He reached her in a blink, sweeping one arm around her back and the other behind her knees.

Her heart gave a little flutter as he lifted her against his chest in one smooth movement that didn't seem to tax him in the least. She released a breath of laughter and clutched his neck as he hiked her even higher.

He returned her grin, then leaned up to press his lips to

hers. Never breaking the kiss, he carried her across the room and straight to the waiting bed.

Once there, he balanced her carefully with one arm while reaching out to turn back the covers with his other hand. Then he laid her near the center of the soft mattress, following her down until he covered her like a warm, heavy human blanket.

The fabric of his tuxedo rubbed along her bare skin except where it was open down the front. The heat of his chest pressed to hers, making her want to wiggle and worm even closer, if possible.

Wrapping her legs around him, she drove her hands inside his open shirt and tuxedo jacket, loosening it even further and pushing it jerkily over his shoulders and down his arms. He moved with her, aiding her efforts until he could shrug out of the garments and toss them aside.

Then he returned the favor, stroking her waist, her rib cage, the undersides of her breasts, but not lingering in any one spot, even though she writhed for his touch. Ignoring her whimpers of need, he finished removing her robe, lifting her when he needed to in order to tug the thick terry cloth out from under her. Then it, too, was gone, hitting the bureau with a *slap*.

His chest heaved as he stared down at her, his gaze raking from the top of her head to where her legs were still twined around his thighs. He took in her bare breasts, the slope of her belly, her triangle of feminine curls.

Everywhere he looked, she broke out in goose bumps. His nostrils flared, and his eyes flashed with a wolfish gleam.

Without taking his gaze from her, he kicked out of his pants and shoes and the rest of his clothes, dislodging her hold on him only when absolutely necessary. In seconds, he was naked and glorious, so beautiful he made her throat close with unexpected emotion. She swallowed it back as he moved over her. Reminded herself that this was just a casual fling, nothing more.

Lifting her arms, she wound them around his neck, drawing him to her even as he met her halfway. They kissed slowly, finally taking time to explore each other's mouths at a leisurely pace. The taste, the texture, likes and dislikes.

Of course, for her, it was all likes. And judging by the feel of him pressing against her inner thigh, he was liking everything just fine, as well.

His fingers tangled in her hair, angling her just the way he wanted while she raked his back, reveling in the play of muscle, the dip of his spine, the row of vertebrae leading down to the delectable swell of his ass.

His moan filled her mouth and his arms tightened around her. She arched into him, wanting to get close, even though they were already nearly as close as two people could be.

Dragging his lips across her cheek, he nipped at her throat, nibbled the lobe of her ear, trailed his mouth over her clavicle and toward her swollen, arched breasts.

Her breathing was choppy, her head getting fuzzier and fuzzier with longing as he teased her mercilessly and her temperature rose. But there were things that needed to be taken care of before they went much further. Before the fuzziness turned to full-blown mindlessness and she forgot everything but her own name.

"Nigel," she murmured, tightening her legs around his hips and moving her hands to his biceps while he nuzzled the side of her breast.

"Nigel," she said again when he didn't respond, resorting to tugging at his hair instead. "Condom. I don't have one— do you?"

It took a second for her words to sink in, for movements to slow and his mouth to halt mere centimeters from the center of her breast.

His head fell to the side and he groaned, the sound vibrating against her skin, making her shiver. With a particularly colorful-but-amusing curse of the British persuasion, he pushed himself up on his forearms to glare down at her.

Without waiting for her acquiescence, he peeled away from her and climbed out of the bed, flashing his sexy bare bottom as he hustled into the other room, where she assumed he had a stash of protection. Thank goodness, because she hadn't exactly packed for Los Angeles *or* Miami with hot, impulsive sex in mind.

Despite his command not to move a muscle, she pushed herself up on the bed, propping the pillows behind her and leaning against the bamboo headboard. She thought about tugging the sheet up to cover her stark nudity, then decided that if Nigel could stroll around the suite completely naked and unselfconscious, then she didn't have to be so modest, either.

He returned moments later, clutching a couple of distinctive plastic packets. Tossing one on the nightstand, he kept the other, tearing it open and quickly shaking out the contents.

Lily watched with barely suppressed eagerness as he sheathed himself in short, competent motions, then rejoined her on the bed, a dark, devilish gleam glinting in his eye as he closed in on her.

"I told you not to move."

His voice scraped like sandpaper, but still managed to pour over her in a rush of honeyed warmth.

She arched a brow, flashing him a wicked, unapologetic smile. "I guess I've been a bad girl. You may have to spank me."

Heat flared low in Nigel's belly, spreading outward until

it tingled in his limbs, pooled in his groin and flushed high across his cheekbones.

"Oh, I intend to do much more than that," he said in a voice gone arid with lust.

If he'd ever seen a more beautiful sight in his life than Lillian George sprawled naked in bed, waiting for him, he couldn't remember it. And now he didn't think he would ever forget.

As aroused as he was, as desperate as he was to be inside her, he couldn't seem to tear his gaze from the delightful picture she made. Her light brown hair falling loose around her shoulders, sexy and mussed from his fingers running through the long, silken strands. Her pale skin flushed with the rosy glow of desire.

Her breasts were small but perfect, their pale raspberry nipples puckered tight with arousal. And the rest of her was equally awe-inspiring—the slope of her waist, the triangle of blond curls at the apex of her thighs, the long, lean lines of her legs.

But what he loved most was her lack of inhibition. She didn't try to hide from him, didn't try to cover her nudity with her hands or a corner of the sheet. She was comfortable in her own skin. And more, she was comfortable with him, with what they were about to do with each other.

Feigning a patience and self-control he definitely didn't feel, he moved beside her, pulling her legs straight and tugging her into the cradle of his arms. She rolled against him, her breasts pressing flat to his chest, the arch of her foot rubbing lazily along his calf.

He brushed a loose curl away from her face, tucking it behind her ear. "In case I forget to mention it later, I'm awfully glad you agreed to come with me this weekend."

Her lips turned up at the corners, her blue eyes going soft and dewy. "Me, too."

"And though I don't mind sleeping in the other room, it will be nice to spend the night in this nice big bed, for a change."

She lifted one dainty brow at him. "I didn't say you could stay in bed with me."

He narrowed his eyes, fighting the twitch of his lips that threatened to pull them into a grin. "Planning to use me, then relegate me back to that dreadful cot, are you? Let's just see if I can change your mind about that."

He watched her mouth curve into a smile just before he kissed her. Her arms wrapped around his neck and trailed down his back as he shifted his weight, bringing her more snugly beneath him.

He'd meant what he'd said—bringing her along on this trip really had been one of his better ideas, even if he hadn't known at the time that they would end up here. He couldn't deny, however, that he'd hoped.

Almost from the first moment she'd walked into his office, every fiber of his being had shot to attention and begun imagining scenarios in which they ended up much like this. He'd known such a thing was dangerous, though, and couldn't—or shouldn't—happen.

But now that it was…he couldn't bring himself to be sorry. Or to worry about the consequences. All he wanted was to continue kissing her, caressing her, making love to her all night long.

And if she thought to send him back to that cramped, lumpy roll-away bed after she'd gained her satisfaction… Well, he would just have to keep her so busy and blinded by passion that she lost all track of the time. He would be spending the night in her bed before she even realized the sun was coming up.

He stroked the smooth roundness of her shoulders, her

arms, her back. Everywhere he could reach while their tongues continued to mate. He could kiss her forever and never grow bored. But there was so much more he wanted to do with her.

With a small groan of reluctance, he lightened the kiss, drawing away just enough to nibble at the corner of her mouth, trailing down her chin to her throat. She threw her head back, giving him even better access. He took his time licking his way down, pressing his lips to her pulse, dipping his tongue into the hollow at the very center, where he felt her swallow.

They rolled slightly so that he was lying over her again, and she welcomed him by hitching her legs high on his hips and locking her ankles at the small of his spine. It brought him flush with her feminine warmth, and brought a groan of longing snaking up from the depths of his diaphragm.

Her fingers kneaded his biceps while he turned his attention to her lovely, lovely breasts. The nipples called to him: tight little cherries atop perfectly shaped mounds of pillowy-soft flesh. He squeezed and stroked with his hands while his lips circled first one pert tip and then the other.

Beneath him, Lillian wiggled impatiently and made tiny mewling sounds while his mouth grew bolder. He kissed and licked and suckled, trying to give each breast equal consideration until the press of her moist heat against his nearly painful arousal grew too distracting to ignore.

Lifting his head, he pressed a quick, hard kiss to her mouth. "There's so much I want to do to you," he murmured, brushing her lips, her cheekbone, the curve of her brow with the pad of his thumb. "So much time I want to spend just touching you, learning every inch of your body. But we may have to wait until later for all of the slow, leisurely stuff. Right now I simply need you too much."

He canted his hips, nudging her with the tip of his erection to emphasize his point. Bowing into him, she brought them into even fuller, more excruciating contact. He hissed out a breath, closing his eyes and praying for the endurance to make it through this night and shag her properly without embarrassing himself.

To his shocked delight, she clutched his buttocks with both hands and leaned up to nip his chin with her teeth. "I'm all for fast first. Slow is overrated."

Nigel chuckled, wondering how he'd gotten so bloody lucky. Hugging her to him, he kissed her again, melding their mouths the way he fully intended to meld their bodies.

Skating a palm down the outside of her thigh, he hitched her leg higher on his hip, opening her to him and settling his sheathed arousal directly against her cleft. He sucked in a breath as her moist heat engulfed him as though the thin layer of latex wasn't even there.

If he was this affected, this close to the edge just by resting against her so intimately, what would happen once he began to penetrate her? Once he was seated to the hilt, with her tight, feminine walls constricted around him? He was almost afraid to find out, and imagined something along the lines of the top of his head flying off and consciousness deserting him entirely.

Lillian ran her fingers into his hair, raking his scalp and tugging his mouth down to hers. Impatiently, she writhed against him, inviting him in, making it more than clear what she wanted.

Peppering him with a series of biting kisses, she murmured, "Stop teasing, Nigel. Do it already."

He would have chuckled at her less-than-eloquent demand if he wasn't just as desperate for her. Sliding a hand between their bodies, he did tease her, enough to draw a ragged moan from deep in her throat. But only to test her readiness and be sure she could accommodate him.

Gritting his teeth, he found her center and pressed forward. She was tight and hot, but took him willingly, inch by tantalizing inch. Their panting breaths and staccato moans echoed through the room while he sank as far as he could go. Filling her, torturing himself.

She fit him like a glove—silken, warm, heavenly. It was a bliss he could have easily spent the rest of the night savoring. If only he hadn't been so desperate to move, the fire, the desire racing through his veins. Lillian's teeth at his earlobe, her softly whispered encouragement, and the way she spoke his name on such a breathy sigh let him know she felt the same.

His whole body taut with need, he drew back. Sliding forward. Slow, even motions that brought exquisite pleasure even as the impulse to thrust faster and harder grew.

Mewling in his ear, Lillian's arms tightened around his neck, her legs around his waist. Her breasts rubbed eagerly against his chest, spurring him on.

"Nigel," she murmured into his neck. The sound of his name on her lips, the feel of them on his skin sent pleasure skating down his spine.

"Please," she begged, slanting her hips, driving him deeper. It was a request, or possibly even a demand, for more.

With a growl he gripped her hips and began to move in earnest. Long, slow strokes followed by short, fast ones. Then the opposite—long and fast, short and slow.

He mixed it up, throwing off any semblance of gentlemanly behavior in an effort to increase pleasure and bring them both to a rocketing completion. With luck, he would be able to hold back his own orgasm long enough to see that Lillian was well-pleased first, though that was becoming more and more of a priority.

And then she started bucking beneath him, her nails raking his back as she cried out. His name, a plea, a litany of *yes, yes, yes, yes.*

Fever heated his blood to a boil while he silently joined in her chorus of need. His muscles tensed, grew rigid. Slipping a hand between them, he drifted his fingers through her downy curls and found the tiny bud of pleasure hidden there.

At the very first touch, Lillian threw her head back and screamed, convulsing around him. Nigel plunged deep, again and again, wanting to prolong the ecstasy, but having no control over millions of volts of electricity setting off fireworks beneath his skin and low, low in his gut.

With a heartfelt groan, he stiffened inside of her, thrusting one last time as ecstasy exploded behind his eyes and spread outward to every cell and nerve ending.

Long, silent moments passed while his heart pounded beneath his rib cage and they both tried to school their breathing. Sweat dotted their skin, sealing them together as he rolled them carefully to one side.

He kept an arm around her, one of her legs thrown over his hip. Her riot of wavy brown hair spilled across the pillow beneath her head, and he smiled, reaching out to pluck a stray strand from where it was stuck to her lips.

At the featherlight touch, she blinked dreamily and opened cornflower-blue eyes to stare up at him.

"Mmm," rolled from her lips in a throaty purr.

Nigel chuckled. "I'll take that as a sign that I left you moderately speechless."

Her mouth curved in contented acquiescence, her eyes fluttering closed again.

Assuming she'd drifted off to sleep, he extricated himself from their tangle of arms and legs and padded to the loo to dispose of the condom and clean up. Returning to the bed, he crawled in beside her, arranged the covers over their still-naked bodies and pulled her back into his arms once again.

She snuggled against him, resting her head on his shoulder and throwing one of her legs over his thigh. Amazingly, the close proximity had arousal stirring to life a second time. But more than mere desire, a warm wash of satisfaction seeped through him unlike anything he'd ever felt before after what was supposed to be only a casual, rushed sexual encounter.

He'd known Lillian George was different—special even—from the first time he'd seen her. He just hadn't known how special, and he wasn't certain even now. All he knew was that she evoked emotions in him he couldn't remember ever feeling before. And created thoughts in his head that he'd never before been tempted to consider.

Stirring beside him, Lillian turned her face up to his, letting her eyes fall open a crack. Her breath danced across his skin and she made a low humming sound deep in her throat before parting her lips to speak.

"I changed my mind," she said drowsily. "You can sleep in the bed with me, after all."

Considering that he was already quite near to doing that already, he couldn't help but chuckle.

"Why thank you," he said, doing his best to feign gratitude when what he really felt was amusement. "That's terribly generous of you."

"I'm a generous person," she mumbled, but he could tell she really was slipping off to sleep this time.

He pressed a kiss to her forehead, waiting until her breathing became fluid and even. "I hope so," he murmured more to himself than to her. "I certainly hope so."

Eleven

They woke up just in the nick of time the next morning. Nigel counted himself lucky they'd woken up at all, considering how…active they'd been throughout the night.

They'd made love once, twice…he'd lost track at three. And that didn't include the time he'd stirred her from sleep by lapping at her honeyed sweetness and pleasuring her with his mouth. Or the time she'd awakened him by returning the favor.

Which made it a miracle that they were up now, dressed quite fashionably, and on their way to the charity runway show that was scheduled to start in a little under two hours, without looking like the walking dead. He was wearing a simple tan suit, white dress shirt open at the throat in deference to both Miami's weather and its casual, oceanside style of dress. It had taken him all of twenty minutes to shower and get ready.

It had taken Lillian slightly longer, but the added time had been well worth it given the results. Her hair was a mass of pale brown waves, drawn up at the sides and held in place while the rest fell down her back in a loose, sexy ponytail. Her makeup was light and flawless, showing no underlying signs of her lack of rest. And she was wearing a short, brightly flowered sundress that definitely hadn't come from the Ashdown Abbey collection. It was, however, perfect for the Florida sunshine, and she looked good enough to eat.

He rather wished he could skip the fashion show altogether, drag her back to the hotel suite and do just that. It took a number of stern mental lectures and dressings-down to keep from telling their driver to turn around and return them to the Royal Crown.

He was Ashdown Abbey's CEO, after all; he was required to be there. And as upset as his father was already with the company's performance since opening stores and a manufacturing plant in the United States, he doubted the old man would be happy to hear Nigel had blown off a big event to spend the day setting the sheets afire with his lovely new personal assistant.

But despite all the reasons he knew he couldn't, he still wanted to. Especially when he reached for her hand in the lift on the way down to the car and she let him take it, leaving her fingers in his on the walk through the lobby, then again in the limousine. And when she sat mere inches from him in the back of the car—still a respectable distance, but much closer than she had the previous night.

They arrived at the event location and joined a line of vehicles waiting to discharge their passengers. People were pouring into the giant white tent set up for the runway show. Slowly, the limo moved forward until it was at the head of the line, and the driver came around to open the door and let them out.

Nigel stepped out first, then assisted Lillian, keeping her

close to his side while camera lenses approached and flashes of light went off all around them. Today's show wasn't exactly a red-carpet event, but there were enough big-name designers showing and celebrities in attendance that it brought out a crowd of paparazzi and legitimate media alike.

Nigel smiled, nodded, played the part, all the while guiding Lillian through the throng with nothing more than a hand at her back. He was careful not to touch her anywhere else or give any hint to the public of the true nature of their relationship. Or what could be considered the true nature of their relationship after the way they'd spent last evening, at any rate.

It seemed to take forever to make it through the tent, stopping every few feet to say hello or speak to people he knew, people who wanted to know him, or simply big associates it was best to share pleasantries with. Until finally they reached their reserved seating near the runway.

Before sitting down, Nigel took Lillian's hand and leaned close to whisper in her ear. "I need to go backstage and check on preparations for the show. Would you like to come with me or stay here?"

Her fingers tightened around his and she looked more excited than he would have expected, her eyes lighting with anticipation. "I'll go, if that's all right," she replied.

He led her along the long, long frame of the raised runway, weaving around bystanders and finding the entrance to the rear staging area tucked off to one side. Backstage was a mad mass of wall-to-wall people rushing here and there, yelling, calling out, trying to hear and be heard over the cacophony of noise and other voices.

He had a general idea of where the Ashdown Abbey staff and collection were set up, and headed that way.

When they reached the proper area, models were at different stages of hair and makeup and dressing in the chosen Ashdown Abbey designs that would be walking the runway today.

At the center of it all stood the head designer of the collection, Michael Franklin. Calling out instructions, pointing this way and that, keeping everyone on task. As frantic as it looked, Nigel knew from past runway shows that it was all a sort of controlled chaos. Once everything was ready and the show was underway, Michael and everyone else would sit back and declare that things had gone off with nary a hitch.

When the designer spotted Nigel and Lillian standing at the edge of the activity, he lowered his arms, took a deep breath and bustled over. *Time to put on a confident air for the boss,* Nigel thought with amusement. Though he wasn't the least alarmed by what he was witnessing. In his experience, what was taking place behind the scenes of the runway was perfectly normal, Michael Franklin perfectly capable of choreographing the necessary stages of preparation.

"Mr. Statham," Franklin greeted, shaking Nigel's hand.

Nigel said hello and reintroduced him to Lillian before asking how everything was going.

"Fine, fine," Franklin replied. "We're short one model, though," he added, glancing to see if she might be somewhere in the crush of people surrounding them. "I'm sure she'll be here, but if she doesn't show up soon, we'll be pushing back the prep for the champagne gown. We had special hair and accessories lined up for it, since it's our final design to walk the runway."

Nigel pursed his lips, wondering if he should put voice to the idea flashing through his head. It was brilliant, of course, at least to his mind. But he wasn't so certain Franklin or Lillian would agree.

Mistaking his drawn brows for upset, Franklin rushed to reassure him. "Don't worry, Mr. Statham, everything is under control. We'll get the model here or find another. If I have to, *I'll* squeeze into the dress and walk it out there myself."

"Actually," Nigel said, deciding to take a chance Lillian

wouldn't slap him for his presumptuousness with so many witnesses standing around, "I have a thought about that myself." Turning to Lillian, he took her arm encouragingly. "Why don't you stand in for the missing model?"

Her eyes went wide, her face pale.

"What? No. Don't be ridiculous."

"What's so ridiculous about it?" he argued. "You're beautiful, poised, more than capable. And we both know you look amazing in the gown, since you wore it to the cocktail party just last night. I'd say it's an ideal solution."

Before she had the chance to say anything more, he turned back to Franklin. "Send her to hair and makeup and get her into the dress. Make sure she looks like a million bucks. She'll be the perfect close to our portion of the show."

"Nigel," Lillian said, shaking her head, looking on the verge of panic.

He leaned in, pressing a kiss to her cheek. "You'll be fine," he assured her. "Better than fine, you'll be marvelous."

When she still didn't look convinced, he added, "Please. We need your help."

He heard her sigh, knew she was on the verge of acquiescence and didn't give her a chance to change her mind.

"Go," he commanded, pushing her toward Franklin, pleased when the man wasted no time grabbing her up and bustling her off to get ready.

With a smile on his face and heady anticipation thrumming through his veins, he made his way back out front, taking his seat and awaiting what he suspected would be the best runway show of his life. Career aspects be damned.

Hours later, Lily was still shaking. She'd never been so nervous in her life. Not even on her first day pretending to be a personal assistant for Nigel.

What had he been thinking? She wasn't a model. Far from

it. She was a designer, for heaven's sake. Her place was well on the other side of fashion—behind the scenes, not out in front, walking a runway with hundreds of eyes riveted on her and flashbulbs going off in her face every tenth of a second.

Not that Nigel was aware of any of that. But that still didn't give him the right to dress her up and shove her out there without warning.

She'd survived, of course. She even liked to think she'd done an exceptional job. At least she'd stayed on her feet, hadn't fainted and had made it all the way down the runway and back without falling off into the crowd of onlookers.

But what if someone recognized her? From the audience or later, from all of the pictures and video clips that were sure to be circulating across the globe.

Too many people knew her as Lily Zaccaro. Even with her hair a little darker than her natural shade and heavier makeup than usual for the runway, somebody out there was sure to notice her and wonder what she'd been doing walking the runway for one of her competitors.

With luck, they would call her cell phone to ask what was going on. But much more likely, they would call the apartment and end up talking to either Juliet or Zoe. Her sisters would be clueless, but they'd begin to put two and two together, track her down in Los Angeles and blow her entire ruse as Lillian George.

Nigel would be furious—for good reason. But worse, she would be kicked out of Ashdown Abbey. Before she'd figured out who was stealing her designs.

Dammit. How did she get herself into these predicaments?

Running her fingers through her hair, she shook it out of its overly sprayed upsweep until it resembled at least a modicum of normal, natural, non-runway style. She was out of the champagne-colored gown and back in the sundress she'd been wearing when they first arrived.

The makeup, however, would have to remain until they returned to the hotel suite and she could take some cotton balls and about ten gallons of makeup remover to it. Not that she looked like a clown. It was just that everything—eyeliner, shadow, mascara, blush, lipstick—was thicker and heavier than usual to be seen from a distance and on camera.

She was about to turn away from the oversize mirror and head back out front when a pair of hands spanned her waist and warm lips pressed against the side of her neck. Her gaze flicked to her reflection, and now Nigel's, close behind her.

"You were wonderful," he spoke near her ear, barely above a whisper. "I knew you would be."

Stepping away before someone noticed his familiarity with the person who was supposed to be simply his personal assistant, he added, "That model never did show up, so thank you for saving the show."

"You're welcome," she said with a touch of reluctance. Then she turned to face him, crossing her arms and hitching one hip in annoyance. "You might have *asked* if I wanted to play supermodel before pushing me out onstage against my will. Do you have any idea how petrified I was? You're lucky I didn't throw up on one of the other models or pass out right in the middle of the runway and ruin the whole show."

To her surprise, he chuckled at her aggravation, a wide smile stretching across his handsome features.

"Nonsense. You were exceptional. And I can't imagine anyone else looking as lovely in that gown…not even a professional model paid to look good in designer creations."

As much as she wanted to hold on to her mad, his flattery was working. She was glad she'd been able to help out in such a way when he'd needed her, happy that he was pleased with her performance.

But that didn't change the fact that she was in trouble. Bad enough they'd slept together last night. That she wanted it to—*hoped* it would, even—happen again.

Now she needed to worry about someone recognizing her and figuring out what she was doing playing out a second identity. That *Nigel* might realize what she was up to and hate her forever.

Her heart gave a painful lurch. She might be lying to him. What they had might be casual, temporary and doomed to be short-lived. But the thought of him finding out who she really was, what she'd been doing pretending to be his personal assistant all this time, nearly brought tears to her eyes.

An ill-fated romantic fling she could handle. Seeing a look of betrayal, possibly even disgust, in his eyes after what they'd shared… No, she didn't want her time with him to end like that.

Which meant she needed to be very careful from this point on. She needed to guard herself against any further attachment to this man. Whatever else transpired between them, she couldn't let it affect her emotionally.

Most importantly, though, she needed to get back to the Ashdown Abbey offices in Los Angeles and find out once and for all who stole her designs for the California Collection.

Oblivious to the twisting, hazard-strewn path her thoughts were taking, he ran his hands down her bare arms, threading his fingers with hers. "If you're ready, we can go. We'll have to make pleasantries as we weave our way through the crowd out there, but the car is waiting to take us back to the hotel."

"Don't you need to stick around awhile?" she asked. "Rub elbows and talk up the company to key account holders?"

"Already done," he replied. "I spoke to several buyers just after the show, while you were changing back into street clothes, and anyone else who might be interested in acquiring our designs has my card. They can call me at the office on Monday."

"That was quick," she said. "I would have thought you'd need to spend the rest of the day schmoozing."

He offered her a gentle smile. "Sometimes I do. But for the most part, these types of events drag on for the public's enjoyment. Those of us who are there for business tend to know each other, look for each other and get straight to the point. Besides," he said, leaning in and lowering his voice to a sultry whisper, "I don't want to be stuck out there, making nice with mere strangers, when I could spend the rest of my time in Miami alone with you."

A flush of longing washed over her, making her catch her breath. She licked her lips, waiting until she thought she could speak without sounding like Kermit the Frog.

"So," she said carefully, "we'll be headed back to Los Angeles soon?"

"Tomorrow. But that gives us the rest of the day and this evening to enjoy the sand and sun."

She cocked her head, unable to keep her mouth from quirking up at one side. "The sand and sun, or our suite back at the Royal Crown?"

He returned her grin with a wink and wicked twinkle to his hazel-green eyes. "I'll let that be your choice, of course. Though I know which I'm hoping for."

She shook her head and chuckled, unable to resist his inherent charm. The man was entirely too tempting for his own good. Or hers.

And though it might not have been the wisest decision for her to make, especially given her current situation, she *wanted* to spend the night with him. Another night, just the two of them alone together.

While she realized it would essentially be digging herself even deeper into her deception and making it that much harder to walk away, she wanted as much time alone with him as she could get. Secret minutes, private hours, cherished memories to carry with her the rest of her life.

She might not have a future with Nigel—how could she when she'd been lying to him ever since they met?—but she could have this. The here and now. And if that was all she could lay claim to, then she was going to grab on with both hands and savor it for all it was worth.

"All right," she told him slowly, teasing him a little. "I'll tell you what. You can take me to lunch, and I'll let you know afterward what I want to do next."

He gave her a look, one that said he intended to do everything in his power to convince her to make the right decision. The one that led straight back to their hotel suite and ended with them both sweaty, naked, wrapped together like kudzu vines.

She shivered a little at the slideshow of pictures that ran through her head. Oh, yes, they would get there. But it wouldn't hurt to make him worry a bit about the day's outcome first.

Turning in the opposite direction toward the curtained-off entrance between backstage and the show area, he offered his arm. As she took it and they started walking, he said, "Fair enough. Just remember that I haven't quite gotten my fair share of time in that big bed back at the hotel. It would be a shame to fly home before I've gotten to use it properly."

Lily bit down on the inside of her cheek to keep from laughing aloud. The campaign to spend the rest of their time in Miami safely ensconced in the suite had begun already, it seemed. Although she didn't see why they had to restrict their activities to the bed he was so preoccupied with. After all, there was also the sofa, the desk, the balcony, the shower, the bathroom vanity...

Leaning into him, despite the fact that someone might see

and perceive that there was more going on between them than mere boss-and-secretary professional relations, she said, "I'll keep that in mind."

The sofa, the desk, the bathroom vanity, the shower and the bed. They'd hit every place but the balcony, at least in part, before checking out of the hotel Sunday morning and boarding the jet back to Los Angeles.

Lily knew how dangerous it was to let herself get so carried away with Nigel. Had reprimanded herself several times while locked away with him, doing all the things she told herself she shouldn't. But she just didn't have it in her to stop before she absolutely had to, so she'd decided to adopt a don't-ask-don't-tell attitude. She wouldn't ask herself why she was letting things go on this way when she knew how they were going to end, and she wouldn't tell herself later what a fool she'd been for letting her time at Ashdown Abbey and her feelings for Nigel Statham get out of control.

Which was how she ended up agreeing to have room service deliver lunch after the runway show instead of eating in a lovely, public five-star restaurant so they could spend more time together, alone in the suite. And how she allowed him to sit so close to her on the flight home, interspersing business talk with naughty whispers about his favorite parts of what they'd done together and what he'd very much like to do in the future. Not the far distant future, but soon after they landed.

As hard as she tried to resist, she even let him talk her into going home with him from the airport. It was a terrible idea. One that could only get her deeper into the hole she was digging for herself. The same hole that was quickly filling with quicksand, threatening to pull her under.

But there was something about his fingers trailing along her bare thigh just beneath the hem of her skirt…his warm breath dusting her ear, sending ripples of sensation all the way down to her toes. It stirred up too many memories from their time locked away together in the hotel suite, and made her weak and susceptible and eager to make more.

So she let herself be persuaded. Let him lead her from the jet to his waiting Bentley, let him *not* drop her off at her apartment, but take her home with him instead, her heart in her throat the entire drive.

She'd expected some dazzling but garish mansion in Beverly Hills, complete with swimming pool and a home bowling alley or some such. Instead, he led her past a uniformed doorman into a very nice redbrick apartment building not far from the Ashdown Abbey offices. Definitely a few steps up from the one where she was staying, especially when she discovered—of course—that his was the penthouse apartment.

The view was spectacular, as were the layout and furnishings. Not his own, he'd explained; he'd rented it that way, but they suited him perfectly nonetheless. A lot of chrome and glass and neutral colors, interspersed with splashes of bright color.

He gave her all of ten minutes to process her surroundings while his chauffer brought in their luggage and he poured them each a glass of wine. Then he'd led her to the bedroom, where he'd proceeded to give her the grand tour of his king-size bed, ocean-blue satin sheets and the eggshell paint of the ceiling over her head.

He'd kept her there for hours…not that she'd minded. Then when she began making noises about going home to her own apartment, he'd insisted she stay for dinner. She'd refused, at least until he'd offered to cook. That was something she just *had* to see.

Unfortunately, she'd also had to eat it with a smile on her face, since she hadn't had the heart to tell him his culinary skills needed work.

After that, he'd very deftly seduced her again, keeping her distracted and too exhausted to protest until morning. Of course, in the morning, they'd had to go into the office.

Thankfully, she'd had enough clothes with her from the trip that she hadn't had to wear the same thing two days in a row. And Nigel had been kind enough to drop her off a couple of blocks from the Ashdown Abbey building so it looked as though she'd arrived by herself, then followed behind several minutes later.

From there, they'd proceeded to fool around in his office, exchange heated glances even when they weren't alone, and—to Lily's consternation and self-reproach—practically move in together. It was comfortable and a lot easier a routine to fall into than she would have expected. At the very least, she found herself spending entirely too much time in Nigel's presence and sleeping over at his penthouse.

Time she was spending getting swept up in the fantasy of spending the rest of her life with this man, inching ever closer to the edge of falling for him once and for all. But *not* getting any closer to discovering the thief of her designs. Every minute she was with Nigel was one she didn't use to snoop around or pore through Ashdown Abbey records.

After nearly a week of sneaking around at work, of them acting like boss and secretary with a professional relationship only, then using the evening hours to act like a couple of randy teenagers—or worse, star-crossed lovers in some romantic chick flick—Lily realized she had to get back on track.

She considered herself extremely lucky that nothing had ever seemed to come of her jaunt down the runway in Miami. Apparently, everyone—even the media—had been more focused on the debut designs than who was wearing them. And the big hair and heavy makeup had certainly helped.

Because no one had ever called to ask what she'd been doing there, or pointed at a photograph from the show and commented that one of the Ashdown Abbey models looked an awful lot like that Zaccaro chick from New York.

Thank goodness.

But even if she couldn't bring herself to break things off with Nigel entirely, she did manage to clear her head enough to insist on spending the night at her own apartment for a change. *Without* him joining her there.

Lily hadn't taken her personal cell phone with her to Florida, only the one provided to her by Ashdown Abbey for company business. And she'd been so distracted by her impromptu stay at Nigel's penthouse that she'd forgotten to grab it the single time she'd managed to swing by her own apartment. It was still in the nightstand beside her neatly made, narrow twin bed, exactly where she'd left it.

So when she finally got inside her apartment, alone, and was able to take a breath, clear her head and focus again, she found her voice-mail box full. As soon as she turned the phone on, it started beeping with notification after notification that she had messages waiting.

Suspecting what she would hear and who most of them would be from, she almost didn't want to listen, but knew she had to. Kicking off her heels, she moved around the living room, gathering papers and folders and notebooks even as she dialed in for the messages.

Sure enough, several were from her sister Juliet. *Where are you? Why didn't you say where you were going in your note? Why haven't you called me back? Please call me back. We're worried about you. Where are you?*

Lily's heart hurt more with each message, guilt biting at her as her sister's voice grew more and more frantic.

Then there were the ones from her private investigator, Reid McCormack. He was anything but frantic. In fact, he sounded downright furious, and darned if Lily could figure out why. He worked for her, after all. Shouldn't *she* be the one to get upset at his lack of progress rather than the other way around?

But while his first couple of voice mails were polite enough, simply requesting an update or letting her know he'd found no connection between Ashdown Abbey and the theft of her designs in New York, they quickly deteriorated into demands for her to return his calls and threats to put an end to their association if she didn't soon come clean with her sisters.

She rubbed the spot between her brows, massaging away the beginning of a headache. This was all supposed to be so simple, and now it was so complicated. She was supposed to be the only one involved, at risk, and now things had spread to encompass so many others. People she cared about and wanted to protect.

With a sigh, she glanced at the phone's display and did the math for the difference between West Coast and East Coast time. If she waited just a little longer, she might be able to call the apartment back in New York and leave a message for her sisters when neither of them would be home. That would give her the chance to reassure them—especially Juliet—that she was fine and hoped to be home soon without having to explain where she was or what she was really up to.

Because if Juliet or Zoe answered, there would be no end to the number of questions they would ask. They'd grill her like a toasted-cheese sandwich, and she just *couldn't* tell them the whole truth. Not yet.

Which brought her to the next and most important item on her must-do list. She *had* to figure out how Ashdown Abbey had gotten enough of a peek at her designs to incorporate them into their California Collection.

Tossing all of the paperwork she'd gathered so far from the annals of Ashdown Abbey on the coffee table in front of the sofa, she trailed into the bedroom and changed from the sundress and sandals she'd worn home from Florida to a pair of comfortable cotton pajamas. Then she returned to the front room, started a pot of coffee—which she suspected would be only the first of many—and hunkered down on the floor cross-legged, with her back to the couch.

Given all the snooping she'd already done and information she'd collected, Lily didn't understand why she couldn't figure out who the design thief was. It had to be there, buried, hidden, eluding her. Worse, she felt as though the answer was *right there,* just out of reach. If only she knew exactly where to look…or exactly what she was looking for.

What she needed was a second set of eyes. Her sisters—Juliet, at any rate—would be terrific at poring through the pages and pages of data. But hadn't the entire point been *not* to get her sisters involved?

The detective would be another excellent choice. But Juliet had contacted him right after Lily had, and now he was smack in the middle of a conflict of interest. From his perspective, anyway—not from Lily's, and she hoped not from Juliet's once she found out what was really going on. It did explain Reid McCormack's souring disposition, though.

On the heels of that thought came another wave of guilt. *All right, all right,* she told her nagging conscience. Grabbing her cell phone, she dialed McCormack's office number first. The better to *not* catch him and be able to leave a message he could listen to later…when she wasn't on the other end of the line, a cornered recipient of his wrath.

And thankfully, it was his voice mail rather than his real live voice that answered.

"Mr. McCormack, this is Lily Zaccaro," she said. Quickly, succinctly, knowing she didn't have much time before the system cut her off and wanting to sound very sure of herself, she continued, "I'm sorry I haven't contacted you, but I got your messages and promise I'm nearly done here. I'm not going to give her any details about my whereabouts, but

I will call Juliet and let her know I'm okay. And I'll explain everything as soon as I get back to New York. I'm sorry if this is causing you problems, but please don't say anything to my sisters—not yet. Thank you."

Heart racing, she hung up, hoping she'd said the right things. Hoping she'd bought herself a little more time and extinguished at least a bit of his anger with her.

She thought about calling her sister next, but it was Sunday afternoon, and though the store was open, the three of them usually took that day off. The chances of both Juliet and Zoe being home were too high. She would wait until tomorrow, when the two of them *should* be back at the boutique and unable to answer the apartment phone. Her message would be waiting for them when they got home, though, which should make them feel better about her health and welfare.

That decided, she went back to flipping through papers and her notes, studying each carefully, just as she had several times before. The letters were starting to blur together, the words branding themselves in her brain. And yet she was clearly missing something or the mystery would have been solved by now.

For the next few hours, she kept at it, sipping coffee to stay alert as she organized and reorganized, straightened and re-straightened. Sighed and sighed again.

She was going over the specifics of the California Collection— memos, instructions, supply lists and sketches—when something caught her attention. Sitting up straight, she leaned forward even as she brought the printout in her hand closer.

Down in the far left corner, in teeny-tiny print smaller than a footnote, was a number. Or rather, a resource code, with numbers and letters mixed together: CA_COLL-47N6BL924.

It meant absolutely nothing to her, except that it seemed to be an identifier for the California Collection. And like one of those 3-D magic mystery image puzzles, she might never have seen it if exhaustion wasn't making her eyes cross and vision blur.

Grabbing up the next page, she glanced down and found the exact same thing. And on the next. And on the next. And on the next.

Her pulse jumped in anticipation. This could actually be something. Of course, she didn't know exactly what and wasn't even sure how to find out.

But on a hunch, she ran for her laptop, popped the lid and booted up. Thanks to her position as executive secretary/personal assistant to the Man in Charge at Ashdown Abbey, she had all the log-in information to tap into the computer system from home—which she'd done numerous times after hours as part of her amateur investigation.

Once she was in, it took her twenty, maybe twenty-five minutes just to locate anything even remotely related to the code, and another ten or fifteen to track down what the jumble of letters and numbers meant.

It was, she discovered, an identifier for all of the sketches and other information related to the California Collection. And miraculously, it brought her to a compilation of scans of the original sketches for the California Collection.

They were definitely rougher sketches than the ones she'd been studying all this time, done by hand in charcoal and colored pencil and with computerized drawing pads and the like. All grouped together, they were miniscule, but thankfully she was able to enlarge them and even run them across her screen in a slideshow fashion.

A flare of annoyance raised Lily's temperature several degrees. If she'd thought the final results of the collection were similar to her work, the original sketches were practically carbon copies. Someone had initially pitched almost her *exact* creations, and they had somehow—thank heavens for small favors, she now realized—been transformed into garments more suitable to Ashdown Abbey.

Refocusing her attention away from her fit of temper, she began to scan every detail of the designs and right away noticed that each of them was signed with the same set of initials.

IOL.

Lily's brows knit. So often with design teams, no one took or was given full credit for initial ideas. She'd suspected someone of using her designs as suggestions for aspects of the California Collection, but not that a single person had offered up complete, nearly identical sketches for all of the designs, which had then been applied to the overall collection.

Apparently, she'd been going at her little investigation all wrong from the very beginning. The thought made her want to smack her head on the nearest hard surface, even as she admitted a newfound respect for folks like Reid McCormack, who did this sort of thing professionally. Clearly, she was better off locked in her studio with bolts of fabric and thread in every color than out in the world playing amateur sleuth.

Not that she could quit now. She'd come too far and was finally, *finally* on the verge of figuring out this whole ugly mess.

It took a minute or two more of tapping at the keyboard, but she found the entire list of employees connected to the California Collection and started scrolling through. No one, *no one* with the initials IOL that she could see. Dammit.

Teeth grinding in frustration, she drummed her fingers on the coffee table and tried to think of what to do next.

Bingo! Payroll records.

Accessing the human resources files, she found the record of every single employee working at Ashdown Abbey, regardless of his or her position. From Nigel as CEO all the way down to the custodial team that came in nightly to clean the offices, she scrolled through every single name, looking for one to match to those three initials.

A ton of *L* surnames popped up, only a few first names that started with the letter *I*. But she kept going, holding her breath in hopes that the mysterious IOL would pop up and bite her on the nose.

And there it was. Her fingers paused on the touch pad, stopping the document's movement. She blew out a breath even as her stomach plummeted and her heart hammered against her rib cage.

Isabelle Olivia Landry. IOL.

Bella.

Lily leaned back against the edge of the sofa, feeling all the blood drain from her face. Bella? Zoe's friend Bella?

Sure, the thought had crossed her mind—*briefly*—after they'd run into one another, but she'd never truly believed anything like that could be possible.

Could she really have done this? To her friend...her friend's sisters...her friend's company?

Why would she have done such a thing? And how did she manage it?

It made sense, though, didn't it? The longer Lily thought about it, went back in her memory, the more things began to fall into place.

Bella and Zoe were friends. Bella had visited Zoe not all that long ago. She'd stayed at the loft with them, toured the connected studio where they worked from home and the space where they worked in the back of the store, too, she was sure.

She couldn't blame Zoe for showing her friend around, either. Lily and Juliet had both given tours to friends, sharing their work space as well as designs they were currently working on. None of them would ever think a *friend* would steal their ideas and try to pass them off as their own or sell them to another designer.

No, this betrayal lay solely at Bella's feet. But Lily still wanted to know how she'd managed it. And *why*.

Had she memorized so much from just a casual glance, or had she sneaked around behind their backs and literally stolen designs, perhaps traced or copied them to take away with her?

Tears pricked behind Lily's eyes even as her fingers clenched. She was sad and angry at the same time. Relieved to have the mystery solved, but dreading what was to come.

Because she had to confront Bella now, didn't she?

Or maybe she shouldn't. Maybe she should turn over all of this evidence to the police. Or Reid McCormack so he could investigate further and gather even more evidence against Bella.

Gather even more evidence. So that they—she—could prosecute someone who at one time had been a close friend of her sister's. The very thought made her want to throw up.

But it had to be done, didn't it? Even though now that she knew the truth, it felt like rather a hollow victory.

And yet it was the whole reason she'd run away from home in the first place. Left without telling her family where she was going and sent poor Juliet into such turmoil over her whereabouts…flown to Los Angeles and gotten a job with a rival clothing company under an assumed name…let herself get carried away by her feelings for Nigel and fall into an affair with him that was going to end badly…so badly.

If she didn't take action against Bella for stealing her designs, all that would be for naught.

Wouldn't it?

Twelve

There were some things makeup couldn't hide, and the shadows under Lily's eyes were two of them. She couldn't remember ever spending a worse, more sleepless night in her life.

For hours, she'd paced her apartment, chewed at her nails, despaired of what to do. Confront Bella herself? Call Reid McCormack for help? Or go home and tell her sisters everything? Maybe talking it through with her sisters would help her decide what to do, and since Bella was her friend, Zoe really did deserve to have a say in the matter.

But no matter what she did where Bella and Zaccaro Fashions were concerned, she found herself having an even harder time figuring out what to do about Nigel.

Oh, how she was dreading that. So many times during the night, she'd considered flying back to New York without a word to him or anyone else at Ashdown Abbey. And in fact she'd started packing her things, because either way, she knew she would be returning home sooner rather than later.

The thought of seeing Nigel again filled her with equal parts excitement and trepidation. Excitement because every time she saw him brought a thrill of delight and desire. Trepidation because she'd been lying to him all along and might now have to come clean, telling him everything.

He would hate her, of course. Hate her, be furious with her, possibly blow up at her before having her dragged from the building like a common criminal. Which was no less than she deserved, she knew.

Her pulse was frantic, beating louder and louder in her ears the closer she got to her desk and the door of Nigel's office. Before leaving her apartment, she'd called Reid McCormack again, this time glad when his secretary put her through and he picked up in person.

He'd been short with her at first, on the verge of reading her the riot act, she suspected. But she'd quickly redirected his anger by filling him in on what she was really doing in Los Angeles and what she'd discovered. They made an appointment for her to bring everything she'd found to his office the following week, where he could look it over and they would decide what steps to take next.

Then she called her sisters. For a change, she'd actually been hoping one of them would answer, but with the time difference between New York and California, she'd gotten only voice mail both at home and on their cells. Instead of the message she'd planned to leave before figuring out who was behind the design thefts, she'd told them where she was and that she'd be home within the next few days.

She hadn't told them *why* she was in Los Angeles or why she'd taken off the way she had, but assured them she was fine and would fill them in when she got back. In fact, she'd ended her message with *there's a lot we need to talk about*. And, boy, was there ever. She only hoped this entire situation wouldn't end up putting a rift between them.

And then she'd picked up her purse and the letter it had taken her most of the night to compose. The ink of which her sweaty palm was probably smearing into illegibility at that very moment.

Her breathing was coming in shallow bursts, her stomach churning and threatening to revolt with every *boom-kaboom-kaboom* of her aching, pounding heart. But as much as it pained her, as much as she wanted to turn tail and run, this was something she had to do.

Swallowing hard, she laid her purse down on top of her—or rather, the future personal assistant's—desk and turned toward Nigel's office. The letter clutched in her hand was wrinkled almost beyond repair. She'd better do this before it became completely unreadable.

Shaking from head to toe, she reluctantly raised an arm and knocked. Nigel responded immediately, calling in his deep British accent for her to come in. His voice snaked down her spine, warming her and causing a shivery chill all at the same time. Pushing the door open, Lily walked inside, her footsteps as heavy as lead weights.

The minute he spotted her, his face lit up…and Lily's heart sank. He was so handsome. So charming and masculine and self-assured. And lately, he'd begun looking at her like she could come to mean something to him.

He was certainly coming to mean something to her. More than she ever would have thought possible, given the fact that she'd originally come here thinking he might be behind the thefts of her designs.

Now it was breaking her heart to think of leaving him. To have to tell him who she really was and why she'd truly been working for him.

She'd tried to deny it, not even letting the thought fully form itself in her mind, but she'd fallen in love with him. With a man who, in only moments, would come to despise her.

"Lillian," he said, and the sound of her name—even her fake name—on his lips nearly brought tears to her eyes.

Pushing back his chair, he rose to his feet and came around his desk. He reached her in record time, before she could register his movements and attempt to stop him. He gripped her arms, leaning in to kiss her cheek and then her mouth.

Heat suffused her, threatening to fog her brain and drag her far, far away from her determination to come clean and tell Nigel the truth. She couldn't help but kiss him back, but curled her fingers into fists to keep from wrapping them around his shoulders or running them through his hair.

Whether he noticed her reluctance or not, she couldn't tell. He was still smiling when he pulled back, which only made her insides burn hotter with regret.

Nigel reached up to brush a stray curl behind her ear, offering a suggestive, lopsided grin. "Did you come in early for our little game of Naughty Secretary?" he asked. "I can't think of a better way to start the day, and would be happy to sweep away all my work so we can make proper use of the desk."

Her throat grew tight and closed on her next breath. She shook her head and blinked back tears.

At her response, his eyes narrowed, his expression growing serious.

"Lillian," he said again, taking her hand and giving it a reassuring squeeze. "You don't look well. What's wrong?"

Clearing her throat, she tried to find her voice, praying she could say what she needed to say without breaking down completely.

"Can I speak with you?" she began, the words thready and weak.

"Of course."

Still holding her hand, he led her to one of the chairs in front of his desk, guiding her into it before turning the other to face her and taking a seat himself.

"What is it?" he asked, concern clear in the hazel-green depths of his eyes.

Hoping he wouldn't notice that she was shaking, she held the letter out to him.

"This is for you."

While he began to open the envelope and take out the piece of paper folded inside, she rushed ahead, knowing that if she didn't get it all out before he began to react to her letter of resignation, she never would.

"I've been lying to you," she said. "The whole time, I've been here under false pretenses. My real name is Lily Zaccaro, and I'm part-owner of Zaccaro Fashions out in New York. I came to Los Angeles and started working for you because someone stole some of my recent designs and used them to create your California Collection. I probably should have handled things differently. I'm sorry," she hastened to add before pausing only long enough to take a much-needed breath.

"I know you'll hate me for this, and I don't blame you. But I want you to know that I didn't do anything to harm you or Ashdown Abbey. I poked around *only* to find out who might have had access to my personal designs and was also involved in the creation of the California Collection. That's all I did. I didn't come here to spy on your operation or steal company secrets or anything like that, I swear."

Eyes stinging, she blinked back tears. Swallowed past the lump of emotion growing bigger and bigger in the center of her throat.

Where only moments before Nigel's features had been relaxed and soft with pleasure when he met her gaze, they were now stone-cold and harshly drawn with both disappointment and betrayal. He stared at her letter in his hand as though it didn't make sense, and she didn't know if he'd heard a word she'd said…or if he'd heard every one and couldn't bear to look at her because of them.

She sat stock-still, afraid to move, afraid to breathe. Simply waiting and bracing herself for his reaction, however ugly it might be.

And then he raised his head, his eyes locking on hers. What she saw there stabbed her straight through: hurt, confusion, betrayal.

"You're leaving," he said, his tone flat, utterly hollow. "You're not who you proclaimed to be, and now that you've gotten what you came for, you're leaving."

She didn't know which was worse—having to explain her actions or hearing him summarize them so succinctly. Both had her stomach in knots of self-loathing.

All she could do was croak out a remorseful "Yes."

The silence that ensued was almost painful. Like nails scraping down a chalkboard, but with no sound, only the uncomfortable tooth-rattling, grating sensation.

A muscle jumped in his jaw, his mouth a flat slash across the lower half of his face. His gaze drifted away from hers, locking on a point at the far side of the room and refusing to return anywhere near her.

One minute ticked by, and then another, while she searched for something, anything to say. But what more was there? She'd already confessed, told him who she really was and why she'd pretended to be his personal assistant. Whatever else she came up with to fill the heavy weight of dead air would only make matters worse.

So she held her tongue, waiting for the dressing-down she knew was coming and that he had every right to level at her.

Instead, he stood and rounded his desk. Still without looking at her, he took a seat in the wide, comfortable leather chair and placed his hands very calmly on the blotter, palms down.

"You should go," he said finally.

Lily licked her lips, swallowed, wished her heart would slow its erratic pace inside her chest. She opened her mouth to speak, even though she had no idea what to say, but he cut her off.

Gaze drilling into her as he raised his head, his voice trickled through her veins like ice. "You're leaving. Your letter of resignation has been turned in, and I've accepted it. You should go."

It wasn't at all how she'd expected things to go. She'd expected angry words and raised voices. Hurt feelings and terrible accusations. This calm, quiet, resigned response was so much worse. Chilling. Heartbreaking. And so very, very final.

With a sharp nod, she gritted her teeth to keep from making a sound. Especially since she could feel a sob rolling up from her diaphragm.

Pushing to her feet, she turned and walked to the door, relieved when she made it the whole way without incident. Reaching out a shaky hand, she gripped the knob and tipped her head just enough to catch a glimpse of him in her periphery.

"I am sorry, Nigel."

Not waiting for a reply, she slipped out of the room and moved toward the elevators as quickly as possible, hoping she could make it inside before she completely fell apart.

Thirteen

One month later...

Lily stood behind the counter of the Zaccaro Fashions store, staring out at the porcelain-white mannequins wearing her designs; the displays of other items, like Juliet's handbags and Zoe's *daZZle* line of shoes; and the handful of customers milling about. A sting of pain made her drop her thumb from her mouth as she realized—not for the first time—that she'd bitten the nail down to the quick. All of her formerly beautiful nails were like that now—short and mangled thanks to her apparent need to work off stress by destroying any chance at a decent manicure.

Clutching her hands together behind her back in an attempt to stop the troublesome habit, she turned her attention to the front of the store. Maybe she should rearrange the window displays again. She'd redone them twelve times in the past four weeks, when normally they changed them only once a month or so.

Her sisters were beginning to think she'd gone off the deep end. She knew this because Zoe had come right out and said, "Lil, you're going off the deep end," just a few days ago when the smoke alarm in their apartment had started shrieking yet again because she'd put something on the stove, then walked away and forgotten what she was doing.

She wished she could claim it was the spark of creative passion distracting her and making her borderline psychotic. What she wouldn't give to have new design ideas filling her head and the need to get them down on paper or fitted onto a dress form keeping her up at night.

But no. Since returning from Los Angeles, she hadn't sketched anything more than pointless, shapeless doodles that had nothing to do with fashion design, and she hadn't sewn a damn thing. She'd tried, but her heart…her heart just wasn't in it.

She was beginning to think it was because her heart was still in Los Angeles with a certain British CEO who probably wished he'd never met her.

Her chest tightened at the thought of Nigel and the expression on his face just before he'd told her to go. That she wasn't welcome in his office, his company or his life any longer.

Well, he hadn't said the last out loud, but it had been implied. And she'd heard him loud and clear.

She'd hurt one person in all of this mess; she was just grateful she hadn't hurt more. Upon her return to New York, she'd spilled her guts to her sisters. Told them everything, from the moment she'd realized her designs had been copied, to her brilliant plan to find the thief on her own, to her ill-fated affair with Nigel. And as much as she hadn't wanted to, she'd broken the news to Zoe that her friend Bella was behind the thefts.

Just as she'd expected, Zoe had been devastated. And angry. And guilty that she'd been the one to bring Bella into their apartment, their studio, and give her access to their work to begin with.

But Lily and Juliet weren't holding anything against Zoe, in the same way Juliet and Zoe didn't hold it against Lily that she'd kept such a secret and run off to Los Angeles without giving them a clue as to what she was up to. It wasn't as though she'd known what her friend was capable of.

And after a long, exhausting discussion that had lasted well into the night, all three of them—Zoe included—had agreed to turn the evidence and information Lily had dug up over to Reid McCormack to let him do some further investigating. Juliet had even offered to take it to him personally, which surprised Lily, since she'd expected her sister to be angry with the detective for pretending to look for Lily while actually covering for her. That had taken a bit of explaining on Lily's part, too.

Then, if Reid thought they had a strong enough case—and they all knew cases like this, concerning "creative license" or the theft of ideas, were hard to prove—they would proceed as necessary, even if it meant taking legal action against Bella Landry. As upset as she was, it was still something Lily would hate to have to do.

Thank heaven for small favors, she supposed. Her broken heart would eventually mend, and the guilt she felt over betraying and lying to a man she'd come to care for—a lot—would eventually dissipate. She hoped. But she didn't know what she'd do without the love and support and forgiveness of her family. Especially her sisters, who were also her best friends.

"Lily!"

Lily jumped at the sound of her name being called very loudly in her ear. She blinked, turning to find Zoe standing beside her, looking extremely put out.

Brows drawn down in a frown, hands on hips, she shook

her head. "I swear, you're about as useful as a zipper on a pillbox hat these days."

Then she sighed, her tone softening. Tipping her head, she said, "There's someone over there who'd like to speak with you."

Lily followed her sister's line of sight, her heart stuttering to a halt when she saw Nigel standing by the far wall, studying the shelves that displayed some of Zoe's finest—and most expensive—footwear designs. Seeing him again made her breath catch. She forgot to inhale for so long that her chest burned and her head began to spin with little stars blinking in front of her eyes.

"What are you waiting for?" Zoe hissed.

Lily shook her head, swallowing past a throat gone desert dry. She couldn't move. She was locked in place, even as every bone in her body turned to jelly.

With a sound of disgust, Zoe put a hand in the middle of Lily's back and urged her out from behind the counter, then gave her a small shove in the right direction for good measure.

"Go," she told her in a hushed voice. Then, in typical Zoe fashion, she grumbled, "And don't screw it up this time."

Nigel watched Lily walking toward him from the corner of his eye. He wanted to turn to her, cross the rest of the distance between them, grab her up and never let go. Instead, he remained turned slightly away, fighting to school his features, keep his heart from breaking out of his chest.

Blast it all, he'd missed her. As angry as he'd been at her... as hurt by the fact that she'd lied to him, pretended to be someone she wasn't...he'd still missed seeing her, touching her, hearing her laugh, watching her lips curl into a smile. Every day since she'd left, he'd wished she were back...then cursed himself for being such a weak, pathetic fool, so easily swayed by womanly wiles. Again, since he seemed to be falling into many of the same pitfalls with Lily as he had with Caroline.

Yet here he was. He'd flown all the way across the country to see her again. And to get some answers to the questions he'd been too bitter and infuriated to ask before she'd walked out of Ashdown Abbey and returned to her real life in New York.

The question was, could he ask them and wait for her response without reaching for her and saying to hell with anything else?

When she was only a few feet away, he turned to face her fully. The sight of her punched him in the gut. If he'd been breathing to begin with, the air would have puffed from his lungs in a whoosh.

Fisting his hands at his sides, he forced himself not to react. Outwardly. She didn't need to know that inside, a team of wild horses was running rampant through his bloodstream.

She stopped. An arm's length from him, which didn't bolster his resolve in the least.

"Nigel," she said on a shaky breath. Then she licked her lips nervously. "I mean, Mr. Statham."

Her tentativeness had a calming effect, letting him know she was just as unsure of this impromptu meeting as he was.

"Nigel is fine," he told her, resisting the urge to shove his hands into his pockets and rock back on his heels. They were a bit beyond polite social etiquette, after all. "Is there somewhere we can talk? Privately."

Licking her lips again, Lily glanced around. There was a handful of shoppers in the store and a blonde who bore a strong resemblance to Lily—a sister?—behind the counter, staring at them curiously. When she caught Nigel's eye, she glowered at him. Definitely one of the sisters.

After Lily had confessed her true identity, admitting that she'd lied to him, he'd been furious, determined to find a way to punish her for her deception. So of course he'd hired a private investigator to discover as much personal information about her as possible.

She came from money, but had worked to open this store on her own, without a handout from her parents, who could easily afford it.

She had two sisters—one older, one younger—who were partners in the design business. They'd gotten involved after Lily had graduated from design school, but seemed to be no less talented. The oldest sister, Juliet, designed handbags and other accessories, while the youngest sister, Zoe, did shoes. Extremely sexy, fashionable shoes, most with enough heel and sparkle to be noticed from a mile off.

Lily designed all of the clothing for Zaccaro Fashions— and she did it quite well. If he'd known about her talent before all of this, he might even have offered her a design position at Ashdown Abbey. She certainly would have been an asset to the company.

And something else he'd been forced to admit after he and the private investigator had both done a good deal of research: she was right about her designs being copied at Ashdown Abbey. How it had been allowed to happen was still a bit of a mystery, but he'd found enough—a link between one of Ashdown Abbey's employees and Lily's sister Zoe, as well as a distinct similarity between Lily's natural design aesthetic and Ashdown Abbey's recent California Collection—to feel confident it wasn't simply a matter of coincidence.

With a tip of her head, Lily gestured for him to follow her, then led him to the back of the store and through a doorway marked *Personnel Only*.

He was surprised to see that it was part storage space, part workroom. There were sewing machines, cutting tables, dress forms and supplies set up, but no one was using them at the moment.

The door clicked shut behind them, and Nigel turned to face Lily, who was standing with her back to the closed panel, hand clinging to the round brass knob.

Taking a deep breath that raised her chest and drew his attention to her breasts beneath the brightly patterned top he now recognized as one hundred percent her personal creation, she said, "Why are you here, Nigel?"

Right to the point. And regaining a bit of her natural confidence, he noticed. Just one of the things he admired about her, and had from the beginning.

"I thought we should talk," he answered honestly. "You ran off so quickly we didn't have a chance to discuss your true reason for being at Ashdown Abbey."

Lily opened her mouth, clearly eager to set him straight, but he held up a hand, stopping her.

"I know—my fault entirely. I told you to go, and at that point, I was too stunned and angry at your confession to hear the whole story. But I've had some time to think and to calm down, and I have some questions that only you can answer."

She considered that for a second, then offered a small nod. "All right. I really am sorry for what I did, for…lying to you. I'll tell you whatever you want to know."

As simple as that, and suddenly he couldn't think of a bloody thing to say. His mind had been spinning with questions for weeks, his body tense with the need for answers. Now Lily was standing in front of him, ready to bare her soul, and all he really wanted was to close the distance between them, clutch her tight to the wall of his chest, and kiss her until the rest of the world melted away.

Minutes ticked by, the silence almost deafening. Her glossy, periwinkle eyes blinked at him, waiting.

Blowing out a breath, he stiffened his spine, telling himself to man up and do what he'd flown all this way to do.

But again, only a single thought filled his head. Not the

desire to kiss her…that was still there, but taking a close backseat to the one question he most wanted an answer to.

"Our time together," he began, forcing the words past a throat gone tight with emotion. "In Florida, and then after we returned to Los Angeles…did it mean anything to you, or was that, too, part of your strategy?"

Seconds passed while she didn't respond, and his heart pounded so hard he feared she could hear it from halfway across the room.

Finally, her lips parted and air sawed from her lungs on a ragged stutter. Eyes glossy with moisture, her voice cracked as she said, "It meant…everything."

Relief washed over him. Relief and…so much more.

"Oh, Nigel." Lily sighed, dropping all semblance of distance—physical or otherwise—and rushing to him. Her fingers wrapped around his forearms, digging through the material of his suit jacket to the muscle beneath.

"I'm so sorry about everything. I was only trying to find out what happened with my designs. I knew they had been stolen, but I didn't know how or by whom, and I knew I would sound crazy if I started tossing out accusations without proof. I just wanted to poke around a little, see what I could find. I *never* meant to lie to you…not really. And I never, *ever* meant to hurt you, I swear."

She shook her head, glancing away for a moment before looking back, the tears on her lashes spilling over to trail down her cheeks. Nigel felt emotion welling up inside his chest as well, and swallowed to hold it back.

"What happened between us…" she continued. "It was never part of the plan, but I'm not sorry. My feelings for you were completely unexpected, and they made everything so much harder, so much worse. But they were very, very real."

Releasing her hold on his arms, Lily stepped back, not sure if her admission had made things better…or worse.

She felt better now that she'd had the chance to tell Nigel the truth, to tell him how much their time together had meant to her. Not because of her "investigation," not because it absolved her of guilt, but because she'd wanted him to know all along that their relationship hadn't been a casual one. Not to her.

He might not share her feelings. For all she knew, she had been beyond casual to him—disposable, even. But she didn't want him to think, even for a minute, that she'd slept with him as a means to an end. That seduction had been just one more way of using him, lying to him.

At the very least, she'd been able to tell him as much and wouldn't have to live the rest of her life with it hanging over her head. Already, her conscience was lighter for having come clean.

Now only her heart was heavy from having him for such a short time, then losing him to her own stupidity.

Taking a deep breath, she braced herself for whatever his reaction might be. Laughter? An angry scoff? An arrogant quirk of his brow when he realized he'd managed to make another of his personal assistants fall madly in love with him?

Not that she could blame him entirely for the last, if that was the case. She wouldn't be surprised if every person who'd ever worked for him had fallen for him. She'd worked for him only a few short weeks and had fallen head over heels.

The good news, she supposed, was that she had the rest of her life to get over him. It promised to be an agonizing forty or fifty years.

But he didn't laugh or scoff or raise an arrogant brow. He simply held her gaze, something dark and intense flashing behind his hazel eyes.

Resisting the urge to squirm, she linked her hands in front of her and said, "I'm sorry. That was probably more than you wanted to hear. And you have more questions."

Another minute ticked by while he stared down at her, making beads of perspiration break out along her hairline.

Finally, he cleared his throat and gave his head a small shake. "I have to say, I'm disappointed."

Her heart sank. She'd bared her soul, confessed all, come close to throwing herself at him and begging him to love her in return. And he was disappointed.

"Did I mention that you were the best personal assistant I've ever had?" he continued, oblivious to the sobs filling her head as every hope, every dream, every might-have-been died a painful death inside of her.

"And now I find out that you're actually a fairly successful fashion designer in your own right, not a personal assistant at all. You know what this means, don't you?" Without waiting for a reply, he murmured, "I have to start over, interviewing for a new assistant."

He sighed. "I suppose it's for the best. The gossip mill tends to run rampant when executives begin dating their employees. It may not be so bad if we're simply so-called rivals in the world of design."

Lily blinked, feeling as though she'd lost time. He wasn't making sense. Or maybe she'd blacked out for a moment and missed a chunk of the conversation that would help her understand what he was saying.

Hoping she wasn't about to make a giant fool of herself, she mumbled, "You don't have to worry about any of that. I won't tell anyone about our involvement. No one ever needs to know what happened."

A single dark brow quirked upward. "Well, someone is bound to figure it out eventually when they see us together."

Lily tipped her head, frowning in confusion. And her confusion only deepened when he smiled at her. A kind, patient smile she would never expect to see on the face of a man who hated her.

"I had a lot of questions in mind when I walked in here," he told her. "More, probably, than you can imagine. But only one question really matters, and you answered it."

He took a step forward, his hand coming up to stroke her cheek. Her lashes fluttered, pleasure rolling through her at even that brief contact. While he spoke, his thumb continued to brush back and forth along her skin, making her want to weep.

"For the record, it meant something to me, too. Our time together. I've never gotten involved with an employee of the company before. Certainly not one of my assistants. But you…" He shook his head, one corner of his mouth tipping up in a grin and desire flickering in his eyes. "You, I just couldn't seem to resist."

Lily didn't know how she managed to remain upright when her whole body felt like one big pile of sand. Laughter—happy, weightless, delighted laughter—bubbled inside of her, building until it couldn't help but spill out.

Smile widening, Nigel leaned down and kissed her, his lips warm and soft and familiar. For long minutes, she clung to him, unable to believe he was really here, kissing her, telling her these things, making her think maybe, just maybe they had a shot.

All too soon, Nigel lifted his head, breaking the kiss, but not letting her go.

"I think I've fallen quite madly in love with you, Lily Ann Zaccaro. And I'd very much like the chance to start over. No secrets, no lies, no ulterior motives. And no mysterious hidden identities, regardless of how adorable you might look in those sexy-librarian glasses of yours," he added, one corner of his mouth twisting with wry humor. "That is, if you're willing."

"Willing?" she squeaked, barely able to believe *he* was willing to give her a second chance after how she'd deceived him. Or that he was so quick to admit he'd fallen in love with her, when she'd been all but certain feelings like those were hers and hers alone.

If it was true, if he was truly in love with her, she was willing to do just about anything to make things work.

He nodded solemnly. "It won't be easy, considering that we're both tied rather strongly to opposite coasts. But thankfully I have access to a corporate jet and am not above abusing the privilege. I also suspect it will require rather a lot of romantic candlelit dinners. Probably a bevy of bold, romantic gestures on my part. You know—flowers, expensive jewelry, blowing off business commitments to spend amorous weekends in exotic locales. And you'll be expected to *ooh* and *ahh* appropriately at each of them until I've won you over completely. Do you think that's something you can handle?"

Lily laughed. *Giggled* might be a better description. She couldn't seem to help herself. "I'll certainly try," she said, striving to match his falsely sober tone of voice.

"I was also thinking we could work together to get to the bottom of how your designs ended up being used at Ashdown Abbey," he said, brows pulling together in a frown as he grew truly serious for a moment. "I've already suspended Bella Landry's employment at the company, but I can't outright fire her without proof that she stole designs from you and applied them to her efforts for us. Especially since she's denying the accusation. We're looking into it, though. We'll turn over every rock and review every slip of paper in the place until we get to the bottom of it, I assure you."

"Thank you," she murmured, touched by his earnestness on her behalf.

"I'm spearheading the investigation myself, but I could use a bit of help from you, since you're the one most familiar with the designs that were stolen and how they were used in our collection. Fair warning, however—it may require spending a lot of hours alone together, many of them running into the wee hours of the night when we may grow tired and feel the need to lie down for a spell."

At the last, he waggled one dark brow and offered her a lopsided grin.

Once again, a chuckle worked its way up from her belly. She'd never expected him to be able to make her laugh so much, especially when it came to something so serious.

"I'll keep that in mind," she replied, her own lips twitching with amusement.

"I also thought you might consider coming home to England with me."

At that, her eyes widened.

"My father has been complaining for months now that I've gone soft, let your American ways dictate how I run the company. I'd like him to meet you, see just how much I've decided to embrace America—and you."

He offered her a wide and wicked grin. "I actually think he'll be quite taken with you. And after he hears what you did in order to protect your company and designs, I'm pretty sure he'll decide you could be a *good* influence on me."

A beat passed while he let her absorb this latest pronouncement.

"What do you say? Willing to give it a go and see if we're as compatible outside of the office as we were as boss and secretary? And if you survive a visit with my parents, perhaps we can discuss making our relationship a little more... permanent."

Ten minutes ago, she'd thought he hated her. Ten minutes before that, she'd been considering joining a convent and devoting herself to a life of silence and chastity because she'd known she could never be truly happy without him.

Now, she was *too* happy not to agree to almost anything. Even meeting his parents, a prospect that she wasn't ashamed to admit scared her half to death.

"I'd say it sounds like you want to use me for some sort of personal gain," she teased after a moment of collecting her thoughts. "But then, I guess I owe you one on that score."

He tugged her closer, until her breasts pressed flat to his chest and his heat seeped through their clothes straight into her skin. "Very true. But only if you love me as much as I love you."

"Oh, I do love you, Nigel. I really, really do," she admitted, the words filling her with emotion and causing them to catch in her chest. "I still can't believe you're here, telling me you feel the same. So I guess my answer is...*yes*." Yes to everything, always, as long as it was with him.

He kissed her again, quick and hard, pulling her against him so tightly, she could barely breathe. Not that she needed air when she was with him.

"Brilliant," he said, sounding slightly choked up himself for a moment before clearing his throat. "Although you should know that I'm not at all opposed to you using me again in the future. Preferably when we're alone and naked. Feel free to use me however you like then."

"Really?" Her gaze narrowed, all kinds of delightfully wicked thoughts spilling through her head.

"Well..." she said, dragging the word out, flattening her palm against the hard planes of his pectoral muscles hidden beneath the thousand-dollar-silk-cotton blend of his suit jacket and dress shirt. "I'm pretty sure my apartment is empty. Zoe is working here at the store, and Juliet is off for the day with her fiancé. We would be completely alone. And if you like...naked."

A devilish glint played over his features, sending a shock of eagerness down Lily's spine.

"I hope this means you're offering to use me again. Slowly and for a very long time."

"I think that can be arranged," she told him in a low voice.

Going on tiptoe, she pressed her lips to the corner of his mouth, his jawline, just beneath his ear. "And then you can do the same to me."

Wrapping his arms around her waist like a vise, he lifted her off her feet and started toward the door, kissing her along the way.

"The key to a successful relationship is compromise," he murmured. "And sharing. And mutual sacrifice."

"And being naked together as often as possible."

Teeth flashed wolfishly as he grinned, swooping in for another ravishing kiss.

"That would be my very favorite part."

* * * * *

A sneaky peek at next month...

Desire™

PASSIONATE AND DRAMATIC LOVE STORIES

My wish list for next month's titles...

In stores from 17th May 2013:

2 stories in each book - only £5.49!

❑ Playing for Keeps – Catherine Mann

& No Stranger to Scandal – Rachel Bailey

❑ In the Rancher's Arms – Kathie DeNosky

& The Fiancée Charade – Fiona Brand

❑ Temporarily His Princess – Olivia Gates

& Straddling the Line – Sarah M. Anderson

Available at WHSmith, Tesco, Asda, Eason, Amazon and Apple

Just can't wait?

Visit us Online

You can buy our books online a month before they hit the shops! **www.millsandboon.co.uk**

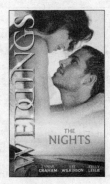

MILLS & BOON®
Book Club

Join the Mills & Boon Book Club

Subscribe to **Desire**™ today for
3, 6 or 12 months and you could
save over £30!

We'll also treat you to these fabulous extras:

- 🌹 **FREE L'Occitane gift set**
  worth £10

- 🌹 **FREE home delivery**

- 🌹 **Rewards scheme, exclusive**
  offers…and much more!

Subscribe now and save over £30
www.millsandboon.co.uk/subscribeme